Stolen Birthright
'There was a crooked man...'

That which is crooked cannot be made straight... **Ecc. Ch1, v15**

JB. WOODS

Dedicated to my long-suffering wife 'Jenny' upon whose family history this book is based, and in memory of my Mother, Edith Agnes Platt, nee Woods, who never lost faith in me.

This book is based on an alleged 19th Century fraud and recorded facts in our family history, therefore certain names, events and places have been altered.

The author also willingly admits to having once or twice stretched history to suit his own ends.

The right of JB. Woods to be identified as the author of this work has been asserted by him in accordance with the Copyright, Design and patents Act 1988

© 2020 All rights reserved. No part of this publication may be reproduced in any form or by any means, or stored without permission of the author / copyright owner.

Acknowledgements:

Hugh Atkinson for his support and help finalising this book.
Marsha Grimes, Ron Sewell and the late Marjorie Tolchard, who read, critiqued and suggested many improvements.

Other friends and colleagues of the **Paphos Writers' Group** for their help and perseverance who taught me a great deal.

Cover graphics: Brian Platt (JB. Woods)

CONTENTS

PART 1
Prologue: 1975: Angus
Chapter 1: 1793: The Promise
Chapters 2 – 8: 1839 – 1842: Fraud, Hope and Adversity

PART 2
Chapters 9 – 19: 1848 – 1886: Eleanor (Ellie)

PART 3
Chapters 20 – 27: 2002: Jenny

ADDENDUM

PART 1

PROLOGUE

May 1975.

Angus Lane raised his hand to knock on the antique oak door when he hesitated unable to make the final effort. It wasn't difficult to understand why he had been summoned the headline of a daily tabloid that morning was evidence enough...

MP DENIES FRAUD
*Mr David Maxwell-Ross MP refutes
allegations concerning his family wealth.*

He studied himself in the brass plaque which announced his tutor *'Prof. J Mildmay'* and a lanky twenty-five-year-old with long blonde hair and the take-away complexion of student life looked back at him.

'What the hell,' he mouthed at his image, 'if I've failed, so what!'

With a surge of defiance he brought his hand down firmly and the booming voice was clearly audible through the ancient woodwork.

'Enter!'

Angus took a deep breath and stepped over the threshold into a Dickensian time warp. The room was dimly lit by wall lights covered with years of accumulated dust and the dark green walls were barely visible behind antique furniture overflowing with books and papers.

Mildmay frowned and looked at his watch. 'Ah, Lane, you've deigned to honour me with your presence?' He pointed to the only available chair. 'Sit.'

Angus sat in a heavy carver chair opposite a robust man of advanced years with a handlebar moustache who peered over rimless glasses. The professor picked up a hefty file, threw it across to him, and said sarcastically. 'Your thesis and your fifteen minutes of notoriety.'

Angus grunted as the file landed in his lap.

Mildmay continued in his forthright manner. 'What have you got to say for yourself? How did it get into the hands of the press?'

Angus screwed up his face, smoothed his hair back and said meekly. 'I left my briefcase on the bus and I suppose someone read my work and gave it to the press, sir.'

Mildmay's fingers drummed on the desk in an impatient tattoo. 'These are serious accusations against this man's family, Lane. Luckily for you I called the newspaper in question and told them in no uncertain terms that unless they stopped using it you would sue.' He paused long enough to take a sip from a glass of water. 'They agreed and are publishing a retraction.'

Angus breathed a huge sigh of relief. 'Thank you, sir.'

Mildmay shook his head. 'Enough of this, let's talk about your thesis.'

Angus's heart sank. This is what he feared most, a post mortem of his labours.

'What do you suggest, sir?'

Mildmay rolled his eyes and sighed. 'Lane, if you're going to use your family history as a documentary on the social history of the nineteenth century you have to convince people of its originality. Relate to me the facts as they occurred.'

Angus paused to gather his thoughts.

'Come on,' Mildmay said impatiently, 'we haven't got all night.'

Angus spoke in a low voice, unsure of himself. 'Err... I recall when I was a child there was a story in the family about a fortune that we should have inherited.'

He pulled himself upright in the chair and started once more with added confidence. 'The story was always a good conversation piece at weddings and funerals. It stayed imprinted on my mind and when it came to finding a subject on social history it was tailor made.'

Mildmay interrupted him. 'One moment. How big was this fairytale fortune?'

'One and a half million pounds in 1839 and at my last calculation that is seventy-five million in today's money.'

Mildmay gasped in disbelief, 'Good God, are you sure?'

'Definitely, sir. In my research I uncovered the original Will of Jane Ross our ancestor and every penny was accounted for. I have Court Transcripts and the most damning of all—the Bank statements of John Reid one of the Trustees.'

Mildmay rubbed his chin. 'And David Maxwell-Ross. Where does he fit in?'

'The family name was Maxwell in 1839, sir. It was William Maxwell his ancestor who perpetrated the fraud.'

Angus paused to glance at his thesis and Mildmay took the opportunity to raise a query.

'Wasn't there a danger that this family fortune was a myth?'

'Yes, sir, but I figured any research into history would serve me twice. If the story was untrue then I would have valuable information on social changes.'

'I see.' Mildmay leaned forward attentively and rested his chin on his hand.

Angus continued, 'I started my investigation by collecting existing family documents. My Great, great, grandfather, Mathew Lane had passed down a leather-bound briefcase containing newspaper cuttings from 1842, some letters from an Aunt Eleanor and his diary from 1866 to 1933, which was pretty comprehensive and disclosed a little philandering within the family.'

Mildmay's ears pricked up. 'Philandering!'

'Yes sir, it would appear that Mathew Lane had an affair with his wife's Aunt Eleanor.'

'Was that the nature of these letters you mentioned?'

'No sir, they were merely asking for donations to the family fighting fund.'

Mildmay sighed, disappointed that the scandal didn't go further.

'Right lad, take a break. Will you join me?'

He took a bottle of *Famous Grouse* whisky and two tumblers from the bottom draw of his desk.

'Just a little with water, sir.'

'This is highly unusual lad.' Mildmay jiggled a tumbler in his hand before giving it to Angus and continuing. 'So the myth turned out to be true, eh?'

'Yes sir.'

'Okay, carry on.'

Angus took a sip before he looked up to the ceiling as if asking for divine intervention.

'It all started in 1793, sir, when Gilbert Ross, the Cashier of the Royal National Bank at that time, travelled down from Scotland to visit his Cousin Sarah…'

***

1

'The Promise.'

1793. Gloucestershire.

The same commotion that made Sarah Bosworth dash to the window set the tongues wagging throughout the hamlet of Moreton Vale with its picturesque cottages and walnut trees in abundance.

A group of high-bonneted women stood discussing the intrusion into their rural tranquillity and an idle bare-footed urchin with an air of studied indifference wandered down to look at the coach-and-horses parked outside the ivy-covered vicarage.

With a careful eye on the driver he reached out with a grubby finger and traced the outline of the Coat-of-Arms emblazoned on the door.

Inside the vicarage, Sarah, a shy, comfortable woman who maintained the vivacious good looks and luxurious dark hair of the Ross women, was talking to her recently arrived Cousin Gilbert Ross of Edinburgh.

Calmer now that the first flush of excitement had passed, she said, 'Cousin, I cannot promise you the fine fare that you're used to, only honest country food.'

'I couldn't wish for better,' he replied.

His long frame stretched out in a carver chair by a rustic farmhouse table, which, with a large dresser filled one end of a flagstoned living room opposite an inglenook fireplace around which were a sofa, an easy chair and a rocker. Sarah had given the place an extra air of homeliness with the addition of homemade rag carpets.

Her orderly life had been thrown into confusion by the sudden arrival of her cousin and her controlled nervous disposition got the better of her. When she called out to her husband instead of her normally composed voice she spoke louder than was necessary for the occasion.

'John!'

Annoyed at herself and to hide her embarrassment she picked up the tray she had prepared and when John entered the room she said, 'John dear, entertain Cousin Gilbert while I take these refreshments out to the driver.'

He gave her arm a gentle squeeze as she went by him and addressed their visitor in his best pulpit manner.

'Cousin Gilbert, it's an arduous journey from Scotland. What brings you to these parts?'

'I was called to London by none other than Mr Pitt himself to give advice on monetary problems in Scotland. Hence, here I am making a detour to visit you.'

'It's only a man of some importance who is called to the presence of our Prime Minister?'

'You make too much of it, sir, I'm merely a banker.'

'Such modesty.' Sarah had returned and with her composure restored she went directly to the pantry and busied herself preparing a snack for Gilbert.

'Here you are.' She placed a plate of ham and cheese before him accompanied by large slices of cottage loaf. 'Would you like some pickled onion to go with our county cheese?'

'Yes, please, and I must say your cheese is one of England's finest.'

She half curtseyed in mock deference to his praise. 'Thank you, sir. Your commendation will be most welcome at the dairy.

'John, Sarah.' Gilbert reached out and took hold of Sarah's arm to distract her from the thousand and one things inside her head. 'I beg of you, please join me. I have something of importance to tell you.'

'Oh, ah,' said Sarah, flustered, her plans thrown into jeopardy.

John was more pragmatic and replied, 'Certainly.'

Sarah fussed about a moment longer before pouring more tea and sat opposite John, nervously twisting her apron in her hands.

'Good, now that we are settled I will tell you my plans. Sarah, I would like to stay a couple of weeks, can I do that?'

'Yes, by all means, cousin, but we have no room for your staff or coach.'

'Fear not, Sarah, they can install themselves down at the Inn.

Bear with me one moment.'

He left the room to return a little later and placed a leather pouch in front of Sarah.

'In there, Sarah,' Gilbert continued, 'is one thousand guineas in gold specie for you.'

He paused to let this windfall sink in.

After a stunned moments silence John shook his head and mumbled, 'Bu…How…Err, I don't know what to say.'

'Be quiet, John,' Sarah said sharply. 'A blessing, I have never seen him at a loss for words. What about your family, Gilbert, do not your wife and children come first?'

Gilbert reached across the table and held one of Sarah's hands.

'I can well afford it. Apart from myself, there are my sisters, Jane and Marion to share the fortune that is ours and we are not of a mind to marry. That makes you the only direct descendants of my Uncle William Ross who came to England after the rebellion in 1715. You will inherit everything when we three pass away. This is merely a down payment of what will rightly be yours in the future.'

Sarah pulled a handkerchief from her cuff and dabbed her eyes. 'This is a great deal of money, Gilbert. Are you sure?'

'As I mentioned previously, Sarah, we have plenty.'

Sarah clutched her breast. 'My goodness I feel quite faint, will you excuse me while I lie down?'

The men stood and Gilbert waited until she had left the room before he spoke again.

'John, on my way here I made some enquiries and tomorrow I wish you to accompany me to Stroud.'

'By all means. May I enquire as to the nature of this journey?'

'No, sir, but I think you'll be well pleased. Let us celebrate. I have in my baggage a good claret. Will you join me?'

'Yes, I will depart from my teachings at this moment as I am quite stunned by events.'

'Fear not, John, does not the church use wine as the blood of Christ in its rituals?'

John nodded. 'You're correct, sir.'

—

The following day.

'Sarah!' John called from the front door. 'Come outside I have something to show you.'

Sarah shuffled into the hallway wiping flour from her hands. 'You men are so inconsiderate. I'm in the middle of baking so this had better be important or being a parson will not save you from my wrath.'

'I beg of you, dearest,' John pleaded, 'indulge me, cover your eyes and have no fear, I'll guide you.'

'What's all this childish nonsense, John Bosworth?'

Sensing her anger he replied, 'Be patient, my love. Hold my hand and step carefully over the threshold.' He gently led her down the garden path to the front gate. 'Now open your eyes.'

A horse and trap with a young sorrel in the shafts, the harness and lacquer panels gleaming in the afternoon sunlight, stood before her. Beyond was a tethered chestnut gelding.

'What's that?' She put her hands on her hips and turned to face her husband. 'Why do you fool around?'

'They are ours, Sarah, a gift from Gilbert. There is also a spare horse so that I may retire the old mare.'

'Oh! I don't know what to say.' She stood wringing her hands for a moment. 'John, we cannot accept. You are not up to looking after three horses and a trap.'

John put a comforting arm around her shoulders. 'Have no fear, dearest. I spoke to old Zac down the lane and he is willing to earn some extra pence looking after them. We will talk more about it over dinner tonight, that is, if you have a mind to cook it.'

'I declare, John Bosworth, you take too many liberties with my patience. Be off with you.'

She punched his arm in mock anger and rushed back into the house her mind a whirlwind of confusion.

Two weeks later, after an enjoyable interlude away from politics and banking, Cousin Gilbert returned to Scotland with the promise of a brighter future in the hearts of the English branch of the Ross Clan…

1975

Angus paused and drank the last few drops from his tumbler while waiting nervously for comment and it was a long minute before

Mildmay spoke.

'Tell me, what happened to this fortune they were promised, it's fairly obvious it didn't come down your side of the family.'

'You're right, sir. It was unfortunate that both Gilbert and his sister, Jane Ross, lived to be seventy-six and ninety-two respectively. They both outlived Cousin Sarah and because Jane Ross was unaware of her genealogy the Will was ambiguous. William Maxwell, who we mentioned earlier, took advantage of this fact and went to great pains to procure the fortune for himself.'

'When was that, lad?'

'Late 1839...'

***

2

Fraud, Hope and Adversity

December 3rd 1839

The death of Jane Ross, millionaire recluse, didn't cause much of a stir in Edinburgh. Her name appeared in the obituaries and society did its duty by attending her funeral before returning to their own misery.

William Maxwell however, retired cashier of the Royal National Bank, was overjoyed—he had been planning ten years for this day.

He was an overweight, ruddy-faced man with immense wealth who had the eccentric habit of wearing an out of date grey frock coat and the double-wrapped neckcloth instead of the more fitting clothes of the time and his cunning far outweighed his generosity.

John Reid, the current cashier of the Bank, found Maxwell in the smoke ridden, dimly lit, **Turnbull's Tavern*** surrounded by other members of the banking fraternity and prostitutes hoping for an early catch.

Maxwell, slumped with his legs outstretched, looked as if he and the chair would soon part company. In his left hand he held a long stem clay pipe and in his right, a tankard of ale.

'Hello John.' Maxwell's alcohol fuelled greeting disguised his animosity towards Reid. 'I'm glad you could make it. Draw up a chair and join me in another jug and vitals.'

Reid nodded and sat down to wait for the ale, a plate of bread and cold beef to arrive before entering into any conversation with the man opposite whom he loathed with an intensity bordering on hatred.

After a few mouthfuls of food and a long swallow of ale Reid at last muttered, 'And to what do I owe the pleasure, as if I didn't know?'

Maxwell growled in a low voice. 'You've heard the Ross woman is dead?'

'Aye, you're right there,' replied Reid, 'What do we do now?'

Maxwell put his finger to his lips and took a guilty look around. 'Be careful man, these damn walls have ears; although it's not before time. I thought she would go on forever.'

'I shouldn't worry too much, William. It is common knowledge that you covet the woman's fortune.'

Maxwell continued in a voice barely above a whisper, 'You carry on as you should. Firstly you must go to the Court and record the disposition. Not too early as we don't want to arouse suspicion. I will handle everything else. Have you told Scott yet?'

'No.'

'Do so, and make sure he does nothing. You must do it all. Have you got that?'

Reid lowered his tankard and looked hard at Maxwell before replying. 'Yes, but it's a bad thing we do here, William. We could go to gaol.'

'Have no fear, John. Declare that you have done a thorough search and can find no other family connection besides me.'

Reid stood up, leaned forward over the table and said with a hint of menace. 'You're right, William, but don't forget the deal. I wouldn't like to be responsible for sending you to prison.'

He touched his hat, nodded and left the premises with the veiled threat hanging in the air.

Fortunes' Tavern*, Christmas Eve, 1839.

'Ah, there you are, John.'

Maxwell remained seated and ignored Reid's proffered hand and instead pushed a letter over the table.

'Read this, and would you like a wet while you're here?'

Reid sat opposite Maxwell at the same time making a mental note of the slight.

'William, I hope it's good news that drags me away from the office. What's wrong with your usual watering hole anyway, and yes, I will have a jug.'

He picked up the letter and began to read…

> Rt. Hon Sir Jas. G Craig
> Lord President of the Court of Sessions

William Maxwell Esq.

Dear Sir,

I accede to your request for Messrs Reid and Scott to be discharged from their duties as executors to the will of Miss Jane Ross and that a payment of £10,000 be paid for their services.

However, further to your attestation I require proof that you are the direct heir to the said estate and I wish also to be satisfied that all possible avenues have been searched to discover the whereabouts of aforementioned relatives in Miss Ross's Will.

It is also my wish that this evidence be shown to me, before, or early in the year of our Lord 1840.

> Rt. Hon. Sir Jas. G Craig.

Maxwell continued the conversation while Reid read...

'I enjoy the fellowship here of likeminded Brothers at least once a week and I think it best that we not be seen together too often because of the nature of our liaison. You will see that the letter discharges you as trustee and is authorization to pay you for your services.'

Reid nodded, 'Very satisfactory, but what of Scott?'

Maxwell reached into the deep pockets of his coat, took out a slip of paper and pushed it across the table.

'Here is a note made out for ten-thousand pounds. You will draw on this and pay Scott half and the other five-thousand each I will pay later.'

Reid's voice took on a more ominous tone. 'Very nice, William. There is however, a problem.'

'Pray what is that, sir?' Maxwell's mocking tone added fuel to the insincerity of his feelings. 'Nothing I'm sure that will deny you this windfall. A man such as you would not let it happen.'

Reid picked up the note. 'This is the first instalment. The price has now gone up to twenty-thousand pounds—Each.'

Maxwell slammed his fist on the table. 'You bastards! I had you for an honest man, John Reid. This is blackmail.'

'Very observant, William, and I am an honest man about to

become a dishonest one. It is not beyond the bounds of possibility that I may go to gaol. Therefore, I want my family well looked after and a pension on my release.'

He leaned forward menacingly and lowered his voice. 'Remember, William, I still get a handsome sum if anything should happen to you.'

'A blackguard, that's what you are. Very well, but not a penny more.'

'You have my word. It's business, William, that is all—business.'

'So it seems. Meanwhile, there is one more thing. I require you and Scott to attend as witnesses on the twenty-seventh of this month at the offices of The Lord President of Sessions.'

'We'll be there, but don't forget what I said.'

Reid stood and with an exaggerated bow, said, 'Nice to do business with you, William, I shall look forward to our next meeting.'

Maxwell waved a fist and mouthed a curse at the back of the departing Reid.

—

Minutes later Maxwell called for his coach. Dray horses, instead of the fine prancing thoroughbreds that he could well afford, drew a heavy lumbering thing from an age gone by, a monster that shook the very foundations of the overhanging buildings as it bounced over the cobbles.

Still angry from the confrontation with Reid he made his way home to a comfortable Adams mansion in the New Town where his wife, Christine, a woman of ample proportions with the charm and demeanour to grace the best salons and drawing rooms of the City greeted him.

'Good evening, William, you're early today. However can the banking business manage without you?'

'Stop your tittle-tattle woman. I'm not in the mood.'

'Oh dear, we have had a bad day, never mind. There is a lady waiting to see you in the drawing room. Maybe that will cheer you up.'

'A lady you say?' His eyes brightened at the thought, 'What would a woman want of me?'

'It's Mrs Beagle dear. You remember her, the widow of Andrew, your assistant cashier.'

'Ah, yes, I wonder what she wants.'

'I don't know, dear, but do remember she has recently lost her husband. Put our best face on and be nice. I shall get Molly to bring some tea.'

'You're not joining us?'

'No, dear, she wants to see you.'

The disconsolate look on his face said it all. 'Very well, if I must.'

As he turned to go into the drawing room Christine took hold of his arm. 'Stop dear, you look a mess in that old coat. I do wish you would get something more in keeping with the times.'

'Ach, woman, it's warm and I can carry a fair bit in the pockets.'

Without further protest he took it off and replaced the scowl with an insincere smile as he entered the drawing room.

—

The early dusk of a Scottish winter made it necessary to light the candles in the modest chandelier aided by artfully placed candelabrum.

The flames from the open fire added light to the room and kept at bay the penetrating winter cold. Flock wallpaper gave the room a cosy feeling but the flowered chintz coverings on the furniture made the ambience fussy and overcrowded.

When Maxwell entered, a petite woman with light brown hair neatly done in a pleat and tastefully dressed in the latest fashion arose from one of the high backed chairs placed either side of the fireplace.

'Mrs Beagle, don't get up on my account.'

She ignored his request and proffered her hand.

Always a ladies' man he bowed deeply and kissed the fingertips.

'It is nice to see you, Rebecca. You're keeping well no doubt?'

'How formal William.' She returned to her seat. 'Yes, I am quite well, thank you, but things could be better.'

'Oh, and how is that?' He found it difficult to hide the feeling of foreboding that came over him. 'Christine said you had business with me, what would that be I wonder?'

'William. A little birdie has told me that a certain Mr Maxwell is coming into a great deal of money by questionable means.'

He mentally cursed before replying. 'Rumours. This town flourishes on 'em. I'm afraid you've been misled.'

'I became a confidant of Miss Ross through Andrew's affairs at the bank, William, and I am familiar with her wishes and if this rumour is true you will see to it that I am no longer a burden on my family.'

The threat put so delicately left him momentarily speechless.

A polite knock on the door stopped the angry outburst that was on his lips and he lamely called, 'Come in.'

Molly entered with the tea tray and placed it on the table between them.

'Thank you, Molly. That will be all.'

She curtseyed and backed out of the room.

Flustered, Maxwell dabbed his brow and began pacing backward and forward the short distance between the door and the settee.

With a disarming smile Rebecca ignored the fuming man before her and said, 'Shall I pour, William? Do you take sugar, it may make you a little sweeter.'

Her demeanour threw him off balance and removed most of the vehemence from his voice and he said through gritted teeth.

'You preposterous little schemer, your name should be Bogle[1] not Beagle.'

'Shame on you, William. How dare you speak ill of my dead husbands name in this manner. I am merely looking after my interests, as are you. What would you do with it anyway—build a castle?'

Maxwell's fallibility in feminine company made him bluster, 'I had no wish to speak of Andrew like that. Shame on you woman that you should turn my words in such a way. There is nothing settled yet but I shall see to it that you are well looked after. Let that be an end to the matter. I shall send Christine in to entertain you while you finish your tea and then you will not show your face in this house again. Is that understood?'

Rebecca gave him her most appealing smile. 'Clearly, William.'

A red tide of anger began rising above his neck-cloth and he hastily did a half bow, turned and left the room.

Christine joined her moments later.

'How was it, Rebecca? He can be a sour old bear at times. Was it something special you wanted?'

'No. It was merely some unfinished business of Andrew's.'

Christine raised a quizzical eyebrow. 'That was some time ago, surely there was nothing left to do?'

'I was going through Andrew's papers,' Rebecca said sweetly, 'and I could not understand one of them but William cleared it up nicely.'

'I am so glad, dear.' Christine took one of Rebecca's hands and gave it a gentle squeeze. 'You must come and see us more often, I have a coffee and wine soirée every Friday afternoon'

Rebecca disguised her innermost thoughts. 'I will see. I really must go.'

'Forgive me, dear, I shall call your carriage.' Reaching around the side of the fireplace she pulled an embroidered sash.

Moments later, there was a polite knock and the butler entered.

'Yes, ma'am.'

'Bring Mrs Beagle's cloak and have her carriage brought to the front.'

'Right away, ma'am.'

He backed out of the room and Christine continued as she showed Rebecca to the door. 'Don't forget now, every Friday afternoon. You may meet a young man.'

Rebecca had no intention of returning. She would never be able to hold her head up in society if anything of this affair were to come out.

***

3

1975

Angus crossed the quadrangle with a spring in his step in contrast to the previous evening when he thought his very future was in doubt. He knocked firmly on the plaque and could hardly contain the urgency he felt as he waited impatiently for the call to enter.

Seconds felt like minutes before he was summonsed. 'Come in.'

The words were barely spoken before he burst in with an eagerness to get started.

He was greeted cordially by Mildmay. 'Steady on, lad, Take a seat and make yourself comfy.'

Angus pulled out the carver chair to a position where he could stretch his long frame and noticed the Professor had anticipated his arrival by placing a tumbler with a measure of whisky and water on the side table.

'If I remember rightly, lad, you were going to tell me about a further addition to those eager to grab a piece of your family estate.'

'Yes sir,' Angus replied with gusto, keen to get started. 'Mrs Beagle was to show her displeasure at the treatment she received from Maxwell but it was late December 1839 when William Maxwell presented his deposition before the President of the Court of Sessions when another interested party sought to ingratiate himself.'

27th December 1839. Edinburgh.

The anteroom to the office of Sir James Craig was cold, austere and barely furnished. The few gilded chairs and occasional tables dotted around and a threadbare carpet broke up the starkness of the surroundings but the small open fire was struggling to fight off the

December air invading through gaps around the window sashes.

John Reid and Colonel Scott were huddled around the fire when William Maxwell joined them a few minutes before the appointed hour and went directly to Scott.

'Good morning, Colonel Scott isn't it?'

The handshake confirmed Maxwell's suspicions that here was a like-minded man. He turned to Reid but declined his outstretched hand and merely nodded.

They waited an hour past the scheduled time watching a steady stream of court clerks and lawyers passing in and out of the double doors that were the entrance to the hallowed sanctuary of the man himself.

Scott pulled his cloak tighter and grumbled. 'I can't take much more of this I am chilled to the very marrow. Five more minutes gentlemen and then I am leaving. My carriage is warmer than this.'

Maxwell was quick to respond fearing that a quick solution to his plans could disappear.

'Gentlemen, were it not so important I would leave also. I beg of you, wait a little longer, it is to your advantage.'

Reid stopped dabbing a runny nose long enough to intervene. 'Why are you in such a hurry? Could we not wait for a more convenient time when it may be warmer?'

Maxwell turned to face him and said, 'Reasons, sir, are none of your concern. You will be well recompensed for your inconvenience and I expect you to stay as long as is necessary.'

Reid replied belligerently. 'If you do not deliver on your part Maxwell we will all go down. I will see to that.'

'That's as maybe, but I have greed on my side.'

Maxwell terminated the conversation by turning his back on them to face the meagre fire and rubbed his hands vigorously.

Minutes later the double doors opened and the clerk called out. 'Sir James will see you now, gentlemen, step this way.'

He stood to one side, took their cloaks and showed them through.

The difference between the two rooms was immediately apparent. Oak panelling and flock wallpaper showed off the finest French furniture the centre piece of which was an enormous walnut desk. Behind this monolith, sweating in the tropical temperature sat a red faced, aging, President of the Court of Session, Sir James Craig.

Rising, he moved to the side of the desk to greet his visitors. He shook their hands his demeanour altering in response to the handshakes of Maxwell and Scott who had guessed correctly the affiliation* of the honoured gentleman.

He bid them take a seat and they arranged themselves, Reid and Scott on one side and Maxwell a little apart on the other.

'Now, William.' Reid and Scott looked up in surprise at the intimacy of the greeting. 'How are you, I trust you have been cautious over the festive season?'

'Yes, sir, the world has been kind to me this year in every respect.'

The repartee was lost on Reid who did not realise the significance of the exchange that would influence the outcome of the meeting.

'Let us get down to business straight away,' continued, Sir James, 'It is always a sad occasion when discussing the benefits derived from bereavement. It is so mercenary, don't you think?' He picked up a letter and immediately dropped it. 'I have your application, William, for the dismissal of the Executors to the Will of Miss Ross. Let me see the proof of your request.'

Maxwell handed over a sheaf of papers before saying with the confidence of a man who already knew the outcome.

'Sir James, I lay before you my family tree with accompanying marriage and death certificates showing the direct family line. These gentlemen,' indicating Scott and Reid, 'will testify that after a long and diligent search they were unable to discover any living relative referred to in the testament of Miss Ross. Therefore, we must assume, because she did not marry, the line is defunct. It is my...'

Sir James held up a hand. 'Enough, William.'

He began perusing the documents laid before him occasionally looking over his pince-nez at Maxwell.

'You seem to have been thorough in your research,' he looked over at Scott and Reid, 'as I hope you gentlemen have been in your search on behalf of Miss Ross. Mr Reid!' Reid jerked upright, shaken from his miserable, cold ridden malaise. 'Surely three weeks is not long enough to have made a thorough search in the South West of England? That would appear to be unseemly hasty in my experience.'

Somewhat taken aback by the directness of the question, Reid hesitated. 'Err... Let me explain.'

'Please do.'

Reid made the most of blowing his nose to gather his thoughts before continuing. 'Miss Ross made her testament and executed a trust to dispose of her heritable and moveable estate in 1832 following the death of her brother. She requested at the time that the trustees should start a search directly. Mr Watson has since died—God rest his soul. So you see, Sir James, we have had ample time to make our enquiries.' He sniffed and dabbed at his nose again. 'Mr Watson, may the Lord have mercy, made several journeys to the Gloucester area.'

Craig stopped him with a wave of his hand and turned to Scott.

'Colonel Scott, do you have anything to add?'

'It is as my colleague described,' Scott replied.

'Very well.' Sir James turned back to Reid. 'Mr Reid, did you not see fit to go south after the demise of Watson?'

Reid sniffed. 'No sir, we concluded that he had been most diligent in his efforts and that further investigation and expenditure would have been fruitless. I was myself as Senior Cashier to the Royal National Bank unable to obtain the necessary leave of absence for such an undertaking.'

Sir James looked askance at Reid over his pince-nez.

'If as you say, you discussed this with Miss Ross. Why did you accept her request knowing you would not be able to give it your fullest attention?'

'Sir James. The Ross family has long been associated with the bank. Miss Ross's brother and father were past directors. Therefore, I felt that it was my duty as a friend to carry out her wishes not knowing beforehand how complex and difficult an undertaking it would become. Believe me, sir, had I known I would have demurred in favour of someone else, although it is my earnest belief that no one would have been any more successful than we three in our efforts to ascertain the truth.'

Sir James removed his pince-nez and addressed Scott and Reid. 'Thank you, gentlemen, I think I have heard all that is necessary, you may leave. William, could you stay a while?'

Reid and Scott left the room bemused. Neither of them spoke as they parted and made their way to their respective employment.

'William,' Sir James continued after they had left, 'let us conclude this unsavoury matter. I see no reason why I should disallow your claim. I will dictate a letter to my clerk saying as much and have it delivered to you on the morrow. Meanwhile, will you join me in a glass of claret? It is the best that France could offer.'

Later, when Maxwell was leaving the premises, the lawyer James Mackenzie approached him.

Mackenzie bowed politely. 'A thousand pardons, sir. You are William Maxwell?'

'I am he, but you have the advantage of me, sir.'

'James Mackenzie, Advocate at Law.'

'How can I help? Be quick, I don't have much time.'

'Firstly, sir, may I congratulate you on your recent good fortune. Secondly, I have information that could be of interest to you. Not that I am acting with any self-interest, you understand.'

Maxwell ran a pitiful eye over this fawning object in front of him and scornfully replied, 'Of course not, why should you? Pray, what is it that would be of interest to me?'

'I saw John Reid in your company earlier, sir. I thought you may be interested to know that he came to see me for advice only a couple of weeks ago.'

Maxwell was curious, but cautious. 'What has that to do with me?'

'Can we walk together, Mr Maxwell? I am now in the area of client confidentiality. Far be it for me to break my oath.'

Maxwell looked at him disdainfully as he spoke. 'But you would if the price was right, which is the reason you accosted me is it not? Join me in my carriage. If what you have to say is useful to me we may come to some arrangement.'

'Gladly sir, this weather is no time to be walking.'

Moments later, cosily wrapped in travel rugs, Maxwell turned to Mackenzie.

'Enlighten me. What is this piece of news that you wish to lay before me?'

Mackenzie began as if he were addressing a court. 'On or about the tenth of December, Reid, on behalf of himself and Scott, who I presume was the other gentleman, approached me in my chambers to enquire of his position in law concerning the Will of Miss Ross.'

Maxwell immediately gave Mackenzie his full attention. 'Whatever for, he is merely a trustee.'

'Precisely. However, you may not be aware that under Scotland's Laws a trustee of a Last Will and Testament may claim a share if it is found that the heirs cannot be traced.'

Maxwell shook his head in amazement.

'The bounder! You're saying he is trying to cheat me of my inheritance?'

'Yes, sir. I did however advise him that your claim was too strong and that he would be unsuccessful were he to pursue it further.'

Maxwell's tone became more conciliatory. 'I am grateful indeed for your information. Advocate you say, bill me for your time. Would you like to make yourself available to me? A retainer would of course be payable for future services. I will expect a receipt to keep our transaction legal. It would not do to flout the Law, would it?'

'It certainly would not, Mr Maxwell. It is nice doing business with you and you can expect my fullest attention in your affairs.'

They shook hands and feeling pleased at the lever he now had on Reid, Maxwell, with unusual generosity said, 'Where can I drop you?'

1975

Mildmay stopped Angus in mid flow. 'So this Mackenzie, through a double cross, sought to ingratiate himself with Maxwell in order to benefit from the legacy?'

'Yes sir, but as is already known about Maxwell, he did nothing without forethought. He could have dismissed Mackenzie there and then, but he knew that in the future he may need a lawyer, a crooked lawyer at that, and here was one ready made.'

'I see. You mentioned that Mrs Beagle became disenchanted with Maxwell. What happened to cause that?'

Angus riffled through his file, pulled out the transcript of a letter and handed it to the Professor.

'The event, sir, that was to change her allegiance, was about to take place. Whether it was Christmas spirit or part of a grand plan, I don't know, but Maxwell showed his dubious charitable side on New Years Day 1840, when he sent this letter to the Bank board of directors…'

Dear Sirs,**
Having lately succeeded to a large fortune by the death of my relative, Miss Ross of Style, I beg most respectfully to resign into the hands of the Directors of the Bank the annuity of £800, which they were so kind to allow me upon retiring from active management of the Bank.

In doing this, I hope they will not think that I am taking too great a liberty when I suggest to the Directors the propriety of their granting an annuity of £200 to the widow of Andrew Beagle, their late Cashier, who was a most zealous and interested servant of the Bank during a very long period of service extending to the whole of his life.

I remain your most trusted servant,

William Maxwell

'…It was charitable indeed,' Angus continued, 'but to recommend a meagre two-hundred pounds a year for Mrs Beagle was a slap in the face.'

Mildmay intervened. 'If my memory serves me right, was not two-hundred pounds a fortune in those days.'

'To the upper class that sum was a mere drop in the ocean. The board would have agreed to more if Maxwell had asked for it and it would have saved him a lot of trouble in the future. As it was, Mrs Beagle determined to avenge the slight and help trace the proper relatives of Jane Ross.'

Mildmay was warming to this saga and eager to know more. 'How did she go about that?

'She was not sure how best to achieve this,' Angus replied, 'when early in January 1840 circumstances were to play their part…'

***

4

January 1840. Edinburgh.

The bitter North Easterly wind blowing flurries of snow before it hindered Robert Mackie and Amy Mitchell as they walked across the New Town. Thankfully it was behind them and the smog that pervaded the city during the winter months had mercifully dispersed giving them a much needed breath of clean air. For the first time in days the Castle was visible as it stood guard on its mound.

It made their mission that little bit easier but they were in no mood to enjoy the view as they huddled deep inside their coats. Amy had a bonnet tied tightly around her head while Robert had a woollen scarf wrapped over his hat and around his face.

When they arrived at 32. St. Andrews Terrace, Robert, in his haste to be out of the weather gave the bell pull a heave much harder than was necessary.

The door opened almost immediately and James the butler, recognizing them, allowed them into the welcoming hall. They stamped their feet and rubbed their hands while James waited patiently as they explained their mission.

'Wait one moment,' he said, 'I'll check if Mrs Beagle will see you. It would have been better had you made an appointment.'

'Thanks, Jamie,' said Robert, 'please give our humblest apologies but it is of some importance.'

Jamie left them while he went to inform his mistress of their arrival and returned moments later to show them into the drawing room.

'Mrs Mitchell and Mr Mackie, ma'am.'

Rebecca Beagle stood to greet them and immediately put them at their ease.

'Robert and Amy, isn't it? You look perished, come and sit by the fire. James; take their coats and bring some hot chocolate and shortbread.'

'Very well, madam.'

He helped then with their outer garments and they sat on a sofa opposite Rebecca.

'Don't be shy,' she continued, 'how can I be of assistance?'

Mackie hesitated momentarily before saying, 'Beggin' your pardon, ma'am, but we don't know which way to turn and being as you were a friend of Miss Ross it seemed likely that you may be the best person to speak to. '

'What is troubling you?'

Amy spoke for the first time. 'It's like this, ma'am. We're not happy with the way things are going with her affairs now that she has gone.'

'Whatever do you mean?'

'Having worked for Miss Jane this past twenty years we had become great friends and confidants. She treated us like family and talked to us a lot, especially after her brother passed away. '

There came a polite knock on the door and Jamie entered with the hot chocolate and shortbread.

'Thank you, James.'

Rebecca helped to clear a space on the occasional table before she returned her attention to Robert and Amy. 'Please help yourself, and continue.'

Amy tentatively took a piece of shortbread unsure of herself in the unaccustomed roll of guest while Mackie took up the narrative.

'We know the family history and Miss Jane often spoke of her poor relations in England who are the direct descendants of her Uncle William. We have a copy of the Will she made to that effect although she does not name them.'

'Why is this any concern of yours?'

Uncertain of himself Mackie paused before answering and then, taking the bull by the horns, he said, 'We had a visit from this fellow Mr Maxwell the other day and he told us as Miss Jane's cousin he was the sole heir and the new owner of the premises. We've never heard of him, madam. If he was indeed a cousin I'm sure Miss Jane would have spoke of him. I think the fact that he is not mentioned in the Will is in itself odd.'

'I know Mr Maxwell. Do you have the copy of the Will with you?'

'Yes indeed, madam.' Amy delved into the depth of her bag and withdrew a neatly rolled bundle of papers tied with ribbon. 'Here you are. I'm afraid the writing isn't up to much.'

'Thank you. Help yourself to the shortbread while I read through it.'

Mackie reached forward and took the smallest piece within reach, while Amy, feeling more confident, helped herself to a larger portion. Mackie gave her a disapproving look but she smiled sweetly at him and continued enjoying the relative freedom of a houseguest while she could.

Five minutes passed before Rebecca looked up. 'It is quite lengthy and as you say, poorly written. It would appear that your concerns may be justified. Tell me more of the family history.'

She listened attentively while between them they told all they knew of the Ross family, especially relating to Jane's, Great Uncle William, who had moved to the South West of England with his wife and daughter Mary after the 1715 rebellion.

Rebecca reflected for a moment on what they had told her before commenting, 'It is interesting to note that William had only a daughter. That would make it easier to manipulate the truth. I see also that you have been well recompensed for your service. There would be no problem there I take it?'

'No ma'am. Mr Maxwell was most vociferous in his explanations and said that after the business of Probate Miss Jane's wishes concerning her servants would be honoured. He has kept us on temporarily to look after the property and the other servants he paid off. Old Page, Mr Gilbert's manservant, receives a pension and is moving in with us.'

'Very good, leave this with me and I will make enquiries. It is noble of you to be so concerned. Most would have taken their dues and departed.'

'Thank you, ma'am, but Miss Jane was a friend as well as a generous employer and in her later years trusted us when we could have taken advantage of her generosity and frailty. We wish to repay that trust.'

'Your attitude is truly commendable and I could find you employment if you should require it. Miss Ross spoke highly of you.'

'Thank you ever so much for the offer, ma'am. However, Miss Jane has made generous provision for our future which leaves us comfortable and able to enjoy our retirement.'

'You speak as if there is some arrangement between you. Is that so?'

Embarrassed, Robert looked down at his boots and said, 'Yes, ma'am, Amy has accepted my offer of marriage after many years of asking and Miss Jane has arranged for us to rent one of her properties in perpetuity at a peppercorn rent.'

'I am very happy for you. Mr Maxwell approves?'

'Yes, ma'am, he seemed quite anxious that we should take it.'

'I imagine he would. If your fears are indeed true then he would want as little fuss as possible. You were right to come to me. I have become a little bored of late and this gives me a new aim in life.'

She determined that here was the way to get her own back on Maxwell for the paltry pension he had arranged.

'Thank you, ma'am, and once more our apologies for taking up your time. I must add that there is a considerable amount of papers at the house should you wish to avail yourself of their content.'

'You're right, of course. Maxwell won't waste much time. He'll remove as much evidence as he can. I'll get on to it immediately.'

Robert and Amy stood up to leave.

'One moment.' Rebecca arose with them, went over to the alcove at the side of the fire and gave a gentle tug on a bell-pull.

Jamie appeared almost immediately. 'Yes madam?'

'James, please bring in the coats and could you have the coach brought around to the front. Also, tell cook we shall have an early lunch today as I have an errand to run this afternoon.'

'Very well, madam.'

He returned with the coats moments later and helped his friends dress.

Robert, concerned they had overstepped there position said, 'There is no need for the coach, ma'am. We have caused enough trouble.'

'Nonsense. It would be churlish indeed to send a dog out in

this weather, let alone one's guests.'

'A thousand thanks, ma'am. How can we ever repay you?'

'You can confiscate those documents you spoke of. I will arrange for someone to collect them. Be careful, you cannot afford the enmity of the man who holds the purse strings. Now run along the coach is waiting.'

When they had left she returned to her chair, pondered for a while the information and formulated a plan to undermine Maxwell.

The offices of A. Beattie, Advocate at Law, were dark and depressing. The clerks strained their eyes in what little light came in through the grimy windows around files and ledgers piled high on the sills and the décor yellowed by years of candle smoke did little to enhance it.

Rebecca breezed into this murky atmosphere and the clerks looking for any excuse to break away from their tedious duties vied with each other to give service.

'Where is that Alistair hiding,' she said cheerfully.

'He's popped out the back, ma'am. I'll go and get him.'

The young clerk jumped up and in his eagerness to please, knocked over his stool. His feet tangled in the upturned legs and he stopped himself falling headlong by grabbing the counter.

Rebecca laughed, 'My word, young man, that is the first time anyone has fallen for me so quickly in a long, long time. I'm flattered.'

He blushed and grinned benignly with embarrassment.

'What's all the commotion in there? Can't a man excuse himself without the place falling apart?'

Alistair Beattie stepped into the front office. He was a man of medium build with an expansive waistline and his tweed suit matched the colour of the walls. When he became aware of Rebecca his ruddy face beamed with pleasure.

'A breath of spring has entered our humble premises. Lovely to see you, Rebecca, dear. How are you?'

'I'm fine, and you haven't changed,' she said while casting a keen eye around. 'When are you going to move into better premises, Alistair? The money lawyers make you could afford it.'

A stifled chuckle of amusement came from the clerks corner as they buried their heads deeper into their work.

'Get on with it you slackers. I pay you too much for you to take part in idle banter.' His admonition went unheeded as they knew their employer and his foibles. Alistair took Rebecca by the arm. 'Come through, my dear.'

Holding the door open for her he followed her down the hall into his office which in contrast to the outer office had a roaring fire but the film of grime the Edinburgh smog had smeared over the glass subdued the light from the only window.

He pulled a chair out for her and he sat behind a desk submerged beneath a mountain of paperwork.

'To what do I owe the pleasure, Rebecca?'

'Alistair, I want you to do some detective work for me.' She took the rolled up Will from her bag. 'Read through that and then I will explain.'

He balanced a pair of battered pince-nez on the end of his nose and spent the next few minutes going over the document every now and then holding it up to the light.

Finally he looked up, put his pince-nez down on the desk, and said, 'This appears quite in order. It is an ordinary disposition but badly written in my opinion. She was inordinately rich this Jane Ross. I have heard of the family although I never moved in such exalted circles.'

'Quite so, Alistair, but it is not the Will I have come to see you about rather the manner in which it is being administered. It would not do for me to inform you of my sources but as friends of Miss Ross, both they and I would like to see her wishes carried out so that others through nefarious means may not benefit.'

She went on to tell him the facts but did not mention her own interest.

'I see.' Alistair rubbed his chin while openly admiring the woman opposite. 'What is it you want me to do exactly, Rebecca?'

'Trace the real benefactors.'

'That will take up a lot of time and expense although I am intrigued.'

He replaced his pince-nez, picked up the Will and perused it once more. After a few moments he said, 'Do you know who the fraudulent benefactor is? Reid I know, the other trustees I don't.'

'Colonel Scott is a family friend.' Rebecca raised her fan a little to shield herself from the fire. 'The other, Watson, is dead. William Maxwell is the person who would have us believe that he is the rightful heir.'

Alistair looked up in surprise. 'Maxwell,' he exclaimed. 'He is rich in his own right, why would he risk all by committing fraud?'

'Greed, Alistair. Money turns many men from their true path.'

'I see. Can you afford this, Rebecca?'

'Hardly, Alistair, but here is ten pounds on account. You will be well taken care of if we pursue this to its rightful conclusion.'

'I will take the matter up right away. Methinks a trip to the Records Office will be forthcoming. That should give us a clue where to look for these people.'

'Thank you, Alistair. I must be going, it's getting dark.'

—

1975

Mildmay removed his glasses, stretched and yawned. 'Stop there, lad. We've done enough for tonight.'

'But that's not the end of it, sir. Lodge nights for the Masons were jolly affairs and it was not long before a loose tongue let slip Mrs Beagles and Beattie's interest. Maxwell, inflamed by this intrusion, hired some villains and bad deeds were done that put Amy's and Robert Mackie's life at risk.'

'You may expand on that tomorrow. Right now it's past my bedtime. Bring some refreshment with you and make sure it's of drinkable quality.'

***

5

1840.

'Mackenzie!' Maxwell stood, leaning over the desk, resting on his hands in a manner that left little doubt about his intentions. 'It has come to my notice there are people who wish to relieve me of my windfall. You will stop them with any means at your disposal, be it legal or otherwise. Leave no stone unturned. I want any connection to the Ross Clan, apart from mine, erased from history.'

'At such short notice,' Mackenzie replied lamely, 'I have only this day taken on a high court case of some distinction.'

Maxwell stabbed his finger down on the desk repeatedly to enforce his words. 'Get rid of it!'

'What of my reputation?' Mackenzie whimpered, cowed by the bully before him. 'I must think of my living in the future.'

'Any reputation you had disappeared when you took your Judas money to tell me of Reid,' Maxwell leaned further forward to emphasize his point. 'And a word in the right ear will secure you a future in yon castle dungeons. Do I make myself clear?'

'You have me over a barrel, Maxwell.' In an attempt to change the subject he meekly said, 'I hear you have a Coat of Arms.'

'You hear right,' Maxwell replied, 'In recognition of my position in the Clan and now that I am the legal heir I have also taken the Clan name. In future I am to be called, William Maxwell-Ross.'

Mackenzie tried to assert himself. 'Don't expect me to bow I know too much. Is there any way your business can wait while I sort my affairs?'

Maxwell's mild response surprised him. 'Aye, but hurry, someone is suspicious of my inheritance and set to put in a counter claim. You must act with some haste.'

Mackenzie sensing that Maxwell's bubble had burst said with some irony. 'Have you anyone in mind or must I search up blind alleys?'

Maxwell threw a bundle over the desk. 'Here's the Ross papers. Trace the family and pay particular attention to William Ross of Kirkston. He was Jane Ross's Uncle, now deceased.'

Mackenzie picked up the bundle and studied the documents for a moment before saying with some alarm. 'You mean me to travel to Aberdeenshire at this time of year. Nothing moves the other side of yon Firth. The snow is horse belly deep up there.'

'Then you're going to be busy.' Maxwell threw a moneybag on the desk. 'Here's five-hundred pounds for whatever expenses you may incur and make sure to go over the house in Picardy Place. See to it that the job is well done and no one is to know of my connection. Remember, any word and I am sure the Sheriff will be only too glad to hear of your misdoings.'

———

Amy Mitchell awoke with a start from deep sleep to instant wakefulness and the cold hand of uncertainty passed over her face. She rubbed her eyes and shook her head in disbelief.

'I must be dreaming,' she muttered.

She lay back on the pillow and listened. The impenetrable silence of the darkness reminded her of her solitude and made her conscious of her pounding heart and she pulled the eiderdown over her head in an unconscious effort to hide only to sit bolt upright immediately as the soft vibrations of a body falling wound its way up the stairs and alerted her clouded senses that something wasn't right.

'What was that?,' she uttered hoarsely.

She shivered as she felt around for the match holder. In her haste she knocked over the candlestick and she held her breath as it dropped and then rumbled across the room every corner of the hexagonal base reverberating in a metallic drum roll.

'Oh, dear,' she said, not realising she was whispering.

Swinging her feet out of bed and feeling around in the gloom she found her wrap and pulled it about her. She searched for the matches but only managed to knock the holder off the bedside table to the floor.

'Damn, damn, damn,' she sobbed.

On her hands and knees she rummaged around until she found it and one of the elusive matches. With a sigh of relief she struck a match and in the brief moment of illumination located the candle and lit it. She relaxed a little as the flickering light pushed back the boundaries of her insecurity and pulling her wrap tighter she grabbed a poker from the fireplace and eased the bedroom door open.

She crept along the landing and down the stairs to the first floor and the family living area. The ghostly wobbling shadows thrown up by the candlelight increased her apprehension as she paused to listen.

Her anxiety lessened as she thought maybe her imagination or the winter winds were playing tricks. She tip-toed slowly to the head of the stairs leading to the ground floor. Hearing nothing, she took the first step. It creaked. She stopped, anxiously listening, unaware that she was holding her breath.

All was quiet. She exhaled, and the noise so fatuous in daytime was magnified in her jumbled brain. Once more, she began to gingerly descend but on the third step she paused and swallowed hard, resisting the urge to scream. In the shadows she could see a body sprawled in the hallway.

Dreading what she might find she continued. The body became clearer in the circle of light and she realised it was Robert. Without thinking she dropped the poker and hurried the last few steps.

'Robert! What is it? What have you done?'

She knelt down beside him, turned him over and saw the trickle of blood from a head wound. 'Oh, Robert, what have you been up to?'

Sixth sense made her look up but too late to stop the blanket thrown over her. Strong arms wrapped around her and lifted her off her feet. She struggled and twisted, kicking out at her unseen aggressor. Her muffled cries went unheeded as her assailant dragged her into the front parlour.

'Stop your caterwauling woman. You'll no' get hurt if yer shut up and be still.'

Her struggles intensified as she lashed out anyway she could.

'Jimmy! Give me a hand with this bitch.'

'What's the matter with ye? Can you no' handle a woman? Gi' her a clout.'

'She kicks and bucks like a horse. Come here, I tell ye, I canna hold her much longer.'

'Auch! Spare me, a'm looking for somebody else after this, yer fair as weak as watter.'

Two of them she could not resist and she gave up the unequal struggle.

'Put her on the chair and tie her up, an' hurry!'

They bound her ankles to the chair legs and then a few loops around her upper arms to secure her.

'Now listen here lady,' an unseen voice said menacingly in her ear, 'If ye tell us what we want you'll come to no harm. Where's the cash and the family deeds?'

'Shut-up, watch what yer sayin',' another hidden voice said, 'Wur only supposed to be robbin' the place.'

That was the noise she had heard. The attack on Robert and rummaging in the study.

'On your way, you'll get nowt here. There's only us servants, and no money. The mistress has died and everything taken away. You wouldn't rob poor serving folk, would you?'

Her isolation beneath the blanket magnified the blow. A bolt of red lightning seared through her head and she collapsed sideways in the chair and tumbled unconscious to the floor.

'Go easy, man, ye dinna wanna kill her. Now we canna mak her talk.'

'It does ne' matter, now we can search unheeded.'

'What are we lookin' for?'

'Any papers that looks important'

'I canna read, how do ah know?'

'If it's got writing on just tak it, and help yourself to anythin' you fancy. It'll add to the measly pickings we're gettin' paid.'

—

The following morning.

'Mrs Mitchell, have you told the Sheriff's men exactly what you told me?'

'Yes, Mr Maxwell.'

'It's all very odd,' he said rubbing his chin with exaggerated concern, cursing inwardly the ineptitude of his hired thugs. 'Why would anyone want the family deeds? Did they leave anything behind?'

'Only the accounts and some bills,' Amy replied, 'anything else that was paper, they took.'

'And they took nothing in the way of goods?'

'A pair of silver candle sticks, sir. They would be of no use with the Coat of Arms engraved on 'em.'

'They would melt them down.'

Maxwell turned away curious about a disturbance coming from the front hall.

'Let me through, I have been called upon to attend Amy and Robert.'

Rebecca Beagle burst into the room and hurried over to Amy.

'Are you alright and where is Robert?' She became aware of Maxwell's presence and bobbed in a sarcastic semblance of a curtsey. 'How do you do William, a dreadful business.'

He nodded in barely disguised dismay and the tone of his reply was equally dismissive.

'Good morning, Mrs Beagle, and to what do we owe the pleasure?'

Amy winked at Rebecca who had begun tending to her and intervened. 'It was my fault, sir, I sent word to Mrs Beagle. Miss Jane always said if there was any trouble we were to do this.'

'These bruises are nasty Amy,' said Rebecca, 'and what of Robert?'

Maxwell interrupted. 'I'll be off. There's nothing more I can do here. Carry on to the best of your abilities, Mrs Mitchell. I will look in again tomorrow. Good day to you, Mrs Beagle.'

She gave him her best smile and said facetiously, 'Goodbye, William. Going to the counting house are we?'

He ignored the barb and raised his hat in response to her exaggerated curtsey before turning on his heel.

Rebecca smirked and turned her attention back to Amy. 'Now then Amy, tell me all about it, and how is Robert?'

'He is being tended upstairs by the Doctor, madam. He needs a couple of stitches to his head.' She went on to narrate the events of the night.

Rebecca listened attentively for a few minutes before interrupting. 'What do you really think they were after, Amy?'

'I don't know, madam. They didn't seem to have a clue either. Only the one said they wanted anything that was interesting looking paperwork before the other one shut him up.'

'How concerned was Mr Maxwell when he arrived?'

Amy looked at Rebecca puzzled. 'What do you mean, ma'am?'

'Was he agitated or did he make light of it?'

Amy nodded as she spoke. 'Now you mention it. He made a big scene with the Sheriff's men about decent citizens not being safe in their beds and what were they doing about it but in the house he only had a cursory look around, sort of, disinterested, if you know what I mean.'

'Mm.' The thoughtful look on Rebecca's face said it all. 'I think we removed those documents just in time. Well done. You rest while I pop and see Robert.'

'Can I come with you? I'm fair worried about him.'

Rebecca saw the furrows of anxiety on Amy's forehead and she did not have the heart to stop her.

'Of course, but you must get some rest also.' Rebecca helped Amy to her feet. 'We'll check on him and then you can give me the key to the tea caddy.'

They met the doctor leaving the patient's room and in response to Rebecca's enquiry about his health, he replied, 'Auch, he'll live. I've given him some laudanum to help him rest. He must have a head made of iron. That was a fair clout they gave him.'

'Thank you, Doctor. See to it that he gets the best treatment and send the bill to Mr Maxwell. You may tell him I said so.'

They went into the bedroom where Robert was lying with a bandage covering his head. The opiate had taken effect instantly and he was snoring fit to waken the dead.

'Oh, my; what a noise,' Rebecca said in amused astonishment, 'shall we turn him on his side?'

'Yes, ma'am, but I've never heard him snore like that before.'

Amy's hand flew to her mouth and she blushed when she realized to what she was admitting.

'Have no fear, Amy,' Rebecca chided her, 'your secret is safe with me. Besides, you did say you have an understanding.'

Amy turned her head away to hide her embarrassment.

Rebecca took hold of Amy's hands. 'Look at me, Amy. Don't be ashamed, yours is a true love, though I do think he should make an honest woman of you quickly before he has any more mishaps.'

Amy smiled with relief, and said, 'Thank you, ma'am, we were going to wait until we moved into our own place, but I think you're right. I'll chivvy him along a bit when he's better.'

'Well Amy, we can do no good here, let's go and have that cup of tea and then I must run along. I had better move quickly as it is my view that they intend to hide all trace of Miss Jane's family one way or another.'

Later

Rebecca spoke with some urgency. 'Alistair, we have to do something quickly. I have an uneasy feeling that this robbery is only the beginning. Have you made any progress since we last spoke?'

'Yes.' He rummaged around amongst the jumble on his desk. 'I paid a visit to the Records Office and was told that I was the second person in a week to make such an enquiry. I have also been through the documents you brought from the house and I can make a reasonable guess as to the location of the English side of the family.'

'Can you get on to it right away?' Rebecca urged.

'Rebecca; that I could. It seems everyone is suing or has some other sort of litigation these days. I am snowed under with work.'

'Alistair, we must do something. Oh, please,' she pleaded, 'we can't wait around and let this tyrant have his way.'

Rebecca could weaken his resolve with a mere flick of an eyebrow.

'Do I detect a little personal feeling in this matter, Rebecca?'

She smiled mysteriously. 'Yes there is. Maxwell offended me and the memory of my late husband. I see this as a way to get my own back and if I can stop him, although I will not gain by it, I will be well pleased.'

Alistair scratched his head for a moment. 'I have an idea. My nephew Stephen, a likeable young man who is recently qualified would be keen to take on this work. Firstly, he must go to Gloucestershire and speak with these people and validate their claim to Ross estate. We will need a letter of introduction from you, Rebecca, as a friend of Miss Jane. Do we know of any other who may substantiate our position in this matter as we are not the legal trustees to her Will?'

Rebecca sat thoughtfully for a few seconds. 'I am afraid not, Alistair. They will have to take us on face value.'

'This shouldn't prove difficult as they themselves will have to attend court here in Edinburgh. We will only be advising them on what action is required.'

'Oh, thank you Alistair, you sweetie.' She blew him a flighty kiss. 'I will go and write this letter for you and have it delivered post-haste. Here is another ten pounds, make it do as my well is not limitless.'

'Thank you Rebecca. We will start at the address of Brother Gilbert's last known visit. By the way, do you know that Maxwell has been declared sole heir and was recently granted Royal licence to change his name?'

'No. What do we call him now?'

'He goes under the exalted name—William Maxwell-Ross of Style.'

Rebecca threw back her head and laughed. 'Let us hope that no one makes the wrong inference with the name, although that is what he is. My upbringing forbids me to say the word. Good day to you, Alistair, I look forward to our next meeting.'

'Goodbye Rebecca.' He took her hand and kissed it. 'It is always a pleasure seeing you, my dear.'

'Away with you, I declare you're flirting, sir.' She gave a slight bob and left the premises with Alistair's eyes following her every step.

'Bastard![2] That's what you meant to say,' he uttered when she was out of earshot.

***

6

Stephen.

1840.

Twenty-five year old Stephen Beattie, a personable, not a handsome man, but one women would call interesting, stretched his legs across two seats in the second-class carriage.

His journey in comparison to Gilbert Ross's to the West Country in 1793 was a pleasant interlude of rail and coach travel over four days. The weather was kind to him and he was able to enjoy the experience with the exuberance of a young man on his first adventure.

The final part of his journey by train from Gloucester to a tiny countryside Halt took half an hour and he was somewhat bemused to be stood on the empty platform in the middle of a rural landscape devoid of any habitation.

He stood for a moment rubbing his chin weighing his options when an elderly man in a rumpled uniform of the Great Western Railway Company appeared from behind the solitary station building . 'Can I help you, son?'

'Yes, sir. I am trying to get to Morcton Vale. I was advised that this would be the nearest place to get off.'

'You'd a been better takin' the coach. Ne'er mind. Cross the track and walk down to the village. It's only about a mile or so. Ya'll get a buggy from Bill the Smithy to take you the rest o' the way.'

'Thanks.' Stephen picked up his valise and set off.

He had only gone a short way when a cart loaded with a variety of produce pulled up along side him. The deeply suntanned driver stopped chewing on a piece of straw long enough to say, 'Can I take you somewhere, young man?

'Yes, please, I'm going to the village.'

'Hop on't back board and hang on, although the old mare goes at no great pace.'

It was somewhat further than a mile and Stephen was glad he had accepted the offer of a lift and when they reached the village he called over his shoulder to the driver. 'Can you drop me at the Smithy, please?'

'Right you are, son. Here 'tis and mind how you go.'

Stephen poked his head around the door of a large ramshackle workshop attached to the end of a cottage and called out. 'Hello! Anyone there?'

The distinctive sound of the blacksmith's waltz rang out to greet him. Bang, ting, ting. Bang, ting, ting.

He ventured further inside and saw the blacksmith hard at work unable to hear him over the noise of his hammering. Edging closer over discarded metal he shouted and waved. 'Hello!'

The Smith stopped in mid-swing and looked up. 'Aye there, what can I do for you?'

'I'm told you can supply me a buggy to Moreton Vale.'

'Yer right there, lad. Can you hang on a couple of minutes?

'Yes, I'll wait outside.'

They were soon on their way and the journey passed easily. Old Bill, the Smith, tried to prise from him the purpose of his visit but Stephen merely replied, 'I'm visiting an Aunt for pleasure.'

This enjoyable interlude lasted forty-five minutes before they pulled up outside the Rectory at Moreton Vale.

'Can you wait, Bill, while I make enquiries? It is some time since I communicated with them and they may have moved on?'

'Most surely, young sir.'

The path to the front door wound through a tidy rose garden. He rattled the knocker and waited a few moments before the Parson, a man of advanced years, dressed in black with the customary white shirt and black necktie opened the door.

'Good day, sir. How can I help?'

Stephen cleared his throat nervously. 'Ahem! Good day, I'm trying to trace the Bosworth family. The last known address I have is this one.'

'You're in luck,' the Parson replied, 'the two previous tenants of this vicarage were indeed Bosworth. Sadly, Thomas, the last one, has passed away, but his wife, Emily, lives with their eldest son, also called Thomas, over Frampton way. It is but a few miles from here.'

'Thank you, sir. Good day to you.' He raised his hat and returned to the buggy.

'Well, Bill, it seems I must travel further. Frampton, do you know it?'

'Yes, young sir, it be a little over three miles from here.'

'Can you take me?'

Bill scratched at the stubble on his chin and thought for a moment. 'Oh, I don't know, that's a fair way to travel back.'

'I'll give you a florin and buy you vitals.'

'That sounds good to me. Jump aboard and let's get going.'

'I'm quite famished now, Bill. Let's stop at the village inn.'

After a tankard of cider, a wedge of cheese, pickled onion and a large portion of cottage loaf, they made their way to Frampton.

It was evening before they arrived in the village and pulled up outside the Red Lion.

'I will lodge here tonight, Bill. Get your fill before you leave and I will pay the bill. Here's your florin.'

'Thank you, kindly, young sir. It was no trouble an' you was good company. I hope you finds your relative an no mistake.'

'Farewell, and give my apologies to your wife.'

Old Bill doffed his cap and with a quick nod they parted.

Stephen stood for a moment inside the door and decided that the Inn was a good choice to lay his head. The spotless shirt and apron of the red-headed barman was a testament to the overall quality of the premises.

He threw his valise down on a nearby bench and the girl who came out from the kitchen instantly grabbed his attention. She was a neat, freckle faced girl of twenty. A starched cap sat atop a mass of red curls surrounding a heart shaped face and her cheery welcoming smile confirmed his decision to stay.

'Good evening, sir. What would you like?'

His weariness fell away as he responded to her in a like manner.

'I would like a room for the night and dinner, but first be so good and make sure Bill over there is well fed. He has done me good service today.'

Oh, Dad'll be glad to speak to a fellow countryman an' don't worry, sir, we'll look after, Bill. Would you be wantin' just the one night?'

'I don't know.' Thinking it best to keep a familiar atmosphere to aid his enquiries he added, 'I'm looking for the Bosworth family. I'm advised that they live in the village?'

'They do indeed. Theirs is the last house on the left on the Arlingham road. You can't miss it.'

'Thank you, I shall look them up in the morning. Where do I lay my head?'

'One moment.' She nipped across and spoke to the barman before rejoining him. 'Take room number two, sir. Will you eat straight away?'

'I'll unpack my bag and rest a little and then if I may dine about eight.'

'That's fine, sir. We have pork and lamb tonight with apple pie to follow. It's my Mum's special.'

'I must say you look good on her cooking. I can't wait.'

She blushed and hurried back to the kitchen.

—

The following morning.

Having ascertained her name as Anne during dinner the previous evening he was able to continue his flirtation over breakfast. She was only too pleased to meet someone her own age and leaning forward to accentuate nature's gifts, she explained, 'The village is only a mile from the main highway, but it may as well be ten. People going to and from the ferry at Arlingham never stop and the young men have either gone to Bristol or Gloucester.'

'Then I must make every effort to stay,' he said, trying to drag his eyes away from the shaded valley of her bosom, 'what do you think might hold me?'

Her eyes twinkled brazenly, 'Oh, I can think of a dozen things. Maybe breakfast by my own fair hand.'

'I can think of no better way to start the day. Already the sun shines.'

'Be off with you, sir, I've not heard a poorer line to my

affections.' She laughed, and disappeared into the kitchen.

He set off much later than intended to find the Bosworth cottage. While strolling through the village he enjoyed the scent of the neat front gardens his mind far away trying to think of ways to delay his departure on completion of his task. Because of his day dreaming he failed to notice the sign over the local store that told all and sundry that the proprietor was one '*Thomas Bosworth Esq.*'

When he arrived at the cottage he was unsure of himself on this his first foray into the world outside the *'Halls of Learning'* and he hesitated before knocking. He had no sooner removed his hand from the ornate brass knocker and turned to look at the garden when a gentle voice addressed him.

'Good morning, you must be the young man staying at the Red Lion?'

He swung round surprised by the melodious voice of the young woman who welcomed him. Her brown dress was buttoned up to the neck with the tiniest of lace frill around the collar and her hair was plaited and fastened in coils either side of her head. She was plain, but attractive, with a pleasant disposition.

Stephen gave a deep bow sweeping his hat across his body and with a ready smile said, 'I'm sorry, madam, but you have the advantage of me. I am indeed, Mr Beattie and I am staying at the Inn.'

'And I am Mistress Esther Bosworth. My brother called at the Inn last night and was informed of your arrival. Oh, please excuse my bad manners, do come in.'

'Who is it dear?' The thin voice of an elderly person came from the parlour.

'It is the gentleman from the Inn that Thomas spoke of, Mama. Wait one moment we are coming through.'

They went from the hall into a pleasant feminine living room.

'Mama, this is Mr Beattie. Mr Beattie, likewise—Mrs Emily Bosworth.'

She was a small fragile woman dressed in black with her grey hair tucked into a white mobcap. He took the proffered hand and kissed the fingertips gently. 'How do you do, madam? It is a pleasure.'

'Thank you. Now what can we do for you, young man.' Her straightforward manner belied her stature.

Esther interrupted. 'Mother, let us provide refreshment before we fulfil our curiosity. Mr Beattie, do you have a first name?'

'Yes ma'am, it is Stephen and I am an Advocate at Law from Edinburgh.'

'Yes, I can tell you come from Scotland. You have a similar accent to Mr Young at the Inn. Would you like a cup of tea?'

'Yes, please, it is a beverage I am growing fond of.'

'I won't keep you.'

She slipped out of the room leaving him under the steady gaze of Emily, who, as soon as they were alone said, 'Now, young man, it is nearly fifty years since we had a visitor from Scotland. The last one came to see my mother-in-law. Do you come on the same errand?'

'How naughty of you, Mrs Bosworth, I can only speak with Miss Esther or Mr Thomas as direct relatives. You're warm though. Hush, she returns with the tea.'

Esther bustled in with a tray and set it down on the centre table.

'I heard voices. She isn't browbeating you is she, Stephen? She does everyone else.'

'We were merely discussing the weather and how mild it is.'

He looked across at Emily and a conspiratorial smile passed between them.

'Oh good, help your self to a biscuit Stephen and tell us what you are about.'

He took a sip of tea and a nibble at a biscuit to collect his thoughts before he cleared his throat.

'Ahem! Late last year, Miss Jane Ross of Style, who resided in Edinburgh, died and left a great deal of money and title. There has been a claim to the estate, however, friends of Miss Ross believe that the direct heirs are your family who are descended from her Uncle William. Alistair Beattie, my Uncle, has been directed to trace you and advise you of your rights.'

Esther looked at Stephen with raised eyebrows and said dubiously. 'I see, and is there a Will?'

'Yes, but it is rather ambiguous and open to fraud. This is

what we believe is taking place.'

'Oh, dear.' Esther sat and thought for a moment before continuing. 'Does that mean all we have to do is go and collect it?'

'It is not that easy. You will have to provide evidence of your ancestry and live in Scotland a short while. Then you must present it to the Court of Sessions.'

'I think Thomas should hear this.' Abruptly Esther stood up and made ready to leave. 'I'll go and collect him from the shop. Make yourself at home, I won't be long.'

———

She returned fifteen minutes later with her brother.

'Thomas, this is Mr Beattie the gentleman I told you about, Stephen—my brother, Thomas.'

They exchanged greetings and while Thomas was reading his letter of introduction Stephen explained once more the circumstances of his visit.

'And there you have it,' he finished with a flourish.

Thomas sat quietly, looking alternately at the letter and at Stephen, unsure what to say. When he did speak, it was slow and deliberate. 'You say all we have to do is collect documentary evidence of our birthright and this fortune will be ours.'

Emily who had sat quietly throughout the proceedings interrupted. 'Excuse me; can I say something?'

'Why yes, mother.'

'A year before your Father and I married, my mother-in-law had a visit from a Scottish gentleman. She always spoke of Cousin Gilbert and the name of Ross in her later years and about how he brought money and said that they would inherit the estate after he and his sister died. We have been waiting all these years for someone to come and fetch us.'

Stephen ears pricked up. 'When was that, Mrs Bosworth?'

'Oh, my memory,' she held a hand to her mouth while she cast about in her aging mind for the elusive dates, 'When did I get married, Thomas, ninety-three or four?'

'Ninety-four, Mother.'

'That was a long time ago,' said Stephen, 'Miss Ross was ninety two when she passed away. Mind you, no one could have expected her to live that long. It must run in the family. I beg your pardon, madam, but you must be four score years.'

Emily laughed and wagged a finger at him. 'I am, but I'm not a Ross,'

'I stand corrected.'

Thomas butted in. 'We are naive in the ways of the law, Stephen. Could you help us? I mean, how will we know what is real proof and what is not?'

Stephen thought for a moment before raising his eyes and saying a silent, 'Thank you,' for the opportunity to stay awhile. He would be able to prolong his pursuit of Anne and assist the family in their quest for truth at the same time.

Trying not to appear too eager, he said, 'I will gladly stay and help. There's one thing, however. I have no means of income or a roof over my head. The expenses I was given will shortly run out.'

Thomas led him over to a corner of the room and said quietly, 'Stephen, I will give you a guinea a week to stay after your expenses have run out and we have a room above the shop which can be yours. Does that prospect agree with you?'

With a suppressed smile Stephen said, 'How can I repay you other than to work hard? I will draw up a legal document to that effect.'

'Let us shake hands on that, young man. It will take a couple of days to straighten out the room I mention. Can you manage at the Inn until then?'

Would he stay at the Inn? He made an effort not to show his delight as the picture of tumbling red hair flashed before him.

'That will be no trouble. I'll get to it straight away. Firstly, I must write a letter to my Uncle. I believe this new fangled postal service works quite well. Then I will get the agreement drawn up and Mr Young at the Inn will do as a witness. Meet me there tonight, Mr Bosworth. Until then.' He bowed to the ladies and shook hands with Thomas. 'Goodbye.'

He took time during his lunch to boldly ask Anne if he could be her suitor to which she consented with barely concealed eagerness and later in the evening after the legalities of his quest had been signed and witnessed he asked the landlord if he might court his daughter.

'So you wanna tak out ma daughter, aye. What prospects do you have?'

'Well, sir, as a legal practitioner the opportunities are limitless.' The white lie slipped effortlessly off his tongue as he omitted to mention that he had recently qualified and had not actually handled anything legal.

'Sounds good.' Young leaned forward on the bar with his chin resting in his hands. 'And what when you move back to Scotland, you'll leave the lass here with a broken heart, no doubt?'

'That is not my intention, sir. As soon as my present task is finished, I shall actively pursue employment here, if there is any to be found.'

'Well now, young man.' Young stood upright and busied himself wiping tankards. 'I could help you there. In Stroud, there is a solicitor by the name of George Innes. He's a fellow countryman and a close friend and I've heard he needs an assistant.

'Thanks for the tip, but first I must honour my word to the Bosworth family. We forget something though.'

Young put down the tankard he was cleaning, wiped his hands on the bar towel and looked intently at Stephen. 'What might that be?'

'My heart leaps at the very sight of her. What if she rejects me?'

'Is that all? She's done nowt but daydream since you arrived. I canna' get a full day's work out of her. You'll be doing me a favour.'

—

Stephen's early travels were local and did not keep him away for more than a day at a time. He used the Bosworth's trap extensively for the first week and the family horse enjoyed the freedom. Stephen's happy mood transferred down the reins and on the return journeys the horse sensed Stephen's urgency to continue his courting.

The daily excursions grew longer as he checked, double-checked and made notes of church records. Moreton Vale, Saul, Hardwicke. He did Arlingham Church on his way to the ferry over the River Severn to Newnham. This saved him a day but it was

Friday before he managed a visit to the offices of George Innes.

Innes looked up from Stephen's introductory letter.

'So you want to settle here, eh? I've no doubt there is a woman involved and I've a mind which one. A fine girl and a good catch for any man.'

Stephen could feel himself blushing and was thankful of the dull light in the office as he hurriedly said, 'I have Mr Young's permission to court Mistress Anne and I am hopeful of employment here about so that I may pursue her most ardently.'

Innes looked at the young man with some amusement. 'My business is picking up and I could do with some help. You'll not be a partner mind as you'll have to prove yourself. Have you got your accreditations with you?'

'No sir, it did not seem necessary when I set out on my errand.'

Innes leaned back in his chair and surveyed the young man in front of him for a few moments before replying. 'This errand of yours, what is it about?'

Stephen outlined the case of the Ross legacy and his search for the descendants.

'And I have contracted to work for Mr Bosworth and do the search on his behalf to trace the family connections. I am obliged to see it through to its conclusion.'

'Rightly so, young man. How long do you think your errand will last?'

Stephen rubbed his chin while he pondered the question. 'I don't know, sir. I have made considerable progress already, but next week I must search further afield. I am hopeful of being finished in a month. Then I can return home and collect my belongings and papers.'

Innes nodded. 'Be as quick as you can, but be diligent. I like you and I shall give you a retainer of ten shillings a week starting Monday and if you can attract some of the work to this office so much the better.'

'I will try my utmost to repay your generosity, sir.'

They stood and shook hands and Innes was quick to notice the lack of response to his handshake. 'I must introduce him at the first opportunity,' he said mentally.

'Goodbye, sir.'

'Goodbye, young man, and take good care of my investment.'

Monday.

Astride a hired chestnut mare Stephen set off early to travel to Newent in the north of the county. He enjoyed the journey through Arlingham and along the rows of walnut trees as he rode down *'The Passage'* to the ferry.

It was low tide but in his present high spirits he didn't mind the wait for the ferryman to make his way from the other side.

After crossing the Severn he trotted at a leisurely pace through the Forest of Dean. Cinderford passed by and when he reached the main highway at Mitcheldean he saw the fingerpost to Longhope.

He reflected on that name for a moment, thinking that his journey entailed a lot of hope.

The landscape changed to rows of fruit trees as he travelled northwards. He felt at ease in the saddle and he allowed his mind to wander from the scenery to the previous evening and the memory of his parting from Anne.

There were many long ardent kisses and cuddles in the moments when she could get away from her chores and later, when her father had fallen asleep, the kisses became more frenzied and the clinches tighter and longer. Their passion had stopped short of intimacy as the desperation of their parting became closer.

Hormones and nature urged them to the boundaries. Her breathing became quicker and her heart pounded inside her corset until she thought she would faint.

He pulled her tightly to him, kissed the top of her head and whispered, 'My love, I will try and make it no more than a week.'

'Stephen, take care. I know 'tis silly of me for so short awhile but your very presence lights my day. I have never been so happy.'

'Likewise I have your vision in my head at all times. The very thought of you makes every day more fascinating. Now I must take my leave and return to my lodgings as I must depart with the cock crow in the morning.' He tilted her head back and kissed her hard.

'Take care, dearest, I love you.'

———

The ride became arduous and he was glad to be out of the saddle that evening as his time at college had left him unprepared for a long day's ride. He was able to walk with barely disguised stiffness.

The proprietor of the local Inn did not inspire confidence. The bulbous red nose on a vein threaded scarlet face suggested he drank most of his profit. The stubble on his chin, an apron stained with all manner of dirt and his drink sodden belly hanging in folds over his belt combined with a white shirt as grey as the bleakest thundery sky emphasized his tardiness.

'Now then, young sor, what can I do for ee?'

Stephen took note of the apparition before him but was too tired to take proper heed. 'I need a bed for the night and stabling for my horse and right now a tankard of your best ale.'

'I'll send the lad for the horse. Will you be wantin' private like, or public?'

The thought of sharing a dormitory with others less desirable made him shudder. 'Private.'

'That'll be an extra three-pence, here's your ale.' He picked up a slate, dabbed a stubby piece of chalk on his tongue an waited, hand poised. 'Will you be wantin' vitals?'

Stephen, with a glance at the grimy apron wondered if he was making the right decision. 'Dinner tonight.'

The landlord's curiosity got the better of him. 'Ridden far?'

'From Gloucester way and my legs are complaining.'

'Wait 'til morning. Going far?'

Stephen grew tired of this conversation. 'I would like to rest awhile. Could you show me to my room?'

'Certainly sir. Dinner's at seven. I'll send the boy for you.'

———

Stephen flopped onto the bed only to find the horsehair mattress knotted in lumps but he was glad to take the weight off his legs.

He lay there dozing and the vision of wayward red hair and long lingering kisses stirred his loins until his discomfort was forgotten and he went to sleep with a smile on his face.

———

The following morning
His visit to the local church took up most of the morning and he had to enlist the aid of the local churchwarden to decipher the scribble of the clerk who had registered baptisms in 1754.

Because Grandfather John Bosworth was a man of the cloth and had been Parson in the parishes of Dymock and Newent before settling in Moreton Vale his name was recorded on wall plaques which made Stephen's search a little easier.

His task completed Stephen made up his mind not to spend a moment longer in this village, not even for lunch. He was feeling groggy from a restless night itching with bedbugs accompanied by a chorus of snores and other bodily functions from the general dormitory and he could not stomach another meal from the table of the landlady whose culinary skills were more suited to the sty.

Without further ado he decided to try his luck on the road to Dymock.

The short ride took him longer than expected. His horse began favouring her right fore and he had to walk the last mile and a half. Stephen shook his head in disgust. 'So much for looking after man and beast,' he muttered. In future, he would be a little more circumspect over his choice of lodgings.

On arrival in Dymock, he left his horse at the Smithy and made his way to the Royal Oak standing across from the Church at the convergence of two highways. It was a large well kept Inn of timber framed red brick on a stone foundation with decorated bargeboards on two bay gables, one either side of the arch left for coaches to enter into the rear yard and the stables.

The outward appearance of the place told him he was going to sleep well that night but his most urgent need was food as it had been a long time since his meagre breakfast in Newent.

He was not disappointed. In contrast to his previous lodgings, the Inn was spotlessly clean and the disposition of Nancy, the serving girl, was most heartening as she was both friendly and pleasing to the eye.

She was a fresh-faced buxom girl with a nipped in waist, whose country charms were almost overflowing the neckline of her blouse. At the sight of a new face, she pushed the shoulders as low as decency would allow. 'Good morning, sir. What can I get you?

'Good morning to you, young lady. I am famished. Cold mutton and the cheese board, please, and a flagon of ale.'

'Oh, you're from up Scotland way. I do like that burr in a man's voice.'

'Do you indeed. Then we must make sure you hear plenty of it tonight, eh.'

He could not help himself and continued the flirtation to help his day along and he gave her a wink as she turned away.

His lunch was plentiful as it was tasty and the feather bed in his room most luxurious, and resisting the temptation to take a nap, he took a stroll before collecting his horse.

It appeared that village life in England, although hard, had a peaceful organised quality about it and the people looked healthier, compared to the squalor and indignity of the crofter's life in Scotland and he thought it was little wonder that so many migrated South.

'That's a fine mare you have there, sir,' the Smithy said, 'a good sixteen hands. You look after her well.'

Stephen gave the horse a pat on the neck. 'She is a hired horse and I may be tempted to buy her.'

'She's not very old, sir, about six years I reckon, so there's plenty of life in her yet and she should prove a good purchase. That'll be three-pence, sir.'

'Is that all?'

'It was nought but a loose shoe.'

Stephen paid and added a penny tip.

—

A bond had grown between him and the horse and she followed him to the Inn on a slack reign.

'Good girl, I shall have to raise a mortgage to get you.' He patted her and gave her a handful of hay as he handed her over to the stable lad. 'Mind and give her the best. We have a long way to go.'

'Have no fear, sir. The landlord makes sure that we give the best treatment to all our guests in the stables. I think he likes animals better than humans.'

'Is that so, then it must be good as he treats us exceedingly well. Here's a penny, give her a good grooming.'

Scooping up the reins the stable lad spoke to her like a friend. 'Come on girl, let's make you pretty.'

———

Stephen took the opportunity to take a bath and have his clothes laundered to rid himself of any unwelcome guests from the previous night's lodgings. Exhausted, he flung himself on the bed and slept.

He was awakened by the clanging of a utensil on a tin tray calling the guests to dinner.

Nancy greeted him in the dining room where a long table was set for dinner. 'Would prefer to dine alone or sit with the other guests, sir?'

He surveyed the assembled company. They were a mixture of commercial travellers and men like him passing through.

'They seem a jolly lot. I will dine with them if I may.'

'Right you are, sir. Come with me and I'll introduce you.' 'Gentlemen!' Her vibrant voice was enough to attract the attention of the other assembled diners. 'If that is what you be. We have a real gentleman with us tonight. May I introduce Mr Stephen Beattie from Scotland? For whatever reason, he prefers to dine with you lot, so mind your manners.' She turned to Stephen. 'I will apologise for them before hand, sir. I know them all and they don't deserve the custom we give 'em.'

The laughter in her voice dispelled any applied insult and they replied with ribald good humour.

One of the other guests, a balding man, took him by the arm.

'You must sit at the head, sir. It is an honour to have you with us.'

For five minutes, pleasantries passed around the table until two large tureens of soup were carried in, and, because he was at the head, Nancy served Stephen first.

'Hare or vegetable, sir?'

'Vegetable, please.'

The man to his right who had nominated him earlier leaned over. 'The hare is best. You won't get any better in the county.'

With an air of jocularity Stephen replied, 'On your head be it, sir.' He turned to Nancy. 'I will have hare, if you please,'

A loud guffaw went around the table at the jest and the

unfortunate recipient rubbing his thinning hair said, 'One to you, sir.'

This set the tone for the rest of the evening.

There followed, grilled sole taken with a light sherry, and then Nancy appeared with, in swift succession, three gigantic silver domes which she removed to reveal to the party, a shoulder of mutton, a chicken overflowing with stuffing and a round of boiled beef all escorted by a mountain of vegetables and dumplings.

Jokes and repartee flashed from one to the other as the diners made their choice, each trying to parry or divert a jest against himself and Stephen's status as a stranger did not spare him.

For pudding, they had rhubarb crumble or roasted apples topped with dairy cream or egg custard.

One of the company shouted. 'Nancy! We want a dark sherry with this pudding. Come on wench, let's be having it then.'

'You be getting it with this skillet if you're not careful.'

There was a roar of laughter as she descended the stairs accompanied by well-meant banter.

She returned moments later with the sherry. The man who had pulled her leg lifted his glass and she filled it. He sniffed it and drank it down with one gulp.

'Give me another, lass. I cannot be sure of it.' She filled his glass once more and continued around the table.

After dinner, port was served. Stephen stood and raised his glass. 'Gentlemen, I drink to you and your amiable company.'

'To you, sir,' they replied in unison.

They lit their pipes and the room became heavy with smoke. Flagons of ale were called for and a fellowship of leisure went on well into the night...

—

The following morning one of his fellow revellers greeted Stephen with a slap on the back.

'Good morrow, sir. How are you this fine morning? Your eyes look a little heavy and methinks I heard Mistress Nancy mewing with pleasure through the night.'

Stephen nodded his head and regretted it. 'Good morrow to you, sir. Yes, I am a little bilious. Nevertheless, well, and I did indeed spread a little Scottish culture.'

'Good man. I never had the pleasure myself but I'm led to believe a lively ride.' Instantly changing the subject he said, 'Excuse me, but whence do you travel?'

'I have a little business to finish here and then I travel to Romsley.'

'What luck,' said his companion, 'I travel frequently on that road selling my wares. It is a pleasant day's ride to Worcester and on to Romsley in the morning.'

'Thank you,' Stephen replied, 'Have a good journey onwards. It's been a pleasure meeting you and our esteemed friends.'

'Likewise, sir, may our paths cross again in such favourable circumstances?'

Stephen turned away and with pangs of guilt stabbing into his heart he made his way to the stables.

His search of the Church records in Dymock didn't take long. Whoever had written them had taken great pains to see that the entries for that period were in his best handwriting.

'Oh, that all records were so,' he said quietly to himself.

He was a little dispirited that he should finish so soon. His lodgings were of the best quality and he felt tempted to tarry another night. Alas, his promise to Anne of his swift return urged him on, as the next stage of his quest would take him two more days.

He shook his head in disbelief at the distances he had to travel. 'This family does move around. Why can't they be like other folks and stay near home?'

After lunch he took the road to Worcester where he stayed overnight. The next day he journeyed to Romsley and he arrived late in the evening. Exhausted, his vow to inspect his lodgings went by the board and he chose the first Inn he came to. It was not a bad choice and he rested well.

'The last day,' he said to himself, 'and then home.'

It was here that he unearthed the family skeleton. Grandma Sarah was pregnant when she married John Bosworth in 1753 and daughter Mary was baptised four months later in 1754.

'He did the right thing by her then,' was his mental comment.

Sarah Hall was born in 1731 in Romsley, the same year that

her mother, Mary Hall, (nee Ross), had married in Longhope, Gloucestershire and moved to Romsley with her husband, William Hall.

Stephen groaned. His chase was taking him back to within a few miles of where he started.

'Must have been dammed gypsies or there was a wanted notice out for them.'

Nothing for it he decided but to return south.

———

He set out early the next morning with his head pounding and any thought of Anne erased by the infernal thumping of his hangover.

His journey south was more direct. He stayed overnight in Tewkesbury and reached Gloucester by late afternoon the following day. His first thought was to push on but Annie, the name he had given his horse, turned her head as they entered the city and gave him a look that dared him to go further.

He patted her gently on the neck. 'Alright, we stay here tonight. You've done well my uncomplaining friend. I must make every effort to buy you.'

She pricked up her ears, and with a snort picked up her pace looking forward to a large bag of hay.

———

Longhope was the quiet backwater West of Gloucester that William Ross and his wife had chosen after fleeing from Scotland in the aftermath of the uprising of 1715. They settled there with their daughter Mary, who in turn, had met and married—Who?

Stephen searched the church records for the marriage of Mary to William Hall and couldn't find it.

'It must be there,' he muttered, 'Mary was from Longhope and according to the custom of the time should have married in her local church.'

He sat for a moment going through his previous searches to see if he had missed anything and then he checked the record books again. Still nothing, and on closer inspection he saw that the books were intact with no pages missing. After one last search he went to look for the churchwarden and explained his dilemma.

The warden peered over his glasses at Stephen. 'Are you certain that your previous work is correct, sir?'

'I have been meticulous with my investigations,' replied Stephen earnestly, 'There is no error I can assure you.'

'Most strange, let me help you. A new eye sometimes sees things that others don't.'

He browsed the book for a few moments before saying. 'These entries are badly written by someone with no experience of a quill. See the little trails around the letters. That's where the quill has split.'

They looked again. 'Very odd,' the Warden said, 'let me see your papers, I think I know the answer. Look here, we have a Mary married to a William Hoyle. There are many Hoyles in this area.'

'And what's that Mary's maiden name,' enquired Stephen.

'Ross. Isn't that the name you're looking for?'

'By golly, yes. As you say, your predecessors have translated Hall into Hoyle. Easily done I suppose. They probably spoke with a Highland accent. Thank you, that's the final piece in the puzzle.'

'It was a pleasure, sir. May I enquire as to the purpose of your search?'

'My client merely wishes to check his ancestors. He thinks he's connected to royalty. I fear not, he's a commoner the same as you or I.'

'Ah, the aspirations of the common man. Good day to you, sir.'

He shuffled away straightening wayward prayer books as he did so.

'Many thanks,' Stephen called after him as he collected his papers and went out to the ever patient Annie. 'Come on, gal, let's go and have something to eat at the Plough and then we're off to our own beds tonight.'

He scooped up the reigns and with her head over his shoulder, they walked to the Inn.

—

'Good day, sir, what can I get you?'

'A plate of ham, cheese and pickle,' Stephen replied, 'accompanied by a tankard, and do you have any fodder for my horse?'

'To that last request, no sir, but you can turn her loose in the back field. Push her through yon gate at the side. There's a trough and there'll be no charge.'

Stephen nipped out, removed the saddle and bridle and turned Annie loose in the field. He watched as she did a few high kicks and took off in a frenzied gallop before rolling in the lush grass.

Inside the landlord placed a foaming tankard in front of him. 'There you are, sir, your food'll be along in a minute, you goin' far?'

'I'm passing through on the way to the ferry and then home,' replied Stephen.

'Where's home, you sound a bit far from it.'

'Ha, ha, you have me. For me home is now Frampton.'

'Frampton you say. We have relatives there. If you meet with the Bosworth family tell them you met Cousin Sarah's family. Here she is now. Sarah, say hello. This young man is staying in Frampton. I was telling him about Cousin Tom.'

Sarah nodded in acknowledgement and said tersely. 'Good day to you. Get stuck into your lunch. I'm too busy for tittle-tattle and give our regards to Tom. Do you know him?'

Stephen replied with caution. 'I've only been there a short while and have not had time to make everyone's acquaintance. If I come across him I'll tell him of you. The name Sarah is popular in these parts?'

'My grandmother was called Sarah, it's a family name. You may also tell Cousin Thomas,' she said with some vigour, 'it's the same distance coming this way as going that.'

She immediately concluded the conversation and turned away.

'Most...'

Stephen's words were left hanging. He turned to the landlord who shrugged his shoulders and said meekly, 'Eat up, lad.'

Stephen dawdled with his meal to give the mare time to enjoy the freedom of the field before they made their way leisurely homeward.

There was a short wait at the ferry for the tide to recede before making the hazardous passage across the treacherous currents. The ferryman was skilful, but there were a few anxious moments before they reached the south bank.

—

Torn between dashing to the Inn to see Anne or reporting his finds, he erred on the side of business and went directly to the Bosworth household where Esther made him comfortable before going to fetch Thomas.

They returned a few minutes later and Thomas enquired directly. 'Well young man, do you bring good news for us?'

'I do, sir.' Stephen gave him a bundle of documents. 'And here is everything I have gathered. In there is the proof you require to show your Ross family lineage. You must now travel to Scotland where one of you must reside for six weeks before presenting them to the courts. My Uncle will represent you in Scotland and I will do so here. In this way, you will have help wherever you are.'

'Sound advice young man,' Thomas replied with a degree of uncertainty, 'but what you suggest does mean paying two legal fees presumably?

'Indeed it does, sir.'

'That we cannot afford. Leave your documents here and I will discuss with the family meanwhile to see if one of us can move to Scotland.'

'Sir,' Stephen said with some urgency, 'wouldn't it be better for me to take these papers back with me to start things moving?'

'Yes, it would be. However, we are not rich people and to employ solicitors and provide enough cash for someone to live in Scotland is beyond our means.'

'I understand.' Stephen realised there was no further point trying to persuade them to take the proper course of action and concluded by saying. 'I will take my leave. Please feel free to call upon me while I remain here. I travel to Edinburgh next week and when I return I will be joining the practice of Mr Innes in Stroud.'

'Thank you, Stephen,' Thomas said, 'will ten-guineas suffice as your fee?'

'More than generous,' Stephen replied. 'I forgot to mention, Cousin Sarah in Longhope sends her regards and hopes to see you soon.'

'Uh, huh, she does aye. Well that's as maybe.'

The two men shook hands and with a polite nod to Emily and Esther, Stephen withdrew. From there he went swiftly to his lodgings to wash and brush up before hurrying to see Anne and prepare her for his departure to Scotland.

—

One week later - Edinburgh.
Alistair Beattie looked over his pince-nez at his nephew. 'Well, Master Stephen, have you good news for us?'

Stephen acknowledged Rebecca before replying. 'Indeed I have, sir, on two counts. There is bad news also.'

Beattie sighed and threw his pince-nez on the desk. 'Out with it, give us the good news.'

Stephen ignored the interruption and continued. 'I have surpassed all expectations of my quest and proved beyond doubt that Miss Ross's legal heirs reside in England.'

'Where's your proof lad?'

'I don't have it as they are of poor stock and cannot travel here immediately. They have kept the documents until such time as they can raise the means for one of them to live here but they do wish to retain your services and have sent five pounds on account.'

Beattie mopped his brow with his handkerchief. 'Damn it! Excuse me, my dear. Time is of the essence. I fear that Maxwell has connections in the highest places.'

Rebecca spoke for the first time. 'Do you know this for certain?'

'Yes, Rebecca, I do,' Beattie replied, 'there are many loose tongues on Lodge nights and our profession lives in these places. It doesn't take long for word to travel.'

Rebecca looked pleadingly at Beattie. 'Can't we help them? They do seem to be coming into a substantial amount.'

'I'm afraid not, dear, it is too great a risk. We cannot guarantee that we are going to win and the investment must come from them. I am willing to reduce my fee, but that is all.'

'I understand, but it seems such a pity. Let us hope they can find the funds quickly.'

Beattie returned his attention back to Stephen. 'And what is the bad news, as if what you say is not bad enough.'

'I am returning to England to live and work, sir.'

'You are what?' Beattie blurted out, shaking his head.

'I have committed myself to a post in England which I was kindly offered by a countryman of ours who is seeking a partner.'

'Stephen, I was hoping you would be interested in a post here. Won't you reconsider? I will pay above his offer.'

'I am sorely tempted but I have given my word not only to him but to another party as well.'

'Let me guess,' piped up Rebecca, 'you have a lady friend? Is she nice?'

'More than words can say. She is the most beautiful thing I have happen to me.'

Beattie groaned. 'Och, spare me. Wait 'til she gets you to the altar, you are subservient for life. It is a contract with the devil and you will be forever poor.'

'Come now, Alistair,' Rebecca said sweetly, 'we're not that bad. It is true there are not enough things in the world for a woman to buy but we bring light into your life and many other pleasures.'

'Enough,' said Stephen, 'my mind is made up and I leave in the morning.'

'So soon, lad?'

'Yes, sir. I need to start earning as soon as possible as I have purchased a horse with not a penny to pay for her. A fine filly, and like my sweetheart, not a bad bone in her body.'

'Listen to him, Rebecca, there is no hope. I wish you well, Stephen.' Alistair stood up and stretched out his hand. 'Good luck.'

They shook hands; Stephen bowed to Rebecca and kissed her hand, 'It has been a pleasure to make your acquaintance, ma'am, goodbye.'

'Goodbye, Stephen. I wish you well for the future.'

A lump came into his throat and a pressure behind his eyes and fearful that a tear might fall he turned and hurriedly left the room.

—

1975

It was past midnight before Angus stopped talking. Professor Mildmay sat with his head resting on one arm with his eyes closed while Angus waited patiently for his tutor to respond.

Mildmay jerked suddenly upright. 'Err... Sorry lad, I was back in the nineteenth century. This Stephen Beattie, what became of him?'

'He took up his position in Stroud with Innes, sir, and married Anne before taking up his own practice in London a few years later.'

'And your ancestors, lad, did they take up the quest after his hard work?'

'No sir. They were not well off and it took them over a year to accrue the necessary funds for someone to reside in Scotland.'

'I see.' Mildmay glanced at the old station clock hanging on the wall. 'I think this would be a good time to break for the weekend. We will continue on Monday.'

***

7

Esther.

1841.

Thomas Bosworth stood with his back to the fire and addressed the family.

'Mother, brothers and sisters and Cousin Sarah, let us drink a toast to Jane Ross our future benefactor.'

'Excuse me, Thomas!'

'Yes, Mother.'

'Thomas, are we not being a little presumptuous?'

'Mother, you're right as always, but don't you remember what young Mr Beattie said, 'We have a right grand case.' I think this justifies our optimism.'

'Maybe so, but I do think we shouldn't get carried away.'

'Of course, Mother. However, it has taken a full year since the visit of Mr Beattie to raise the funds. We now need to decide on who should go. I myself, have commitments with the shop. Cousin Sarah has the Inn to maintain in Longhope. How are, Mr Jackson and Julia these days, Sarah?'

'He is well and seeks to move to a bigger place. Julia is Julia.'

'Excellent,' Thomas continued, 'Brother William meanwhile, fares less well with his health and is dependant on Mr Bush, his father-in-law. Beth's husband is beholden to his job on Gloucester docks. Are Ted and Ellie both well, Beth?'

'Yes, he works hard but is healthy and he is now an overseer so things are a little easier and Ellie is over the measles.'

Thomas turned to Maria. 'Brother James, how is he doing in Canada?'

'He sounds well enough from the letters I receive.'

'Esther!' Thomas went over to his sister sitting quietly in the background. 'That leaves you. Would you mind doing this thing for us?'

'Thomas, I have no knowledge of worldly things. I have never ventured further than Gloucester.'

'Then we must find you a companion. Your fiancé's sister, Hannah, would she join you?'

'I will ask her, but she spends a lot of her time looking after her grandmother.'

'On the assumption that she says yes, this is what you must do on your arrival. You must first go to this lawyer, Beattie. He will advise you on your course of action. Ladies, please make sure that Esther is well equipped for the long stay in Scotland. Esther, you must tell Hannah that she needs to prepare for at least six weeks away. Money and the documents for Mr Beattie I will give you on the day of your departure.'

'I am afraid, Brother, that I may fail you. It makes me frightened that a mission of such importance should fall on my shoulders.'

'Have no fear, Esther. You merely have to be present in Scotland. No harm will come of you and Beattie will guide you every step of the way. We have alerted him to your imminent arrival in Edinburgh. Elizabeth; give our guests more refreshment while Esther and I go to see Hannah. On our return we will sit down to lunch so that you may all journey home in daylight.'

—

Ten days later.
Alistair Beattie greeted Esther and Hannah and kissed the hand of each in turn. 'Mistress Bosworth, how do you do, and your companion also. Please take a seat, you must be tired after your journey. May I get you some refreshment?'

'A cup of tea would do wondrous things, Mr Beattie.'

'Excuse me one moment while I arrange it.'

He left the room and hurried down to the front office.

'One of you laggards go down to the store and get some tea and milk. Does either of you know how to make tea?'

'I have watched my mother, sir. It appears quite easy.'

'Good. Make tea for two, nay, three, and hurry.'

'We require a pot, cups and a milk jug, sir.'

'Get them, and get a move on.'

He hurried back to his guests. 'Ladies, your tea will not be long. Now what have you got for me?'

Esther handed over her letter of introduction from Thomas and after a few moments reading Beattie looked up.

'You have brought your proof with you?'

'We have, sir.' Esther rummaged in her bag and gave him the bundle of documents.

'H'mm... Young Master Beattie did a good job and I think you should have no trouble. Where has that tea got to?'

At that instant there was a knock on the door and one of the clerks carried in a tray. 'Earl Grey, sir? Would that be to your taste?'

'Most certainly, do we not always drink Earl Grey?'

The startled clerk looked at him blankly. 'Err...'

Beattie waved him away.

'Ladies, do help yourself.'

'Thank you.' Esther concealed a smile wondering if she dared ask the next question. 'Do you have any sugar?'

'I waste my time on these two. How many times have I told them. One moment.'

He opened the door and bellowed down the corridor. 'Sugar, you dolts! Bring some sugar!'

Esther and Hannah smothered a laugh as he returned to his desk. 'Excuse me, where were we?'

'Documents, Mr Beattie.'

'Ah, yes. These are excellent. Can you leave them with me?'

'No, sir. I am under instructions that they must never leave my person.'

'Very well. There is not a lot we can do yet anyway.'

'Sugar, sir?' The clerk nervously placed the missing sugar dish on the desk and beat a hasty retreat.

'Where was I,' Beattie said aloud. 'Ah, I know. Have you lodgings, Miss Bosworth?'

'No, we came to you directly.'

Esther fanned herself, flushed by the warmth and the untoward situation she found herself in.

'Tonight,' Beattie continued, 'you and your companion must stay in the hotel and I will contact Mrs Beagle who will assist you in finding a permanent address where you must live for six weeks before you can present your case.

'Who is, Mrs Beagle? We had a letter of introduction from her when your nephew visited, but we don't know her'

'It is to her that you owe a debt of gratitude for alerting us to your predicament. She is an interested party, but has no claim. Do you understand?'

'Yes, but however can we thank you for your help, Mr Beattie?'

'My thanks are my fee.'

Seven weeks later at the Court of Sessions (Outer House)
'Your honour, this claim is brought by my client, Miss Esther Bosworth of 13 Field Street, Edinburgh, on behalf of herself and her relatives. I wish to show, your honour, that this claim to the Ross estate is the only true and honest one and that the trustees to Miss Jane Ross were not only negligent but I also believe them to be untrustworthy and that nefarious acts have taken place which I consider to be of criminal intent.'

Beattie's opening words could not have been more damning, and a sharp intake of breath was audible around the courtroom.

James Mackenzie jumped to his feet. 'Your honour! I object!'

The judge leaned forward on his elbows twiddling a pen between his fingers. 'So soon, Mr Mackenzie. We have only just begun.'

'The statement by my learned friend is malicious in its content, sire, and should it not be proved the muck will stick.'

Mackenzie stopped, at a loss for words. He had not expected a legal attack, merely thinking it was a straightforward claim and counter affair.

The judge nodded and turned to Beattie. 'Mr Beattie, do choose your words carefully. Mr Mackenzie is correct and unless you have proof of these allegations it would be foolhardy to pursue this line.'

Beattie waved his bundle of papers. 'Your honour, it is my intention to prove what I say is in fact true and I believe I have the necessary ammunition to do so.'

'Very well, but I might point out that this is a civil court.'

'Thank you, your honour. However, there may be criminal charges forthcoming.'

John Reid sat at the back of the courtroom and inwardly shuddered. 'What had these people found out?'

Beattie continued. 'It is my intention to show that rather than do their duty and search for the direct relatives of Miss Ross the trustees did take payment to do otherwise. Had they extended their search with diligence, as in fact I did, they would have discovered the direct line from Miss Ross's Uncle William is the Bosworth family in England.'

Mackenzie banged his fist down on his table and stood up. 'Your honour! I object. Let the opposition prove their claim to the estate of Miss Ross as that is what we are here for. Any case of alleged fraud and mismanagement should be investigated by the right authorities.'

'Mr Mackenzie is correct, Mr Beattie,' the judge warned. 'Keep your comments confined to proving your client's claim. Your words so far have little or nothing to do with this hearing and I want to be finished early.'

'Your honour, I merely wish to prove that all previous claims are based on corruption and as such have no bearing on this application, which is the only true and legitimate one.'

'Get on with it, Mr Beattie.'

'Sir, I wish to submit these documents. They are the marriage and birth certificates of the claimants and their ancestors. They show a direct line to the Ross estates and family not that of a cousin-in-law'

'Thank you Mr Beattie. I will call a recess here so that I may read them in the privacy of my quarters.'

'Your honour!'

'What is it, Mr Mackenzie?'

'Sir, we have no knowledge of these documents.'

'Should I believe them to be true, Mr Mackenzie, you shall have time to look at them. We are adjourned.'

—

Maxwell accosted Mackenzie in the corridor outside.

'Mackenzie! What is going on? I thought you had removed all trace.'

'I did.'

'Then who are these people? Where did they spring from?'

'They are nothing but upstarts from England. Have no fear I will deal with it.'

'They seem mighty clear on their facts to me. This Beattie, who pays for his services?'

'I know not, he is merely a second rate advocate.'

'That's as maybe, Mackenzie.' To emphasize his words he stabbed his finger into Mackenzie's lapel. 'I don't care how—Stop them!'

—

The judge banged his gavel on the block with barely disguised irritation.

'Mr Mackenzie! I believe these documents to be true copies. You and your client are free to read them.'

'Thank you, your honour. May we have an adjournment so that my client and I can take them away and study them?'

'No, Mr Mackenzie, you may not. You may read them at your leisure in the courtroom. I am a man of great patience. Clerk—give these to Mr Mackenzie.'

Maxwell and his advocate spent some time huddled together arguing amongst themselves before the judge interrupted them with a polite cough.

'Gentlemen are you finished?'

'Yes, your honour.'

'Be so good as to return the documents to Mr Beattie.'

Beattie stood up. 'Thank you your honour, may I continue?'

The judge pulled out his watch, muttered and looked up. 'Yes, Mr Beattie. Try to be brief.'

'I would like to call Mr John Reid to the stand.'

The clerk called his name out and Reid took his seat in the witness box.

Beattie shuffled his papers for effect before he addressed him.

'Mr Reid, you were an appointed trustee to the Will of Miss Jane Ross.'

'Yes sir.'

'On the passing of Miss Ross, what did you do?'

'I and my fellow trustee searched most diligently for her relatives. On her instructions we were searching before her death.'

'What did you find?'

'We found that there was no direct line and that Mr Maxwell as Cousin-at-law was heir to the estate.'

'You were paid for your services were you not?'

'Yes sir.'

'Would you tell the court how much?'

'Five-thousand pounds.'*

A gasp of disbelief went around the courtroom.

'Mr Reid! I put it to you that you were paid to find no one.'

Mackenzie jumped to his feet. 'Objection, your honour. This line of questioning is absurd.'

'Mr Beattie,' the judge said wearily, 'did I not say earlier that you should stick to the facts.'

'Yes, your honour. I beg forgiveness, I have only one more question.'

'Very well, but be cautious in your choice of words.'

Beattie looked at the judge with surprise at the hidden warning before continuing. 'Mr Reid! I have it on good authority that you in fact deposited a further nine-thousand pounds in the Royal Bank a little after New Year last year. Can you explain that?'

Mackenzie jumped to his feet. 'Your honour, indeed! This is all hearsay and has nothing to do with the case.'

The judge sighed and shook his head. 'Mr Beattie, what do you mean by this?'

'I meant to show, your honour, that Mr Reid did not tell the truth and in doing so has proved himself untrustworthy.'

'My chambers, Mr Beattie.' He then addressed the Court. 'We are adjourned for the day. Court resumes at ten o' clock tomorrow.'

—

The next day.

'Mr Beattie, where is your client?'

'I don't know your honour. Can we continue without her? I am knowledgeable of all the facts of this case.'

'No, Mr Beattie, we cannot. We will recess for half an hour.'

The doors at the rear of the room burst open and a breathless policeman pushed his way in and hurried to the Judge's bench.

'What is the meaning of this, Constable?'

'Excuse me, sir. I bring grave news.'

The judge leaned forward in order to hear better.

'Tell me.'

The officer took a few moments to catch his breath before blurting out. 'My Inspector sent me here sir, post haste. He said a certain Miss Bosworth and her companion have had a terrible accident during the night. A gas pipe fractured and they succumbed to the fumes.'

'Mr Beattie, step forward, please.'

'Yes sir.'

'Mr Beattie, it appears that your client has had a terrible accident overnight. Owing to a broken gas pipe they have died in their sleep. Thank you, Constable. Mr Mackenzie if you please.'

Mackenzie joined Beattie at the bench.

'It seems gentleman that this case has come to an untimely end. The litigant has passed away and is no longer able to pursue her claim. Therefore, this case is closed.'

'Your honour,' Beattie protested, 'I am fully aware of the facts. Can this case not proceed as it was brought on behalf of her relatives?'

'Are they resident in Scotland, Mr Beattie?'

'No sir.'

'Then we can no longer continue. The case is closed.'

Mackenzie looked over to Beattie. 'Kismet, sir, fate has dealt them a poor hand.'

'I wonder who was doing the dealing. Methinks there is dirty work afoot.'

'What are you suggesting, Beattie. Choose your words carefully as once outside this courtroom what you say may be construed as slander.'

Beattie continued packing his papers and looked at Mackenzie with distaste. 'I cannot be sued for my thoughts, sir, unless of course there is something to hide. Good day to you.'

—

Maxwell addressed his advocate after the court had cleared.

'Mackenzie, you did well. Did you make absolutely sure they stole nothing this time?'

'Only the papers as you asked.'

'Gas, aye, that was clever.'

'It was easy. They poked a hole through the wall and fed a

pipe through from the street lamp. When they returned later they broke in and made it look like an internal fracture and left everything as they found it.'

'Good, here's a bonus. How you share it is your affair.'

—

Three weeks later.
Thomas Bosworth addressed the assembled family once more.

'This occasion is very sad and it falls upon me to tell you that Cousin Esther* and Hannah, her companion, have died.'

No one spoke; they sat stunned, looking from one to the other until Elizabeth could restrain herself no longer and let out a sob.

'Ooh… Oh, dear…' She wiped her nose and sniffled. 'Wha.., What ha… Happened?'

'They were overcome by gas during the night and did not suffer. Even worse is the fact that we cannot afford to transport them home. However, the people in Scotland have been extremely kind and have given them a decent burial, asking only that we send a nominal amount to cover their costs.'

'Is there nothing we can do and what of our cause?'

'I will come to that. It does appear that things were not as they seemed. Mr Beattie informs me that all our documents are missing and there were signs of tampering with the pipe work and illegal entry into the house. The police are treating the deaths as suspicious but more he could not tell us.'

A tearful voice spoke up from the back of the room and Mother Sarah dabbed at her eyes. 'Our claim to the inheritance, Thomas, what happens now?'

'Because there is no one residing in Scotland and no documents of proof we must start again. I am going to Stroud in the morning to seek guidance from young Mr Beattie and start collecting more evidence to further our claim. I would like to ask you for a donation to a fighting fund to finance these travels. May I suggest five pounds per household and I will keep a book showing where the money is being spent.'

'Five pounds is a lot. I can pay two for now and we will seek to send some more when we have it.'

'Donate what you can, Cousin Sarah.'

'We are moving from Longhope,' she continued, 'to a new inn

down Chepstow way and until business picks up we are going to find things difficult.'

'I understand, but that will be some way to travel to our meetings.'

'It's not so far. We are moving to Beachley by the ferry and the railway has made things easier and I find it safer.'

Thomas clapped his hands.' If there's nothing else let us go through for refreshments.'

***

8

1975

'Sad times, eh,' Professor Mildmay remarked as Angus prepared for the evening session.

'Yes sir, and all the accounts I have found in diaries and such like say that Esther was a lovely girl. Shy, modest and well liked throughout the village and she was sorely missed in church, not just for her flower arranging but for her singing also.'

'Did they catch anyone?'

'No, sir. I have checked Police records for the day and the case is still open. Filed, but not forgotten.'

'One thing you forgot to mention, young Lane. What did they do next these would be millionaires?'

Angus flicked through the file and read for a few moments, turning pages backward and forward in an effort to find the missing information.

'It appears you're right, sir. I don't know how I came to miss that.'

Mildmay sighed and shook his head. 'Now maybe a good time, aye?'

'Yes sir.'

Angus took a sip from his tumbler.

'Thomas Bosworth, the patriarch of the family, was as good as his word and set about covering the ground that Stephen Beattie had done before him. Meanwhile, Maxwell was also busy arranging insurance against further claims and fulfilling a dream.'

1842

The everyday life in the village of Longhope was undisturbed by the presence of two strangers. The locals paid scant attention to Oates and Barley as they rode through and stopped at the end of the village, talked for a moment, turned and made their way back to the Plough Inn.

Minutes later James Mackenzie arrived. He sat apart enjoying his lunch before he engaged them in casual conversation.

The landlord served more ale and ignored the trio thereafter.

Leaning forward and speaking in a lowered tone Mackenzie said, 'Did you get a good look at the church?'

Barley, the taller of the two replied. 'Aye, we did that. It's convenient having the rectory opposite like that.'

'Good. There is extra work for you tonight. I want you to deface a couple of gravestones. I will walk the churchyard this afternoon to locate the graves of William Ross and his daughter Mary, so that you may go directly to them while I do what I have to. You will have to work quickly as the noise is bound to wake someone.'

He raised his voice so that all around could hear. 'Gentlemen, let us be on our way. Good riding and luck be with you.'

They emptied their tankards and stamped out laughing and talking meaningless banter before going their separate ways.

———

It took Mackenzie little time to break into the vestry and locate the burial records and there were plenty of candles and matches to aid him with his search.

Using the stolen records in his possession as his guide, he was able to go directly to the years he required. With a sharp tug he removed the offending pages.

He moved onto the marriage and baptism records and scoured them repeatedly.

'That's odd,' he muttered, 'there's no record and it cannot be. Beattie's documents clearly show them to be here.'

There was a creak, and he jumped, his heart pounding. He paused and listened. Breaking into a cold sweat the hairs on his neck prickled. The flickering shadows thrown by the candles in the darkness of the church made his flesh creep.

'Why am I doing this. I'm a lawyer not a thief and why does the house of God feel more like a morgue?'

He continued his search, nervously jumping at every sound and flickering shadow, mystified why he couldn't find the name, Hall.

He became aware of noises outside and slammed the books

shut in disgust, doused the candle, hurried from the vestry, and rushed through the darkened church cursing as his thigh encountered a hidden pew.

In his haste he slipped on the polished tiles and crashed to the floor. With a barrage of colourful language he ran from the place that tormented him.

Outside he became aware of the commotion coming from the Rectory. Angry voices carried over to him and lanterns were lit as people made themselves ready to investigate.

'Oates, Barley! Where are ye?' Mackenzie called in a hoarse whisper, 'You drink sodden louts, show yourself.'

The voices were growing louder and with no time to linger he ran towards the surrounding wall where his companions should be waiting for him with the horses.

'Mackenzie! Over here, where the hell have you been?'

'It's a long story. Let's get away from here.'

Quickly untying the horses they walked unhurriedly following the line of the walls behind some cottages until they reached the road. They continued on foot until they were clear of the village before mounting and melting away in the darkness down the Gloucester road.

'Did you get those gravestones done as I said?' Mackenzie enquired. He had little faith in the bar scourings he had been forced to hire.

'Aye! Just the surnames like you said. We was almost done afore they woke over the road.'

'Good. A day's rest and then I'll leave you while I take a look at Frampton.'

—

Mackenzie had little trouble finding the Bosworth household. He gave himself a quick brush down before he knocked with some authority. He had to wait some moments before he heard shuffling steps and the door opened a little. The time weary face of Emily peered at him suspiciously.

'Yes?'

He raised his hat and bowed slightly. 'Good morning, ma'am. I'm James Mackenzie, Advocate, down from Scotland to see

Thomas Bosworth on the matter of his inheritance. My card.'

She ignored the card and said abruptly. 'He's not here. You'll have to go over to the store,' and she closed the door firmly in his face.

With a shrug of his shoulders he said to no one in particular. 'Methinks I've been rebuffed.'

He found the store without difficulty and presented himself to Thomas who stood behind the counter in readiness for his next customer.

'Good day, sir, can I help you?'

'Do I have the pleasure of addressing Thomas Bosworth?'

'I am he, but you have the better of me.'

'James Mackenzie, Advocate, and I am down from Scotland on the business of your inheritance. My card.'

Thomas took the card and gave it a cursory glance before replying, 'Mr Beattie is my solicitor in Scotland.'

'Correct, sir, but Mr Beattie is exceptionally busy and he has sent me on this errand which is of extreme importance. Time is of the essence and owing to the unfortunate demise of your sister, Esther. I beg your pardon—it was your sister?'

Suspicious of this sinister character Thomas replied with a cautionary, 'Yes.'

'In that case we must hurry as the judge has closed the case. It is a matter of some urgency to get it back into court as quickly as possible before it goes out of statute. I need whatever information you have as proof.'

Thomas rubbed his chin thoughtfully for a moment. 'Does not one of us have to live in Scotland?'

'You're right, but at the moment all I need is for you to sign a power of attorney naming me as your representative and we can present it to the court on your behalf.'

'Why couldn't we do that the first time?'

'Because it was the first time.'

Thomas looked askance at Mackenzie, 'Oh, I see.'

Mackenzie pulled out what appeared to be a legal document and spread it on the counter. 'I have one prepared. All you have to do is sign it and give me all your documents.'

'I will sign it,' said Thomas, 'but I will not give you my proof, such as it is, and we are unable to get evidence of the last marriage anyway.'

'I must have the documents,' insisted Mackenzie.

Thomas shook his head. 'No, they stay here in my safekeeping up at the house.'

Mackenzie snatched his paper from the counter and said angrily, 'You're wasting my time, good day to you, sir,' and as he was leaving he turned in the doorway and said as an aside, 'You have little time to waste if you wish us to help you. Keep in touch by letter and we will advise you on your position.'

He turned on his heel and left, cursing under his breath.

—

Barley and Oates crept up the garden path of the Bosworth household and around the side of the building

'Bloody hell,' Oates cursed as he stumbled on a carelessly left garden utensil and made a grab at Barley for support.

Barley swore under his breath. 'Quiet, you damn fool. Have you got the jemmy?'

'Yes.'

'What are you waiting for? Open the bloody window.'

Oates inserted the jemmy under the kitchen window and applied downward pressure. The window stayed firm and Oates cursed, 'Bugger! Of all nights we had to get a tough one. I hate these people with new frames. Give us a hand, Barley.'

'It's not new, they use oak hereabouts.'

'They're still a bloody nuisance.'

They applied further pressure until, with a sharp crack, the catch gave way and after waiting a few minutes Barley whispered, 'Let's do it. I'll go first.'

The sash window pushed up easily on the counter weights. 'At least he keeps his runners well soaped,' muttered Oates.

'Shut up, it's your mouth that needs soaping.'

They wedged a convenient piece of wood under the window and Barley pulled himself over the sill, held onto the edge of the kitchen sink, twisted around and lowered his feet to the floor.

Oates thrust himself enthusiastically over the sill and missed the sink, sliding instead, head first into the waiting Barley sending them both crashing to the floor.

They spent the next minute cursing, fighting, and slipping on the flagged kitchen floor while trying to untangle themselves in the darkness.

Barley grabbed Oates around the throat and shook him. 'You clumsy dolt,' he cursed. 'Why did I have to pick you?'

Finally settled, they stood silently for a few minutes before searching the kitchen for a candle. With the light of a couple of matches they found one and lit it.

'What are we looking for,' muttered Oates.

'Documents, like we did before, you oaf.'

'What's with the bloody paperwork?' Oates complained in little more than a whisper. 'Don't they want something of value for a change. A thief can't make a decent living like this.'

Barley could hardly suppress his anger. 'Shut up and get looking. Here's another candle.'

Satisfied that there was nothing in the kitchen of any importance they tried the connecting door, eased it open and cringed at the loud squeal.

'Shit! He doesn't oil his hinges.'

They squeezed through the half open door and waited briefly before crossing on tip-toe to the bottom of the stairs.

Oates stepped on one of Emily's walking sticks lying unseen on the floor and his feet went from under him. With a loud crash he hit the floor and his candle went scattering across the hallway and came to rest against the drawing room doorjamb and set light to the draught curtain.

The racket awakened Thomas who shouted. 'Who's there? I have a gun and I shan't hesitate to use it.'

'Let's get out of here,' Barley shouted. 'Leave the bloody curtain.'

The pair of would be burglars crashed back through the kitchen door fighting with each other to get through. In their haste they overturned an unlit oil lamp spilling its contents across the floor and Oates's trousers. Barley pushed Oates aside, threw his candle down, and ignoring the screams from Oates as the oil on his trousers exploded into flames scrambled out of the window .

'You bastard, help me,' Oates yelled at his disappearing companion.

Barley turned, grabbed Oates by the collar and dragged him bodily through the window and beat at him with his hands to dowse the flames.

'You're alright now,' Barley growled at the hapless Oates. 'Let's get out of here.'

They dashed off pell-mell into the darkness. At the end of the path they looked back to see the interior of the house lit up by flames which had an intense hold on the tinder dry woodwork and the draught from the open kitchen window was fanning the flames.

Thomas dashed down the stairs and immediately saw the hopelessness of chasing the pair. With no time to fight the fire he scrambled back to his room, threw a gown over Elizabeth his wife and pushed her to the top of stairs.

'Wait there, I'll get the children.'

He raced along the landing and into the children's room to find his daughter Charlotte cuddling her brother.

'Come on you two, put a blanket over your heads and follow me, hurry!'

He shepherded them to the head of the stairs where Elizabeth was shielding her face..

'Follow me,' he shouted over the noise created by the flames.

The heat coming up the stairs was intense but passable. Keeping to the side farthest away from the flames he led them down into the hallway.

'Out through the front door, quickly.' He ushered the reluctant Elizabeth towards the door. 'I'm going back for Mum.'

'Thomas, be careful.'

'Go, before it's to late.' He gave her a helping shove and turned to go back upstairs.

She urged the children forward past the flames and opened the door. The sudden inrush of air made the fire explode up the stairs and Thomas screamed as the flames engulfed him and set his nightshirt alight.

Through the haze of pain he fought his way into his mother's bedroom, threw himself on the bed and rolled in the quilt to quench the flames.

'Come on, Mother,' he yelled as he pulled her out of bed and dragged her over to the window. He pushed it open. 'It's out of here for us.'

He helped her onto the ledge. 'Jump, Mother, jump, it's getting hot in here.'

He gave her a gentle nudge and she leapt into the flickering semi–darkness. A quick glance backwards was all that he needed to see that the situation was hopeless and he followed her out.

Landing awkwardly, he stumbled over something and crashed to the ground. Laying breathless, drawing fresh air into his lungs, he realised he had fallen over the inert form of his Mother.

'Mum, Mum, are you alright,' he shouted, cursing the pain of his burnt back and legs. He dragged himself over and shook her, crying out in disbelief as her head flopped sideways at a crazy angle.

'Mother, what have they done?'

He cuddled up to her prostrate body and sobbed uncontrollably trying not to believe that he had rescued her only for her to break her neck in the fall.

—

The village people turned out to help but a bucket chain was of little use against the inferno and it was two days before the ashes cooled enough for them to poke around and search for any possessions that may have survived.

—

1842: The offices of James Graham (architect), Edinburgh.
William Maxwell ignored the proffered chair and spoke to Graham with little regard for courtesy. 'Now here's the way of it. I have purchased the land and the old castle at Eaton and I want to build myself a grand house in the Scottish manner.'

Graham answered with great forbearance instinctively disliking the man in front of him, 'I posses a little experience of that. Did you have anything in mind?'

'I think something on the lines of Walter Scott's place, or the one over to Duns. I like them pointed turrets.'

'I know what you mean. Come over here, I have my plans of Brodick Castle.'

Maxwell joined Graham on the other side of the room at a long desk covered in drawings. He studied them for a moment and hovered over the side elevation of a rather grand pinnacled design.

'That's it, something like that.'

'Would you like it finished in sandstone?' Graham enquired, aware that Maxwell knew little of architecture.

'Yes, and this tower.' Maxwell jabbed his finger down on the plans, 'At the top I want a room built with no windows and no landing and decorated in a certain way. Can you do that?'

'Anything you desire.' Graham was mentally calculating how much he could squeeze out of Maxwell. 'Let me know, but I beg of you give me plenty of warning of any changes you may require before we get too far advanced.'

'Very well, but can you put a price on it,' Maxwell asked in the hope that their joint affiliation of the Brotherhood may give him a discount.

'I will have to look at the site before I can estimate but probably in the region of thirty-two thousand pounds.'

'As much as that,' Maxwell said, horrified at the thought of dipping into his vast purse.

'Do you want a castle or a croft,' Graham said irritably. 'If it's a croft yer wantin' then you have the wrong man.'

'No, no, you go ahead,' said Maxwell, holding his hands up in alarm fearing the price could rise even higher, 'I am ignorant of the cost of building, it came as somewhat of a surprise that is all.'

'If I am hearing correctly Maxwell, you have funds aplenty. I was an acquaintance of the Ross's.'

Maxwell looked a little sheepish and wandered around the table scrutinizing the plans to hide his discomfort. 'I don't know what you have heard. It's a castle I want and a castle I shall have no matter what the cost.'

'I shall have the surveyors out to it shortly. Meanwhile, if you could leave a deposit to cover my expenses.'

'I have no specie with me. Here is a note to draw on the Royal National Bank for five thousand pounds.'

'That will do nicely and speaking of the National Bank—you have something to do with that, do you not?'

'I am a Director.'

'Is that so? I also hear John Reid the cashier has been put out to grass.'

'Aye, right he has. There was a rumour of corruption and they terminated his employ.'

'You know what it was then?'

'Yes, but I am not at liberty to discuss bank business. I will bid you good day. I have tarried long enough.'

'Goodbye, sir.' Graham took Maxwell by the arm and walked with him to the door. 'You leave yourself in the hands of a master.'

'You don't mind blowing your own trumpet do you?'

'I have to. No one else does it for me although you found your way here.'

'It was by word in the Lodge,' Maxwell replied, 'they speak well of you and your generosity to charity.'

'Then I must make sure that I live up to their word.'

1975

Mildmay mopped his brow before scribbling on a piece of scrap paper and when he had finished he peered over at Angus.

'Thirty-two thousand pounds, aye, that makes the value in today's money, one point one million. Oh, to have the freedom of the rich, what do you say, young Lane?'

'I'm not sure money brings happiness, sir.'

'Maybe you're right, lad.' He glanced at the clock. 'We're about one third through your work and I noticed when I read it you left a six year gap. Did people stop living for six years?'

Angus sat quiet for a moment pondering, turning pages before putting the file down and rubbing his chin.

'It was a difficult time for the family, sir. There had been two deaths caused by doubtful means and the loss of the cottage. Thomas Bosworth became depressed, blaming himself for his mother's demise and so the family lost its leader. Then of course, there was the money factor. They were not rich people and could not afford to keep paying for a dream.'

'They lost the will to go on, is that what you mean?'

'Yes. That is until 1848 when a very inquisitive thirteen year old called Eleanor Hinchcliffe pestered her Mother, Thomas's sister Beth, to tell her the story of their '**stolen birthright**.'

***

PART 2

1848 – 1886.

ELEANOR

(Ellie)

9

1848.

'That's the way of it, young Ellie. Your Uncle Tom lost his house and his Mother on the same day.'

It was evening in the Hinchcliffe household at the end of damp autumn day. The heavy curtains were drawn and there was a log fire blazing in the hearth.

The combination of warmth and dinner was too much for father, Edward, who, after a long day at Gloucester docks was physically tired and he was asleep in his favourite armchair with the family tabby curled in his lap.

Ellie, her long dark hair tied in rags sat at her mother's feet her hazel eyes wide with excitement, the sampler of cross-stitch forgotten as her Mother related the family history.

'What happened next, Mum,' she said excitedly.

'They went to live above the shop while Uncle Tom recovered from his burns. Auntie Elizabeth looked after the shop with the help of the children and the family gave what they could in the way of clothes and furniture. The village people also helped and donated thirty pounds.'

'Why didn't they build the house again?'

'Your Uncle became depressed and for a long time could do nothing. The house had too many memories and to lose his Mother and Sister in so short a time was very distressing. He loved his Mum and missed her immensely. When your Uncle got better, they sold the land and built up the shop.'

'Were Cousins Charlotte and Thomas hurt?'

'No dear. Your Uncle's quick action got them out in time.'

'Is that why we are still poor?' Ellie sighed as her dream of fantastic riches dissipated before her eyes.

Beth laid a reassuring hand on Ellie's shoulder. 'Yes, dear, and after lots of hard work we are still no nearer our right.'

Ellie changed to a kneeling position, placed her hands on Beth's knees and declared with some determination.

'When I grow up I'm going to Scotland to get our money back.'

Beth stroked Ellie's hair affectionately before holding her hands. 'Are you now, young lady? Very well, but right this minute you're getting ready for bed.'

'Mum, how do I go about looking for our money?'

'More questions, my goodness.' Beth stood up and helped Ellie to her feet. 'There are so many things you need, dear. You had better speak with your Uncle Tom next time we visit. Now leave me be and run along.'

Ellie badgered her Mother to take her to visit Uncle Tom and they went that weekend. The passenger barge along the Sharpeness canal cost them a penny-halfpenny and the short walk to the village of Frampton took no time at all. When they alighted Ellie ran on ahead, so eager was she to find out more about the family mysteries and the task she had sworn to carry out.

She burst through the shop door and set the bell ringing in a solo campanile performance.

Uncle Tom stood up quickly from under the counter where he had been refilling shelves.

'What's going on then,' he enquired, pretending he had not seen Ellie. 'Who's in such a hurry to tear down my door?' He raised his hands in mock surprise. 'Oh, it's you, sweetheart and to what do I owe this pleasure, and where's your Mum?'

Ellie giggled at her uncles antics. 'Oh, she's coming, she can't run anymore.'

'What's so urgent my little one that you have to run? Surely it's not the pleasure of seeing me?'

'No, Uncle. Oh, dear,' her hand flew to her mouth. 'I didn't mean that. Of course I want to see you.' And then standing with her legs braced apart, hands on hips, she pronounced, 'I'm going to Scotland to get our money and I want you to tell me how.'

The doorbell once more rang out its manic virtuoso to reveal Beth holding tight to the handle and gasping for breath, her face red with the exertion.

'Hello, big sis,' Thomas said cordially, 'how are you and what nonsense have you been feeding your offspring?'

'One moment,' she took a few deep breaths, 'Ellie has near dragged me off my feet coming up from the canal.'

Beth paused again, sucking air into her starved lungs.

'That's better. I'm very well, Thomas, and how are you and Elizabeth?'

'We're both well. Come through and I'll send one of the children to watch things.'

He ushered them through the door separating the shop from the family quarters at the rear and into the living room come kitchen where Elizabeth was preparing pastry.

The room, comfortably furnished with the large black range at one end surrounded by armchairs and a settee and behind them the table where Elizabeth was working. A dresser covered in plates, dishes and kitchen utensils stood against the door wall. Rag rugs, which Elizabeth had painstakingly made, were scattered over the stone-flagged floor.

'Oh dear,' Elizabeth stopped working and grabbed for a cloth to wipe her floury hands, 'What are you doing here? I'm not ready for visitors,' and she added anxiously. 'Nothing wrong is there?'

'No, no, Elizabeth, Ellie has her mind full of this foolish idea of going to Scotland to rescue our money and she wanted to see Tom and it's a good excuse for a cup of tea and a chat.'

Tom interrupted the social chatter, 'Sit down, sis and young Ellie, you come over by me on the settee.

Beth sat by the table talking to Elizabeth and Thomas continued his conversation with Ellie.

'Now, tell me all about it, young lady,' he said.

'Mum told me about us having money in Scotland and that we could not get it because some naughty men kept stopping us. I want to go and get it when I grow up and I need to know where to start.'

'Well, young lady, you have picked a hard task as you will need to travel and search church records for all the family connections right back to your Great-great-grandma. The longer you wait the longer the list grows.'

'Do I need everyone's record, Uncle Tom? Can't I just get the first one because we know the later ones are related?'

'No, my love, you have to show everyone is connected like the rungs of a ladder.'

Ellie sighed 'Oh, dear.' She shrugged her shoulders in resignation and said, 'Where do I start?'

Thomas sat deep in thought and after what seemed an age he said, 'It's a sorry state of affairs, Ellie, but I have absolutely nothing to start you with. Everything was lost in the fire. I can only suggest that you go over to Stroud and see Mr Beattie, the solicitor. His was the first search for us and he will be able to point you in the right direction. It's a funny thing. They had no need to burn the house down as we didn't have all the information needed to prove our claim.'

'Why was that, Uncle Tom?'

'Because,' he continued, 'we couldn't find the proof of the last marriage connecting us to the Ross Clan. It was lost. You could stop by Longhope Church while you are collecting the documents close to home and look for the marriage of Mary Ross to William Hall, about 1730. It's the last link in the chain but no good without all the other material.'

Ellie called over to Beth. 'Mum, can you help me? Can we go to Stroud, and Longhope?'

'Maybe, dear,' Beth replied. 'Finish your schooling first, and then we shall see. You will have to be patient as it takes money to do that sort of thing.'

'I'll save all my pocket money,' Ellie said in earnest.

Beth looked at her daughter full of pride and unspoken love. 'What it is to be young, eh, Thomas, and have the exuberance of a child.'

'I wish I had the will again,' Thomas replied, 'I owe it to Mother really.'

He suddenly sat bolt upright and flicked his fingers. 'I know!' In one swift movement he sprang from his chair and left the room to return almost immediately. He handed Ellie a small bundle. 'Here you are, young lady, a guinea to help you on your way.'

Ellie unrolled the bundle and in it was a mounted gold coin.

Thomas continued. 'It is a George III coin that belonged to your Grandma and is said to be from the original specie brought down from Scotland in 1793.'

'Oh, thank you, Uncle Tom.' She threw her arms around him, and gave him a hug, 'You're my favourite uncle of all time.'

He stood, picked her up and swung her round. 'And you're my favourite niece.'

Ellie squealed with delight and ran over to her aunt. 'Auntie Elizabeth, look what Uncle Tom has given me. It's Grandma's guinea.'

'Oh, he did, did he? You wait here while I pop up to my room. Thomas put the kettle on the fire for me.'

Elizabeth was absent a little longer but when she returned she gave Ellie a shining bundle of gold.

'Here you are poppet. This is your Grandma's belcher chain to hang your guinea on. You must look after it, mind.'

The gold chain was so long Ellie had to loop it around her neck three times.

'Elizabeth you can't,' Beth protested.

'We're all going to die one day,' replied Elizabeth, 'so I may as well give it up now.'

'What about your children, doesn't it belong to them?'

'They'll get the shop so don't bother yourself. Tom doesn't mind, do you?'

The habitual way that women answered their own questions left him bewildered and he replied with a tame, 'Yes dear,' whereby he turned to Ellie and said lamely, 'Give them to your Mum to look after, Ellie, and let's have that tea.'

On Ellie's thirteenth birthday Beth took her to Stroud to meet George Innes, Solicitor. Standing proudly before the desk in the front office, Ellie said in her best voice.

'Can I see Mr Beattie, please?'

The stony eyed, grey haired receptionist looked over her glasses at the diminutive girl in front of her, sniffed in a patronizing way and answered haughtily.

'I'm afraid not, he no longer works here.'

Ellie could hardly stop herself from laughing when a disconnected voice called from the back, 'What is it, Mrs Bright?'

'We have someone for Mr Beattie, sir, a young lady.'

Innes entered through a door in the corner of the room. He was a kindly looking man with straight white hair and looking over his half glasses, he said, 'Who is it that wants Mr Beattie?'

Ellie liked the look of him. 'Me, sir. My uncle told me to come here as Mr Beattie may be able to help us.'

'You had better come through.'

He led them down a narrow passage to his office and pulled a chair out.

'You sit there, young lady, while I get a chair for your Mum. It is Mum, isn't it?'

Beth spoke for the first time. 'Yes, but I'm taking a back seat today.'

'I understand.' He turned his attention once more to Ellie. 'Now, young lady, let us introduce ourselves. George Innes at your service and you are?'

'Miss Eleanor Hinchcliffe, but my friends call me Ellie,' she answered brightly.

'Ellie aye, may I call you, Ellie?'

'Oh, yes sir, it's much shorter, and easier to say.'

'Ellie, what is the business you have with Mr Beattie? He has moved on to his own practice in London, but maybe I can help.'

She looked earnestly at Innes, 'Will I have to pay?'

'Ellie!' Beth exclaimed. 'You don't say things like that.'

'Your daughter has a sound practical head, Mrs Hinchcliffe. Yes, Ellie, for all business you have to pay, but I have not heard what it is you require and I am sure that some consideration may be given to your income and status.'

'Very well,' she replied. 'My Uncle is Thomas Bosworth of Frampton and I'm going to get our money from Scotland. Can you help me? Tell me what I should do.'

Innes put one elbow on his desk and scratched his chin reflectively.

'Umm, Mr Bosworth, aye, an unfortunate business that, but I'm afraid that I know nothing of your case, young lady as Mr Beattie did it all before he joined me.'

He picked up a pen and scribbled something on a piece of scrap paper. 'Here you are, this is his London address. Write to him and I am sure he will help and don't forget to tell him I suggested this line of enquiry.'

Crestfallen, Ellie replied, 'Thank you, and how much do I owe?'

'There is no charge as I did nothing for you and I expect nothing in return.'

Beth stood up and put a comforting arm around Ellie. 'Thank you, Mr Innes.'

'The pleasure is all mine, Mrs Hinchcliffe. It was a delightful interlude from the moaning, avaricious malcontents which I normally deal with.'

———

That same evening, Ellie unfolded the writing slope on the kitchen table, and in her best handwriting wrote a letter addressed to – *Mr S. Beattie…*

Four days later when she returned from school, there on the mantle piece was a reply with the stamp precisely placed, addressed to – *Miss E. Hinchcliffe…*

Feeling proud and grown-up at receiving her first letter and a little apprehensive about its contents she left it unopened.

At the tea table later, Beth, who had been on tenterhooks all day, could stand it no longer.

'Eleanor,' she demanded, 'will you open that letter?'

Ellie smiled, she knew when her mother was getting angry or tense because she always used her full name. 'I don't want to,' she replied sincerely, 'I'm a little scared of what it might say.'

'Don't be silly, girl. Come here, I'll do it.'

'No, Mum, it's my letter. Let me finish tea and then I will open it.'

There was both anger and pleading in Beth's voice. 'Oh no, come on, stop teasing. Here's a knife, open it now, please.'

To delay the opening as long as she could Ellie slid the knife in a slow deliberate slice along the top flap until her mother was nearly screaming with the tension.

'Hurry up, will you? I can't stand it, give it here.'

She made a grab over the table, but Ellie was too quick and pulled it away.

'No Mum, it's for me.'

The letter, neatly folded and written on the best velum began…

Dear Miss Hinchcliffe…

It made her feel grand to be addressed in such a manner. She pulled herself upright in her chair, held the letter firmly with both hands and started again…

Dear Miss Hinchcliffe,
It gives me great pleasure to be able to assist you in your endeavour to reach the truth of your family history and so bring to an end the saga that has gone on long enough...

The letter went on to explain in detail the travels she would have to undertake to put together the family documents.

Beth was getting impatient now. 'Have you finished yet? Don't keep it to yourself. What does he say?'

'Here you are, Mum. He says he is glad to help and we should get in touch again to keep him up to date on our progress.'

Beth read it through twice before putting it down.

'There is a lot of hard work there Ellie, and expensive.'

'Yes, Mum, but there is something I can do now. Uncle Tom's marriage and birth certificates we have already and I can write to Auntie Sarah for hers. Mr Beattie also said that now the postal service is working it would be quicker and I thought that I might put a note in to Cousin Julia at the same time.'

'What a good idea, it's a long time since we met them. To send a letter would be an ideal way to catch up on the news. I have their address somewhere and while you're at it, Ellie, write to your Auntie Maria. I know it's only Arlingham but it will save both time and money.'

Ellie's course was set and she wondered about the future.

—

Some weeks later.

Beth met Ellie at the front door, put an arm around her daughter's shoulders and in a sombre voice said, 'Sit down, Eleanor, I have something to tell you.'

Ellie felt uncomfortable. 'You're using your serious voice, Mum? Have I done something wrong?'

'No dear.' She gave Ellie a hug. 'I have some terrible news

and I don't know how to say it.'

'Mum, you're crying. What is it?'

Beth pulled a handkerchief from her sleeve, dabbed her eyes, and shook her head, unsure what to say.

'Ellie, dear, there was an accident on the docks this morning involving your Dad and he died soon after. Darling, your Daddy is no more.'

Ellie ran into Beth's enveloping arms and cried, huge sobs wracking her slight body.

Beth pulled her in tight and consoled her grief stricken offspring, 'There, there, dear, let it all out.'

After some moments Ellie wiped her eyes on her mother's apron, sniffled and said in a quiet voice, 'Mum, what are we going to do?'

Beth stood back, held Ellie by both shoulders and looked down at her. 'I will have to find work and now you are approaching your fourteenth birthday so will you.'

Ellie's hand flew to her breast and she said, wide eyed with shock. 'Me too!'

Beth nodded, 'Yes, dear. It was only because of your Dad's money as overseer that we were able to leave you at school as long as we did. Wait until after the funeral then we shall see.'

A loud knock on the front door interrupted their grief.

'I'll go, Mum.'

Without thinking, Ellie had changed from a child to a helpful member of the household.

'No dear, you splash your face while I pop and see who it is.'

Beth patted her hair and straightened her dress and apron as she walked down the hall. She could tell by the cut of his clothes and the coach at the roadside that the tall portly man at the door was of some importance. He raised his hat and announced himself. 'Good afternoon. I'm Mr Armcoat, your husband's employer.'

'Oh dear, you had better come in. I'm sorry for the mess, I wasn't expecting visitors so soon.'

'Don't apologise, Mrs Hinchcliffe,' he said as he followed her down the hall.

Beth flicked at a chair it with her apron. 'Please, be seated Mr Armcoat and let me take your coat.'

'There's no need, I'll not take up much of your time, and who's this young lady?'

Ellie put an arm around her Mum.

'This is Eleanor, our daughter.'

'How do you do, young lady.' He abruptly turned back to Beth. 'I have come to offer my condolences for the untimely death of your husband. He pushed someone out of the way of a falling bale. It was an act of heroism that killed him and I know that nothing will replace him, but here's his week's wages, plus a little extra.'

He pulled out a small moneybag and placed it on the table alongside the wages. 'And this is a collection from the men and by the weight of it they thought well of him.'

A tear came to Beth's eye and she wiped at it with the corner of her apron.

'Thank you very much for your kindness, Mr Armcoat and please give our thanks to his workmates for their generosity.'

'I'll do that and let us know when the funeral is. Goodbye, I wish it was under more favourable circumstances.'

Beth showed him out and hurried back to Ellie who could not control her tears. Putting her arms around her she hugged her to her bosom.

'There, there, baby, have a good cry,' and her own tears dropped onto Ellie's hair.

After a few moments, she held Ellie at arms length and said, 'I know. You can count the money while I do some tidying up.'

She tipped the contents of the bag onto the kitchen table and was surprised to see that there was a large amount of silver and two gold sovereigns.

'Oh my, you get stuck into that little lot, sweetheart.'

Through a mist of tears, Ellie sorted the money into little piles while reminiscing about her Dad and the good times they had together.

How they held hands as they went to Church every Sunday, or he would lift her onto his shoulders as they walked along the canal bank. In the summer, they would go to a little beach on the south bank of the River Severn where, mindful of the Severn bore he watched her closely while she paddled.

Other Sundays he would potter about in their small garden and after dinner he would light his pipe and fall asleep in his chair. She loved the smell of his pipe and many were the times they had to dowse the glowing embers of tobacco to stop them burning the rag pile carpet.

She dabbed away a tear, fearful of what the future might bring and continued counting.

'Mum, mum, come quickly, they've given us a fortune. There is twenty-four pounds, thirteen shillings and sixpence.'

Beth stopped what she was doing and came to look.

'My heavens, he must have been well thought of. That'll give him a good send off.'

'Mum, please can I have some of it to do my family search and then we might be rich?'

Surprised, Beth could only stand at look at her daughter in admiration. Still grieving and already planning the future.

'I'm sorry, love. We have to pay the rent and the corner shop and then buy what we need to run the house until we get work of some kind. It won't last very long, you'll see.'

Another loud knock on the front door interrupted them.

'I'll go, Mum.'

Ellie ran to the door and opened it.

The Reverend Robin Bolton raised his hat, 'Hello, Mistress Hinchcliffe, is your mother at home?'

'Mum,' she shouted down the hall, 'It's the vicar.'

'Show him in then, don't keep him on the doorstep.'

'Won't you come in?' Ellie bobbed and stood to one side.

'Thank you, young lady.'

She followed him down the hall thinking, 'He doesn't look like a vicar he's far too good looking, and all that red hair.'

Beth met the vicar at the kitchen door and he took her hands.

'My deepest sympathy, Mrs Hinchcliffe, it's a sad loss, not just for you, but also for the community. He will be sorely missed and who could forget his vibrant singing on Sunday's.'

'Thank you Reverend, you're most kind.'

'Is there anything you need most urgent, Mrs Hinchcliffe? We have a fund at the church to help the bereaved in their darkest hours.'

'No, thank you. His work mates have been most generous and with care we will be able to manage.'

'That is excellent and I have arranged the funeral for Saturday, next week. Will that suit?'

'Yes. I think I can let people know by then, this new fangled post is a wonderful thing.'

'Very well. Join me in the Lord's Prayer and I will be on my way.'

They clasped their hands together, bowed their heads, and in unison they recited – *'Our Father, which art in Heaven...*

When they had finished he laid a hand on their heads and recited – *'In the name of the Father, the Son, and the Holy Ghost, Amen.* Take care, Mrs Hinchcliffe, and you young lady.'

He patted Ellie patronisingly on the head as he walked down the hallway. She hated it when people did that and pulled a face at his back. At the door he turned to say. 'Don't forget. If you need anything please get in touch.'

'Thank you, Reverend.'

Beth closed the door behind him before turning to Ellie. 'Now, young lady, we have to get busy. You're good at writing and I want you to write to all our relatives telling them about the funeral and first thing in the morning you can go to the corner shop and post them.'

'What do I say, Mum?

Beth thought for a moment. 'Oh, just keep it simple, like... I know; I still have the notice from your Uncle Tom about Grandma's funeral. You can copy that, but in your best handwriting mind.'

'Yes, Mum, I only have best handwriting.'

'Don't be cheeky. Here you are, use those words and just change the names.'

Ellie set up the writing slope and with her favourite pen set to work.

―

It took her the best part of an hour and a half to finish the list, not counting the two she had to re-write because a tear had made the ink run and her fingers ached when she finally put her pen down.

'Finished Mum, can I have a read now?'

'No love. I'll make you some hot milk and then you can go to bed. We have to be up and about early tomorrow. I have to clean and you have to run down to the shop before eight o' clock to catch the post.'

'Oh Mum, please.'

'All right, but only ten minutes mind. I don't know what you find in those books anyway.'

Thomas Bosworth consoled his sister. 'That was a right good showing for your Ted, Beth. I've never seen a funeral so well attended and there was many a man from his works, including his boss.'

'Yes, Tom,' Beth said with pride, 'he was well liked and he'll be missed a great deal.'

Her brother William wandered over to join them.

'A good turnout, aye, Beth,' he said, glancing around the room. 'And not without justification.'

'Thank you, William, and you're looking better these days.'

'I'm feeling better, sis, and able to work now.'

Beth looped an arm in his and enquired with an air of mock concern. 'What was your ailment, William? Did the doctors find anything?'

'They had no explanation for it, Beth. One said I was malingering, another thought it some sort of arthritis, but I had no strength and was unable to move at times. Tiredness accompanied me all day as if I had not slept. About a year ago, I began to feel easier and now I am ninety-five percent fit. It is a relief, and Mary's father has found me a position so I now have an income. I can't thank Mr Bush enough for his forbearance.'

Beth looked up at him earnestly suppressing a smile, 'Oh good, and might we expect an addition to the family, or is that the five percent?'

'Beth, I declare! It is merely an aching in the muscles at the end of the day that ails me now. One hopes that such a misfortune would not happen at our age.'

She gave her baby brother's arm a squeeze and said with a sisterly smile, 'So true. I'm glad to see you well, William. Excuse me, I must find Ellie, have you seen her?'

'She was entertaining her cousin, Julia, on the back step a little while ago.'

'Thank you, William.'

Before she could move her older brother grabbed her attention once more. 'Beth!'

'Yes, Tom.'

'We must be going, Beth. It's an hour's journey to Frampton. A letter travels quicker than that horse of ours.'

William butted in. 'We will leave also, Beth, although Saul is not so far.'

'Very well, but first let me round up Ellie to fetch your coats.'

She went out to the kitchen and found the cousins deep in conversation and they did not hear her approach. 'Ellie! Fetch the coats from upstairs, there's a love. I'm tired to the marrow.'

Ellie jerked around at the sound of her mother's voice. 'Very well, Mum. Julia can help me.'

Julia jumped to her feet. 'You can show me the bed I'm sharing with you tonight.'

'Alright, come on.'

The two Ross cousins, so alike, dashed away with the boundless energy of youth.

—

Upstairs, Ellie gave Julia the tour.

'That's Mum and Dad's room. Oh, I forgot.' A tear rolled softly down her cheek as she realized her mistake.

Julia put an arm around her cousin and gave her a hug. 'Never mind, Ellie. It must take a long time to get used to.'

'I know, how silly of me.' Taking control once more Ellie pointed into the master bedroom, 'Your Mum and Dad are sleeping in there tonight and Mum's on the settee downstairs.'

—

Laden down with coats and cloaks the two girls staggered into the living room and Ellie called out. 'Here we are everyone.'

Uncle Thomas with wife Elizabeth, children Charlotte and Thomas and Uncle William with wife Mary and Auntie Maria, whose husband worked in Canada, made their way out to their traps where the horses waited patiently, loosely tethered with their heads deep into feedbags.

The following morning, Cousin Julia and her parents, left to catch the train that would take them to Chepstow and when all was quiet, Beth and Ellie sat down to take stock of their situation.

'Well, young lady, that's that. We'll spend today cleaning up and tomorrow we go looking for work.'

'Do you think we'll find any, mum?'

'I'm sure of it. Work is there if you look hard enough and besides, we have a letter of introduction from Mr Armcoat. First stop is that soap factory down in the basin. He said to go there as they're always looking for people.'

'Why do they always want people, Mum?'

'I don't know, love.'

On the stroke of six a.m. they watched as the workers clocked on and it didn't take Ellie long to find out why there was a large turnover of staff even in hard times. The smell was disgusting, unlike anything she had come across before.

As the last worker disappeared into the factory they plucked up the courage to give their letter to the overseer.

'Oy, right posh, eh! A letter from old Armcoat, no less. Wait here while I go and see what to do with it.'

Beth whispered into Ellie's ear, 'That a good sign. He has to see his boss first. Are you alright, lass, you're shivering?'

'It's only nerves, Mum.'

Beth put a sympathetic arm around Ellie's shoulder. 'Try not to worry too much, I'll look after you. It's all part of growing up.'

A large swarthy man came from the back office dressed in a suit whose jacket buttons were straining against his bulk. His neckcloth was rumpled and stained and hanging from his lapel was a pair of half glasses held together with cotton binding. In ludicrous contrast he wore a gold half-hunter watch and chain across his middle.

'Well now, what have we here? You come with good references so you can start in the packing department.' He glanced down at the letter. 'Mrs Hinchcliffe; it's ten shillings a week for you, and the lass seven. Sign on at the front desk. Start at six every morning. It's twelve hours Monday to Friday and Saturday you finish at one.'

The overseer hovering in the background called them over.

'You've got a start then. Right put your mark here and I'll take you down to meet Edie.' He watched as they signed their names. 'Educated a bit, then. I was thinking you looked a bit smart for this place.'

Beth put her arm around Ellie. 'My husband was killed on the docks. You can't sit on your hands under those circumstances.'

'I'm right sorry to hear that. It's hard work and you'll be knackered for the first month 'til you get used to it. Edie will look after you.'

They followed him into a building of Cathedral proportions with lines of steaming vats of what looked like boiling fat with a white sludge floating on top. By each vat were stacked the ingredients for the next mix, including barrels of some type of oil.

Pipes of all sizes criss-crossed the room with no apparent design and Ellie likened it to a giant cat's cradle puzzle. Dozens of gaslights lit the place creating an eerie incandescent glow and the cloud of steam hanging amongst the roof girders was not unlike a blanket of cotton wool.

The heat and humidity made them perspire after only a few paces and their clothes clung to them.

'Oh, my, how do you work in this?' Ellie shook with anxiety at the prospects of what was to come.

They were passing the end of the line of vats nearest to them when she was surprised to see some men breaking open coconuts and tossing them into a grinder. They added the resulting creamy white substance to the contents of the vat where a man, stripped to the waist, stirred it with a wooden paddle.

Ellie called out over the noise. 'Excuse me, mister, why do we have coconuts?'

'Nice to see you takin' an interest, missy. We add coconut oil to the solution to make your softer household soap an' give it a bit of colour. The other hard soap all goes to the woollen mills to wash the wool before they card and spin it or whatever it is they do.'

'Thank you.'

'Pleasure, miss.'

After the vats the mixture was poured into wooden trays to

cool and solidify before a man operating a guillotine cut it into handy bars.

They walked through into a smaller cooler building where the smell was less overpowering. The lines of soap bars were coming through holes in the wall on rollers where women collected them, stuffed them into wooden boxes and pushed them down the line to the next gang of workers.

They in turn, with a one tap and a bang rhythm, nailed a lid onto the boxes, eight nails to a box before passing them on to the stackers who carried them through to the warehouse. On the line farthest away from them the bars were thrown into a grinding mill where they were turned into flakes and measured out into one-hundredweight sacks.

'EDIE!' The overseer hollered over the noise.

A pleasant faced woman in her early thirties, her hair tied up with a scarf turban looked up and signalled that she was coming over.

She stopped between Ellie and Beth and gave them the once over.

'What have we here, Ben?'

'A tiddler and her mum,' he replied, 'and the boss said to start 'em in here.'

Edie gave Ellie's upper arm a gentle squeeze. 'Not much there have you, love? Never mind, you go on the nailing and packing. What's your name?'

'Ellie, ma'am.'

'Ma'am aye, I like a girl who knows her place. You call me Edie love, and this is your Mum?'

Ellie clung onto her mothers arm. 'Yes.'

'Hello there, Mum, an' what's your name?'

'Beth,'

'Right, Beth, you go on stacking. See that blonde woman over there, she'll show you the ropes. I expect you up to speed next week and don't worry about the young one. She'll be tired out at the end of the day and all she'll want to do is sleep, but you must make her eat.'

'Thanks, Edie,' Beth replied. 'She's a good worker, and clever.' She unclenched Ellie's fingers from her sleeve. 'Go on, love, you'll be alright.' She gave her a final hug and went off to join the stackers.

Edie put a friendly arm around Ellie's shoulder.

'Ellie eh, right, let's get you sorted. Go behind those boxes and take off your extra clothes. Just keep your dress and pinny on and when you're ready come back to me.'

A few moments later Ellie returned.

'Done that?' Edie gave her a reassuring smile. 'Ellie, small you may be, but you have to do your share. Here's your hammer and you keep the same one so's you get used to the weight. Get some nails and go over to that pile of finished boxes and practice. One tap to hold it and then—wallop—in it goes. You won't do it straight away. After one hour of that, go to the packing and do an hour there, got that? Nails is over there. Off you go, and if you have any trouble, come and see me.'

Ellie dragged a box into a corner, watched the others for a moment, and then tried her first nail.

'OW,' she howled. Peals of laughter rang out across the bay.

'Ooh,' she sobbed, and sucked her throbbing thumb. Tears came to her eyes, but she was determined not to give in and she prepared to strike another nail.

'Hold on, lass!' An older woman about her Mum's age joined her. 'Let's have a look. You'll have a right bloody one after that and your nail'll probably go. Now watch. Keep the tack between thumb and forefinger like this and just give it a tap, see. That should hold it. You can let go of it and if you've done it right it'll stay in place. Until you get used to it tap a little softer otherwise you'll have no fingers left. An' don't worry, lass, we all did it.'

'Thank you, I'll soon catch up, you watch, but it does hurt.'

'Good girl, now go and put your hand in yon cold water for a few minutes and that'll ease it somewhat.'

Reduced to the obscurity of nailing and packing, life changed dramatically for Ellie. Her fine slender fingers, after the initial bruising and bleeding, became calloused and her life became a drudgery of waking, walking and working...

Meals prepared on a Sunday were warmed up and eaten half-asleep. Days ground into weeks, weeks into months, never seeing the light of day until the weekend.

Breakfast was a hurried affair, followed by a fifty-minute dash along the canal bank in all weathers. A risky walk in the summer, but in the winter, when ice formed in the puddles left by the horse's hooves, you had to be extra careful. It had become the favoured short cut into the town since the opening of the canal and there were always someone about in case of trouble.

The walk home was slower. After a twelve-hour shift their feet dragged and at fourteen years of age Ellie was asleep on her feet and leaned on her Mum.

A cold house welcomed them and the fire in the range had to be lit before the evening meal could be prepared.

There was no relief on the demand for time. Ellie went shopping on Saturday afternoons, while Beth stayed at home to do the washing, keeping an eye on the weather, a set of clothes kept in reserve in case the washing did not dry in time for Monday morning, but there was always time for church on Sunday.

The service was the barometer which showed their change of circumstances. People were polite and friendly but as their fortunes dwindled their circle of friends grew smaller and their declining social status meant they had to move to the rear pews of the church. Apparently only the vicar was unaware of their diminished well-being.

—

Ellie learned quickly and after three months Edie arranged to have her wages raised to the adult rate. Ellie also endeared herself to her colleagues, when, with her education, she was able to check their wages to see if they were being correctly paid.

The news of the young girl in the factory who was good at Math's and English spread to the office and a little over a year later, she was summoned upstairs to meet the office manager, but before Ellie went to meet her destiny Edie gathered the packing crew around her.

'Listen girls, young Ellie here has been called up to the office. She has done nothing wrong. I know what it is but I'm not going to say because I don't want to spoil the surprise. Let's tidy her up. Sit down Ellie and give us yer boots. Doris, you're good at hair.' A hidden flat iron was brought out. 'Get your skirt off, lass.'

When they were satisfied Ellie looked presentable Edie put a comforting arm around her. 'Off you go, lass and don't go through the factory or the steam will make your hair droop. Come back and tell us what goes on.'

With feelings of misgiving and quivering inside Ellie presented herself to the Office Manager.

'Good morning, young lady, Ellie is it?'

'Yes sir.'

'Sit down. Now then, word has it that you're good at sums and things and I have a proposition for you. Old Will has passed away, God Bless him, and I'm offering you his job in the accounts office. You will have to check all money coming in and all the money going out, besides balancing the books. Can you do that?'

Ellie clenched her fists to stop herself shaking and replied with a quiver in her voice. 'I... I think so, sir, I was good at problems in school.'

'Good, the pay is nine-shillings a week.'

Ellie's face dropped.

The manager shook his head in disbelief. 'What's the matter, girl, aren't you pleased to get out of there?'

'Yes, sir, but can I ask my Mum first? I don't know if we can manage with less money.'

'Oh, I see, of course. Let me know by lunchtime and if you can you start tomorrow at seven o' clock until five of the evening. You must be smartly dressed, mind.'

Ellie ran back to the packing shed and straight to her mother.

'Mum! Mum!'

'Yes, lass what is it?'

Everyone gathered round to hear the news.

'Mum, I've been offered a job in the office, but it's a shilling less pay. Can we manage?'

Edie stepped forward. 'Well can you manage, Beth? I'll fix it that they don't replace Ellie, and that way we can share the wages she would have had. How about it? Let's get her out of this hellhole. She'll have good prospects up there.'

Beth nodded as she wiped away a tear, 'I would have said yes, anyway, Edie, I'm just so happy for her.'

After dinner they spent a couple of hours preparing for Ellie's new job. Ellie ironed her best blouse while Mum altered a couple more to give her a change and her Sunday best outfit became her office clothes. They would have to make do until she could afford to replace them.

While polishing her boots a tear came to Ellie's eye. She remembered her father who did the family boots every Saturday night ready for church the following day.

Later, Beth put Ellie's hair in rags to give it some extra bounce and after a cup of warm milk Ellie went to bed, but, excited at the prospects the future might hold, sleep wouldn't come.

Visions and doubts flashed before her eyes. What if, or—that would be lovely—and what about clothes? Hundreds of things lined up one behind the other until she was going mad with the desperation to sleep.

Fitful slumber came eventually although it felt like she was conscious as her dreams were so visual.

Concentration had been difficult on her first day and understandably, she was tired. Five o' clock couldn't come quick enough and she hurried home to grab a nap before preparing dinner.

A routine was soon established where they were both able to take advantage of Ellie's shorter hours. Ellie did the cooking and cleaning while waiting for Beth to come home and during the extra hour in the morning she was able to tidy through. A little money was put aside each week to build up Ellie's wardrobe and they found that they were able to cope with her lower wage.

Ellie studied, and pestered the senior members of the office to show her the finer details of accounting and as the years progressed, she took on more and more responsibility.

On her twenty-first birthday she was offered the position of Assistant Accountant which she accepted and a little over a year later she was promoted to Senior on the recommendation of her mentor.

'That's it, Mum. No more long days at the factory for you.'

'I can't Ellie. We need to live.'

'I earn enough for both of us, Mum. You can prepare our meals and look after the house and make use of your seamstress skills by taking in a little light work.

'Oh, thank you, Ellie. I do feel tired these days and I don't know if I could have done much more. Edie covered for me a lot of the time, but it was still to much some days.'

'I will tell them on Monday when I go in and they won't argue as I'm now looked up to, which is hard for them, me being a woman and all.'

The transformation into womanhood had not gone unnoticed in the dingy office. Gone were the calluses and she held her head high showing her newfound self-confidence. She had developed into a striking, slim young woman and her long midnight black hair, courtesy of her Scottish ancestors, complimented her vivacious smile and deep hazel eyes and that she always had her way in the male dominated office came as no surprise to those who knew her.

The fortunes of William Maxwell during this time had also been on the rise. With the additional wealth of the Ross Clan added to his own personal riches he was able to indulge himself in all manner of things.

He became a substantial shareholder of the Royal National Bank and subsequently a Director. He furthered the family name by subscribing to many charities and it was not long before he indulged in local politics attaching his name to many urban improvements for the more unfortunate people of Edinburgh.

With his star in the ascendancy his influential and secretive connections rewarded him with the Baronetcy of Witchell from the area where he was building his castle.

His problems appeared to be over and with no further claims on his inheritance he moved into his new stately home during 1851.'

***

10

1851

William Maxwell-Ross banged the long mahogany dining table with a spoon to attract the attention of the people around it.
'Gentlemen! I thank you for indulging me by having our Lodge dinner in this my new home. This is the first function under this roof and my thanks go to Brother James Graham for a grand job. It does me great honour to have so many highly esteemed people around my table. I propose a toast to you and our honoured guest. Gentlemen! I give you – His Most Worshipful, the Grand Master, Your Royal Highness.'

They all stood and raised their glasses.

'Your Royal Highness.'

Maxwell kept the jollities moving by announcing in the same stentorian manner. 'Fill your glasses and follow me. We have a young man waiting who wishes to join our number. What better place than this to initiate him.'

'Excuse me, sir. Should not this ceremony be done in the temple as is customary?'

'Indeed, sir. Come with me and I will show you.'

He led the way from the great hall into the magnificent black and white tiled entrance hall and subsequently the grand staircase. 'Gentlemen, we go up four flights of stairs but don't be alarmed, the risers are low for our benefit.'

The staircase ended in front of a heavy oak panelled door. Maxwell with a show of ceremony flourished a large key and opened it.

'Gentlemen, I give you the finest Temple of our Brotherhood. Enter and be amazed.'

They followed him in and he listened to the ooh's and aah's with pleasure as the secrets were revealed. What confronted them was a large windowless room with a high pointed ceiling painted in a luminous blue paint. Decorating the ceiling was a gold crescent moon and stars and in the centre of the floor a gold five-pointed star with a painted golden circle joining the lower valley points and between the outer points were drawn the signs of the zodiac and other sinister symbols.

The eerie luminous blue glow was enough to see the six-pronged candleholders dotted around the walls and a large altar draped in blue velvet standing at one end of the room adorned with Masonic symbols. On the altar were laid out two five pronged candelabrum, a gold chalice and a jewelled dress sword with the point facing out. Along one wall hung a tapestry of a rearing goat.

They lit the candles much to the relief of the guests who had been troubled by the overt symbolism of the occult that was within.

'Is this not more in keeping with witchcraft than our society,' said one of the guests.

'It depends on the meaning of religion and your definition, sir. Does it not fit the bill? Will it suffice?'

'It will indeed, sir, but have you had it consecrated.'

'No, that is not the way of the Brotherhood. I call upon our Holy Royal Arch to read out the sacred tenets and bless this place in the name of the Great Architect, as only he knows the name. Will you do that, sir?'

A tall, bearded gentleman stepped forward and speaking with a heavy Germanic accent replied, 'I most certainly will.'

They all stood in a circle until the ritual of consecration was finished and in the silence that followed Maxwell said, 'Let us bring in our initiate and then we can move on to greater sport. I've had some entertaining packages brought down from Edinburgh especially for this occasion.'

One of the guests enquired, 'What's the name of the young man who wishes to join us and what is his calling?'

'It is John Mackenzie, Brother James's son, and he is an up and coming lawyer.'

'A lawyer, aye, he could be useful.'

'Lawyer, huh.' One of the older members chipped in. 'Leech more like. I pay more out for them than I do for my house. These packages, Maxwell, I want two.'

'So shall it be. It will be an interesting sight to see, you old letch.'

'Ha, ha, I have a yearning to be the meat in a nubile sandwich with the bread warm and moist. A generous helping of butter would not go amiss, I can tell you. I trust cook has enough in the pantry.'

The ceremony completed, the bedrooms became the next object of their business.

The following morning his guests took their leave in various states of weariness, except the special guest who, smartly attired in a suit of tweed and high gaitered polished brown boots was his usual immaculate self.

Maxwell bowed deeply. 'Goodbye, sir, I am told the road to Balmoral is a particularly good one.'

'Farewell to you, sir. Here is a small gift of appreciation for your hospitality.' With little ceremony he handed Maxwell a red box with a gold inlayed Coat of Arms.

Maxwell bowed again. 'Thank you, sir. Words fail me.'

They left in turn. Sir James Craig, James Mackenzie, Advocate, and his son, the newly initiated member, closely followed by Lieutenant-Colonel Scott, Sir Ronald Stirling and others of Edinburgh's and Scotland's leading men.

It was past ten o'clock before he looked at the present he had received and he was most pleased with the contents of the satin lined box. It was a triangular half-case silver watch encrusted with diamonds, the enamelled face decorated with Masonic symbols.

William Maxwell-Ross enjoyed the fruits of his ill-gotten fortune for another ten years and died in 1861 at the age of 81. The title and estate passed to his eldest son, Alexander Maxwell-Ross, MP, who was also granted the immovable assets of Jane Ross's estate and he remained an MP until he retired.

***

11

1857

A couple of years after her rise to the top, Ellie came to the attention of a young sea-going officer in the merchant marine. He called on Beth while Ellie was at work to enquire if he may call upon her daughter.

'Your name, sir, and does she know you?'

She surveyed the young man before her on the doorstep in his dark blue uniform. He was tall, about five foot eleven she fancied, with dark brown eyes and thinly clipped moustache over a full mouth. It was a pity about his nose, which had a bump near the top, but he held himself well. When he removed his cap, it revealed a shock of dark brown wavy hair.

'David Chalmers, ma'am, and I am acquainted with your daughter merely by chance. I was fortunate to be at the post box at the same time she dropped her letter, which I retrieved. I then made the most of the opportunity and asked if I may walk her home. I was immediately attracted to her as she is bright beyond words and speaks so eloquently. If I may be so bold, who could miss those eyes and the smile that would charm the most stubborn of birds from the trees.'

Beth rolled her eyes and shook her head. 'You had better come in.'

When they were settled she said, 'And what have you to offer my daughter?'

'I'm a Lieutenant in the mercantile marine with hopes of promotion to Captain someday. I have my certificates and wait only for a ship.'

'A dangerous occupation, young man?'

'Indeed yes, but I serve on the new steam driven vessels, ma'am. They are much less risky as they depend less on the frailties of the weather and I tend to be home more often.'

'I see, but I'm dependant on my daughter as my husband died

some time past. What will become of me if you are successful in your courtship?'

'You would be a companion for her when I am away. It is an ideal solution. You would be most welcome in my household, but I must warn you—I will tolerate no meddling in our relationship.'

'Well said, young man. I owe a lot to my daughter and I only wish to see her happy and I give my word there will be no interference. I must warn you that she is very strong willed and doggedly determined on her path, but she would also be loyal to the right person.'

'Do I understand that you have given your permission?'

'Yes, how silly of me, we'll see you at seven thirty.'

'Yes ma'am.'

She stood up to show him out and he took her hand and kissed it.

'Oh, a gentleman indeed, it is many a year since anyone kissed these gnarled hands.'

'Gnarled they may be, but they show the honesty of years of toil and have the beauty of age like a well worn piece of furniture.'

She laughed, 'Get on with you. I have already said, yes. There is no need for further flattery, but I like you even more.'

'Goodbye, seven thirty it is then.'

—

Ellie paced backwards and forwards across the front parlour stopping occasionally to look in the mirror, pat her hair and pinch her cheeks.

The clock on the mantelpiece said seven twenty-five. She twisted her handkerchief nervously in her fingers and did another turn around the room unable to concentrate her thoughts.

This is ridiculous she thought, 'I have dealt with men all my life so why am I acting like a silly child.'

She glanced at the clock once more – seven twenty-six.

A further look in the mirror confirmed her opinion that she was pale and looked ill. She turned from left to right to check that all was correct at the back undecided if she had chosen the right outfit for the occasion.

She wore a crinoline with the new flattened front. The floral pattern on a cream background highlighted her dark hair, which she had tied back in a bow of the same material and hung between her shoulders.

The décolletage had an infill panel of broderie-anglaise which buttoned up to a small frilled collar. Fragile lace gloves complimented the flared three-quarter sleeves fluffed out with layers of lace.

A sharp rap on the front door jerked her from her melancholy and she absentmindedly patted her dress, pinched her cheeks quite unnecessarily, and stood facing the door forcing herself to stop clenching and unclenching her fingers.

She heard her mother answer the door and address the caller before letting him in. Beth added to the tension by knocking politely on the parlour door and waiting a moment before ushering in the equally nervous David.

'Eleanor.' Ellie grimaced at the use of her full name. 'I would like you to meet Mr David Chalmers, who quite graciously asked my permission if he may court you.'

Ellie stepped forward her right hand outstretched.

'Mr Chalmers, a pleasure to meet you, although we are acquainted.'

She liked the look of this man before her in his immaculate uniform with his cap tucked under his arm and a ready smile.

'Quite handsome,' she thought.

'Mistress Hinchcliffe.' He kissed the fingertips of her outstretched hand. 'The pleasure is all mine and the circumstances more favourable than our previous encounter.'

Ellie smiled and she was finding it hard not to laugh at Beth who was stood behind him and looking heavenwards mouthing, 'Oh, my God.'

'Mr Chalmers, please take a seat.' She showed him to the sofa at one side of the fireplace. 'Can I offer you tea or would you prefer a glass of wine?'

David tactfully opted for tea and smiled to himself as Beth mockingly bowed at Ellie's request for tea for two.

Ellie sat opposite David and now that they had been formerly introduced her earlier nervousness disappeared.

'Mr Chalmers, tell me about yourself?'

He liked her direct approach. 'Mistress Hinchcliffe, or may I call you Eleanor?'

'Mr Chalmers,' she smiled in the manner that had been the instant attraction on their first encounter. 'This merely our second meeting and therefore it must be understood that I shall call you David in retaliation.'

Beth brought the tea and David laughed out aloud when she bobbed and whimsically enquired, 'Will there be anything more, ma'am?'

'Mother, behave yourself, and no listening at the door either.'

She left the room to the young couple but ignored Ellie's request not to listen and was gratified when she heard laughter coming from within.

Ellie and David's courtship lasted two years and after they married it was a solid partnership based on love and trust.

David's merchant navy career suited Ellie as she was able to carry on working and with their combined income it was not long before she was building a nest egg. Once a month she wisely invested in factory shares and watched it grow.

In the early summer of 1860 when Ellie was eight months pregnant, Beth, hardly able to contain herself, met her at the front door as she arrived home from work.

'Ellie, Ellie, there is wonderful news today. We have two letters, one from David and the other from your Cousin Julia inviting us to her wedding.'

'One from David? Where is it, it may be bad news?'

'Don't be silly, dear. David would wait until he got home, he would not have you worrying. Here it is.'

Ellie opened it with trembling fingers and read for a few moments and then she laughed with tears of joy flowing down her cheeks.

'What is it, Ellie, why all the excitement?'

'It's David, Mum. He writes to say that he has been promoted to Captain and will take over his new ship, sailing out of Liverpool, on his next voyage. Just in time for,' she patted the bump under her dress, 'our addition to be born. Now what was that you said about Julia?'

'I said she is getting married and has invited us to her wedding in July.'

'It is out of the question in my condition. This is all very sudden. I hope they've done nothing silly.

'Ellie! How could you even think it?'

'I will write to her. Oh, my memory. What's her fiancé's name, Mum?'

'It's Walter Crosswell, the railway engineer from Newport who works for the Great Western. It is said that he has good prospects and he has been courting her for nigh on eighteen months now.'

'We will go to Gloucester this weekend and find a suitable gift. Meanwhile, I am famished. Let me change and we will have dinner.'

Their daughter, Zoë, arrived on time and Ellie was absent for only one week before resuming work. Beth took on the role of nanny, and Ellie expressed enough milk to give the baby feed during her absence.

David, not happy with this arrangement, was quite vociferous in his arguments against it, but Ellie prevailed and gently explained to him that she had seen the devastating effect that her father's death had caused and she was not letting it happen again.

It was twelve months later when he broached the subject again and Ellie stayed calm and soothed his fears.

'David, my love, if you should, God forbid, have an accident on the high seas, what of us? Would you have me work fourteen hours a day just to eat, or our child sweating in a factory for a few extra shillings, like I did?'

'No, you're right of course, my love, but it just feels wrong that my wife still works. I would feel more, what is the word? I don't know, but a man should support his family.'

'You do, and how fortunate we are. It is an admirable arrangement we have and I would be bored waiting while you were gallivanting across the oceans. I also intend that our offspring should have the best education and not have to work under factory conditions.'

'Darling, you said offspring, does that mean?'

'No, my love, but it does signal my intention to try for more. Are you tired or do you feel in the mood for some after dinner activity.'

'Let us indulge in another glass of this excellent wine and then retire. We should save on fuel and snuggle together under the quilt early on these dark autumn evenings.'

'My, my, David, how discreet. If you don't persist now.' She lowered her eyes and smiled coquettishly. 'The mood may pass.'

'You lynx, come here.'

She sat on his lap, hooked an arm around his neck and wriggled provocatively as his hand manoeuvred its way under her voluminous skirts.

She squirmed as his fingers teased her. They embraced each other tighter and kissed passionately. Her heart pounded inside her corset and she said breathlessly, 'Take me now, David, the warmth of the fire adds to my flame.'

He lifted her and lowered her gently to the rug where their bodies entwined as one.

Their passion never faltered throughout their marriage but a further addition to their family never arrived.

—

Meanwhile, in the spring of 1861, Ellie's cousin, Julia, gave birth to a daughter, Julia-Jane.

The soap factory modernized and became larger and Ellie's responsibilities grew with it. Her knowledge of the industry made her invaluable and on her thirty-fifth birthday she joined the Board of Directors as a non-executive.

Ellie thought it time that she and David should own their own property and after much consideration, they chose the village of Hempstead and settled in a modest house with its own grounds and a stable. She employed a housemaid and cook so that Beth could live the rest of her life without stress, although Beth quibbled about that.

'I can still cook and clean with the best of them. Besides these young girls don't do it right. I had to show her how to change a gas mantle the other day.'

'Mother, you leave them alone and only help when you're asked. They have orders from me to let me know if you interfere. I shall lock you in your bedroom.'

'I know, and I quite like Bella, the maid. She walks with me after she has done her chores.'

'Good. Do you think I can go to work now?'

'Yes, but why don't you hire someone to drive the trap for you?'

'I enjoy driving myself and the provisions for the horse at the factory are good.'

It was a busy, but ideal life. David came home every six weeks and Zoë stayed on at school.

―

This comfortable existence lasted for seven years before Beth passed away after a short illness and she was buried in Hardwicke alongside her beloved Edward.

Two more years passed before Zoë, tired of schooling and with her mind full of the exploits of Florence Nightingale, begged her mother to allow her to go into nursing.

'Darling, do you know what they do in hospitals? It is not an easy life and hard work.'

'I know, Mum, but I don't aspire to an academical career and I do want to help people, especially sick people.'

'If that is what you want, then that is what you shall do. You're eighteen now and old enough to decide your own future.'

Zoë gave her mother a hug. 'You're the best Mum in the world.'

'Yes dear, but have you done anything about it as yet? It's silly of me to ask, I know.'

'Yes, I can start next month. They have a new intake every so often and I could live in if I wanted to, but I said, 'No.''

'Right too, I've heard stories of those living in places and besides, I'm cheaper.'

―

Ellie was tired. She had been working at the factory for thirty years and as she no longer had to pay for Zoë's education, she retired. It was time to fulfil the promise she had made to her Mother all those years ago.

Her fingers strayed to the guinea and the belcher chain which would normally be worn around the waist. It was so long she had to coil it around her neck twice. Her eyes moistened as she remembered the childhood days when Uncle Tom had given it to her.

Way back then life always seemed to be sunshine and picnics by the river and at the end of the day her Dad carrying her home, dog-tired, on his shoulders. The smell of tobacco was all around her as she imagined him in his favourite chair after dinner with his feet up, half asleep, his pipe resting on his stomach.

'Enough of this moping girl, let's prepare dinner.'

She spoke aloud as she poured water from a large willow pattern jug into a matching bowl and splashed her face.

They tried to persuade her to stay on at the factory, however, she was adamant and they graciously awarded her an annuity of £100 a year for her long and faithful service. It was quite unexpected, but it meant they would live quite comfortably.

Fate, however, had other plans and snatched her beloved David from her in late 1880.

When the letter arrived, addressed to her from the Cunard Shipping Company, it was most unusual, as they never wrote to her directly, always to David. She had a dark feeling of foreboding and her fingers were shaking as she slid the paperknife along the fold hardly daring to read it. She gave a little cry and bit on her clenched knuckle as she read…

Dear Mrs Chalmers,

We are sorry to advise you that your husband, Captain David Chalmers has been lost at sea.

His ship capsized with the loss of all hands off the North of Ireland in the great storm of Friday last while passing through the North Channel. Great efforts were made to mount a rescue, but the notorious seas of this Channel thwarted all attempts.

We are hereby advised by the Board to give you an annuity of £175 for his distinguished service.

Yours sincerely,

The bottom fell out of her world for the second time. Devastated, she ran upstairs and threw herself across the bed sobbing.

Zoë found her there when she returned and, although older than Ellie when she had lost her father, the news for Zoë was no easier to bear and they sat and hugged each other, crying.

An hour later Bella, the housemaid, disturbed them enquiring if she should set dinner.

'Yes, yes, please do, we will be down shortly, and Bella—the master will not be coming home again. He has been lost at sea.'

Bella's hand flew to her mouth. 'Oh, ma'am, I'm dreadfully sorry, I didn't know.' She sobbed as she pulled a handkerchief from her cuff to catch the tear.

Ellie calmed her. 'It's not your fault, dear, we have only just learned of it ourselves.'

Dinner was a sombre affair that evening as neither knew what to say to console the other.

—

During Sunday service special prayers were said for David and when they returned home, they sat together over hot chocolate to sum up their situation.

'With your contribution Zoë, we will have a reasonable income. I shall pay off the mortgage with my shares and some of my savings. Bella will have to go, but I will retain cook and we will continue to use the horse and trap. Yes, I think we'll manage quite well.'

'Do we have to lose Bella, Mum?'

'It's Bella or cook, Zoë. Seven shillings a week will be quite a saving.'

'Can't we pay her with the money I earn from the hospital?'

'No dear, that is yours. You will maintain yourself from now on and all I ask is that you pay towards your upkeep.'

'It's a shame; she's part of our family.'

'I know, dear, and it's a hard decision to make. We will hang on to her until she finds another position and give her an excellent reference. I will tell her tomorrow, although I'm sure they know one of them must go.'

'Thank you, Mum, I know you'll do your best for her.'

Ellie took to wearing the now traditional black, swearing that as soon as was decent she would discard this drab attire and retain the more colourful dresses she liked.

Three months later when she received another letter from Cunard telling her that the cheque enclosed for £613-17-5½d was for tonnage bonus accrued by her husband while in their employ.

She needed no further stimulus to start her search for the family fortune she had promised all those years ago.

***

12

1881.

Ellie wrote to all her known relatives asking for documents of birth, marriages and death, or any other information they may have in their possession, but above all, they must search most carefully for a marriage in the eighteenth century occurring in Gloucestershire connecting them to the Ross name.

She built up the family tree until, tantalizingly, only one marriage remained—the same one which had evaded previous searches, that of Mary Ross to William Hall.

She went over the list time after time, often late into the night, but no amount of candle grease could bring the connection. All trails ended at Romsley with the birth of Sarah Hall and frustratingly there was no trace of her parents.

She knew that Mary Ross had been in Longhope so she made that her starting point badgering the churchwarden to the end of his tether.

'It must be here, are you sure there is not a page missing?'

'No ma'am, there's no pages missing.' His voiced was starting to rise with anger. 'See here in the burial records, there is a page missing. You can tell 'cos the dates don't follow, but the dates are all consecutive in the marriage book so nothing is missing, see.'

'Are you sure? Try one more time,' she pleaded.

'Look here, I've been through this damned book dozens of times already. It's not there and I've never heard of the name Ross or Hall in these parts anyway.'

'I'm terribly sorry and I do apologize, my behaviour is intolerable. Please forgive me, but I am so close to my goal that it has become frustrating to say the very least. I know it exists this marriage because I was told as a child but I can no longer find a record of it which I must have.'

'Don't worry, ma'am, it is I that should apologize for speaking so short to you. I can offer no explanation other than the writing of the time was so appalling.'

'Thank you for your help, I must seek elsewhere.'

Using Longhope as her base, she set about searching the church records in a ten-mile radius. She left adverts in shop windows and in all local newspapers offering a twenty-pound reward for information leading to the discovery of the final piece in the jigsaw.

A lady wrote from Ross on Wye suggesting she may look there because of the similarity in the name. Ellie politely wrote back telling her that the family name and the town were not connected, but merely a coincidence.

A letter from Hereford offered a better prospect so she packed a day bag and set off to investigate, undaunted by the prospect of another days travelling. All her life she had never ventured further than a few miles from her home, and now, the more she did it, the more she enjoyed it. Every journey was different with the never-ending variety of people and the changing scenery as the trains rumbled along, singing to her as they clacked over the joints in the track.

'Ellie is here, Ellie is here, she's never been there, clickety-clack, no going back.'

—

The new sights and sounds as they crossed from Gloucestershire into Herefordshire amazed her. The rolling pastures of the southern Cotswolds changed to rows of lime washed fruit trees and before the eye could settle nature had moulded into the rich verdure of the Wye valley its idle red coated cattle with their white faces feeding at the edge of every stream. They passed over the bend in the river where the green country stretches to the Welsh hills and down into Hereford with its red sandstone Cathedral standing guard.

She decided she liked Hereford and thought she might stay over and explore it further, but first she had business to attend to. A short ride in a hired trap took her to her final destination, a three-storey cottage on the Monmouth road.

'Please wait, driver, there may be no one at home.'

'Right you are, ma'am.'

A few moments after knocking a uniformed butler answered the door.

'Good day, ma'am.'

Ellie presented her card. 'I understand this is the Ross household. We have exchanged letters and they are expecting me.'

'Please step inside and wait one moment, ma'am.'

He disappeared only to return seconds later.

'Major Ross will see you, ma'am, dismiss your man.'

She paid off her cab and followed the butler, who, after taking her cloak, introduced her to a greying gentleman of advanced years and military bearing standing stiff and upright in front of an open fire in the drawing room.

'Mrs Chalmers, sir.'

'Good day to you, ma'am. Major Ross at your service. Please take a seat.' He pointed to a settee positioned across the front of the fire and when she was comfortable, he continued, 'What can I do for you?'

'As I mentioned earlier in my letters, Major, I am tracing my ancestors.'

Before she could finish a lady entered the room who although foregoing the dowager black Ellie thought she resembled Queen Victoria in her manner of dress. Her hair was pulled back in a bun with a small mobcap pinned on top and she wore a neck to floor bottle green gown with the tiniest of lace collars.

'Roger, I heard voices.'

'Aah, Marion dearest, did you sleep well?'

'Yes, I did, thank you. Now tell me, who have you here? Are you not a little old to be entertaining young ladies?'

'This is Mrs Chalmers my dear, and no, I do not think I am beyond a little entertaining.'

She turned to Ellie. 'Wishful thinking my dear, although I can see the attraction if he did. Has he offered you sustenance? Of course not. Will you take tea with me?'

'I would love to.'

She was warming to this couple who she could sense still had great affection towards each other.

'Pull the bell, dear.' She sat down beside Ellie and the butler immediately appeared. 'Ah, Evans. Bring some tea and refreshments, please.'

'Yes ma'am.'

'Now young lady, tell me what we can do to help.'

'You flatter me, I'm not really that young.'

'Nonsense. With those eyes and that hair you would slay any man and you dress well.'

'Thank you. Coming from another woman it is indeed a compliment, but back to business. I understand your family name is Ross?'

'That is right.'

'I am seeking a family connection to this Scottish Clan that has so far eluded me. It is most important.'

She went on to narrate the family history as briefly as possible.

The Major spoke for the first time since his wife had entered the room. 'I'm sorry to say, dear, that we come from a line of the Ross's who settled in the Bristol area. Wait one moment, I will fetch my papers.'

While he was absent there followed polite small talk about the family and their respective backgrounds and although they were dissimilar Ellie was established as being middle class and worthy of their patronage.

The Major returned forthwith and spread a selection of documents before them on the occasional table. 'Here we are, compare them with yours.'

For several minutes they perused the papers before them but could establish no link between the two branches of the Clan.

'I'm sorry, Mrs Chalmers,' the Major declared, 'it would appear that we are not related. I would suggest that you continue your investigation in the Bristol area. In the aftermath of the 1715 and 45 rebellions many of the Ross Clan of Aberdeenshire did move down here either to emigrate to America or settle in the area like as not your ancestor William and his family.'

'Thank you for your help, you have been most kind.'

Mrs Ross patted her arm. 'It was no trouble and a welcome diversion, my dear. Would you like more tea while I have the carriage brought around?'

'Please don't go to any trouble, I can make my own way.'

'Wouldn't hear of it, my dear,' said the Major, 'you are our guest and will avail yourself of our hospitality.'

He gave a tug on the bell pull and the butler who must have

been hovering close by appeared instantly.

'Yes sir.'

'Have the carriage brought around, please. Where are you going Mrs Chalmers?'

'I thought I would stay in the City overnight, can you recommend a good hostelry?'

'Mrs Chalmers will be going to the Royal Oak, Evans. That will be all.'

'Very well, sir.'

'Good luck in your search, Mrs Chalmers. Do let us know how you get on.'

'I certainly will, and many thanks once more. You have been most kind.'

Ellie spent the afternoon visiting the Cathedral and wondered at the ancient Mappa Mundi. The warden, who opened the oak doors protecting it, showed her this queer version of the world on a large sheet of vellum.

'Methinks my David would have trouble finding his way home with this map,' she said, as she explained to the warden her late husbands occupation. 'And may I also take a look at the Cathedral marriage records for the early part of the last century, please?'

'Certainly, ma'am. Come this way.'

She drew a blank much as she expected and travelled home feeling a little dejected.

Her next port of call was Bristol. Trains there were fast and frequent so she commuted on a daily basis leaving adverts in windows and in the local papers as she had done many times previously. She had no urge to explore the city but she was impressed by the number of bowsprit that seemed to separate every street as if the very ships were land-locked.

In the tramway centre ships mixed with the trams, their masts like a forest overshadowing the men working below unloading bananas. One could step off a boat straight onto a tram although it was unlikely that any sailor ventured beyond the taverns placed tactfully on every street corner. Her search proved fruitless. It appeared the whole Ross Clan had moved to Bristol, but all she found was a large community of hitherto unknown members of the Clan.

———

A few days later while taking hot chocolate with Zoë before retiring for the night she spread all her documents and papers over the dining table until there was only one letter left in the box addressed to her. She picked it up and immediately her thoughts rushed back to the day she had received it more than thirty years earlier. She had been so proud that day to receive her first letter and she began to read… *Dear, Miss Hinchcliffe…*

Her eyes filled up as she remembered the events in her life since that day which had delayed the promise she had made to her mother. Something stirred in the back of her mind and suddenly the reality came to her.

'Of course, Mr Beattie,' she said aloud. 'The man who started the quest to retrieve our birthright in 1841. Why didn't I think of him before?'

'What's that, mother?'

'Zoë ! I'm going to London.'

'What for?'

'Don't you see? Mr Beattie, he who did the first search. He moved to London and he may still be able to help me.'

'Why don't you write and save yourself the trouble of travelling.'

'That makes sense, Zoë, but I intend to kill two birds with one stone. I will explore our capital and visit Mr Beattie at the same time. Come on, you can help me dig out my best dresses. The shroud is coming off. I mean to travel as a lady.'

'Mother, you will behave yourself, won't you?'

'Yes dear, but I think I may be better treated if a man thinks he has a chance, so a little flirting may be in order.'

'Take care, Mother. I know you're forty-six going on thirty, but you're new to city life. Please, go in your mourning clothes, people have more respect for a widow.'

'No, dear. My mind's made up. Let me try on some silks, I have the need to feel alive again.'

———

Ellie sunk into the plush cushions of first class carriage intent on enjoying herself. The thought that David wouldn't have approved of her spending his bonus in such a manner crossed her mind but these opportunities only came once.

On arrival at Paddington Station she stood transfixed marvelling at Brunel's high vaulted glass canopied roof.

'How do they get that to stay up there,' she pondered.

A porter eager to earn a copper was at her elbow. 'What's that, ma'am? Can I help?'

'Oh, sorry, I was talking to myself. I was marvelling at your roof.'

'Yes ma'am, t'is a grand affair and keeps me dry all the year. Can I carry your bags?'

'Yes, please do. I need a cab to take me to a hotel.'

'Which one, ma'am?'

'A clean and honest one, where I can feel safe.'

'Follow me, the cabbies will know.'

'Very well.'

The porter hailed a hansom cab and explained to the driver her needs while he loaded her bags, accepting her penny tip with a doff of his cap.

'God Bless you, ma'am.'

The driver lifted the flap in the roof and spoke to her. 'I knows a good hotel just made for you, ma'am. Real smart it is.'

'Oh, good, I will have to accept your recommendation as I am a stranger to London.'

'Have no fear, ma'am.' He dropped the flap and with a brisk, 'Walk on,' pulled out into the hustle, bustle and mayhem of the city.

Her first experience of London was a noisy and terrifying affair that left a lasting impression. One full of movement and mud mixed with straw as there had recently been heavy rain. The many wheels churned mounds of horse dung into the mix and she held a handkerchief to her nose to dampen the nauseating smell.

She used her fan to ward off the flies that invaded the cab and although quite used to the country smells of animals and horses in particular, nothing had prepared her for this.

The jumble of traffic appeared to have no direction as horse drawn trams mixed with four-wheel carts, hansoms cabs, and private broughams. Everyone it seemed was cracking a whip or shouting and there was the perpetual jingle of harness and the thudding of the horse's hooves mixed with the cries of the street traders. They knew each other intimately apparently as bawdy pleasantries were exchanged whenever they stopped and the remarks between the drivers and public made her both blush and smile simultaneously.

She saw a Hogarthian London with a vocal lower class and a city full of animal noises and street bands, hurdy-gurdies and peddlers. Shop owners were competing with this cacophony touting for customers.

She was eternally grateful when the cab turned into the quieter thoroughfares of the Adelphi area on the Savoy side of the Strand and pulled up outside the Hotel of the same name that stood on the corner of John Street and Adam Street.

She thought there was an air of ancient grandeur about the place as she entered the lobby. The marble floor of the foyer was a chrysanthemum pattern under quite the biggest chandelier she had ever seen. Down one side a mahogany reception desk polished so vigorously the wood grain tumbled like a waterfall.

Her enquiry for a room was greeted with a polite, 'I'm sorry, Madam. We have only the one room left and that is a large suite for which we charge fifteen shillings a night.'

'Oh dear, that's far too expensive, could you recommend another hotel?'

'What seems to be the matter?'

Ellie turned to face the inquisitor, and found herself confronted by a woman of similar age with quite the largest blue eyes and heart shaped face, dressed in mourning clothes which were made of the most expensive fabric. She held out a gloved hand. Ellie responded and noticed the firm confidant grip.

'I'm Mrs Clarke, the proprietor of this establishment.'

Ellie responded in like manner. 'Mrs Eleanor Chalmers.'

'What appears to be the problem, Mrs Chalmers?'

The receptionist intervened. 'I'm sorry ma'am. 'We have no room to offer the lady, only our best suite.'

'Have we any bookings for it?'

'No ma'am.'

'Very well, give it to Mrs Chalmers.' She turned to Ellie. 'You look honest and presentable. You shall have it at our standard price.'

The room quite took her breath away. It was a magnificent affair with a ceiling in the Adam fashion and decorated with painted wall panels. In the centre of this splendour was a large four-poster bed.

She hardly had time to take it all in when there was a polite knock on the door and a maid entered with a bottle of champagne in an ice-bucket.

'Compliments of Mrs Clarke, ma'am.'

'Thank you. Please convey my thanks to Mrs Clarke.'

'Yes ma'am.'

She gave a polite curtsey and left the room.

Ellie poured herself a glass and stretched out on the bed revelling in the luxury.

'Oh my, oh my, David, if only you could see me now. My bed at home will never be the same.'

Dinner that evening was a drawn out affair. The headwaiter placed her at a quiet table in a corner from where she could view the evening's guests and she purposely took her time dining to enjoy the spectacle unfolding before her. It was a one act play with many leading players.

The many changing faces and mannerisms with the regular comings and goings as people, all seemingly in a hurry to go somewhere, passed before her. There were artistes dining before going to work closely followed by the theatregoers themselves and finally, tourists tired from a days sightseeing.

There were one or two she couldn't place into any category but she noted they were friendly with the staff and had a particular table. She assumed they were regulars who enjoyed the experience and the atmosphere of the hotel.

A few admiring glances were cast in her direction but remembering her daughter's words she did not respond. There would be plenty of time for that after she had concluded her business. She forced herself to leave this fascinating scene and retired early to bed.

A double step was provided to enable patrons to climb into the bed and she lay there with a last glass of champagne feeling absolutely decadent. She smiled to herself as it passed through her mind that she could get used to this life quite easily.

Ellie had a leisurely breakfast the next morning and it was a little after ten o' clock when she requested the concierge to call her a hansom cab.

'Where to, ma'am?'

She showed him the letterhead. 'Temple Bar, please.'

It was only a short cab ride down the Strand and within minutes the cabbie dropped her outside the practice of Beattie and Driscoll – Solicitors and Barristers'.

A quick check assured her that the premises were indeed correct, although the name had changed. A young lady in a crisp white, high-necked blouse and grey skirt greeted her with a cheery,

'Good morning, ma'am, how may I help?'

'Oh, good morning, I'm Mrs Chalmers and I have this letter from Mr Stephen Beattie. It's quite an old one. I was hoping that I may see him to enquire about some business he did for us some years ago.'

'May I see it?'

'Yes, of course.'

'Aah, I see, please take a seat while I go through and speak to young Mr Beattie. I won't keep you a moment.'

She disappeared down the corridor from the entry hall to return a few moments later. 'Mr Beattie will see you now, please come this way?'

A tall red haired man of about forty stood as she entered.

'Good morning, Mrs Chalmers.' He came around his desk and shook her hand. 'Please be seated.' He waited while she made herself comfortable before returning to his seat and continued, 'Firstly, I must advise you that my father, Mr Stephen, passed away a couple of years ago.'

'Oh! I am so sorry.'

'Thank you.' He picked up the letter. 'Tell me about this unfinished business of his.'

Ellie related the story of the family inheritance and the misfortunes which had befallen them since Stephen's enquiries and now that she had taken up the search how the final link, proof of the marriage that connected them to the Ross Clan, was the one link that eluded her.

She concluded with a hint of exasperation in her voice. 'The marriage cannot be found. That is why no one else in the family has tried. They have given up, but I know that your father found it in his initial enquiries.'

Beattie remained silent for a few minutes while he perused her collected paperwork. Finally he said, 'It would seem that on the face of it you have done a very thorough job and on the strength of what you have told me I believe you have a good case. I will get our Miss Hope to check our archives. This may take a day or two, so if you could call around on Thursday. You are staying in town, are you not?'

'Yes, I am residing at the Adelphi Hotel. I had decided on some sightseeing while I was here.'

'A good choice. You should see some of our prominent artistes of the day as they prefer to stay there, including Mrs Langtry who is currently taking the town by storm.'

'I must watch for her, although to be very honest I have not frequented the Theatre in my lifetime so I am not familiar with the faces of today's artistes.'

'Mrs Clarke is very discreet, which is one of the reasons for its popularity. I am sure she would be very obliging and point out a few of our current celebrities.'

He stood up, came around the desk and walked with her down the corridor to the front of the premises. He flagged a cab and helped her in.

'It has been a pleasure talking to you Mrs Chalmers. I look forward to your visit on Thursday.' He called up to the cabbie, 'The Adelphi, please, driver.'

'Right you are, sir.' He touched his cap and wheeled the cab into the traffic.

On her arrival back at the hotel Mrs Clarke met Ellie as she walked into the foyer. 'Good morning, Mrs Chalmers, I trust you slept well last night?'

'Yes, thank you, most comfortable, I hardly think I shall sleep so well in my own bed after that.'

'Excellent. I am finished here Mrs Chalmers will you join me for coffee. I would enjoy the pleasure of female company for once instead of these fusspots.'

Asked to join one of the leading lights of London society came as a surprise to Ellie, and she hesitated.

'Oh... I... Ah, yes, I would like that. I do apologize you caught me by surprise. My mind was elsewhere.'

Mrs Clarke dismissed her entourage. 'Come this way, Mrs Chalmers, you can tell me what's on your mind.'

She led the way into a small discreet lounge and sat in a position that would give her a clear view of events taking place in the foyer.

'Shall we dispense with the formalities, call me Frances.'

Ellie nodded. 'My name is Eleanor, but I prefer Ellie, Mrs Clar... I'm sorry, Frances. It's difficult to drop the lessons of one's upbringing.'

'Don't worry, Ellie. I think you and I will get along fine. I didn't always move in such distinguished circles. I think if you looked into our backgrounds you would find similarities. Tell me about yourself.'

A waiter delivered the coffee after which they gossiped for about an hour when Frances asked what she was doing for the rest of the day.

'I did think of doing a little sightseeing.'

'In that case you shall use my carriage. Have some lunch and it will be waiting for you outside at one-thirty.'

'Oh, no, I couldn't possibly.'

'Nonsense, Ellie. It will give my idle coachman something to do. You will find him very informative on all aspects of London history. You must also join me for dinner tonight. I have a number of guests and you will balance the sexes. You may meet some surprising people.'

'Are you sure?'

'Positive. Until dinner then.'

Ellie stood and acknowledged her with a slight nod of her

head and sat down again with a bump, her head spinning.

'Oh dear, what have I done? I hope I can live up to it.'

Precisely at one-thirty the concierge came to fetch Ellie.

'Your carriage is here, ma'am.'

'Thank you, I shall come at once.'

She followed him out and after he had made her comfortable in the open Brougham the coachman spoke for the first time.

'Mrs Clarke says to take you to the City today, ma'am, and tomorrow you are to join her at ten o' clock when we go down Rotten Row, the Palace and around to the Houses of Parliament. Sometimes it's hard to hear above the noise, ma'am, but if you listens carefully I will tell you all about it as we go around.'

'Thank you so much. I am entirely in your hands.'

The tour took her down the Strand and Fleet Street to the gate at Ludgate and on to St Paul's Cathedral, along Cheapside to the Bank and the Royal Exchange. From there, they went down to the Thames to see the Tower before following the line of the old city walls. They came back into the City at Moorgate. On to the Guildhall, around St Pauls once more, and out the way they came in and finally into Gough Square to see Dr. Johnson's house.

When they arrived back at the hotel her head was spinning with information and she didn't think she would remember the half of it.

'That was wonderful. I never knew the Romans had built London.'

'Not much was known about that, ma'am, until the 'Great Fire' in 1666. When they started rebuilding they found artefacts buried under the ruins. They re-laid part of an old Roman paving when they extended the Bank.'

'My, my, what secrets are you going to impart tomorrow, I wonder? Thank you, very much, I enjoyed this afternoon. You made it so interesting. Here, take this.' She pressed a shilling into his hand.

He tipped his hat, 'Thank you, ma'am, enjoy your evening.'

That Evening
Apart from nagging doubts about accepting the invitation in the first place Ellie agonised over what to wear. She eventually decided on a princess line dress in bottle green with a close fitted bodice and the slim skirt skimmed over her hips and thighs. It had no bustle to speak of and a short train hung from the hips.

Her décolletage came low enough to show the genetic Ross mole at the top of her cleavage and she pondered for a moment, only a fleeting moment, if this was the occasion to show it. Released from her mourning she quickly decided to tease the opposite sex with its allure.

Her hair was pulled back and fastened with a black velvet bow allowing it to hang down between her shoulders. Three quarter black lace gloves and a cameo brooch on a black velvet choker completed her ensemble.

The room maid, who had helped her, said, 'Ma'am, you look wonderful, you will captivate the men folk tonight.'

'I don't look like mutton dressed as lamb or to provincial?'

'No ma'am, you looks a real lady, an' no mistake. You has such a fine figure.'

Ellie pressed a silver three-pence piece into Polly's hand. 'Thank you, Polly.'

Polly curtsied. 'Thank you, ma'am. You have a lovely time now and you can tell me all about it tomorrow.'

Finally, Ellie declared herself ready. She picked up her favourite ivory fan, a present from David, did a twirl in front of the mirror, took a deep breath and went down to dinner.

—

She descended the wide staircase slowly, her head held high. Some would say arrogantly but it was a guise she had adopted to hide her shyness. Her self-confidence began to dwindle however, when she saw heads turning to watch her. The comforting voice of a young porter eased the tension.

'Good evening, ma'am. I've been instructed by Mrs Clarke to escort you.'

'Thank you, young man. I could not think of a better person for the job. Give me your hand while we walk.'

Slightly nonplussed at the request he nevertheless raised his right hand. Ellie rested her hand on his and said, 'Tell me about yourself, young sir.'

Their conversation helped to dispel her butterflies. To her surprise they passed the restaurant and went instead to a private room.

'Here we are, madam. One moment, please.'

He knocked and they waited a couple of seconds before the double doors opened. She had a glimpse of the assembled company inside and doubts about the wisdom of her decision welled up inside her.

The porter nodded and informed the doorman of her name. 'Right lad, run along.' He turned into the room and announced in a stentorian voice, 'Ladies and gentlemen—Mrs Eleanor Chalmers.'

Ellie took a deep breath and said silently, 'Brace yourself girl, here we go,' and stepped into the room.

Frances excused herself and came to welcome her.

'Eleanor dear, you look absolutely wonderful. Allow me to introduce you.' Taking her by the arm she led her across to the assembled group standing in an arc around the fire. 'Ladies and gentlemen, I would like you to meet Mrs Chalmers, her husband was in shipping. Eleanor; Mr Brown and Clara from America.'

'How do you do, pleased to meet you.'

'Next we have, Mr Beecham and his wife Victoria.'

'Ma'am.'

'Their companion, Mr Lloyd, and where is your charming wife, sir?'

'She is temporarily inconvenienced, but I am pleased to make your acquaintance, ma'am.'

'Ellie, here is a most interesting couple from Scotland. I would like you to meet Mr Alexander Maxwell-Ross MP, and his charming wife, Joanne.'

Ellie covered her surprise by raising her fan and giving it a few whirls. She stole a glance at Frances, who with a wicked twinkle in her eye, smiled and nodded.

Quickly pulling herself together Ellie said, 'I do beg your pardon, it's quite warm in here. It is a pleasure to meet you.' In her confusion she added quite unnecessarily, 'My ancestors come from Scotland.'

Maxwell-Ross took her hand, bowed deeply and kissed it gently on the tips. 'Good evening, Mrs Chalmers. It is a pleasure to meet you. We must talk about your family later.'

'Oh, I don't think you would be interested,' Ellie added quickly, 'They were quite ordinary people who lived their lives quietly.'

Frances stepped forward to save Ellie from further embarrassment. 'Last but not least, Eleanor, meet Mr Albert Edwards. He is here by request but I think he only comes for a free dinner.'

Ellie realised she should have known this person sooner. When she first noticed him through the open door he looked familiar with his portly figure and trim beard, thin on top and clothes of the finest quality.

She did a deep curtsey. 'Your Royal Highness.'

He bowed and kissed her hand and his eyes stayed riveted to her cleavage. 'Charmed, Madam, the pleasure is all mine, but you have been hiding too long in the counties. Such beauty should be seen around our better salons. Frances, can you not persuade her to live amongst us?'

'Bertie, you cannot have all things. You have to share with the rest of the country. Come let us dine.'

—

Dinner was a gregarious affair. Frances had seated Maxwell-Ross to the right of Ellie but had the forethought to seat the American on her left and she was able to divert attention away from her ancestry and include Maxwell-Ross in discussions on the current situation in the States.

After dinner the gentlemen remained to enjoy their cigars and brandy while the ladies retired to the salon. They had been there only a few moments when the head-porter announced.

'Mrs Emily Langtry!'

Frances stepped forward to greet her. 'Mrs Langtry, welcome. Did it go well tonight?'

'Yes, thank you, a very enthusiastic audience. I wish we could have the same people every night.'

'Would you like some refreshment or have you eaten?'

'I'm famished. I did eat before the show, but all that smoke and the excitement seems to make one hungry.'

'I shall order something. Have some champagne while we wait. I have someone desirous of meeting you later Mrs Langtry. He is a fan of yours so I took the liberty of asking him to dinner. Meanwhile let me introduce you.'

'Please call me Emily, we are amongst our own kind.'

Frances turned and called to her circle of guests. 'Ladies, I want you to meet Mrs Emily Langtry. She is currently appearing in Oliver Goldsmiths—She Stoops to Conquer—at the Haymarket Theatre.'

Ellie thought her quite beautiful, but not in an English way.

The ladies joined the men later where Ellie noticed Albert Edwards remained a close companion of Mrs Langtry for the rest of the evening. Small talk continued amongst the guests and around midnight Ellie made her excuses and left, the encounter with the family adversary and Royalty indelibly imprinted in her mind.

Wednesday passed quickly with the planned tour of the West of the city. She thought Rotten Row most amusing with the rich and famous parading their latest fashion acquisition, be it a horse, a dog or a dress.

On the return journey they called in at Frances's dressmaker where Ellie chose some of the newer fabrics to take home but she avoided all arguments to persuade her to stay longer and have the dresses made up.

On the Thursday Ellie had a late breakfast in her room before taking a hansom cab to Beattie's office only to be disappointed at the news.

'I'm sorry to tell you Mrs Chalmers that we can be of no help to you. According to the notes my father left in the file a Mr Thomas Bosworth took all documents and papers into his safekeeping. We only have a copy of your original letter, however, his notes do suggest that you have a strong case and should you find this missing marriage we would be only too happy to take on your case here in London. You have a good claim and I see no difficulty.'

'Thank you. I only came on a whim and was not expecting much. It is still a disappointment though. Will there be anything to pay?'

'No. As we were unable to help you there will be no charge. There is one thing however, if I may suggest it. You could bring the case in Scotland and it will probably be a lot cheaper. My father's Uncle had a practice in Edinburgh,' He rummaged in a desk draw. 'Here we are, this is the address. I will write to them by way of introduction and I will have it delivered to your hotel this evening.'

'I am much obliged and thank you, again.'

He stood up and came around the desk. 'I'm sorry we could not have been more help, goodbye and good luck.'

Disheartened, she walked back to the hotel unaware of the hustle and bustle around her. Feeling the need to be alone when she arrived she ordered coffee in her room.

The coffee came with a note from Frances asking if she was free to join her at the Theatre that night to see Mrs Langtry.

Ellie accepted feeling that a trip to the theatre may shake her from her lethargy and she was glad she did as it was one of the Jersey Lily's better performances which called for five encores.

Frances sensed Ellie's mood when they returned from the theatre and asked her as they entered the lobby. 'Will you join me in a glass of wine before you retire, Ellie?'

'Yes of course, but only one. I have an early start tomorrow.'

They retired into the lounge and when they were comfortable Frances enquired. 'What do you think of our capital, Ellie?'

'For the most part I have enjoyed myself immensely and you have looked after me extremely well.'

'It was a pleasure. You never told me, Ellie, but what did you make of our illustrious Mr Maxwell-Ross?'

'That was very naughty Frances. I could hardly look at him let alone speak to the man. Good manners alone made me acknowledge him.'

'It was a coincidence, Ellie. He is a close friend of our Bertie and already invited, but I do admit to a touch of mischief when I invited you.'

'Your friend, Bertie. He was quite taken by Emily?'

'Oh, yes, he has a thing about Mrs Langtry. She is the latest in a line of conquests.'

'How does his wife feel?'

'Very tolerant, a good way of avoiding an unwanted pregnancy, don't you think?'

'I'm not sure I could accept that situation. I must go now, Frances. Thank you for making my stay here so wonderful.'

'It has been a pleasure. You must stay with us again if you come to London.'

They parted with a kiss on either cheek.

***

13

1881-82.

'We have been here before, Zoë?'

'Yes, mama, and I don't know why you carry on like you do. We are comfortable and I enjoy my work at the hospital. Why do you pursue this dream? It's years old.'

'Pride; and you cannot let people run all over you. It was our money and they stole it.'

'Yes, Mama, but it was such a long time ago, when was it?'

'1839, dear.'

'Surely they have forgotten by now.'

'Maybe so, but I will give it one last try. I am going into Gloucester tomorrow to search the Probate records in the Town Hall. If I can't find them alive, then maybe I can find them dead.'

—

'Here we are, ma'am, the records from 1600-1850. The best of luck.'

'My, my, it doesn't seem possible that all these people died in this area.'

'These books cover all of Gloucestershire, ma'am, not just the immediate locality. Have you tried your local church?'

'Yes, and a few more besides. Thank you for your help'

She went to the task with the same determination which had carried her through life and after an hour's search success was hers and she declared loudly, 'I have it.'

'What was that, ma'am?'

'I have found what I am looking for. William Ross—Died 1756, and he is buried in Longhope. Now let us see if we can find his daughter.'

After another hour of searching she conceded that it was hopeless. 'I think she must be in Romsley.'

Catching the attendant's eye she called him over. 'I have

finished with these, do you have the Cathedral Marriage Registers also?'

'Yes ma'am, we keep all records here now.'

'Can I see them?'

'Now look here, I've had a busy day and these books are heavy.'

'I insist. I want the books from 1700-1800 if you please. This is most important to me.'

'It bloomin' must be the time you've been here.'

Muttering under his breath he grudgingly fetched the ledgers as requested. 'Here you are, but no more. That's it!'

'Thank you.'

It was quite late in the day when she found what she was looking for and she couldn't hold back a shriek of delight.

'Eureka!'

The startled attendant came over. 'Is anything wrong?'

'No, no, look here, quite the opposite.' She pointed to an entry on the page. 'Mary Ross married William Hall 1731 in Longhope. It has taken my family years and here it is all the time. We didn't know there was a copy of all County records in the Cathedral.'

'Oh, yes, ma'am. Since 1538 records have been kept both locally and in the Cathedral to cover the diocese.'

'If only we had known.'

'You mean you couldn't find it in the church records?'

'No, it's not there.'

'If it's here, then it's there. First check and see if a page is missing and if not, examine the handwriting. Some of the peasants who wrote the records couldn't spell their own name. See this number here on the left, that's the entry number in the church register so you should be able to go straight to it'

'Thank you, I will go and look again, and I am sorry if I was so much trouble.'

'Glad to see you happy, ma'am.

Longhope Church.

'Not you again, what are you after this time?'

'The same thing, but this time I have a copy of the Cathedral register.' She took the document from her bag and gave it to him.

'The attendant said that this number here,' she pointed it out for him, 'should match the entry in your books.'

'That's right ma'am, let's go and look.'

She waited for him to bring the book out and they went through it together.

'Here we are ma'am, but it's not the same bridegroom. It says Mary Ross and William Hoyle. Look closely though and you see that the writing is poor and the quill poorly sharpened. It had a split in the end, see the double line and they were poorly educated in them days so he has misunderstood the dialect and written in a local name. There's plenty of Hoyles hereabouts.'

'That's good. I need a copy of that entry to show the mistake and now for the burial register. We are looking for William Ross.'

She showed him her copy.

'Right you are. Let me change the books, what was the index number?'

He turned the pages over and back. 'It's not here ma'am, but look, you can see that the pages are not in sequence. Someone has torn it out. We know the year though, 1756, and people from that time are buried in the eastern part of the graveyard. Shall we look?'

'Are you sure, I can do it if you're too busy.'

'No, ma'am, you have me intrigued. Why someone should pull out pages from a burial register is weird, follow me.'

It didn't take long to walk to the eastern plot and they had only been searching for a couple of minutes when the warden called her over.

'Here, we have a gravestone, ma'am, and it's been defaced. If you look closely you can make out some of the letters. See, we have William and what looks like a **P**, but look closer there has been a tail on it like an **R**, and this here could have been a **3** but I think it is the end of an **S**. The date is **17** something, but hard to tell. I think this is your missing ancestor. I have some charcoal so let's do a rub and you can take it with you.'

'Are you sure? I don't want to put you to much trouble.'

'It's no trouble, ma'am. A little mystery helps to break a humdrum day. I wonder who did it, these marks are quite old.'

'About forty years, I think. Searches have been made by my family since 1841.'

'Someone is trying to stop you finding the truth, aye.'

'That would sum it up, yes.'

'Let me get that charcoal.'

She wandered around looking at gravestones and noted the high number of infant mortalities to adults. She shook her head sadly, 'Why can they not find cures for these childish ailments?'

'Here we are, ma'am and we'd best hurry as it looks like rain.'

Using the side of the charcoal stick they got a fair facsimile of the gravestone and hurried inside to shelter from the passing shower.

Safely out of the rain, she thanked him for his work. 'This will be of enormous help to me.'

'Glad to be of service, ma'am.'

Early 1882.

The winter of 1881-82 was a harsh one with unprecedented falls of snow and long periods of severe frost. The death toll from airborne viruses reduced only to be replaced by an increase of those less well off dying of cold. It was late April before Ellie thought it fit to travel to visit her Cousin Julia in Newport.

Julia greeted her cousin with a kiss on either cheek. 'Cousin Ellie, how lovely to see you, did you have a nice journey?'

'Yes, thank you. It is a pleasant ride following the river in the spring.'

'Give me your coat and come through, Jane's fiancé is here.' Julia led the way into the living room. 'Ellie, meet Mathew Lane and Mathew; my cousin Eleanor from Gloucester.'

A tall, slim young man with piercing blue eyes, dark blonde hair and a military moustache, attired in a pale grey suit, stepped forward. He looked disconcertingly straight into her eyes, smiled and kissed her hand.

'Oh dear,' thought Ellie, 'one could get into trouble with him.'

'Pleased to make your acquaintance, ma'am, I see beauty is not confined to one line of the family.'

She gave a slight curtsey. 'I believe you are flirting, sir, but don't stop. It makes me feel, what is the word?'

'Wanted?'

'Young man, behave yourself and be off with you.'

Julia interrupted the banter. 'Mathew, take Jane for a walk. Come along Ellie, we have much to discuss, not least, what brings you here.'

'I have come to ask a favour of you as well as a social call.'

'Oh, and what is that Ellie? You can tell me while I make some tea.'

'Ever since my David passed away I have spent a lot of time researching our family history.'

'Are you still trying to solve that old cherry? It's long gone, why don't you leave it?'

'Hear me out, Julia. I have found the marriage and the grave that connects us to the Ross's. All that remains is to go to Scotland and prove our connection to that branch of the Clan and I need someone to accompany me.'

'Come through to the parlour Ellie, we can discuss this in comfort.'

When they were settled on the sofa before an open fire Julia addressed her cousin once more, 'Ellie, I must tell you that it is out of the question for me to go with you to Scotland. We are shortly moving to Southall on the outskirts of London with Walter's job. He has been promoted and is going to work in the railway depot and workshops there.'

'Oh dear, I was rather hoping that you could come. I don't know who else to ask.'

Sounds of laughter came from the hall and Jane poked her head around the door.

'Can we join you, mama? I would love some tea, and I think Mathew would like some too.' She giggled. 'Stop that at once, Matt. Sorry about that, he's tickling me.'

Jane looked at Ellie who nodded and said, 'Let them join us, I haven't seen my niece for some time now and we have finished the serious business of my visit.'

Jane pulled Mathew into the room and they sat on the sofa.

'What serious business is that, Aunt Ellie?'

'Oh, nothing really. I wanted someone to accompany me to Scotland for a few weeks but you are in the middle of moving.'

Mathew spoke for the first time. 'Excuse me interrupting, but why do you want to go to Scotland?'

'It's a long story, young man, but I will try to tell you briefly what it is I'm doing.'

She gave him a potted history of the family saga and the ground she had covered.

'How interesting, I have always wanted to go to Scotland and I have no objection to helping you. After all, this summer I will be part of the family.'

'That is very kind of you, Mathew. I would feel extremely safe with you along. What about Jane?'

'Jane can come too. Unfortunately, it cannot be soon. There is the wedding to consider and I am going to be busy at work taking over Mr Crosswell's job. If you could be patient and wait awhile.'

'This is wonderful, and there is no hurry. We have waited forty years, another delay is of no consequence. We must write to each other and I'll see you at the wedding. There will be plenty of time to prepare.'

They spent the rest of the day in idle chatter talking over the old days until it was time for Ellie to leave and she thought when the subject of her leaving was mentioned Mathew offered his services a little too quickly.

'Let me drive you to the station, Ellie.'

'Are you sure?'

'Positive, I'll get your cloak.'

He made unwarranted haste to fetch her cloak and later in the buggy Ellie was surprised when he sat close to her and even more amazed when a little way down the road he moved his leg so that they were touching from hip to knee.

He turned, smiled and looked straight into her brain with those piercing blue eyes. She was unsure of herself but enjoying the experience, flattered that a younger person should openly make a pass at her. His hand dropped onto her knee and rested there a moment.

'Mr Lane, you are engaged to my niece. Could you pay more attention to your handling of the reins and not me?'

'I beg your pardon.' He smiled and she could feel herself melting inside. 'I shall be more circumspect in future, Aunt Eleanor or can I call you Ellie?'

The urge to put this young man in his place was uppermost in her mind but when she spoke she tamely replied, 'You may call me, Ellie.'

She was disturbed by her feelings but she was barely able to hide her disappointment when they wheeled into the station forecourt.

He came around to help her down, fumbled, and grabbed her around the waist before lowering her slowly. As she slid down the front of him he held her close and she stifled a cry when she felt his ardour through the thin suit material as their bodies pressed together their lips almost touching.

Her heart was pounding against the restriction of her corset and she blushed as she looked into his eyes and fought the stirring in her loins.

'Mr Lane, put me down. What on earth would Jane say if she saw us and I am a lot older than you?'

It was all rather lame and not the rebuke she had intended.

He gently lowered her and said quietly. 'But Jane cannot see us and I find myself attracted to you like no other. My body stirs like never before. It is some kind of magnetism I am unable to control.'

'Mathew, I am flattered and it does my ego a power of good. However, nothing can come of this. Now please carry my bag to the train while I catch my breath.'

'My apologies and I'm sorry if I caused you any alarm. Please forgive me.'

'Forgiven. Now will you carry my bag?'

The remainder of **1882** passed quickly. The Crosswell's moved to Southall, closely followed by the wedding where, much to Ellie's relief, Mathew was on his best behaviour and paid full attention to his bride. There had been a few tears as Julia-Jane left home to make a new life with Mathew in Newport.

Ellie made contact with the old Beattie law practice in Edinburgh and told them of her intentions and discoveries. They in turn wrote back and informed her that a Mr Morton was now head of practice and they had re-opened the file and would be glad to be of any help.

Christmas came and went and she was raring to go, impatient at the delay but a letter from Mathew advised her that any trip to Scotland before the spring would be inadvisable owing to the inclement weather conditions north of the border at this time of year and would she mind if Jane did not travel as she was expecting their first child.

Ellie acquiesced and they settled on late April 1883 as the best time for their journey.

***

14

1883.

Tired, after travelling fourteen hours, the spectacular entrance to Edinburgh's Waverley Station, with Princes Street and its emporia high on the left and the Old Town and Castle on the right, could not raise their spirits.

They booked into the 'Railway Hotel' too exhausted for pleasantries and after a silent dinner they both retired promising an early start the next day.

Ellie wandered down to breakfast some time after Mathew full of remorse for her lateness.

'I slept right through, I feel so boggy eyed. I think if we do this again we will stay overnight somewhere.'

'We might try going via London.'

'What a good idea. We shall return that way?'

Ellie contented herself with coffee and scrambled egg on toast feeling unable to consume anything heavier.

'I'm ready, Mathew. I have all our papers in my bag. If you will excuse me while I go to the cloakroom we can be on our way.'

Mathew stood when she left the table and watched her cross the room. He knew she was a shy person and covered her uneasiness with deliberate bravado. She walked tall with an upright posture, head back and looked straight ahead. It gave her overt sex appeal and she was obviously unaware that her adopted manner focused every appreciative male eye towards her but he imagined that to women she would appear quite unapproachable.

The offices of what had been Alistair Beattie's practice were now luxurious compared to the days of 1840 when Stephen Beattie had set off to unravel the mysteries of Jane Ross's *'Last Will & Testament.'*

Gaslights had replaced the candles and the walls newly whitewashed. Haphazard documents were now housed safely in tall wooden filing cabinets and the previously grimy windows were clean making for a much more agreeable and inviting environment. The counter behind which the clerks had worked had disappeared and been replaced by a desk and a single male receptionist.

'Good morning, may I help you, ma'am?'

'Yes, I'm Mrs Chalmers. I believe Mr Morton is expecting us.'

'One moment, I'll let him know you're here.'

He disappeared through a door off to the side, which had formerly been the open corridor, to return a few moments later.

'Mr Morton sends his apologies and asked if you could wait for a few minutes as he has a client with him. Would you like a cup of tea?'

'Yes please.'

They were about to take their first sip when a gentleman, bordering on the portly, of average height with a trim military moustache came through to greet them.

'Good morning. I'm sorry to keep you waiting. Please come through and bring your tea with you.'

They followed him down to the refurbished office which had formerly been Alistair Beatties'. Morton showed them in and made them comfortable before introducing himself.

'Henry Morton, at your service.'

'And I am Mrs Chalmers. This young man is Mr Mathew Lane, my chaperone.'

'How do you do,' Morton responded. 'Let me explain matters. Mr Beattie, my Great Uncle, passed away some time ago. Mr Forbes, my partner, and I, now run the business. However, your file is quite comprehensive and I have been doing a little investigation on your behalf.'

'Thank you very much, it is most kind. I have only the rumours that have dribbled down through the family and copies of marriage and death certificates to go on so I am unaware of previous investigations.'

'If you don't mind me saying so, Mrs Chalmers, it has been an uncommonly long time since anyone made enquiries about this matter.'

'The events that have occurred over the years to frustrate us have been many and there is of course the substantial cost.'

'Just so. In the beginning a Mrs Beagle was your voice in Scotland and did much to push the case along. However, she passed away last year. Mr Mackie and his wife, Amy, nee Mitchell, the servants of Miss Ross, are still alive, although very old. I have arranged for you to visit them tomorrow at their home at ten o' clock. I shall be there with a Justice of the Peace at this address.' He handed a card to Mathew, 'They will swear on oath and tell you of Jane Ross's wishes as relayed to them during their service. Notes will be taken and I will have them signed and witnessed. Mr Mathews will do for a witness. They did give a previous account, but that was forty years ago and any judge would probably dismiss it. Page, the manservant of Mr Gilbert, Jane's elder brother, is now dead. However, we have his account on file.'

'I am in your debt, Mr Morton.'

'It is not over yet, Mrs Chalmers. We have to present all this to the Court of Sessions and then you will have to reside here for six weeks at some time to register as residents in Scotland. May I look through your papers?'

'Certainly.' She rummaged in her bag and gave him the bundle of documents.

Morton browsed through them for five minutes or so before looking up. 'It is my opinion,' he said at last, 'that you have a right grand case here. I see only one possible problem.'

'Oh, and what is that?'

'Jane's uncle, William Ross. You are going to have to show his lineage as he could be anyone called William. For instance; is he in fact Miss Ross's Uncle?'

'I had never thought of that. Have you any idea how I may go about finding this information?'

'Yes, we have a good records office here. Far more advanced than your English equivalent. Here's the address. You will have to present yourself at the office to make an appointment and tell them which records you wish to see. If there is no queue you may get it done straight away or more than likely go the next day.'

'We will go directly.'

'Glad to be of help.'

He came around the desk and escorted them to the front door

and flagged a passing cab for them.

'Goodbye, Mr Morton, you have been a great help.'

'It has been a pleasure. Good luck with your search.'

Mathew helped her in and followed suit, sitting close to her.

'The Railway Hotel, please, driver,' whence he turned to Ellie and at the same time his hand came to rest on her thigh. 'I thought we may have lunch before we go to the records office.'

'What an excellent idea.' She lifted his hand away but did not release it immediately.

When they arrived at the hotel he alighted and made no pretence when he helped her down, clasping her around the waist and holding her close as he lowered her to the pavement.

They stood momentarily, their bodies touching, looking into each others eyes, the unspoken message passing between them, before he escorted her through the doors held open by a patient Porter.

Lunch was a slow affair with little spoken. There was lingering touching of hands and eye contact through glistening irises moist with anticipation.

Ellie broke the spell. 'I think we had better go or they will close before we get there.'

Mathew shook his head as if he had been asleep. 'Oh dear, yes. I was dreaming and had quite forgotten our business. I apologise for my lapse. One moment while I settle and we will be on our way.'

Their arrival at the record office was a little later than two o'clock and the clerk looked at them with the air of a civil servant who delighted in giving bad news.

'You're too late for any reading now. We shut in an hour and you cannot do anything in that time. Give me your name and what you require and I will have it ready for you in the morning.'

Ellie smiled and gave him her most appealing look. 'Are you sure we won't be done in an hour?'

'Yes, ma'am, by the time I get them there won't be moment to turn a page. Then you'll have to pay again tomorrow.'

'Oh, I see.'

'Complete the application and as I said they will be ready in the morning.'

She filled the form in requesting all the deeds and records available on the Ross Clan from 1650 to 1839.

The clerk looked at it. 'I'll leave them out ready. You'll have to do the search for whatever it is you want, we don't help with that.'

'I want marriages, deaths and births for those dates.'

'Very well ma'am, all of them you shall have. Ten o' clock it is.'

'We can't come at ten tomorrow Ellie, we have a meeting at the Mackie's house. Let us make it for two o' clock.'

'That's not enough time, sir. You best make it the day after.'

'Thursday, ten o'clock.'

Outside Ellie turned to Mathew. 'You can take me up to the Castle now, young man. It looks so grand looking down upon us mere mortals.'

'Your humble servant, ma'am.'

They took a cab to the Esplanade at the front entrance of the Castle.

Before they alighted the driver said to them. 'Welcome to Canada.'

'What do you mean, Canada?'

'This Esplanade was made the territory of the Nova Scotia Baronets by Charles the First.'

'Oh, and why was that?'

'I don't know the whole story, but I know the decree has never been lifted.'

They thanked him for the unsolicited information and spent an hour and a half wandering around the Castle precincts admiring the Norman Chapel and the Honours of Scotland. Mathew insisted on viewing an assorted collection of weaponry in the military museum before they walked down Castle Hill to the Old Town and then took a cab back to the hotel.

Refusing the offer of coffee Ellie retired to her room until it was time for dinner.

She demurred long and hard over her choice of dress for dinner and talking to her reflection in the mirror she said, 'I think we will tease our young Lothario tonight.'

She chose a deep red gown trimmed with black. It had a close fitting bodice but in keeping with fashion it had the larger bustle that sat high on the hips. The off the shoulder décolletage was low enough to display her Ross birthmark and she smiled with anticipation of its effect.

She enlisted the help of the room maid to tie-up her hair and decorate it with a black velvet bow before lacing her corset and fastening the innumerable tiny buttons down the back of her dress. A black velvet choker with a diamond clasp added extra allure to her translucent skin.

Mathew called for her at seven forty-five and he stood speechless as he admired the ageless woman before him who carried herself with dignity and elegance.

'You're beautiful,' he said, 'I feel proud and honoured to be your escort tonight.'

'Thank you, young man,' she said with a twinkle in her eye, 'I shall recompense you later for those kind remarks.' She picked up her favourite ivory fan mindful of its memories. 'Shall we go down?'

Her customary shyness evaporated in the presence of her young companion as he escorted her down the wide staircase and into the anti-room.

Standing close and exchanging small talk they lingered over a glass of wine with the other guests before they entered the restaurant its décor and subdued lighting designed to give an oyster pink glow.

Dinner was a pleasant interlude with four courses complemented by excellent wines and Mathew took every opportunity to touch her. He reached across the table and held her hand while his knee gently massaged hers. Mesmerized, helpless as a rabbit hypnotised by a stoat, his eyes never left her face the reason for their being together in Edinburgh forgotten.

'Mathew dearest, do stop looking at me like a lovesick calf. I think people may have noticed and you should remember that we are here on business.'

He jerked upright searching for words. 'Oh… Aah, yes. Your spell had completely erased that from my mind. Ellie Chalmers, unlike medicine, I think you're not good for me. Oh, that I had met you sooner.'

'Mathew, you are twenty years my junior so nothing would have become of your meeting me then. I was happily married anyway.'

'I know, but a man can dream.'

'Possibly. Let us go through to the lounge these dining chairs were not designed for long conversations.'

'By all means.' He came around the table to hold her chair and as she turned to move away he leaned forward and whispered, 'I want to make love to you.'

'Behave yourself, young Casanova, people are watching.'

'I care not. I am drunk with your very presence.'

'Then you will have to be patient. I would like another glass of wine before bedtime.'

So determined was she to make this young gigolo wait that she took the small talk to its outer limits and made every sip of wine deliberate.

'You should linger over a good wine,' she told him with a sly provocative smile, 'the pleasure lasts that little bit longer.'

Every second was adding to his ardour for this woman and he tried to suppress his feelings worried that further delay would see an early climax to his passion.

At last, she relieved him of his torment. 'I think it late enough Mathew. Shall we retire?'

—

Outside her room they paused. 'Mathew dearest, I need someone to undo me. Could you oblige?'

Overcome with desire for this woman the direct invitation into her boudoir had caught him off guard. 'Aaah, hem, err, yes,' he stuttered.

Taking his hand she led him into the room and stopped in front of the long winged dressing table mirror where she could watch him from all angles.

She stood on tip-toe and nibbled his ear before whispering,

'Undress me.'

He stood behind her and with shaking fingers tentatively undid the top button, then the next and the next, becoming bolder with each one. He paused, leaned forward and kissed the perfect skin between her shoulder blades and caressed her backbone with his tongue. He felt her shiver as the sensation travelled down her spine.

She pulled on each sleeve in turn and let her dress fall to the floor. Turning quickly, she grabbed his jacket and almost tore it from his shoulders and then frantically pulled off his bow tie and waistcoat. The pile of clothes grew as the mutual undressing continued.

When she stood naked before him wearing only her choker he dropped to his knees and kissed her in that most feminine place.

His tongue flicked and massaged the tiny lobe that led to heaven while his hands teased, searched and fondled.

She sighed and writhed, her breath coming in short gasps. She pushed her hips forward to meet him and pulled his head in to her as the tension mounted. Throwing her head back she dug her fingers into his shoulders and moaned.

He held her at the peak of her climax, picked her up and carried her to the bed.

Their first coupling was wild, his lovemaking that of a Stag in heat, not the slow ministrations of an older man but the rampant urgings of a young bull intent on propagating his harem.

Twice, their ardour was uninhibited before the exhaustion of their lust made them rest.

Later, as they lay curled together like forks in a cutlery box, she felt him rising again between her buttocks and she took control by climbing above him. Her lovemaking was slow and deliberate. She held him at his peak and showed him where to touch her so that their eruption was simultaneous and intense.

Passion spent, they slept, entwined in a passionate Gordian knot.

In the early hours she heard him moving around as he prepared to leave. She feigned sleep and was glad of his forethought to leave the – *Do not disturb* – sign hanging on her door.

Breakfast was a late affair and she greeted him with a smile. 'Good morning, Mathew, I trust you slept well.'

'Yes, jolly fine. The beds here are very good. How was yours?'

'Excellent. Most comforting on the spine but I thought I could have laid a little longer this morning.'

The innuendo was not lost on him and the sparkle in her eyes told him so.

'Hurry now, young man, we have just a short while before we are due at the Mackie residence.'

He shook his head in disbelief as he mentally said, 'This woman is amazing. She seduces her niece's husband and carries on as though nothing has happened.'

They arrived at the address given at the same time as Morton with his clerk and there was little time to wait before the Justice of the Peace made his presence known with a knock on the door loud enough to waken the dead.

The Mackie's living room was of modest proportions and severely cramped with seven people in it. Mathew stood in the doorway and the clerk managed to find a place on the dining table for his writing slope. The others stood or sat in a circle around the Mackie's.

Morton spoke first. 'Robert and Amy, we want you to recall your life with the Ross family. In particular what were the wishes of Miss Jane with reference to the disposal of her assets?'

'We did all this forty years ago. Who was it, Amy dear?'

'A Mr Beattie.'

'Yes, Mr Beattie,' reiterated Robert Mackie.

'We have Mr Beattie's papers, but it is so long ago that we need to hear it for ourselves. Before you start I would like you to say your names, and you Mrs Mackie, your maiden name.'

With the formalities out of the way they told as much as they could remember of the events that took place when they were in service to Jane Ross. Memories had faded with age but they prompted each other until they had exhausted their minds of all detail.

Morton turned to his clerk. 'Did you get all that?'

'Yes sir.'

'Very well, everyone sign at the end of those notes? I will have proof copies sent to you by tomorrow afternoon and thank you. Robert, Amy, we will be going now and I hope we have no further need to bother you again.'

Mathew called for a hansom and when they had boarded, he said, 'Would you like to go to the hotel for lunch, Ellie, or to the records office a day early?'

'Lunch by all means and later I'm going shopping. You may come if you wish.'

'Fait accompli! I will join you. Shopping is a dangerous thing for a lone woman in a strange city.'

After a couple of hours shopping and exploring the Old Town they returned to the hotel to rest until dinner. There was to be no repeat of the previous evening and Ellie retired early and left Mathew to his own devices.

—

At ten-o'-clock prompt the next day they presented themselves at the Record's office to find the books they had ordered laid out ready for them.

'Where do we start, Mathew?'

'May I suggest that we look up Jane Ross first and then work back? If I am correct, we should come to Uncle William.'

'Good idea.'

Mathew was correct with his predictions. Going back two generations brought them to Jane's—Grandfather Gilbert, the eldest son, and William the second son, Jane's uncle. There were three other brothers— James, Robert, and Alex.

'William was born in Kirkston, Aberdeenshire, and his father came from Tortestone, also in Aberdeenshire. That is where we go next, Ellie. Get copies of these and we travel tomorrow.'

It cost a guinea for the copies and the search and they were free for the afternoon.

'Shall we do Holyrood House after lunch, Mathew?'

'If that is your wish, most certainly.'

—

Their visit to Holyrood was not a long one and when they came out Ellie expressed her disappointment.

'That was rather a waste of time. There is very little there and those portraits of so called Scottish monarchs were quite the worst I have ever seen. How many were there?'

'One hundred and seven, I believe. I lost count'

'Did you notice that there was a similarity in all of them, as if the same half dozen people had sat several times.[3] It is an unlikely coincidence to have the same appearance over so long a time.'

'I was not paying that much attention after the first dozen or so.'

'Come,' said Ellie, 'it's a fine afternoon, let's walk for awhile.'

They had quiet evening and retired early as they were to rise at six o' clock the next morning to catch the first train.

They changed trains in Aberdeen and it was late afternoon before they arrived in Petershead. It was a short buggy ride to the hotel where the landlord was a veteran of the Crimean War and had a peg-leg.

'I'm verra sorry. Ah have ney twa single rooms. Ah have the best room, tha's all.'

Mathew intervened. 'We'll take it. We only have two rooms because I snore terribly and keep Mrs Smith awake.'

The landlord raised his eyebrows. 'Weel, yeell hav to bury ya heed under yon pillow ma'am. Smith, ya said...' He rolled his eyes and looked heavenwards, '...tha's a rare name, sign here.'

The room, cosily furnished with a modest four-poster, a wardrobe and a chest of draws with a jug and washbasin in blue willow pattern was warm and friendly.

'Oh, Mathew, how could you? Mrs Smith indeed, and who said that I consent to this arrangement?'

'I didn't hear a protest, Ellie, my love, so I took your consent as read.'

'It's my love now.'

She walked around the bed and stood in front of him, grabbed him by the lapels and pulled his head forward.

'Nothing will ever come of this, Mathew. When we return home, that will be the end. The infatuation will cease. I will not pretend that I don't enjoy it and I am flattered, but it cannot go on.'

'Ellie, I adore you, you are quite the most beautiful creature I have set eyes on. You have this irresistible magnetism, I cannot help myself, your very smell sends me wild with expectation.'

She kissed him lightly on the lips. 'You must try. Now let us go down for coffee, if they serve it this far north. We can also arrange a carriage for the morning.'

Mathew, determined to make the moment last was most attentive like the perfect husband and pandered to her every need. Ellie revelled in the attention bestowed on her, but did not take advantage of it, feeling instead feminine and protected in the way she had felt with David.

She realized that she missed the companionship of a man in her life and at the same time guilty, which made her flush with excitement at every little touch and intimate contact.

After dinner he applied himself equally to her needs making their lovemaking a partnership where they both enjoyed the intimacy of the moment.

In the morning, they wrapped up against the cold north-easterly winds that blew in from the North Sea and snuggled against each other for the five-mile ride to Kirkston only to find that James Mackenzie had done his job well.

'The pages are missing for 1676, Mathew.'

'Here let me look. By golly, you're right. Someone has taken a lot of trouble to make sure that your family is not traceable. Where next?'

'We had better look for his elder brother Gilbert. It's in Rora.'

The driver welcomed the extended journey to Rora. These were difficult times and any increase in his income was welcome.

The thin-wheeled carriage had to travel slowly to negotiate the bumps and many potholes and the two mile journey over rough un-surfaced back roads took them almost an hour.

The Church records in Rora revealed more information.

'Mathew, we have Gilbert here. They obviously thought that removing William was enough and let me see,' she turned a few more pages and clapped her hands. 'And yes, we have his brothers James and Robert also. Let's get these copied and stop for lunch at the local tavern and then we'll search for great-grandfather on the way back.'

The driver advised them that they could go to Tortestone. 'But you'll have a bumpy ride as it's no'but tracks and we go nearly to Petershead before turning west again. T'is the only way over the River Ugie.'

'So be it. Let's get the unpleasant travelling over in one day.' She enquired of the driver. 'You don't mind taking us do you? It's been a long day for you.'

'No ma'am. You pay the fare and I drive and thank you for the vitals, ma'am.'

In Ellie's opinion the trip was worth the discomfort. She was able to establish the birth and death of the patriarch of the family, one, William Ross. Sen.

'Let us hope that is enough,' she remarked over drinks later, 'We shall retire early Mathew and catch the first train back and it will be single rooms from now on. You will behave with utmost propriety when we get back to civilization. It will be remembered as no more than a delightful interlude.'

'Yes, my love, that I should have had this time with you was a blessing the memory of which will remain with me forever. You're right of course, nothing can ever come of it.'

Henry Morton's office, Edinburgh.
Morton took his time studying their documents before saying, 'You've done well, it's a great pity about Uncle William. You must leave these with me and tomorrow morning we will present them to the Court of Sessions.'

'I'm sorry.' Ellie shook her head as she spoke. 'But after previous mishaps I wish to keep all paperwork in my possession.'

'That could be a problem. Never mind, can you leave them with me now and I will have a clerk copy them for my files?'

Ellie looked at Mathew for guidance. He gave a slight nod of his head to affirm his opinion that all would be well.

'Very well, Mr Morton. I shall return at five o'clock.'

Mathew interceded. 'One moment. Let me count them and if you will indulge me, could I have the use of a pen?'

'I think, sir, that you are being preposterous. This is a grave insult on my integrity and that of my employees.'

'My apologies sir, no slur was meant, on you, or your staff, who, I am sure, are most honest. It is merely a precaution owing to previous circumstances. You must realize that this investigation has been ongoing for forty years. Unfortunate accidents have happened along the way and I wish only to protect Mrs Chalmers.'

'Apology accepted, sir, I will initial each page and count them for you. I will not be present when you call this evening as I have an important function to attend but our Mr Corbett will see that everything is in order.'

'Thank you, sir. We look forward to doing more business with you. Until morning then.'

They shook hands and turning to Ellie, Morton bowed and took her outstretched hand. 'Ma'am, it has been a pleasure.'

Outside, Mathew hailed a cab. 'What should we do with the rest of our day, Mrs Chalmers?'

Ellie gave him a sideways glance and smiled to herself. 'I have an urge to go to Picardy Place to see where my ancestors lived and then we shall take a leisurely lunch. This afternoon you can escort me along Princes Street.'

'Picardy Place, driver.'

'Any particular number?'

'Number two.'

'Right ye are, sur.' He guided the cab into the traffic and pushed the horse to a gentle trot.

Picardy Place was the south facing terrace of a square of granite four storey Adam style houses facing outwards. The stables were in the rear quadrangle out of sight.

It was only a short walk through the houses of Greenside Place to the parkland surrounding Calton Hill with its Observatory and the inevitable Nelson Monument.

'It is not such a grand house for a family of millionaires,' observed Ellie.

'You must remember Ellie. Scotsmen are not renowned for

spending their money and if my memory serves me correctly they were a banking family and the house is ideally placed for the business centre of town. They also had two large estates, one at Style, I forget where the other one is.'

'Canonside, in Aberdeenshire.'

'Yes, that's right, and she also lived on her own for the last seven years of her life so I don't expect she left it very often, although by all accounts she was a sprightly woman.'

'You're right, of course, Mathew, as always.'

'Thank you. Now Mrs Chalmers, shall we go for lunch?'

'Yes, Mr Lane.' She laughed, 'How formal we are.'

They turned toward each other and gently kissed.

He held her at arms length and looked directly into her eyes, which were moist with undisguised passion, and said, 'Should we go directly to the hotel or try a restaurant in town?'

'The hotel I think. It is quite reasonable and I believe the maître de quite favours me.'

'Mrs Chalmers, you are incorrigible.'

'I know, dear, but I am enjoying myself. Are you prepared for shopping this afternoon?'

'Quite, and you know I would be proud to be seen anywhere with you. Have you noticed some strange looks when we are out? I'm sure the women of this parish think I am a gigolo.'

She laughed, leaned back and pushed her hips provocatively into him. 'And a handsome one at that. Julia-Jane is a lucky woman, although you will have to overcome this penchant for older women. Come now, I am famished.'

'Not just any older woman, a special one.'

'Enough.'

***

15

The Parliamentary offices of Alexander Maxwell-Ross Jun. MP.

'Excuse me, sir, the morning mail and this one is marked—Personal. It has been re-directed from your country house at Eaton and is written in exceedingly fine handwriting. Could be legal perhaps.'

'Thank you, Wilson, and how is your wife this morning?'

'She is much improved, sir.'

'Good. Leave the letters in the tray I will attend to them shortly.'

'Very well, sir.'

He waited until his secretary had left the room before he picked up the letter and studied it curiously for a moment. Normally a decisive man, for some unknown reason he was apprehensive about its contents and it was some moments before he opened it...

Dear Sir,
I wish to inform you that a petition has been presented to the Court of Sessions in respect of the Last Will and Testament of your late Aunt, Miss Jane Ross of Style.
No date has been set for a hearing as yet, but if you would oblige me by giving me instructions on this matter I will make all the necessary arrangements.
A felicitous reply would be greatly appreciated.
I remain, yours faithfully,

J. Mackenzie.
(Advocate at Law)

'Damn and blast these people,' he said aloud, 'can they not take no for an answer?' He went to the door and shouted. 'Wilson!'

His secretary obligingly appeared within seconds. 'Yes sir?

'Wilson, I'm going to Scotland immediately. Make the necessary arrangements and excuses. I shall be gone for a week or so.'

'Sir, you cannot leave now, you have the debate and vote on the *Reform and Distribution Bills* this afternoon.'

'I know. You will make my apologies. Tell them I have been taken ill or something. My wife will be staying in London and I will be obliged if you will look out for her.'

'Before you leave sir, I have some papers for you to sign.'

'Very well, get a move on as I wish to catch the two o' clock train.'

—

The London home of Maxwell-Ross

'Alexander, dearest, what are you doing home? Has the vote been cancelled?'

'No, Joanne, my love, I have received this letter from our solicitor in Edinburgh. Here read it. I must go there immediately.'

'Alex, darling, I cannot possibly get ready in so short a time.'

'You must stay here, I have instructed Wilson to look in on you. Come help me pack, it is only for a week.'

'You must eat dearest. Katy will help me pack a bag, you go to cook and see what she can do for you.'

'You organise so well my love. I will stay at the Railway Hotel of course.'

'Why not the house, dear. Picardy Place would be nice this time of year.'

'It is only for a short stay and I could not imagine rattling around inside that place. We must sell it. It is far too big for our needs and the city is spreading around it. We will have Eaton and the London town house and if needs be we can keep a suite available in an Edinburgh hotel.'

'We will discuss that when you return, dear, go and eat.'

—

The Railway Hotel, Edinburgh.

'Mathew, I am ready, shall we go down?'

'Yes, my love, I could eat a horse tonight.'

They proceeded down the wide staircase and mingled with other guests making their way to the restaurant.

'Mrs Chalmers!'

Ellie stopped and looked around to see Alexander Maxwell-Ross pushing his way through the throng.

'It is Mrs Chalmers?'

'Indeed it is, Mr Maxwell.'

He took her outstretched hand and kissed it. 'Your memory is only exceeded by your beauty, madam.'

'Thank you, sir. May I introduce my chaperone, my nephew-in-law Mr Lane. The two men nodded, sized each other up and shook hands.

'Mrs Chalmers, what brings you to our fair city?'

'I have been looking up an old Aunt and included a little sightseeing. Mr Lane chose to escort me thinking me too air-headed to find my way around.'

'Are you staying long? We must make time to see each other.'

'I'm sorry, but we leave early in the morning for Gloucestershire.'

'A great shame, it has been a pleasure meeting you again. If I don't see you before, have a pleasant journey and goodbye.' He half bowed and kissed her hand once more before turning to Mathew and nodding. 'Mr Lane, sir.'

Mathew acknowledged and they went their separate ways.

Later, at dinner, Mathew leaned over and whispered to Ellie, 'That was a close call. Do you think he knows anything?'

'I think not, Mathew, or the greeting wouldn't have been so cordial.'

'How does he know you then?'

'We attended the same dinner party in London.' She went on to recite the events that had led up to her previous meeting with Maxwell. 'I felt quite put out but was able to cover my frustration by conversation with other guests. I don't think he'll be so cordial the next time we meet.'

The Office of Mackenzie & Mackenzie, Advocates.

'John, what is the meaning of this? I thought your father had cleared up this mess. We now have the immovable rights. How can they be allowed to do this?'

'It is a fact of law, Mr Maxwell, that people, if they so desire, can contest any Will if they think they have a right and can prove it.'

'Have these people the right, and can they prove it?'

'They have a very strong case, and, if what I hear is true, they have found the connection to Jane Ross which evaded earlier claimants. You must be prepared for the worst.'

'Who are these people?'

'Their names are on the petition to the Court of Sessions.' He rummaged around on his desk a moment, found what he was looking for and peered at it intently before giving it to Maxwell.

He gave it a cursory glance before exclaiming angrily, 'Chalmers and Lane, the scheming, avaricious, cunning bitch. She smiles so sweetly and then goes for the jugular. I spoke to these people only last night. All charm and courtesy and they were staying in my hotel. You must do something. Stop them at any cost.'

'How do you suggest I do that, sir?'

'How did your father manage it?'

'I believe there may have been a little leverage applied through a well known fraternity in one way or another.'

'What are you suggesting?'

'Let us say that my father acted outside his sphere of Advocate to help this case to a satisfactory conclusion at the time. I cannot believe that you were not aware of it.'

'I was a young man enjoying the trappings of wealth and military service. I took little notice of my father's business, only that which benefited me. How he achieved it, I did not care.'

'May I make a suggestion, sir?'

'Please do.'

'You are of the Brotherhood, as was your father. Is it not possible to use them to your benefit again? You have the names of the plaintiff and their legal representative. I do not wish to know how, but if you succeed, it will help your case enormously.'

'What's needed?'

'You need to remove their proof, or them, or both.'

'What are you suggesting?'

'That's not for me to say. I wish to have no complicity in

whatever action you may take other than to be your legal representative. It is your business.'

'I can make you a wealthy man. Can you not see your way to handle this affair for me?'

'No sir. The temptation is great, but the sins of the father shall not be visited upon this son. It's your problem to deal with.'

***

16

1884 – 1885. The Jervis affair.

'Mathew! What a pleasure it is to see you, how are Julia-Jane and the baby?'

They embraced and Ellie was careful to keep it formal.

'They're fine,' Mathew replied, 'and we have called her Gertrude. It's not of my choice, but Jane insisted.'

'Mathew, what is going on?'

Ellie picked up a letter from the occasional table and waved it towards him.

'Henry Morton has written saying he can no longer represent us. Most of his clients have left him without reason and he has had to close. He's moving his practice to Manchester and a fresh start. No reason was mentioned other than something peculiar is happening which has driven his business away. He has asked his colleagues in Edinburgh to take our case but no one will touch it. They do not say why, only that they are to busy, or some other such excuse.'

'There's something afoot, Ellie. Things have been made intolerably difficult for me at work. They find fault with everything I do. So much so that I have been demoted and moved to the engine sheds at Southall to join Mr Crosswell as his assistant.'

'What are we to do?'

'We can do nothing at the moment. It appears something or someone is conspiring against us and I know not what. We must be patient until things settle down and then try again.'

'Mathew, all that money I have spent is wasted. My nest-egg is much depleted. I thought that once we had the last link things would be over quickly.'

'It is not to be, and you're not going to have your day in court. You must find new legal representation.'

'Oh dear,' Ellie clenched and unclenched a handkerchief and

paced back and forth, 'When do you move, Mathew?'

'In two weeks.'

'That's quick. Do you have accommodation already?'

'Yes, we are very fortunate. Only last week a house in St. Johns Road, a few doors down from the Crosswell's came on the market. Mr Crosswell has bought it and agreed we are to rent it. It is tolerably large, with room for a servant girl in the attic. It is not far from the Union canal for nice walks along the towpath.'

'What an ideal solution. It keeps your money in the family which one day you and Julia-Jane will inherit.'

'That is precisely what Mr Crosswell had in mind. Meanwhile Ellie, you're not to worry. This quest of yours appears jinxed, but as soon as I am able we will go to Scotland and start again.'

'Thank you, Mathew. I have great faith in you. I will enjoy Zoë's company for awhile.'

They embraced and made their goodbyes and as they parted he gave her some encouragement.

'Don't get too downhearted, Ellie. Things will sort themselves out, you'll see.'

—

Early 1885.

Ellie was distracted from her morning chores by sharp rapping on the front door. It was a relief from the daily grind but alternately it disrupted her solitude. Stuffing a duster into the pocket of her apron she opened the door and found to her consternation a total stranger.

He lifted his hat and bowed slightly and spoke with a slight Scottish accent. 'Good morning, Madam. Abraham Jervis, Solicitor at your service. Do I have the pleasure of addressing Mrs Eleanor Chalmers?'

He proffered his card which Ellie accepted with alacrity. She noted that it was an introduction to Jervis and Son, Solicitors of London and Edinburgh.

'Yes,' she replied in a manner that showed her displeasure, 'How can I be of help?'

'I bring news of your inheritance and I have had the pleasure of meeting your cousins Charlotte and Thomas concerning this very same matter.'

'Oh...' She did not like this skinny man with shifty eyes and pointed features. His suit was out of sorts and a little on the loud side she thought but undecided on what to do next she meekly said, 'I suppose you had better come in.'

She stood to one side to allow him into the hallway before leading him into the parlour. 'Be seated, Mr Jervis, and explain yourself.'

Jervis settled himself in one of the armchairs and placed his bag by his side.

'Your case, Mrs Chalmers, has been given to us by our Scottish colleagues after they were approached by a Mr Morton who asked them to take up the case on your behalf. Unfortunately Morton left none of his files so we have to start afresh with whatever documents you may have. We will need only a small retainer to continue. Your cousins have obliged me with the little paper work they had and have given me twenty pounds each on account. If you can give me whatever documentation you may have I can be in London by tonight and get started right away.'

'Why should I give to you what has taken me years to collect? I don't know you. What assurance can you give me?'

He reached into his inner pocket and withdrew a paper.

'Here's a letter from your cousins introducing me with their greatest confidence. May I see your documents?'

He flashed the letter in front of her but took great care not show it in any detail. Ellie deep in thought took him at his word.

'One moment,' she replied, 'I'll get them for you.'

She left the room to return a few moments later with her workbox. Removing her sewing, she pulled from the bottom a sheaf of papers and gave them to him.

He spent a few minutes perusing each one with deep intensity. At last he looked up, shook his head and muttered, 'Hmm... I don't know.'

'What do you think,' Ellie said anxiously, holding one hand to her breast.

'I'm not sure that these are good enough. You've been very thorough, but there does seem to be holes in your case.'

'Mr Morton said we had a right grand case.'

'Yes, I believe you have. I will consult with our senior partner who is experienced in Family law. However, one or two anomalies need to be looked at. When all is done we can send them to Scotland for furtherance of your case. You will not have to do anything until it is time to appear in court.'

He rolled the documents together and tied them in a bundle with some blue ribbon.

'May I take them, Mrs Chalmers?'

'I am loathe to let them out of my sight, but I suppose so.'

He dropped them in his bag and then rummaged around before partially withdrawing a couple of other bundles similarly tied. He nodded towards them. 'Your cousin's. You are doing the right thing. Can you oblige me with a pen and ink and some paper and I will write you a receipt.'

Ellie provided the requested items and waited while he wrote in an exaggerated hand. He blotted the ink dry and handed her the finished document.

'There you are, hang on to that. You can contact us any time and immediately they have been copied I will return them. That should only be a few weeks, but we are very busy so I apologise beforehand for our tardiness. Now there's the business of our retainer.'

'I find it difficult at the moment to raise any significant amount. How much do you need, Mr Jervis?'

'Our initial fee was two hundred pounds as the amount we hope to gain for you could be in excess of a million. If we get a large amount then we will expect half of one percent.'

'My cousins, you say, have paid twenty pounds each? I will give you the same amount, but it is difficult.'

'Come now. We are talking millions and you offer me a measly sixty pounds total.'

'That's all I have.'

'Then we cannot do it.' He reached into his bag and pulled out the bundle of documents. 'You had better keep these and forget your inheritance.'

'Wait one minute. I can give you twenty pounds more but that's all.'

'Mrs Chalmers, you try my patience. I will accept it, but I shall be severely reprimanded on my return to London.'

'I'm sorry. One moment, I will retrieve it for you.'

While she was out of the room he spent a few moments writing a second receipt.

'Here you are.' She gave him the forty pounds. 'More you cannot have as there isn't any.'

'Thank you. Here is your receipt. I will be in touch as soon as your documents are ready. Take care, Mrs Chalmers, and good luck.'

Ellie showed him out with a feeling of misgiving in her heart.

She agonised for some months before she made up her mind and took the train to Southall to tell Mathew of her blunder.

'Mathew, I've been such a fool.'

'Why, Ellie?'

Wringing her hands and twisting her handkerchief nervously she told the circumstance of her dealings with Jervis.

'And I've heard nothing since. I think we may have been tricked, but he did give me his card and receipts.'

'Um, let me give these to our company solicitors to see if they can trace this firm in London.'

'Very well, but I feel such an idiot as he deceived our cousins also.'

'A thorough chap. He gets your documents with expenses thrown in. You must stay with us for a while. We have plenty of room here and Jane would love your company as she is expecting a companion for young Gertrude.'

Ellie's heart skipped a beat. 'Mathew, are you sure that would be the wise thing to do under the circumstances?'

'What circumstances are those, Aunt Ellie?' Julia-Jane had entered the room unheard behind them.

Ellie looked anxiously towards Mathew.

'Your Aunt was referring to your condition Jane. Will you be up to a visitor?'

'Of course. It's early days yet and I would enjoy it. Someone to talk to while you work.'

'That's settled then.'

Ellie let out a quiet sigh of relief but the feeling of guilt would not go quite so easily.

'Come, Aunt Ellie. Let's enjoy a cup of tea and then we can

go for a stroll along the canal. It's a lovely evening and the weather is mild for this time of year.'

———

Three days passed before Mathew returned home with the bad news. 'There is no law firm called Jervis in London. However, there is a man wanted in Scotland for fraud and false pretences by that name. I have no idea how he came by our case but he must have obtained it from someone. I think it's all part of a conspiracy to stop us.'

'We have lost everything, Mathew, what can we do?'

'I have an idea but it means me going to Scotland for a few days. Ellie, can you stay here and keep Jane company until I get back?'

'Why yes, so long as I'm welcome.'

Julia-Jane was quick to give reassurance. 'Of course you are, Aunt Ellie.'

'Mathew,' Ellie turned towards him. 'About expenses, can I help? After all it was my silliness that caused this problem.'

'We railwaymen work together, my fare and lodgings are taken care of.'

'Are you sure?'

'Yes, perfectly, I have obtained leave of absence and I travel in the morning. Now for a last drink and I am retiring.'

'We'll join you, it's been a long day.'

———

The Express train from London to Edinburgh took a little over six hours to reach its destination. Mathew lost no time in dumping his bags at his lodgings and went directly to the Bridewell opposite Calton Hill. Looking around before he went in, he wondered what Nelson would have thought about overlooking a police station and the local jail.

The desk Sergeant was a man who Mathew guessed must have been six feet four and almost that in girth with a large handlebar moustache.

'Afternoon, sir, what can I do for you?'

His voice was gentle in contrast to his impressive presence.

Mathew pulled out the receipts and business card left by Jervis. 'I'll be as brief as I can Sergeant. I pursue a man called

Abraham Jervis who's fraudulently extracted money and valuable documents from members of my family.'

'Jervis you say. We know of him, where did this take place sir?'

'Gloucestershire.'

'He's spreading his wings. He must have been done at least three times and the silly bugger uses his own name every time. We know where to find him, but you'll be unable to charge him here. You'll have to do that at home.'

'Can you arrest him for me? I would like to retrieve the documents if I can.'

'We can't arrest him, but I will send a constable with you to his lodgings and see if you can persuade him to give them back. That's all I can do. When you get home, report him to your local nick and they will send up an arrest warrant for him. I'll make a note in the log to have someone ready to assist you at nine o' clock.'

'Thank you, I'll be here.'

'Right sir, give me your name and address, the precise nature of your complaint, and we will see you in the morning.'

—

The following morning.

'Good morning, sir, I'm Constable McEwan. I've been assigned to help you. We're looking for our old mate Jervis, I believe?'

'That's correct. Is it far?'

'It's over in the old town sir, quite a stroll.'

'Am I allowed to carry you in a cab?'

'Yes sir, at your expense.'

'By all means, wait while I call one.'

It was only a few moments before a hansom cab came along and they set off along Princes Street, over the Mound to Bank Street, into Lawnmarket and alighted on the junction by Melbourne Terrace.

'Here we are. Thank you cabbie, don't wait.'

The cabbie refused the fare, touched his cap and muttered, 'On the house.'

Mathew turned to the policeman, 'He wouldn't take any fare.'

'No, they don't charge us, that's why I said you must pay.

Then if you get a free ride it is not me that's sponging.'

'Oh, I see. This looks a mighty rough area, although I felt quite safe when walking around a couple of years ago.'

'Don't worry, sir. This is probably the safest place in town. If you get your money nicked the Caddie fund* will pay you back. See those rough looking layabouts hanging around. They're caddies and by now every crook in the Old Town knows we're here. Follow me.'

They walked across the street to where three caddies* were lounging by a doorway.

The constable spoke first in a conversational manner. 'Jervis, lads, have you seen him?' He fumbled with his handkerchief and as he pulled it free a sixpence fell to the floor.

'Ee ad a big un on last night,' replied the older of the bunch, 'In is digs ah should'ne' wonder. Di ya wanna guide.'

'No thanks, but you might watch the Grass for me.'

'Aye awreet, but it'l cost ye anither tanner.'

'Here's three-pence.'

'Skinflint!'

The constable ignored the jibe and turned to Mathew. 'Come on sir, this way, and stick close by, it's a rabbit warren in there.'

A few paces down Melbourne Terrace they ducked into a narrow close and Mathew felt suddenly claustrophobic as the buildings closed around him blocking out all but the faintest of light as they moved into the permanent twilight of the slum.

A little way down they turned into a Close and up a flight of stone steps onto a walkway that took them over dingy backyards. It followed the contours of the houses and over a couple of narrow entries before they stepped down into another Close.

'Okay, sir, we're almost there.'

They arrived at a rickety wooden door that was hanging on one hinge and it pushed open with difficulty. Hurrying past a foul smelling communal privy and up the outside stairs that led to the top storey, they came up against a heavy door, which, even in its dilapidated condition wouldn't budge.

The constable hammered on the door with his truncheon at the same time shouting, 'Open up, Police!'

It must have been a minute before they heard shuffling feet

and the bolt slamming back. A woman of repellent ugliness opened the door and her body odour drove them back.

'Who's makin' all that friggin noise? Can ah woman no' have a sup in peace now?'

'Out of the way you drink sodden hag.' The bobby used the tip of his truncheon to persuade her. 'Jervis. Where is he?'

'Aye, up yon stairs,' she said sullenly, 'and then bugger off and leave us in peace.'

They went into the house which stank of urine, gin and stale food where a couple of dirt smeared toddlers played on the floor. A line of washing hung across the room and discarded clothes and nappy cloths lay around in heaps on the floor.

Holding their breath, they hurried across the room to a door that led to a staircase and dashed up making no attempt at stealth. Wasting no time the officer put his shoulder into the door at the top and the flimsy latch showered the floor with wood splinters as it exploded from the doorjamb.

'Ere, wos going on?'

The unshaven figure of Jervis dressed in the previous night's spew stained clothes scrambled off the bed.

'Jervis! We've come to see you about a job you pulled in England.'

'Oh, no you don't.'

Jervis, wide awake now, swung a punch and knocked the constable to the floor, shoved Mathew out of the way and ran out and down the stairs.

The policeman picked himself up, retrieved his helmet and brushed himself down. 'Come on,' he said as he led the way unhurriedly from the room, 'He won't get far.'

Mathew followed bemused at the lack of urgency.

Down in the Close at the back of the house there was a caddie leaning against the wall. He made a slight motion with his forefinger pointing to his right. They set off at a quick walk turning this way and that. At every turn there was a caddie showing the direction Jervis had fled.

They crossed Victoria Street into another Maze of alleys and out into the junction of Grass Market and Candle-makers Row. They turned right along Grass Market and crossed to the South side. A little way along they turned into another Close and halfway down there was a caddie leaning on the wall by a gate. As they approached he nodded his head towards the gate and moved off.

Not a word had been spoken during the whole pursuit, just a nod of the head or a motion of a hand.

They stopped by the gate and the constable raised a finger to his lips and whispered, 'Quietly now,' as he eased it open.

They tip-toed into the yard and Mathew breathed a sigh of relief to find it cleaner than the previous enclosures they had come across. The back door was ajar and slumped in a chair was Jervis holding his head.

In a voice that brooked no argument the constable said, 'Jervis,! You're nicked, put your hands out.'

Jervis moaned and clutched his head. 'Can ya no see I'm hurt?'

'Stop your moaning, it was only a sock full of sand. Hands!'

The constable slipped the cuffs on Jervis. 'Come on, move. You're lucky, you get to ride in a cab.'

They led him out into Grass Market and hailed a passing hansom.

'Three of you an one a prisoner. That'll be double,' said the cabbie curtly.

'The Bridewell,' commanded the constable, 'and be quick about it.'

Settled in the cab and on their way Mathew asked why it had been so easy to catch Jervis.

'Why did they help like that?'

'The caddies like to think of the area as their own and they have their own discipline. The head caddie even dishes out fines if one of them causes trouble. They don't want us poking our noses in making life difficult so when they get a bad apple they get rid of it as quick as they can. When he's finished his stretch they'll let him back until the next time.'

'When he's been to prison? I don't understand. I thought I had to go to the English police first?'

'You do, but he hit me so he's in for at least six months hard and by that time you'll have your warrant.'

'Oh, I see. Can I ask him a question?'

'Go ahead.'

'Jervis?'

The disgruntled Jervis replied in a manner that suggested he was not going to be very helpful. 'What?'

'What did you do with the documents you took from Mrs Chalmers and her cousins?'

'I give them to the bloke that paid me. Some toff that was staying at the Railway Hotel. He took me to London and told me what I must do and I delivered them to him at Kings Cross Station on my return journey.'

'Mrs Chalmers said you spoke like you knew the law.'

'I'm a failed law student. A colleague who was at University with me introduced us.'

'Does this gentleman have a name?'

'No. We never spoke apart from his instructions.'

'Did he tell you to charge for your services?'

'No, that was my idea. It made the story appear genuine and it gave me a little extra on top.'

'What did he pay you?'

'One hundred pounds, plus expenses.'

'These people have been struggling for forty years to right a wrong done to their family and you have ruined everything.'

'A man has to live.'

Mathew resisted the temptation to strike the loathsome creature next to him.

—

Southall, two days later.

'Jane! Mathew's coming. Come on, Gertrude, come and meet daddy.'

Jane came to the front door wiping her hands on her apron in time to watch Gertrude run up the road on her unsteady little legs to meet her Daddy while a worried Ellie hurried behind.

Mathew dropped his bag, scooped Gertie up into his arms and swung her around. She squealed with delight. 'Hello, young lady, what a welcome.' Ellie arrived breathless a few moments later. 'And what a day! A man loves to be welcomed by the women in his life.'

Ellie stopped smiling and spoke to him quite sharply.

'Mathew! The woman in your life waits yonder expecting your second child. Please remember that.'

'I deserved that, Ellie. How are you all the same?'

Ellie picked up his bag as they turned to walk towards the house. 'I'm well, and what of your little venture?'

'Prepare me a cup of tea and I'll tell you all about it. Hello Jane, darling.' He put his free arm around her and they kissed. 'Have you been well while I've been away?'

'Yes, I have. I think pregnancy is good for me and Aunt Ellie wouldn't let me do a thing and young Gertie loves her.'

Mathew changed from his travelling clothes while Ellie made tea and when they had settled he related his adventures in Scotland.

'And we are left with nothing, Ellie. There is no money and we have fewer documents than we had before. The only satisfaction we get is that Jervis is going away for a long time.'

Ellie pulled out her kerchief from her sleeve and wept. 'All my hard work wasted and we were on the brink of success.'

Jane embraced her. 'Never mind, Aunt Ellie. Everyone appreciated your efforts. Can we start again?'

'Oh, that I had not been so spendthrift with my money. It will take longer, Jane, and I don't know if I can carry on.'

'You must have a rest from it and then decide.'

'Yes, you're right. I have everything written down. I just need to retrace my steps and luckily most of the work is local. Romsley and Aberdeenshire are the most difficult. We will see.'

Mathew eased himself into the conversation, 'Ellie, my current position with the company allows me to travel extensively throughout the country. Whenever I can, I will help.'

'What is it you do with your railway company, Mathew? Were you not demoted?'

'Yes, I was, but what a relief. I'm a little poorer maybe, but a lot happier. The company are seeking to build a new line in locomotives and have delegated me to pick the brains of the best engineers in the country for their latest developments. Come, the weather is fine, who is going to join me for a walk by the canal?'

'No thank you, Mathew,' Jane said, 'I'll lie down for awhile.'

'I will stay with Jane, Mathew, and look after Gertie.'

'Gertie can come with me,' Mathew said eagerly, 'I won't be long.'

He swooped up his daughter and she giggled and squealed as he carried her from the room.

He had only been gone a little while when Jane approached Ellie.

'Aunt Ellie, are you and Mathew getting along alright?'

'Whatever do you mean dear, of course?'

'I noticed that Mathew seems to avoid you. If you pass him he steps back, or he moves to another part of the room. He walks around you, not past you, if you know what I mean, like he is trying to avoid contact.'

'Oh, I think he's just being a gentleman dear. We get along very well and I find him most trustworthy.'

'That's good. You would tell me if there had been any trouble?'

'Yes dear, don't go worrying your head, everything is alright.'

'I love you, Aunt Ellie.'

For a moment Ellie was speechless, unsure what to say, when she reached up behind her neck and after a few seconds fiddling took off the gold belcher chain with its guinea attached.

'Jane! I want you to have this. It is a family heirloom which has survived from the visit of Gilbert Ross in 1793. It was he who came to tell the family that one day his fortune would be ours and it is the only piece of our inheritance to come South of the border.'

'Aunt Ellie, you can't. It is Zoë's by right.'

'Don't worry. She has all my other belongings and Mathew has been a great help on my quest. All I ask is that you pass it on to your eldest daughter, and so on.'

'I can't.'

'You must, it is my will, no more argument. Here let me put it around your neck.'

'Aunt Ellie, you are naughty, I don't know what to say.'

'Say nothing. There, it suits you.'

A few minutes later Mathew returned much invigorated from his walk.

'I must say young Gertie loves walking,' he said, 'and what have you two been up to while we were away?'

'Mathew, speak to Aunt Ellie. Look what she's given to me.'

He turned to Ellie and said earnestly. 'Ellie are you sure about this. You and that guinea are never parted.'

'I'm quite sure. Now let that be the end to it.'

Mathew turned to his wife and shrugged. 'I'm sorry, darling. Your Aunt is the most stubborn person I know and I for one am not arguing.'

Ellie stood up and straightened her dress. 'That's settled then. Tomorrow I am going home to decide what to do next but right now we should do something about eating?'

The following evening.

Zoë sat by her mother holding her hands. 'Mum, what are we going to do?'

'I don't know darling,' Ellie replied, 'I feel quite dispirited. I shall spend some time sharing my life with you before I make up my mind.'

'Why don't you drop it altogether? We're comfortable and you're not getting any younger.'

'I can't. I made a promise to my mother when I was thirteen and I intend to carry it out. I'm quite well. Mathew told me I look ten years younger and I feel that way. Mind you, I don't know how you're supposed to feel at fifty.'

'Most people at your age are a little bent and grey. You are a freak mother, no grey hair and perfectly straight. How do you do it?'

'Hard work mostly and your Grandfather Tom kept his dark hair until very late in life. It must run in the family.'

'I hope I take after you, Mum. I have an idea. Let me finish this stint of night work and I'll ask for a week's leave of absence. That way we can do the local searches together and visit our relatives at the same time. It will do me good to travel and see a little of our county.'

'What a splendid idea. We are due some time together and can do something practical at the same time. It was doing this self same thing in **'81** that gave me the travel bug.'

'Right, that's it. I'm going to work while you prepare the

itinerary for next week.'

They started their search at the Gloucester Central Records Office and retraced Ellie's footsteps and day by day they extended their travels.

Ellie was prepared this time with paper and charcoal to take rubbings off the gravestone in Longhope and finally they went as far afield as Dymock.

In the Gloucester area they caught up with their relatives and these were many. Only Aunt Julia and Cousin Julia-Jane had moved to new pastures.

For Ellie it was déjà vu, but also sadness as she remembered when she had previously started out in 1881 on this same quest. The countryside had not changed although she did notice there appeared to be less people in the fields.

It wasn't all work. Ellie insisted that Zoë should see and experience as much as possible and it was an expense that Ellie considered well spent. 'If you're having a holiday then it must feel like one,' was her argument when Zoë protested.

The week was over all to quickly, but Ellie was satisfied with what they had achieved and now there was only Romsley and Scotland left to do.

Fortune smiled on them when a few days later a letter arrived from Mathew saying he was going to a place called Ellesmere Port in Cheshire to oversee some engineering work on new sidings at the Telford dock and he would do their search in the Midlands on the way back. Could they send him details of where to go and what names to look for, etc…

'Thank heaven for Mathew, he comes to the rescue again.' She smiled as she remembered guiltily their time in Scotland but without any real regret as the episode had rejuvenated her. It was if Mathews youthful zest had been instilled into her through their delightful and vigorous entanglement.

She carefully placed all the collected documents in the bottom of her workbox as before. 'This time no one gets them and I must have copies made for Mathew.'

It was six months before Mathew posted the missing Church records and photographs of his youngest child. A brother for

Gertrude called Percival.

'Percival! Who calls a child, Percival. The poor boy, he will never live it down. He will get Percy all his life. What were they thinking about?'

'What is it Mum, you're talking to yourself again?'

'Zoë, your cousin Julia-Jane has called her new son Percival.'

'Oh, goodness me, where did they get that from. They call pigs, Percy.'

'Zoë, behave yourself. The poor boy, my heart bleeds for him. But now the real business calls. We have the final piece of the puzzle. All we need to do now is to go to Scotland once more.'

'How are you going to do that, Mum?'

'I will need to live there for at least six weeks to qualify for residency. This is most important, but quite beyond me. I will attempt to save and meanwhile I will write to all our relatives and try to raise funds.'

'Can't you do this in one trip?'

'No. It will take approximately a year from presenting the petition before it gets to Court. That means I will have to travel twice and there are lawyers to pay also. Speaking of such, this time I intend to employ legal representation from England, which entails a trip to London. I will write to Beattie & Driscoll and ask their advice before I spend out on train fares.'

Ellie was most careful with the wording of the letters to her relatives. She avoided the mistake of making it a begging letter, rather one of raising funds for a venture that they were already aware of and which would be to their mutual benefit if it were successful. She did not ask for a specific amount, only as much as they could afford and then add to it as funds became available. This way she hoped to have a steady income into the fighting fund as she called it, and soften the burden on people's pockets at the same time.

Mathew said he would accompany her once more to Scotland at his own expense. Beattie & Driscoll of London were favourable and would she please present herself at her own convenience with the necessary documents.

'I can't afford the Adelphi this time Zoë. I will have to do the trip in one day. There is a train at eight in the morning which will give me ample time to do what I must and return on the five o' clock.'

***

17

1886. The London offices of Beattie & Driscoll, Solicitors.

She followed the clerk down the corridor and it reminded her of school days when you were called before the headmaster. She giggled as she mused silently, 'Maybe I should appear forlorn and plead forgiveness for disturbing his day.'

As she opened the office door the clerk looked at Ellie curiously before dismissing her with a shake of her head.

Beattie came forward and kissed the fingertips of her outstretched hand, 'Good morning, Mrs Chalmers. It has been five years, and if I may say so, you have not changed a bit.'

'Older perhaps.'

'Please take a seat and tell me, are we still pursuing the same cause?'

'Very much so.'

'I was under the impression that you were well on the way to achieving your goals. Has something changed?

'How long have we got, Mr Beattie?'

'My clerk can earn her keep for once. Wait one moment.'

He left the office to return moments later. 'My next appointment has been transferred to my colleague, please continue.'

Ellie related to him as briefly as possible the events of the last five years, in particular, that which had occurred after they had presented their case to the Court of Sessions in 1883.

'And now I would like you to take the case.'

'Mrs Chalmers, listening to your problems and those of Mr Lane, I have some idea of what may have happened. It is only a theory you understand and I am not at liberty to expand on it. However, I can say with some assurance that it will not happen again should we go forward with this case.'

'Whatever do you mean?'

'Let us just say that we are nearer to head office.'

'Very well.' Ellie was puzzled by this insinuation and thought it better to remain ignorant. 'But can you help me?'

'Yes, indeed. It is your good fortune that I have made a partnership with my cousin in Edinburgh only last year. That means I can do all the work here and they promulgate it from there. Give me your documents and let us get started.'

Ellie handed over her bundle of papers with apprehension, the memory of a previous occasion when she had entrusted the family documents into the hands of another still uppermost in her mind.

She waited patiently while he went through them. He examined every detail meticulously and while he read he drew a family tree and double-checked every so often to make sure of his facts.

Finally he laid down his glasses and looked up. 'You have been very thorough with your investigation, Mrs Chalmers and as I said previously, 'You have a jolly good case.' I see no problems but you will of course have to reside in Scotland for six weeks at some time and I don't expect that to happen for at least another year or so. Can you prove Uncle William's connection to the family in relation to Jane Ross?'

'Yes, we have done this before. I know where to go and what to do.'

'Good. You retrieve those records during your six week residence qualification and present them to my colleague and that should seal your case.'

'Oh good, I thought I was going to have to travel twice to Scotland.'

'Can you leave these with me? I will have them duplicated and send the originals back to you.'

'I am loath to do that. We have lost them so many times before.'

'I understand your caution, Mrs Chalmers. Please understand that we are a leading practice at the very centre of the law in this country and our reputation is our lifeline.'

'Very well, but should you not come up to scratch I will camp on your doorstep.'

'Have no fear, as soon as I have the case together I will dispatch it to my colleagues in Scotland so that they may submit it to the Court of Sessions. The moment we have a date for a hearing

I will let you know and then you can book your stay up there. Do you know anyone there you can lodge with?'

'No, I would have to stay in a hotel.'

'Not to worry, I will have them look around for a nice respectable hotel for you. There is time to worry about that later. Meanwhile be patient and we will be in touch.'

'Your fee, Mr Beattie, how much?'

'Could you manage twenty pounds as a retainer? The rest we will work at depending on the outcome.'

'I have only ten pounds, may I forward the remainder?'

'By all means, let me give you a receipt. Mrs Chalmers, you appear to be, how shall I say this? You seem to be less well off than on your previous visit.'

She lowered her eyes with embarrassment and she could feel the warmth in her cheeks as she blushed. 'Yes, with all the nonsense that has gone on before, our resources are somewhat depleted. I am now reduced to begging off my relatives to sustain a fund.'

'In that case we will enter this case, *'en forme pauperie'*. It is a poor man's court. Something the Law does for people that are less well off. If your case is won, you have to pay the court a percentage.'

'Thank you, Mr Beattie, I am most grateful, but I did not come here to beg for charity.'

'It is not charity, look upon it as a loan. Now let me get you a cab.' He stood, and they shook hands. 'The best of luck, Mrs Chalmers, let us hope the next time we meet it is in more favourable circumstances.'

He went out with her to the front office and waited while the clerk hailed a cab.

'Where to, Mrs Chalmers?'

'Paddington Station, please.'

***

18

The Edinburgh office of Mackenzie & Mackenzie, Advocates.

Alexander Maxwell-Ross very much like his father before him leaned over the desk and punctuated his words by stabbing the polished mahogany with his finger.

'Mackenzie! What is the meaning of this? I understood that this affair was finished. In fact, you promised it was, and yet the same people present me with another claim. What are you going to do about it?'

'Nothing.'

'What do you mean, nothing?'

'Sir Alexander, if you recall, I refused to take part with any arrangements you made other than the legalities of the case. Whatever else you organised is your affair.'

'Then who is their brief this time around? We shall have to do the same with them.'

'That is out of the question as they are represented by a legal firm at the centre of *'The Temple'* which is one of the leading Lodges in the British Isles who have privy to far more senior members than you or I. If it were to come out that we used our status for illegal means I cannot imagine what the repercussions would be.'

'What is the answer?'

'I don't have a legal one. It would seem that you are going to have to find some other method of which I want no knowledge.'

'What about your man, Jervis?'

'He's serving time in Gloucester Jail.'

'Does he have any friends?'

'I don't know, I represent the lawful citizens of this parish, the lowlife I want nothing to do with. Now sir, was there anything else?'

The Maxwell-Ross residence, London.
Wilson, the secretary of Maxwell-Ross addressed his employer in the manner of a confidant. 'I have arranged a meeting with a man called Bill Roughley, sir. It's at the *Rose and Crown* in the East End at nine o' clock this evening. He's an ex-serviceman and an old pal of my brother. You must not draw attention to yourself, wear a faded red flower in your buttonhole and be careful how you speak. The gentleman in question, sir, is rough by nature as well as by name.'

Maxwell's venture into the East End was not a happy one. With the darkness came fog and the London cabbie not known for his gregarious qualities became even surlier when told of the destination.

'Sorry, Guv, I ain't going down there in this bleedin' fog. It gets worse as you move aart ov the city.'

'I'll pay you double.' Maxwell didn't plead, but there was a hint of anxiety in his voice.

'It's bad enough da'an there wiv aart fog, guv. It'll be treble fare, an I ain't angin' araand either.'

'How do you propose I return?'

'That's your problem. I'll tell the lads to look aart fer ya if'n they're in the area.'

His senses were at odds with reality as the fog became thicker and hung like a sodden blanket. The buildings on either side moved on a conveyer belt. Pedestrians glided by on rollers and the cab stood still in time. The hallucinatory gloom muffled sound and instead of the sharp clip clop of the hooves there was only a series of tuneless thuds.

Within five minutes he had lost his bearings as the cab progressed from the fashionable West End through the City towards the East End. He couldn't see the Tower as they proceeded down towards the river into Wapping. The fog became smog as they went further into the labyrinth of terraced houses with each chimney stoking the already grimy atmosphere with thick clinging, yellowish green smoke.

His mouth was dry and tasted of coke as the smog gripped his throat and made his eyes water. It hung like a theatre curtain with illuminated cones around every streetlight. Ghostlike two-dimensional figures glided into each murky spotlight and were instantly lost as they passed out of it.

He grew increasingly anxious as they turned into Limehouse and he questioned the sanity of his decision, debating with himself the pros and cons of his actions. The affairs of state were easier to discuss than this conundrum but the possibility of losing the family fortune persuaded him to continue with his plan to rid himself once and for all of the pestilent upstarts who had their sights set on his wealth.

When the cab finally stopped the silence was deafening in the choking, murky mixture that cloaked them. The dislocated voice of the cabbie through the communication hatch made him jump.

'Ere we are, guv, the Rose and Craan.'

He paid the fare and then made an unusual request. 'How much for your cap?'

'Can't sell that guv, I'll catch me death.'

'Ten shillings.'

'Two pounds.'

'Two pounds for a two bob cap? Fifteen shillings and no more.'

The cabbie threw his cap down and eagerly accepted the proffered money.

Maxwell waited until the cab had disappeared into the gloom before putting on his newly acquired headgear, thankful that it was a size too big. He was doubtful of the wildlife that may lurk within but it did hide his neat haircut and it made his ensemble just that little bit more imperfect.

Wilson had dressed him in borrowed clothes that didn't fit too well and he had scuffed his shoes against the wall to make them look as if they had seen better times.

His last words were, 'There you are, sir, now you appear second hand. Keep your head down and try not to look anyone in the eye. Drop your shoulders and shuffle your feet, not too much, because you're not down and out. Just enough to make them think you've seen better times, and remember, if anyone gets too inquisitive you're a public school boy who has gambled away the family fortune. This may explain your accent if you have to speak.'

With this advice ringing in his ears, Maxwell entered the pub. When he opened the door the sounds of merriment and chatter were swallowed up by the smoky green soup before they got beyond the doorstep.

It was questionable whether the atmosphere inside was any better than outside. The smell was different. The main ingredients being stale beer, body odour and smoke from many pipes and cigarettes. The gas lamps had an incandescent halo that made them appear detached from the wall.

He moved slowly to the bar, rubbing his hands and looking right and left of him, making sure not to stare or dwell on one person. It was a corner building and the L shaped bar followed the contours. Around the walls high pine settles divided the room into little alcoves.

Above the bottles and decanters behind the bar hung a pair of horse pistols and he wondered if they worked. It looked the sort of place where you might need them.

The barman leaned on the bar his grubby fingers barely discernible from the grimy surface. 'What'll it be?'

'A pint of your best, please,' Maxwell mumbled in a feeble attempt to disguise his accent and he pushed a shilling over the bar.

As he went to pick up his change, a hand appeared between his.

'Buy a box of matches, guv, 'elp an old soldier.'

He gave a penny and took nothing in return.

Strangers were not welcome in these parts and he sensed the silence as people stopped their chatter to weigh him up. He made his way to a corner table taking heed of Wilson's warning. A slight shuffle, bent shoulders and don't look at anyone.'

Gradually the chatter and laughter grew louder as they looked upon him as no more than someone taking respite from the ghastly choking slime outside.

He took a mouthful of the warm brown liquid and immediately recoiled as the palate used to fine wines tried to rebel against swallowing.

'How do they drink this stuff,' he muttered to himself, 'It has the odour and taste of dishwater.'

He sat brooding in his corner forcing himself to drink when a glass banged down on the table, jolting him upright.

'Put one in there, Commander.'

The man who confronted him was balding, of medium height and stocky build. His dirty grey shirt, which had once been white, was pushed into baggy trousers held up by a belt with an enormous brass buckle. Around his neck was a garish coloured neckerchief and his coat was thick navy blue serge of the type favoured by seamen.

'Bill Roughley, at your service.'

Maxwell recoiled at the body odour, but was surprised that a man of this ilk should speak with little or no discernible accent. He pushed a sixpence over the table and said testily, 'Here, fetch it yourself.'

'Would you be wantin' a top-up then?'

'No, thank you. One glass of this muck is about as much as I can take.'

'I see. You can't stomach the fare that we live with, but you're quick to come to us for help.'

Maxwell watched as Roughley went to the bar and wondered if he could trust this man with the task he had in mind.

On his return Roughley pocketed the change and pulled up a chair. It took willpower not to recoil from the smell of sweat that accompanied the man wherever he went.

'Right, Commander, what's your problem and have you any cigarettes?'

Maxwell took his silver cigarette case from his inside pocket and offered it to him.

'For God's sake,' Roughley said quickly, 'don't flash the family silver in here.' But not before he had helped himself to a couple of cigarettes.

Maxwell glanced around fearful of being be set upon, before continuing. 'My problem, Mr Roughley, as you so delicately put it, is there are two people who are being a nuisance. I stopped them once, but now they have come back to haunt me.'

'You want me to harm them, or get rid of them?'

'I don't want to hear about them or their wretched plan ever again. What you do is your affair.'

'How much are you paying?'

'Five-hundred pounds.'

'Not enough, Commander, double it.'

'Five-hundred now and five-hundred when you complete the job.'

'That's fair, who are they, and where are they?'

Maxwell took a folded piece of note-paper from his pocket. 'You will find what you need there. Names, addresses and description.'

Roughley looked the details over. 'Give me fifty quid for expenses. There's some travelling to do here and I need to improve my attire.'

'Very well.' Maxwell surreptitiously removed the required amount from his wallet and passed it under the table. 'Here you are. You will contact me through my man's brother when the job is done. I want proof and I don't want to see you again.'

'Aye, aye, Commander.'

'Thank you, now can you help me get back to the city?'

'It'll be hard tonight, but come on. I'll walk with you until we spot a cab.'

'That's very kind of you.'

'No, Commander. I'm looking after my investment.'

***

19

On an early spring day after a pleasant Saturday excursion into Gloucester, Ellie and Zoë were travelling home in the trap at a brisk pace. A short distance from Hempstead the hairs on Ellie's neck bristled.

She intuitively glanced back along the road and saw a shadowy figure on horseback. There was something odd about him and it was some moments before she understood why.

'Zoë, I think someone is following us and he doesn't ride.'
'What was that, Mum?'
'I said; he doesn't ride.'
'Who?'
'That man following.'
'What do you mean?'
'Look at him, Zoë. He's bouncing up and down like a sack of potatoes, poor horse.'

Taking her eyes off the road Zoë glanced over her shoulder.

'Hmm, you're right, he does look awkward. Probably a sailor going back to Bristol.'

She tried to sound unconcerned but urged the horse to greater efforts.

They reached the edge of the village and a few minutes later Zoë swung the trap into the drive of their cottage and went directly around to the stable block at the rear.

The lone rider slowed, took note of the premises and rode on and both Ellie and Zoë breathed a sigh of relief to see him disappear into the approaching dusk.

Some time later Ellie felt uneasy when, from the window of a darkened bedroom, she thought she saw a shadowy figure lurking in the bushes.

The incident faded from Ellie's mind until the following weekend when she ventured into Gloucester to look for some lining material to match the latest outfit that Zoë was making for her.

It was a mild day and Ellie took full advantage of the weather to do some window shopping along Northgate Street taking great care to stay on the inside of the pavement to avoid horse droppings flicked up by the many hooves and carriage wheels.

She stopped to look into the window of the shoemaker to admire the latest line of footwear when she became ill at ease.

She shivered inexplicably and glanced back, positive that someone had ducked into a shop doorway. Had she imagined it? Other pedestrians walked by unconcerned and she could see no reason for her uneasiness.

Nevertheless, ignoring the child road-sweepers plying for her business, she crossed to the other side of the street carefully picking her way around mounds of horse dung. A sixth sense made her hesitate and look back.

A stocky man of medium height stood on the opposite pavement watching her. There was something familiar about him and she noted that although he was well dressed, he seemed uncomfortable in his clothes as if he were unused to such finery.

She pondered a few moments, when recognition flashed into her mind. The awkwardness, the build. It was the man who had followed her and Zoë the other evening although his features had not been recognisable then.

Something told her he was up to no good and with her heart pounding, she gathered up her skirts and went quickly into the City Shopping Emporium.

Mingling with the other shoppers she tried to appear unconcerned and edged further into the store. Distracted, she went from counter to counter until she was startled by the polite cough of an assistant who enquired if she might help.

Flushed with embarrassment, Ellie uttered a confused, 'No, no thank you,' and moved hastily into the haberdashery department.

After a short deliberation she chose a subdued brown material and feeling calmer, and somewhat safer she made her way to the exit onto the main street.

Glancing left and right she saw the cause of her earlier anxiety was not in sight and she determined to visit the Cathedral for a few moments contemplation before retrieving the trap and making her way home.

The timeless atmosphere inside the Cathedral was comforting. The ancient building sensed the need for solitude from its visitors and wrapped a serene cloak around them. Ellie chose a pew midway down the long aisle and sat quietly reminiscing about the previous thirty-eight years.

She smiled at the early memories of her father before his premature death on the docks not far from where she sat. Her thoughts were more subdued by what followed. The gruelling twelve-hour shifts in the soap factory before her promotion, which led to her marriage to David until his demise on the high seas. Life had been busy since then and she had a secretive inner flush when she remembered her love tryst with Mathew in Edinburgh. She giggled and hid her face when a nearby worshipper gave her a disapproving look.

The mellow tones of an organ whispered down the nave and she bowed her head. Long forgotten prayers swirled around her and an ethereal premonition made her shiver involuntarily. She hastily gathered her things and made her way to the entrance.

There was chill in the air and she pulled her coat tighter around her and stepped out onto the long pathway to the gate. With her head lowered against the breeze she unexpectedly bumped into someone.

Startled, she looked up and stepped back with a cry when she recognised the man who had followed her earlier.

He knuckled his forehead and said, 'Sorry ma'am, I had no intention of shocking you like that. It's Mrs Chalmers isn't it?'

This very action alerted her to the fact that the clothes did not match the person.

'Er, yes, but you have the advantage of me, sir.'

'I'm doubly sorry, ma'am. Bill Roughley, I'm an old shipmate of your husband. I worked the clippers with him in his later years.'

Zoë had been right. His demeanour was that of an ordinary seaman. She could tell by the way he touched his forelock instead of raising his hat, but he hadn't sailed with David for he had been on steam ships, not clippers.

Ellie kept calm although her heart was pounding. 'It must have been nice for you as I understand he was good to his crew.'

'Oh, yes ma'am, and he could haul on a sheet with the best of us and we had many a drink in Bristol afterwards.'

His lies were becoming an embarrassment and she realised she had to get away.

'If you will excuse me, I have arranged to meet my daughter in town so I must leave. It has been nice talking to you.'

'Of course Mrs Chalmers, my apologies, maybe we can talk some other time.'

'Yes, maybe.'

He knuckled his forelock again and stepped to one side. She gathered up her skirts and fled as modestly as she could muttering under her breath, 'Not if I can help it.'

—

Monday

'Oh, Mum, must you visit Mathew, can't you write?'

'No darling, I need his advice. This man, whoever he is, was obviously lying as he knew absolutely nothing about David and he gives me the creeps. Besides, now that we have a Court date I want to go over last minute details.

'Are you sure?'

'Don't worry, Zoë. I also want to tell him how generous the family have been, I can manage six weeks in Scotland easily. Why don't you come with me?'

'I can't, Mum. We've had a rush of Diphtheria and we're short-handed, but I'll come and see you off.'

—

They joined the throng waiting for the London train and Zoë commented. 'There's a lot travelling today, Mum, you should be alright.'

'It's usual for a Monday, darling, but there will be plenty of room. Here it comes.'

A thrill went through the crowd and they moved forward expectantly. The iron monster, belching smoke and hissing steam crawled along, its metal brakes squealing in protest as the driver did his best to stop at the appointed place.

It was barely ten yards from them when there was a commotion in the crowd and Roughley, crudely shoving people aside, crashed into Ellie and with both hands shoved her hard in the back.

Ellie staggered towards the edge of the platform with arms flailing trying to maintain her balance and for a moment, it appeared she might save herself. She teetered on the edge wobbling, her upper body swinging back and forth as she fought to regain control until Roughley, in desperation, lunged forward again and gave her a final push. Her dying scream brought everyone to a mesmerised standstill as she fell beneath the wheels of the slowing train.

'Stop that man,' yelled Zoë.' Stop him! He's pushed my Mother under the train.'

Roughley, slowed by the crowd clamouring for the train, fled along the platform. A policeman, alerted by the furore took up the chase and to further his escape Roughley jumped down onto the track in front of the now stationary London train in a desperate attempt to cross to the other side, but in his haste he forgot to check the through centre line.

Too late, he realized that a fast goods train was bearing down on him. He tried to turn, his foot slipped on the worn rails and he went sprawling, his screams drowned by the noise of the leviathan.

Ellie's funeral was well attended and she was laid to rest in Hardwicke churchyard alongside her Mother, Beth and Father, Edward.

It was later when they were all gathered at the house in Hempstead that Mathew and one or two others asked Zoë if she would carry on where Ellie had left off.

'No, I'm not. There's been enough misfortune in this family chasing this fantastic dream and now it has taken my Mother away and it is time to stop. Allow me a little respite and I will reimburse everyone who has donated towards the journey to Scotland. Should anyone decide to follow Mother's footsteps I will gladly help, otherwise—It's over.'

Mathew spoke up for them all. 'Well said Zoë, I fully concur, enough is enough. By the way, I had a word with the police earlier and all they know of the man who committed this foul deed is that he had five hundred pounds in his wallet and a return ticket to

London. He wore brand new clothing, which was very odd, and they think he was paid to do it but there is no evidence of who might wish to harm Eleanor.'

'Mathew.' Zoë took him by the hand to gain his full attention and said seriously. 'I think it would be wise to stop, I have a feeling that you will be next.'

'By golly, I never thought of that. Wise words, young lady.'

'Please stop saying that, Mathew.'

'What?'

'Calling me a young lady. You're only a few years older. I am twenty-six, a year older than your wife. Talking of which, while we are alone, you had a relationship with my Mother, didn't you?'

'Eleanor was a very special lady and we had an understanding, like that of brother and sister. She was young at heart and did not act, or look her age. Believe me, I had a hard time keeping up with her.'

'Is that all, Mathew? She always had this secretive smile on her face when she spoke of you.'

'My dear Zoë, what are you suggesting? There was no impropriety between us.'

'Careful, Mathew, you are a little red around the collar. Do we listen for a cock crowing?'

'I loved your Mother dearly, and I'm greatly saddened by her loss. Let her rest in peace.'

'Very well, that will be the last you will hear of it. I knew there was some attachment after your first trip together. She came back a different person that only another woman would recognise. Help me say goodbye to the other guests Mathew. You can be my right hand man for today.'

'Gladly, and Zoë, if there is anything you should need, please get in touch. Will you be able to manage?'

'Yes, we have no debts and mother left me well provided for and I also have my job. Helping others keeps me occupied.'

'Good, all the same you must visit.'

1975

Mildmay stretched and smothered a yawn. 'That was intriguing, It was a great shame about Ellie. I had grown quite fond of her.'

'I'm glad you agree with me on that score, sir. By the time I had finished Ellie's life I had fallen in love with her. She was alive, she hurt, was naughty, but not promiscuous.'

'I couldn't have put it better myself, lad. About the rest of the family, we may as well carry on now that we are nearly there. What happened to them? They had lives, did they not?'

'Yes, sir, but no further attempt was made to retrieve the legacy and it went out of statute. Life just continued, she died, he died.'

'Angus Lane,' Mildmay sounded exasperated, 'When you write about a family you must include everyone. We know they died, everyone does eventually, but tell us a little about them.'

Angus pulled his notebook from his inside pocket and scanned the well-worn pages.

'Zoë, sir, did not marry, became a Matron in the Hospital and devoted herself to looking after the sick until she retired and when the Second World War started, even in her advanced years, she volunteered for the WVS until she passed away in 1942, aged 82.'

'And what of our young Casanova?'

'Mathew Lane, my Great-grandfather, worked all his life for the railways and it is believed he drowned in the Union Canal after suffering a heart attack in 1933, aged 76.'

'The guinea, what happened to that?'

'Aah, the guinea, one moment.'

Mildmay lowered his head and looked over his glasses with a pained expression as Angus consulted his notebook yet again.

'The present holder,' Angus blurted out, 'is my cousin, Mrs Jenny Beaumont.'

Mildmay pointed to the file. 'Well done, lad. Take that away get it revised and back here a.s.a.p. One more thing.'

Angus suppressed a groan. 'Yes, sir.'

'Have you used real names?'

'That occurred to me sir and I changed the names and called the Clan 'Ross', after my fish finger tea.'

'Why don't you write to your family members and tell them about this saga. I'm sure they'll be interested.'

'Yes sir, I'll do that, and give them a copy of Eleanor's last letter also.'

'Off you go, lad. Congratulations, and get a hair cut before you try on a mortar board.'

***

PART 3

2002

JENNY.

20

20a Village Farm,
Middlemere,
Cheshire

08/07/2003

Dear Prof. Mildmay,

Many years have passed since we last communicated and I was glad to read in the University journal that you and your wife are well. This would have nothing to do with your favourite tipple of course.

I hope you don't mind me taking the liberty of extracting your address from the magazine librarian. She was adamant that it was a breach of privacy or some such thing and it cost me an expensive meal and a few bottles of wine before she would submit to my appeals.

On a positive note, we are now dating on a regular basis.

My reason for writing is to fill you in on what happened to the Ross Legacy. If you remember we discussed this at great lengths in my final year.

I am glad to say that the family saga has come to a satisfactory, although rather eerie conclusion, and in a manner which no one would ever have imagined.

Here is the way of it. Mrs Jenny Beaumont, a cousin of mine, found the letters I sent to her parents and made a search of her own. She concluded rightly that there was no point pursuing the matter as it was out of statute, but a rather coincidental thing occurred...

Cheshire, England. 2002

Jenny Beaumont was a complex woman in many ways. Slim, medium height with tumbling dark hair, green eyes, a dazzling smile and a complexion that belied her fifty years. She was both vivacious and shy, a quality that made her own gender wary of her and confused the opposite sex.

The urgent rattling of a key in the front door of the bungalow on the outskirts of a Cheshire industrial town shattered her daydreaming in the conservatory. The front door burst open, followed by the living room door, which, defying the laws of mechanics, stayed on its hinges.

'Mum! Mum!' Elaine, her daughter, similar in appearance, although slightly taller, came bouncing through the house and stopped, gasping breathlessly at the conservatory door.

'Mum, I have some great news. I tried phoning, but I couldn't get an answer.'

'Oh, steady on, darling, I've been on the Internet, that's all. What are you doing here anyway. You're not due until next week.'

'Mum, I have some wonderful news.'

'I know dear, you said. What is it?'

'Andrew has asked me to marry him.'

Jenny's heart sank at the very words she didn't want to hear.

'Mum! I said, Andrew has asked me to marry him. Aren't you pleased? He would like you to come and meet his father next weekend. I'm so happy.' She leaned over and gave her Mother a peck on the cheek.

'It's a bit sudden isn't it?'

Elaine sighed. 'Mum, you don't sound too happy. Is something wrong?'

'Elaine, sit down, I have something to show you.' Jenny rummaged around in her workbox and pulled out a sheaf of papers. 'I think you had better read these before you reach any decision.'

'What are they?'

'Read them, and I will explain later.'

Elaine spent the next few minutes reading two letters from the past. One dated 1976 to her grandmother and the other dated 1886 to her great-grandmother.

'Very complex, but what do they mean?'

'It means, dear, that the person you wish to marry is a direct descendant of William Maxwell-Ross who stole a lot of money and land from this branch of the Ross Clan in 1839. His family home was built with our money.'

Elaine's hand flew to her mouth. 'Oh...' She stood up and began pacing up and down deep in thought.

After a couple of minutes Jenny could stand it no longer.

'Sit down, dear.'

Elaine paused in mid stride. 'This changes nothing, Mum,' she said sharply, 'I love him and I don't intend to lose him over some silly ancient allegations.'

'Don't raise your voice, Elaine.'

'How long have you known about this?'

'Keep calm, darling. About six months.'

'Mum! How could you,' her voice rising in anger, 'You find something that could ruin my life and you keep it to yourself. Where did these letters come from anyway?'

Jenny cut short her daughters belligerence. 'Stop shouting and remember who you're talking to young lady. As it happens, I found them in the attic amongst your Grandmother's effects. The reason I have never told you is because I wanted to check first, so I took them to a solicitor.'

'And?'

'Do calm down, Elaine. These allegations are true. I also have a copy of the Will left by Jane Ross, but the whole issue is now out of statute. This means we cannot claim even if we wanted to.'

After a moments reflection Elaine said quietly. 'Mum, I don't care if we could claim. I would still marry him.'

Jenny gave a long sigh. 'Are you sure?' Elaine nodded. 'In that case we shall forget the whole thing. This week-end you said, what am I going to wear?'

'Oh, Mum, come here.' They put their arms around each other and hugged.

'I know,' Jenny said, holding her daughter at arms length, 'Now you're here, we can go shopping and see if I can find something decent to wear.'

'Mum, your wardrobe is full to bursting. Andrew is always

saying how well dressed you are. I think he would rather marry you than me. It makes me wonder if he has mother-in-law fantasies. You keep away from him, do you hear.'

With a mischievous glint in her eye Jenny replied, 'Oh, if I must. On second thoughts, you have no need to worry, dear. I couldn't be bothered starting again, I've been on my own too long, and a younger man—you must be joking. I haven't got the energy. Although…' With the same slow, sensuous smile that turned her late husband to jelly, 'I suppose the boy's got something.'

'Watch it. I'm warning you, there'll be no wedding cake for you.'

Jenny's disguised insecurity welled up. 'I still want to look my best for you. Andrew does come from quite high society doesn't he? I mean, he lives in a stately home.'

'It's a mock Scottish castle actually. Mum. They're just ordinary people with a bit more silver in the cabinet and a huge garden, that's all.'

'Well, they accepted you so their taste can't be that high.'

She laughed and ducked away from the playful cuff aimed at her as Elaine turned to go into the house. Jenny got up from the chair, fluffed up the cushions and flicked at imaginary dust on plant leaves before following her daughter.

'Elaine, I know Andrew lives with his father, but what happened to his mother?'

'Didn't I tell you? She died in a riding accident.'

'Oh yes, my memory; how sad.'

'Mum, it was ten years ago.'

Saturday – One week later.
It was mid-afternoon when they crossed the border into the Southeast of Scotland and a little while later they turned inland off the **A1** and followed the old road which was little more than a country lane.

After several miles of rolling countryside, swooping hollows and little woodlands scattered here and there as if dropped by the searing easterly winds that came in off the North Sea, through the trees, standing haughtily on a hillock, could be seen Eaton Castle, a sandstone, turreted mansion, which had a commanding view over the Eye valley.

Jenny pulled over into a gateway and surveyed the scenery around her and the building that was to be home for the week-end.

'Cold and austere, Elaine, like a disapproving aunt. It makes me feel chilly just looking at it.'

'You'll love it once you get inside. It's one of those old houses that Dad used to like. Full of wood panelling and high ceilings, paintings and ornaments, clocks by the dozen and they still use the open fires which adds to the atmosphere. I know what Dad would have said.'

Together, almost in unison they said aloud, 'I'd love to get up in that attic.'

Jenny's eyes filled up at the recollection. Although widowed almost two years she still thought of him fondly as their twenty-five years of marriage had been close and loving.

'Oh, I'm sorry Mum, I never thought.'

'It's alright, darling.' She put an arm around her daughter and gave her a quick squeeze. 'But you're right, your Dad would have loved this place as well as the countryside around, and he wouldn't like us moping around feeling sorry either. He said that life has to go on and if anything happened to him I was to start afresh and look out for my happiness.'

Jenny suddenly stopped talking, looked over her shoulder and then up and down the road.

'What are you doing, Mum?'

'Your Dad always said he would come back and haunt me so I'm just checking.' They both chuckled, which turned into a chorus of laughter. 'Come on, I'm dying for a cup of tea.'

They followed the low stonewall of the estate boundary and passed the little gothic Parish Church of Eaton until they arrived at high red sandstone facade with a studded wooden gate that was the main entrance to the estate.

A few words into the inter-com at the side and within moments the gates swung open and they drove through.

Jenny gave an involuntary shiver as they entered and a feeling of déjà vu swept over her. This is peculiar she thought, 'I've never been here before, so why do I feel like this?'

They drove through rolling parkland behind the church this

time and the castle minarets were the only thing visible beyond the trees. Driving up a slight gradient they went into the woods where the trees arched over them like a pastoral guard of honour. At the end of the wood they were immediately confronted by the impressive sandstone house built in the Scottish style with a central tower.

The French influence was apparent by the pinnacle turrets, a throwback to the days when Scottish Pretenders were to be found in France rather than in their own country.

Jenny parked and with a sigh of relief, switched off the ignition and unfastened the seatbelt. The door opened with an invisible hand and as she swung her legs out a leather belt over brown cords confronted her. Her eyes travelled upwards before she saw the face of Alexander Maxwell-Ross, a tall handsome man in his mid-fifties with thinning silver hair who spoke with a soft Scottish burr.

'Excuse the cliché; Jenny, I presume.'

'Err… Yes,' Jenny replied, self-consciously patting her hair, worrying about her appearance and wanting to give a good first impression. She stood up glad that she had chosen to wear trousers that day.

'I'm sorry,' he said profusely, 'I should have known. I'm afraid Andrew is busy with some week-enders and I got thrust into the fore.' He pushed out a hand. 'I'm Alexander—Andrew's father.'

She took the hand and the grip was firm, but precisely pressured.

'As you so rightly guessed, Alexander,' she said with emphasis on his name, 'I'm Jenny.' She smiled, feeling embarrassed for no good reason.

The tension was relieved when Elaine came around the car. 'I see you two have met. Open the boot, Mum.'

Jenny reached into the car and pushed the appropriate button. She used the opportunity to grab her Gucci leather jacket from the back seat and slip it over her shoulders.

Alex took the suitcases from the boot and with the enthusiasm of a Scout troop Brown Owl he called, 'Follow me!'

He led the way to the front door, which, for a building of this consequence was not much larger than the front door of your average suburban semi. Above the entrance the Ross Coat of Arms was engraved in the granite lintel.

They entered a large entrance hall with a chequered tiled floor and wood panelling and spiralling upwards was a polished wooden staircase.

'Leave the cases here.' Alex spoke louder than was necessary and seemed agitated. 'Andrew can bring them up later.'

Jenny smiled to herself when she realised that Alex was just as nervous as she was.

He came over to Jenny's side and showed her through a side door and into the Great Hall.

She felt more relaxed now and a quick peek in a huge mirror assured her that the image was not too shabby after the long drive.

Elaine broke the silence. 'I'll leave you two. I'm going to look for Andrew.'

'You'll probably find him in the stables with the American group,' said Alex, 'they've just returned from a hack.'

'Thanks.'

They walked to the middle of the hall. It was a large oblong room with open fireplaces on two sides and a polished wooden parquet floor reflecting the light from the small windows.

The walls, panelled in dark oak, had crossed swords, pikes and muskets fixed to them and in between were the family portraits. The centre of attraction were two extravagant chandeliers suspended from an exquisitely decorated plaster ceiling in the French style which was in character with the outside of the house. Down the centre of the room was a long mahogany dining table set for twenty-one people and across the top, at right angles, a smaller table set for four.

'Are we expecting guests, Alex?'

'It's Saturday and for our week-enders we have a banquet of sorts. They have the pleasure of our company and get to eat with the Lord of the Manor. We shall be sitting at the top table. The Americans love it and it's mainly for their benefit.'

They stopped in front of one of the fireplaces with its engraved Coat of Arms and the slogan 'A Ross, A Ross' underneath.

Jenny felt cold and she shuddered as a clammy mustiness surrounded her, akin to a moist fog. In her subconscious she became aware of a whisper.

'Welcome home, Jenny Ross.'

She looked around, but there was only herself and Alex in the room.

'Is anything wrong,' said Alex, concerned for his guest's welfare.

'No, no,' she said hastily, 'I thought someone had followed us into the room. You know that feeling you have when someone is watching. It's probably the atmosphere getting to me.'

As they left the hall she looked towards the fireplace and gave an involuntary shudder. 'Ghosts, rubbish, there's no such thing,' she said mentally.

They went into the east wing, across the bottom of the broad staircase and into the drawing room where the décor was predominantly blue. Oak panelling reached to door height with blue flock paper up to a dado rail and in the centre of the ceiling a decorated plaster carnation surrounded the base of an elaborate electric chandelier.

A luxurious Egyptian rug covered most of the parquet floor and the swirling patterns of dark blue and gold inlay made a perfect backdrop to the mahogany furniture and a sumptuous blue three-piece suite.

Above the open fireplace hung quite the biggest ornate mirror Jenny had ever seen and the alcoves either side were crammed with books up to the ceiling.

She thought it was all a bit gloomy as the windows, which were small to keep out the winter cold, did not allow much light in.

'I would change this if I lived here,' she thought, 'it needs a woman's touch.'

Alex broke into her thoughts. 'This is where we live. We call this the blue room for obvious reasons. The other wing has been given over to visitors because like all stately homes we have to make a living.'

He rang a Chinese lobster pot bell and a few seconds later a middle-aged lady entered.

'Lily, could you get us some tea, please? Oh, I beg your

pardon let me introduce you. Lily, this is Elaine's Mum, Jenny. Likewise—Jenny, meet Lily our housekeeper and my right arm.'

Both women spoke simultaneously. 'How do you do,' and laughed together also.

'A good start,' Jenny thought, as Lily left the room.

'Please sit down, Jenny, and let me take your jacket.'

Alex took the jacket from her and laid it over the back of an armchair and as she sank down into the settee her feet disappeared into a deep sheepskin rug.

'First impressions of our family pile, Jenny?'

'I think it to early to make judgement. From the outside quite austere, but the inside is very much like all stately homes. This one does have a lived in feeling and it's not very old is it, Alex?'

'No. This is the third castle on this sight. The first built around **1130**. The Earl of Surrey flattened that in **1498**. Rebuilt, it was destroyed again by fire in **1834**. Then my great-grandfather four times removed bought the land and the Baronetcy of Witchell and built this one.'

'Oh, I see. The family has not always had a title then?'

'No, and I'm not completely sure of our family history. Apparently, the Maxwell's were in banking when the last of the Ross line died intestate. Investigation found that William Maxwell was a cousin three times removed and it all passed to him. That's as much as I know. I suppose it's all stored somewhere and I might try and trace it one day.'

Lily arrived with a tray laden with tea and a triple tier cake-stand loaded with goodies and placed it on the occasional table between them.

'I'll play, mother,' said Jenny, 'milk and sugar?'

'No sugar, thanks.'

She poured the tea, handed one to Alex and offered him the cake stand. He dallied for a moment before choosing a ginger nut.

'Looking after our figure, are we,' she teased.

He smiled and blushed. 'I have to. Take a look at our family portraits and you can see that being overweight runs in the family. Once a week on our banqueting night I make up for it.'

The small talk carried on a little longer until Jenny excused herself by saying she would like to rest before dinner.

'By all means,' said Alex, 'let me show you to your room. I think you'll like it, from the window you have a nice view of the park.'

They walked up the winding staircase and she trailed her hand along the broad mahogany banister. The silky touch of the polished wood sent a sensuous tingle through her fingers and she warmed to the feeling of this big house.

On the first landing stood a tall long case clock.

'Oh, I love that, it's beautiful, is it very old?'

'It is an 18th century Northern clock.'

'Tell me, Alex. What's the difference between that and a Southern clock?'

'It's something to do with having an excess of mahogany brought over in ballast from the West Indies and left lying around the docks at Liverpool.'

'My husband used to talk about North and South clocks, but I never asked him what the difference was. You learn something every day.'

'Was he in antiques then?'

'No, he just loved old things. He said that's why he married me.'

They stopped by a bedroom door and stood facing each other and she had to bend her head backwards to look up at him.

He looked down at her and said earnestly. 'This is your room. I hope you like it. Your husband was pulling your leg. I can assure you that you are not old but very attractive and it will give me great pleasure to have you as my companion at dinner tonight.'

She felt the warmth of the flush creeping up her neck and she said hastily, 'Thank you, Alex, I shall look forward to it,' and she turned quickly into the room to hide her feelings.

―

A four-poster bed was the centrepiece of a room filled with antique furniture and decorated in modern pastel shades of peach and rose with a brightly coloured flower patterned duvet cover. On the dressing table was a pink willow patterned bowl and jug and a rattan screen hid the en-suite shower.

Leaning against the door to reflect on the events that so far did not seem believable she pinched herself to make sure that it wasn't a dream.

'Now you silly thing, what are you going to do,' she said out loud, 'this is not possible. You come here with a secret and find yourself fancying the one person who you should rightfully despise for living in your birthright. I wouldn't mind but I'm enjoying the experience. What do I do?'

'Follow your heart, Ross. This will be yours one day.'

Jenny's heart skipped a beat and she shivered. Her hand reached to her throat as she looked around anxiously but there was no one there.

'Oh... No, I don't believe in ghosts, they only happen in fairy tales.'

Unsure of herself she undressed and lay on the bed and before long sleep overcame the mental gymnastics.

Saturday Evening.

She lay on the duvet savouring the cosiness of the four-poster. The awnings enclosed her in a cocoon of warm homeliness. Stretching she gave a deep sigh, turned over and snuggled deeper into the feathers, until a guilty conscience got the better of her. She and peered through half open eyes at her watch and jerked upright, suddenly wide awake.

'Oh, my God,' she said aloud, 'Look at the time, I'll never be ready.'

Sliding off the bed, she dashed to the shower discarding underwear as she went.

'Oh, oh, where's my hot brush?'

Conscious of her nudity, but enjoying the covert sexual caress of the air on her body, she did a quick U-turn back to the suitcase stand and hastily unpacked.

She lay things out for the evening and put other unwanted items in drawers and wardrobes and she heaved a huge sigh of relief when she saw that the skirt she was wearing that evening had survived the journey.

The gas hot brush she found lurking in the bag reserved for the shoes. She switched it on and dashed to the shower.

While rummaging in her toilette bag for a shower cap she spilled the contents on the floor.

'Bloody hell!'

She scrambled to pick things up and knocked her elbow on the corner of the vanity unit. Naked and on her hands and knees, she sobbed, berating herself for her clumsiness. 'Silly girl, pull yourself together, you're behaving like a lovesick child, calm down,' and similarly excused herself, 'A lady should make a late entrance.'

Taking a few deep breaths she retrieved the remaining items before stepping into the modern full body shower.

She squirmed as the surrounding jets of water caressed her body, soothing and cleansing. After a few minutes, feeling relaxed, she lowered the temperature slightly and changed the setting to power. The needle jets of water massaged every muscle and explored every crevasse as she sensually used her hands to caress and stroke the pivotal points of her sexuality.

Hormones activated, nerve ends stiffened and tingled with anticipation. She mewed quietly, her breathing became quicker, her stomach muscles tensed and suddenly her body jerked uncontrollably and she moaned with pleasure as multiple waves of passion rolled over her.

She turned off the shower and held on to the tap sucking in huge gulps of air until her breathing became easier and her heart stopped pounding. As the glow of sensitised nerve ends lessened, she sighed, and somewhat bemused she said to herself, 'Where did that come from?'

Stepping out of the shower, she pulled off her shower cap, shook her hair loose and studied herself in the long mirror, still glowing in the aftermath of her exertions. Smiling secretively, she flexed a delicate six pack and did a pirouette, pinched her firm buttocks and said aloud, 'Not bad for fifty.'

Drying herself, she slipped on a set of *'Agent Provocateur'* best and sat before the dressing table mirror. Moments later while she was picking through her jewellery box, there was a light tap on the door.

'It's only me, Mum, can I come in?'

'Yes, it's all clear.'

Elaine entered. 'Mum, you're not dressed and they're assembling in the library for aperitif's.'

'Darling, I'm determined to get it right and I refuse to be

hurried.' Holding one clear pear-drop earring up, she said, 'Should I wear these? I think they would reflect nicely under those chandeliers as they give off the most brilliant rainbow colours under lights, or the guinea with the matching chain loops?'

'I think the pear drops, are you wearing that skirt?'

'Yes.'

Jenny tip-toed over to the bed, picked up calf length black leather skirt, and did a twirl.

'Mum, I'm not sure I like the opposition.'

'Darling, you look wonderful, how can I possibly steal the thunder from someone twenty-five years younger?'

'You're impossible, mother. I'll see you downstairs and don't be too long.'

———

Jenny was met at the bottom of the grand staircase by Andrew dressed in the traditional Ross Red Tartan kilt, dress jacket and doublet and neck cloth.

He held out his hand to help her down the remaining stairs, openly admiring her as he did so. Her skirt fitted close around the hips and flared out from mid-thigh. A cream silk blouse with frill collar cut low enough to show her Ross birthmark and a wide patent leather belt and high-heeled sandals completed her outfit.

'Good evening, Andrew, you look resplendent. I should think any girl would fall for those calves.'

'Thank you, I will escort you to father.'

'By all means, where's Elaine?'

'Circulating, being first lady comes naturally to her.'

They went into the drawing room where the other guests were assembled and into the library where, over her shoulder, she overheard someone say, 'Hey, who's the dame, is that Mrs Baronet?'

Confronted by a crowd of people who turned to observe her, she hesitated, her disguised shyness over-riding her bravado. Alex was quick to notice and came hurrying over.

'There you are, Jenny, how wonderful you look.'

'Why, thank you, Alex.'

He put an arm around her waist. 'Let's mingle, but don't worry we shall be going into the hall in a few moments.'

Her nerves were subsiding and the closeness of him was comforting as the gentleness of the big man surrounded her, it felt so natural.

The deep resounding boom of the huge dinner gong reverberated around the mansion and with stentorian equanimity the major domo announced—'DINNER IS SERVED!'

'Follow me, ladies and gentlemen,' Alex called out to the assembly. 'Look for your place names and be seated as quickly as possible.'

Taking Jenny by the arm he guided her through into the hall.

When everyone was seated, Alex and Jenny in the middle, Elaine and Andrew either side of them and the guests stretching out in front, Alex gave a sharp rap on the table with a wooden gavel to attract attention.

'Once more, ladies and gentlemen, good evening. As we are an uneven number Mr Bloomberg, you will be entertained by a rose on either side. Is that to your liking?'

'Sure is, Baronet, sir.'

'Good, and as you so rightly say, I am the Sixth Baronet of Witchell of the Clan Ross. I welcome you to my table, but first I would like you to meet our guest of honour for tonight. My son's future Mother-in-law, the lady on my left—Mrs Jenny Beaumont.'

'Hear, hear, bravo,' the effervescent Bloomberg shouted, 'I wish my goddam mother-in-law looked like that.'

For his pains he received an elbow in his side from Mrs Bloomberg and the spontaneous laughter which followed broke the ice around the table.

Jenny blushed and laughed along with them.

Alex persisted above the hubbub. 'Jenny's daughter, Elaine, has consented to become the wife of my son, Andrew. Let us raise our glasses to the couple and wish them a long and happy life.'

Applause and well wishes came from the table and Alex had to restore order with a sharp rap of the gavel, 'Ladies and gentlemen, tell the staff your preference for starters and wine and later I have a surprise for you.'

A polite clap went around the table and everyone got down to the business of consuming the first of the night's fare. After twenty minutes of eating and drinking interspersed with small talk the dishes were cleared away and Alex once more called for attention.

'Ladies and gentlemen! I would like you to be upstanding and pay your respects to—'The Haggis.'

The humming of a drone, followed by the full-blooded sound of the bagpipes assailed the room. The piper entered the hall playing—*'Scotland the Brave'*—followed by the chef bearing the Haggis. In steady procession they did a circuit of the hall before coming to a halt in front of Alex. He took a dirk from his stocking and sliced into the haggis.

'Ladies and Gentlemen, I give you—'The Haggis!'

The assembled party raised their glasses. 'The Haggis!'

Alex continued. 'This is not Burns night but, please, try the haggis. *Bon appetite.*'

The Chef went around the table serving the haggis while the remainder of the evening's feast, Venison and Roast beef was laid on the table for the guests to help themselves.

Conversation dwindled as everyone set about devouring the mountain of food set before them.

They were only a few minutes into the meal when Jenny had the feeling of being watched. Looking up she noticed Bloomberg nudge his wife and the guest on the other side of him, say a few words and point with his knife to emphasize something.

She gave herself a quick once over. 'Elaine,' she whispered, 'Is there anything wrong with me?'

'No Mum, you look fine, why?'

'That man Bloomberg is pointing at me.'

'I'm sure you're imagining it. You know these Americans, he probably talks with his hands, don't worry.'

'But I do worry, darling.'

'Mother, don't be silly.'

The remainder of the dinner passed without incident and Alex announced that coffee would be served in the library and the guests were free to wander around the hall to view the artefacts.

Unable to hold her curiosity any longer Jenny stood and looked behind her. There was nothing untoward, only a portrait of a lady wearing a pale blue dress with a Ross tartan sash over her right shoulder and around her waist a gold belcher chain with an ornate enamelled crucifix dangling from it.

She walked over to stand beneath it and thought there was something familiar, but could not make up her mind what? Was she imagining things or did the lady in the picture—smile.

'Don't be daft,' she said mentally, and then the whispering voices began again. She shuddered and felt cold and clammy at the same time.

'Welcome Ross, your birthright awaits. I have been waiting a long time for you.'

Startled, Jenny looked around, shook her head and said quietly to herself, 'I must be getting senile.'

'Hi, there, Mrs Beaumont.' The intervention of Bloomberg made her jump. 'I was just saying how much alike you are to that lady in the portrait. Is she a relative?'

Alex came to the rescue. 'That lady was our Clan benefactor. She is Jane Ross on her fiftieth birthday and when she died forty-two years later she was the last of the direct line. On her death the Clan name, lands and wealth passed to my family. That is why we are called Maxwell-Ross. The additional surname and Coat of Arms was granted by Royal licence in 1840.'

'That's unbelievable. From my seat this lady could have been her sister. The likeness is uncanny and I swear that the eyes moved. They were watching Mrs Beaumont.'

'I can assure you, Mr Bloomberg, Jenny is no relative and the eyes were probably a trick of the lighting. The portrait artist paints the eyes centrally so that they appear to follow you around. The Mona Lisa is a good example.'

'This gentleman here.' Bloomberg pointed to the adjoining painting. 'Who is he?'

'That is William Maxwell-Ross. He is the ancestor who inherited the fortune of Miss Ross.'

Jenny felt the clammy chill envelope her once more accompanied by feminine laughter. Looking around she noticed that nobody else appeared to be affected and she hurriedly suggested they rejoin the others for coffee.

Glancing over her shoulder one last time as they were leaving the hall she smiled up at the picture and walked out shaking her head muttering under her breath, 'Pictures don't wink.' It was then she realized what was familiar about the painting. 'She has a mole just like mine.'

The evening drew to a close and the last of the guests were leaving to go to bed or retiring to the small bar in the West wing. Alex put his arm around Jenny and asked if she would join him for a nightcap in the drawing room.

Bending backwards to look up to him, enjoying the cosiness of his arm, she obliged by giving him a huge smile and nodding, 'Yes,' at the same time feeling uncomfortable at the thought that she had feelings for this man who should by rights be her enemy.

He escorted her through to the drawing room and made sure she was settled comfortably on one of the sofas.

'Would you like a last glass of champagne, or would you prefer something stronger?'

'Champers would do fine, thank you.'

'I'll just pop through to the library, there doesn't appear to be any left here. I won't keep you.'

'Alex, you don't have to.'

'Oh, but I do. One moment.'

She felt at home in the warmth of the fire. 'Elaine was right,' she thought, 'this big red pile is quite homely.'

Alex returned with two flutes, gave her one and flushing slightly asked if he may sit beside her.

'Of course, Alex, I wouldn't have it any other way.' Taking a sip she turned to him and said, 'It's been a lovely evening, Alex. Thank you for having me. I've only been here a short while and I feel comfortable already.'

'The pleasure is all mine, Jenny. This house needs someone like you in it. The feminine touch is missing around here although Elaine has brightened it up immensely.'

'Alex, that almost sounded like a proposal.'

'Oh! I... I...,' he stammered in confusion. 'I do apologise, I didn't mean to offend, I mean, oh dear.'

She took his hand. 'Alex, you poor boy, I'm not offended. In fact I'm quite flattered, although it is rather sudden. Changing the subject, Alex. I know it's been ten years since you lost your wife, has there been anyone else?'

'No. I immersed myself in this place and time passed. There

were one or two flings, but no one caught my attention, until you came along.'

She squeezed his hand. 'Do you have any other children besides Andrew?'

'No. There were complications when he was born which meant Sarah, that was my wife, could have no more children. A bit sad really as we had planned on two. Andrew makes up for the disappointment though. He has been the ideal son all his life, but don't you ever tell him. Elaine makes a lot of difference, she is like a daughter to me. We get on wonderfully well. It's a pity Sarah never met her as they are very much alike. How about you?'

'Elaine, of course, and then there is her brother, Ian, in Australia. He's been over there ten years now.'

'Is he doing alright?'

'He's fine. He has his own computer business, a partner and two children. Goodness me, look at the time, I really must be going to bed.'

'Let me show you to your room.'

'You don't have to, I can manage.'

'I insist, it is the Laird's duty to look after his guests, and besides, I enjoy your company.'

'I'm flattered, Alex, but don't stop.'

Alex put his arm around her and they made their way upstairs and stopped outside Jenny's room. She opened the door and left it ajar, before turning to him.

'I've enjoyed being here, Alex. Thank you once again for a lovely evening.'

'It's an honour and a pleasure,' he took her hand and kissed it, 'Goodnight,' and he made to turn away.

'Alex.'

'Yes.'

She felt her strategic nerve ends tingling, but gently said, 'You're too old fashioned, goodnight.'

Closing the door behind her, she leaned against it and let out a sigh. 'This is not right surely. I didn't come here to do this.'

'I have told you, Jenny Ross. Follow your heart.'

Jenny's heart skipped a beat and her body stiffened. In the shadows on the far side of the room she could make out the misty figure from the portrait.

Suppressing the desire to run from the room, she said, 'It's Jane isn't it? What do you want?'

The ghostly figure replied. 'Myself and many friends would like to restore the family fortunes, although, Lord help us, there is very little left after the Maxwell's squandered it. It has been so long coming but now the time is right. You have found your way here and here you should stay.'

'I didn't come to claim any title or wealth. My daughter is marrying the son.'

'And you are falling in love with the father, how appropriate. I will be able to rest peacefully and you will be able to live the rest of your life happily.'

'You make it sound so cold, it wasn't planned.'

An urgent knocking on the door broke the spell. 'Mum, it's me can I come in.'

The vision of Jane Ross spoke one last time before disappearing. 'Be careful, Ross. There are evil forces about who wish you harm. You had better let her in.'

'Come in,' Jenny blurted out.

Elaine entered the room. 'Mum who were you talking to,' she gave an involuntary shiver, 'It's cold in here.'

'Hello dear, you're up late,' Jenny said a little too light heartedly to be convincing; 'I was having a little sing to myself. I've had such a lovely time I was trying to hang on to the atmosphere.'

'I heard talking as I was going past the door.'

'Darling, there's no one here and I certainly don't talk to myself.' She glanced around to make sure.

'Then why are you acting so nervously?'

'Oh, darling, do stop, I am getting a headache and it's way past my bedtime.'

'Okay. Mum, do you like Alex?'

'Yes, very much so.'

'Good, I think he fancies you.'

'I shall keep that in mind, dear. Now let me go to bed.'

Elaine crossed the room and kissed her mother on the cheek.

'Are you sure you're alright?'

'Yes, yes, now run along.'

When the door closed she had another nervous look around before preparing for bed.

***

21

Sunday

That it was morning there was no doubt as Jenny could see daylight forcing its way around the heavy brocade curtains. That she also had a headache there was also no doubt as the thumping in her head reminded her.

'I should never have had that last glass of champagne. Why not,' she reasoned, 'it was nice, and I haven't enjoyed myself so much for a long time.'

Easing herself up, she filled a tumbler with water from the decanter on the bedside table and had a long drink in an effort to relieve the pounding behind her eyes.

With a moan, she flopped back, but not for long, as the revving of high-powered engines and loud voices shattered her peace.

'Who's making a noise at this time of the morning?'

Pushing herself up onto her elbows, she peeked at the clock.

'My goodness, it can't be.' She was fully awake now. 'Oh, my God, nine thirty.'

Frantically she rushed over to open the curtains and let the full blaze of sunshine into the room.

'What's going on?'

With the muffling effect of the curtains removed the roar of a Rolls Royce V12 engine reverberated around the room and looking out over the parkland towards the woods she saw a large tank moving through the trees followed by a smaller one.

'Don't tell me he lets the Army use his land on a Sunday. Haven't they heard it's a day of rest, we lie in, at least civilised people do.'

Resigned now to staying up, she flung off her nightdress and bolted for the bathroom.

Feeling much refreshed after her shower, dressed in slacks and sleeveless T-shirt she made her way down to the lower floor where Elaine greeted her with a peck on the cheek.

'Good morning, Mum, how are you this morning?'

'I'm fine, thank you. Why didn't you wake me?'

'Mum, you're on holiday, besides, Alex told me not to disturb you. He sends his apologies, but he and Andrew are out directing operations for the guests.'

'Which guests are those, darling? I saw tanks driving through the grounds, is it the Army?'

'No Mum, they have a collection of old army vehicles here. It's a hobby of Alex's. He was in an armoured Regiment when he was in the Services so now he has a museum of World War two and many more modern army vehicles. The guests are allowed to drive them as it's all part of their weekend. Have some breakfast and we'll go and join them.'

Feeling much refreshed after a bite to eat and coffee, they made their way around the back of the house and through the woods to the Museum a little way from the house.

Breaking away from a party of tourists, Andrew greeted them both with a peck on the cheek. 'Good morning, how are we? Dad won't be long, he's near the end of a drive with our Mr Bloomberg. Give me one moment, I have to get this little party of ramblers on their way, take Mum into the Museum, Elaine, darling.'

'Come on, Mum, I hope you like khaki.'

Alex joined them a little later. 'Good morning, ladies, did you sleep well, Jenny?'

'Yes thanks, although it was a bit of a shock to see the Seventh Cavalry.'

'That's Stan's department. A wonderful chap, ex-Army technician, he services everything and drives them whenever anyone wants to try them out. I can drive them all modestly, but to get reality I leave it to the expert. Would you like to try? He loves teaching the ladies.'

'Oh, I'm not sure I should.'

'Come on, I'll introduce you.'

Taking her hand, he led her outside to where the tank was parked on the hard standing.

'Wait here, he's probably drinking tea somewhere.'

Moments later, he reappeared accompanied by a man about

the same age, of slim build with a shock of grey wavy hair, carrying a small stepladder.

'Stan, meet Elaine's mother, Jenny.'

'Morning, ma'am, excuse me not shaking hands, but I've been doing a spot of greasing, nice to meet you.'

'Please call me Jenny.'

'So you want to drive a tank, eh?'

'Not really, I've been talked into it,' she said, nodding towards Alex.

'Don't worry, if you're anything like your daughter you'll find it easy.'

'Elaine, you never told me about driving tanks.'

'I didn't want to worry you, Mum. It's not exactly a girly thing is it?'

Stan placed the steps at the front of the vehicle. 'Right, ma'am, up you go onto the trackguard and then lower yourself into that hole there. You're about the right size for a tank driver. Hold it one moment!' He dashed off to return moments later with a pair of overalls. 'Try these for size.'

Suitably attired, she lowered herself into the driver's hatch. Stan climbed up and sat to the right, while Alex wedged himself over on the left against the turret, which was in the reverse position.

'Right, ma'am, this is a Mark 10 Centurion tank. Seat adjustment is just like a car. Down between your legs for backwards and forwards...'

'That's not all that's between the legs. What's this thing?'

'That's the gear stick.'

'Oh, very macho.'

There was spontaneous laughter all round and she blushed.

'Mother, behave yourself.'

Stan brought her attention back to things in hand. 'Before we were interrupted, the up and down is that handle at the side. Raise your chin above the front edge and then pull forward until you can depress the clutch comfortably. Press the pedal a few times, is it okay?'

'Yes, but surprisingly light for such a big vehicle.'

'Now fasten the seat harness, pull down on those toggles to tighten it. By your right arm is a red switch, turn it on. Directly above your right knee is the control panel. Turn the ignition switch to on, press the green button, at the same time gently depress the throttle. As soon as you hear the engine, lift off.'

Following the instructions, she was surprised that the engine did not make more noise, feeling, rather than hearing a deep rumble coming from the rear.

She gave a little wave to Elaine who had moved the steps.

'Steering is by those levers either side of your legs, gears the same as your car. Select first, build the revs and off we go.'

Gingerly she let out the clutch and stalled. 'Oh dear.'

'Don't worry, ma'am. This thing weighs over forty tons so give it a few more revs. Let's go.'

'I do wish you would call me Jenny, you make me sound like an old maid or royalty, and I'm neither.'

She went through the routine again and this time managed a reasonable, if somewhat jerky start.

'Now stop, into neutral and pull your left lever and rev the engine. Stop, now the other way, stop.' He quickly explained double de-clutching to change gear. 'Okay, Jenny, ma'am, let's go.'

They moved off the hard standing onto a track and disappeared into the woodland.

Safely parked some half an hour later, she clambered out and slid off the front. As she dropped to the floor, Alex caught her and clasped her to him.

Looking up to him, her face flushed with excitement, she said, 'Oh Alex that was wonderful, can I do it again sometime, I'll pay you for the petrol.'

'Yes you can, and no you can't.' He bent to kiss her and then remembered the company.

She whispered, 'You can, you know.'

He brushed a hair from her face. 'Thank you, I'm a little shy, and I am not sure what Elaine would say. Come on, let's go to the house and have coffee, thanks, Stan.'

'Yes, thank you, Stan. Have you thought of doing driving instruction for a living?'

'No maa-ah, Jenny, I haven't the nerves for it.'

'Jenny,' Alex intervened, 'I would like to speak with Stan for a moment. You go on ahead and I'll meet you in the drawing room.'

'Of course, I'll walk through the gardens for a while.'

The gardens were only a short distance away, situated at the east end of the house and she wandered aimlessly for ten minutes to soak up the country air before she made her way along the path at the side of the house.

Suddenly, an invisible wall stopped her. She was unable to move. Something was holding her back and try as she might she couldn't put one foot in front of the other. Paroxysms of fear swept over her.

'Help! Anyone there, I can't move, help!'

Crumbling masonry began falling around her and looking up she realised she was directly beneath the tall east-end chimney which was teetering on its base.

In sheer terror, she shouted again. 'Help, help! Someone help!'

The stack broke loose and began tumbling towards her as Andrew came around the corner.

'Help,' she cried.

Taking in the situation quickly, Andrew desperately covered the ten metres between them and hurled himself forward in a rugby tackle, taking Jenny around the waist and knocking her to the ground.

Masonry exploded around them as it crashed to earth where moments before Jenny had been transfixed.

'How the bloody hell did that happen? Are you okay?' Andrew helped her to her feet, dusting her down as she removed bits of debris from her hair.

Alex came running around the corner. 'What's going on? Jenny, are you alright?' He threw his arms around her and pulling a handkerchief from his pocket he wiped her face and dabbed at a couple of scratches. 'Are you hurt anywhere?'

'No, only my ego. Where's Andrew, he saved me. I can't understand it, I couldn't move. I was paralysed. Oh, Andrew, thank you so much, are you alright?'

'Yes, I'm fine, Dad, didn't we have that chimney fixed last year after the winds?'

'Yes. I'll get on to the builders, they can return and do a proper job. Come on, Jenny, let's get you tidied up. I think a strong pick me up is required.'

He hooked an arm around her and helped her into the house.

Indoors Jenny reached up and kissed him on the cheek. 'I'll lie down for a while, Alex. You have that drink. I think you need it more than me.'

Sunday afternoon

Much refreshed after her rest, Jenny joined the others in the kitchen for lunch and Alex greeted her enthusiastically, 'Come in, come in, how are you, are you quite recovered?'

'Yes, I'm fine, honestly, a little peckish though.'

'Grab a seat while I sort the out the tea, meanwhile you dig into that pile of sandwiches and cakes.'

'Why did you make all these, there are far too many.'

'I can't tell a lie, Jenny, the chef sends them over from the guests' restaurant.'

'They do well over there, what do you do for your evening catering?'

'We send out for a takeaway or we eat the same as the guests. It keeps the staff on their toes as a lot of our business is done by reference.'

'Do you get many return bookings?'

'Yes we do, most come for the rest away from the big city and if we can keep them out of the local hotel, the chefs have done their job.'

'Alex, to change the subject, I would like to ask a question. Is this place haunted? I mean, aah... I don't believe in ghosts normally.'

'It has been alleged that we have residents from the after life. A lady in blue is the most reported and an old man in a grey frock coat. The Americans love it so we don't discourage the rumours. Why, you're not worried are you?'

'No, no. It just seems the sort of place that should be.'

'Oh, I see. Is that incident still troubling you? I tell you what. Let's go for a drive this afternoon. We'll leave this pair to look after the guests and I will show you around the Borders countryside. It has a great history. Is that alright with you two?'

'I'm okay,' Andrew replied. 'How about you Elaine?'

'Fine by me, you fuddy-duddies buzz off, we can handle it.'

'We've been dismissed, Alex.'

—

They were driving along the border that follows the river Tweed, through countryside where even the most hardened of city-dwellers would have their senses awakened.

The appeal to the eye was everywhere. Little glens, belts of trees, the burbling of water tumbling over the pebbled beds of small burns. All in the majestic sweep of moorlands with clouds bouncing off the hilltops.

Alex pulled over before they reached Kelso, short of the bridge that crossed the river.

'How's that for a view. The bridge, does it look familiar, Jenny?'

'I'm not much on bridges, Alex, but I have a feeling that I have seen something similar.'

'It was designed by Rennie, the man who built Waterloo Bridge. Some would say it was a try out.'

'I love that view, Alex. Is that Kelso Castle in the background?'

'Close. It's the ruin of Kelso Abbey. Let's have a look at the town.'

Moments later they entered the town square.

'Oh, Alex you were right, it is so French. Shutters and a Gendarme are all that's missing.'

'I believe our architects got their influence from France with our Royalty spending a lot of time there. It is funny though that our most French town never provided any recruits to Bonnie Prince Charlie's Army.'

'Alex, you're a fountain of knowledge.'

'Most of it useless, I'm afraid, but you would be surprised at the questions we get asked over dinner so the information I absorbed on local history comes in handy. Come on let's walk a little.'

They walked arm in arm into the square in the heart of Kelso.

'An interesting place this, Jenny. In **1715** James Stuart was proclaimed James VIII in this very square and thirty years later came Charles Stuart with his army. Perhaps the town has never recovered from the French it heard in '45.'

They continued their journey through the Borders, and when they arrived in Selkirk Alex suggested a cup of tea. They parked a short way from the market place with its oddly spired town hall and made their way to the Fleece hotel.

'Oh, Alex, this town is frenchified also. It only needs the three musketeers.'

'You have an imagination very much like mine, Jenny.'

They settled into the historic atmosphere with its low beams and panelling. Foregoing the array of offerings that go with a Scottish tea, they settled for a pot of tea and biscuits and after a few minutes of small talk, Alex reached across and took her hand.

'Jenny?'

'Yes, Alex.'

'I feel so awkward. I've forgotten how to do this.'

'Don't be shy, Alex.'

'Ahem... Jenny, could you possibly stay on for a little while longer instead of going home tomorrow. I enjoy your company so much I feel I have known you forever. Err... I... Oh... I feel so stupid, like a tongue-tied teenager.'

'It's all so sudden, Alex.'

'Oh, I'm sorry. I do apologise. Have I offended you? It's,...aah...It's. I'm making a fool of myself aren't I?'

'No, you're not. Alex. Thank you for asking, and yes, I would love to. I can manage, Elaine always says I travel with far too much and as she and I are both the same size I can borrow off her.'

'You won't get in trouble at work will you?'

'No. I am of independent means so I only do voluntary work. A quick call in the morning will sort that out, and Alex?'

'Yes.'

'I like your company also and I'm sure Elaine will approve.'

'Jenny, you make me a happy man. Let's take a walk and then make our way back home.'

They wandered around the town until they came to a memorial monument with just three words upon it—*O Flodden Field.**

'Oh, how sad that inscription, Alex. Is Flodden near here? I heard of it in history lessons, but that's all.'

'It's a little way out of town. A stone cross on top of a green hill is all that marks one of Scotland's saddest occasions and Scotland became a graveyard after that battle, one they should have won.

'All battles are sad, Alex, you must tell me more, later. Let's go back and I shall pass judgement on your guest's cuisine.'

Later that evening, when they were alone in the drawing room with only a fire and the wall lights for illumination Jenny took his arm.

'Alex, sit closer.'

'Err…, yes, can I get you a drink first?'

'Please, a glass of red wine will finish the evening nicely.'

He poured the wine and rejoined her on the sofa.

She pulled him to her and keeping hold she laid against shoulder. 'This is cosy, Alex. Don't be shy, I feel content tonight. I haven't felt like this for a long time and thank you for a lovely day.'

He placed a hand casually on her thigh. 'It gave me great pleasure to have you there with me. Do you believe in love at first sight? There I go again, like some love struck adolescent.'

'Yes I do, or as my husband would say—Love at first smell. He used to ramble on about pheromones or something.'

'You loved your husband dearly, do you miss him, I mean…'

'I know what you mean Alex, dear. Yes, I miss him a lot. We were good friends as well as lovers, but we made an agreement that if either of us passed away early and the other was still young enough to enjoy another relationship they must not go through life grieving. What about you?'

'I've been alone ten years now, so I don't think she would mind and like I said previously—I've never met anyone before you I had feelings for.'

He turned towards her and looked into her eyes. 'Jenny, I'm really taken by you. I light up at the very sight of you, and I miss you when you leave the room. Oh, there I go again.'

'Don't stop. Kiss me…'

***

22

Monday.

This day came with its own problems, not least, what was she going to wear? A suitcase suitable for a weekend had its limitations.
Clean underwear packed for the return journey would suffice for today but washing and drying used clothes would need some organising. Elaine's knicker drawer was definitely going to come in handy. Size was not a problem but her daughter's taste was mostly of the thong variety and she detested them.

'Beggars can't be choosers,' she mused.

A quick shower refreshed her and checking the weather, she decided on a jumper rather than a T-shirt. The previous days slacks were brought into service and with a quick pat of her hair she made her way downstairs to breakfast.

In the kitchen, Lily greeted her warmly. 'Good morning, ma'am.'

'Lily, please call me Jenny. You make me feel old.'

They both laughed simultaneously for a moment or two before Lily said, 'Jenny it is. Can I get you some breakfast, the others are all done and out to work.'

'Yes please, have you any muesli?'

'We have it all. Elaine has similar tastes. She does enjoy it here and she's one of the family now. I'm sure Alex can't wait for them to get married and then maybe he can relax a little. There I go chatting away. Excuse me while I get your breakfast.'

Jenny propped herself up on a kitchen stool. 'You don't mind me coming into your domain, do you?'

'No, not at all, everyone else does. Besides I enjoy the company. It gives me a good excuse for a cup of tea and a chat.'

'Is Alex a good employer?'

'Oh, yes, he just leaves me to get on with it while he runs the business.'

'I notice you only have Sunday off.'

'Officially I have Thursdays off as well, but I quite often work. Being a widow, I wouldn't know what to do with myself if I didn't work.'

Jenny thought she probably wouldn't take kindly to a new woman moving in to her territory either. Lily placed a steaming mug of fresh coffee and a bowl of muesli in front of her. 'That's lovely, thank you.'

For a few minutes there was silence while she ate, but eager to cement the friendship Jenny spoke immediately she had finished.

'Lily, have you worked here long?'

'Twelve years, all told. Two as cleaner before the mistress died and after that, Alex, Mr Maxwell-Ross, that is, asked me to stay on as housekeeper.'

'I'm not being nosy, Lily, but have you noticed or felt anything strange about this place?'

'Like what specifically?'

'It's very hard to explain. You know that feeling you get when you're being watched as if there's someone there.'

'You mean is this place haunted? I'll say it is.'

'Please don't think me silly, but I think I have been visited by a ghost. I spoke to her. Either that or I was dreaming.'

'That will be Jane, the lady in the picture. There's supposed to be another one, as yet unidentified. People have reported hearing two people arguing, but we are used to it and leave them to it. In fact, Alex actively advertises it, especially in America. He says it brings the punters in.'

'I see, but it's a little bit nerve racking to have that experience first hand. Before I came here I didn't believe in ghosts. I treated it as some sort of myth or hallucination. Now I'm not so sure.'

'I think there was some shifty goings on in the early days of this castle and there is a room at the top of the tower that I won't go in. It's done out in the most unusual way and it frightens me. I don't know why he doesn't redecorate it.'

'I suppose it's because the castle and its contents are a family heirloom and he doesn't wish to spoil the history attached to it.'

'I've never thought of that, more coffee?'

'Yes, please, and where is everybody?'

'Mondays are change over days. Old guests out and new ones in. They are over in the West wing helping the weekenders move out and later today we have a crowd of salesmen on one of those corporate do's, moving in. Lots of testosterone flying around and rowdiness for a week and they make such a mess. I don't know why he puts up with it.'

'Money, Lily. It must take a lot to run this place.'

'Yes, it's hard work. Alex hasn't taken a holiday since the mistress passed away and some days he looks totally worn out. He likes it when the youngsters are here. It gives him a much wanted break.'

Jenny nodded in agreement. 'Thanks for breakfast, Lily. I'll go and find the others and see if I can do something useful.'

'My pleasure, feel free to pop in, I enjoy a chat.'

Jenny left the kitchen and spent the next fifteen minutes exploring the nooks and crannies on the way to the West wing.

—

'Hi, Mum, you must have slept well?'

'Yes I did.' She gave Elaine a peck on the cheek. 'That bed's lovely, it wraps itself around you but I spent a little time chatting to Lily over breakfast.'

'Lily likes you. She told me what a pleasure it was to speak to someone her own age.'

'I'm glad to have some uses. What are we doing today?'

'I thought we might go shopping in Berwick. The boys are busy with change over so we won't be missed. You'll like Berwick, Mum. It's a bit like Chester.'

'Okay, but what am I going to wear?'

At that moment Alex joined them and kissed Jenny on the cheek.

'Good morning. Did you sleep well?'

'Yes, thanks, Alex. I was telling Elaine how comfortable that bed is.'

'You don't know how glad I am to hear those words. I worried when we were preparing the room if that bed was going to be all right. It's antique with a modern mattress.'

'Mum and I were just planning a day's shopping in Berwick, Alex.'

'What a coincidence! I'm going to the Trading Estate to pick up some bits for Stan. How about I drop you off and join you for lunch at the *Three Bells* later?'

'That would be lovely, is that alright, Elaine?'

'Yes, let's be chauffeured.'

'That's settled, Alex, you've got the job.' Jenny linked arms with her daughter as they turned to go back into the main house. 'Elaine, I want to speak to you about clothes.'

Alex stood and watched as mother and daughter, so much alike, disappeared, deep in conversation. It was then he realized how fully he missed her whenever she left his company.

—

In Berwick the girls disappeared into the backyards and narrow streets of the historic town to indulge in retail therapy while Alex went about his business.

Sitting in the hotel some time later he anxiously looked at his watch and wondered how much time women needed for shopping. Resisting the temptation to phone he decided to give them a little more time. Not that he minded waiting, he liked the hospitable atmosphere of the 18th century hostelry. It gave him a pleasant respite from the hurly burly of running the castle.

Five minutes later the reason for his being there came through the door looking suitably flushed with their exertions and laden down with innumerable bags. He got to his feet to greet them and put his arm around Jenny to give her a hug.

'I had given you up for lost. Have you left anything for anyone else?'

'Alex, dear, it's not everyday I get to shop with my daughter. We've had a wonderful time and got quite carried away. We haven't kept you long, have we?'

Tongue in cheek he replied, 'No, I've only been here a few minutes.'

Jenny noticed the near empty glass and guessed he was being economical with the truth.

'Right ladies, now you're settled, what'll you have?'

'A plate of mixed sandwiches and a glass of red wine,' they replied simultaneously.

He gave their order and a coffee for himself and then enquired as to what they had been up to realising too late the folly of his query as the contents of numerous bags were revealed with accompanying anecdotes of changing rooms and shops they had visited. Their laughter raised a few eyebrows amongst other patrons in the library dull atmosphere, but he enjoyed the attention feeling rather proud to be in the company of his two attractive companions.

Lunch arrived before the pile of assorted ladies apparel could overwhelm the table and decorum was restored once more

Sandwiches and two glasses of wine later they made their way reluctantly to the Range Rover and home in high spirits.

Dumping their bags the girls joined the men who were busy with the new arrivals and it was a couple of hours before they were able to relax over a cup of tea and then get ready for dinner.

After dinner Jenny and Alex excused themselves and retired to the lounge leaving the youngsters to do their own thing.

Alex poured two glasses of wine and sat close to her unconsciously resting a hand on her thigh while they talked about the events of the day. With a sudden change of subject he surprised her by saying.

'Jenny, please don't think me forward. I enjoy your company so much. Oh dear, I feel such an utter fool. How is it we forget the ritual of courtship?'

'Alex, the feeling is mutual. I'm very comfortable in your company the like of which I have never experienced since I was courting Brian.'

At the mention of her husband's name he quickly removed his hand.

'Oh, please don't Alex. It felt so right and I didn't mind at all.'

'Are you sure, I didn't mean to be so presumptuous.'

'Oh, oh, this sounds serious.'

'I know we've only known each other for a short time, Jenny, but would you consider coming to live here?'

'I can't answer you straight away, Alex, but I will give it some thought, I promise you. I like you very much, in fact, I think I'm falling in love with you. Every time I see you I get a lump in my throat and a lovely cosy feeling, but I will not rush. To do something in haste or lust would be terrible. Elaine, by the way, thinks it would be a wonderful idea. Only today she said a double wedding would be nice. She is such a romantic.'

'I understand your feelings and reasoning Jenny and likewise I miss you when you're not around. Don't take too long.'

'Alex, look at me. Now kiss me and shut-up.'

He needed no second bidding and they became lost in each other, the large sofa enveloping their passion. After a few moments she whispered, 'Alex, let's go somewhere more private.'

***

23

Tuesday.

Jenny awoke feeling at ease with the world and sleepily stretched. Reaching behind her she was disappointed to find the bed empty, but she could still feel the warmth of his body. She rolled over, pulled his pillow into her, and cuddled it.

It was two years since her husband had passed away and although there had been the odd date and invitations by well meaning friends, this was the first man who had stirred her feelings and reached into her affections with such an impact. She was lucky enough to have met two men in her life who had affected her this way when most women had trouble finding one.

At that moment she felt the luckiest woman in the world and nuzzled his pillow harder with the thought that breakfast would have been late that morning if he had dallied a little longer.

He had been gentle and with his old-fashioned manners had made her feel like the only woman in the world. His lovemaking was tender and unselfish, fulfilling her needs as well as his own. Passionate waves of sensuality had flowed through her on a conveyor belt.

That this man had stepped into her life was now causing doubts as well as feelings of well-being. It created a dichotomy that she was not sure how to manage.

Rolling onto her back she mulled over her crisis. She had accepted the invitation with the knowledge that the fortunes of the Maxwell-Ross family were the result of the fraud which had robbed her ancestors of their rightful inheritance. This had made her instinctively dislike them, but on the other hand there was the need to see what the opposition was like.

The coincidence of her daughter meeting and falling in love with the heir to this inheritance was fate, as was her meeting with Alex. Memories of the previous night's passion flooded back and the contradiction of emotions clashed. Suddenly she doubted herself.

Speaking out aloud, she said, 'Jane Ross, to quote an Oliver

Hardy classic—'What a fine mess you've got me into.'

Her heart skipped a beat when a familiar voice answered her whimsical query.

'Kismet, Ross. Let love take its course and you will achieve three things. Happiness. You will release me from my quest and last, but not least, an evil wrong will have been righted. You must beware, Ross, your path is not easy. There are evil powers who will try to thwart you in your endeavour. Persevere, an unrequited love is not for you as it was for me.'

The feeling of a presence disappeared.

'Jane, don't go, help me, tell me more.' But she was left with her own thoughts. After a few moments reflection she decided the message had been plain enough. That she must do away with any feelings of revenge to right what had been an enormous wrong to her family, but follow her instincts about her relationship with Alex.

'The result will be the same,' she mused, 'so I may as well enjoy it.'

In a happier frame of mind, she allowed the shower to have its way with her, dressed, and made her way down to breakfast where, still glowing from her exertions, she greeted Elaine and Andrew. 'Good morning you pair,'

They looked at each other and nodded knowingly. 'Morning Mum, you sound happy this morning.'

'I am, dear. A great weight has been lifted from me and I have made a decision about my life. I'll tell you some other time.'

Lily entered the room at the sound of her voice. 'Morning, ma'am, what can I get you?'

'Could I have lots of coffee and some Muesli, please, Lily, and do call me Jenny.'

'Certainly, it won't take a minute.'

She turned to make her way back to the kitchen and Jenny followed her out.

'Lily?'

'Yes, maa... Jenny.'

'Lily, can you recommend a local hairdresser?'

'Yes. The little place I go to in the village, Elaine uses it too. Young Sally is very good. You take your breakfast through while I make a phone call. Today alright?'

'That's fine if she can manage it.'

Jenny returned to the dining room to continue her conversation with the two youngsters and a few minutes later Lily popped her head around the door.

'Jenny, any time after eleven o' clock, being Tuesday it's very quiet.'

'Thanks, Lily.'

Jenny finished her breakfast and caught up on the days news before setting off in search of Alex.

Wandering aimlessly she walked through the gardens, looked at the scaffolding around the chimney and wondered with idle curiosity what had caused the sudden collapse which so nearly could have had more serious consequences.

She inhaled the smell of the flowers and herbs and decided all was well and with some certainty she felt she liked this sandstone monolith even though it had nearly killed her.

Still musing she bumped into Alex amongst his toys in the living Military museum. He clambered out of a restored WW11 half-track on which he had been working and without thinking, enveloped her in a bear hug.

'Good morning, Jenny, you're a sight for sore eyes, did you sleep well?'

She revelled in the warmth of the big man and almost purring, replied, 'Yes,' and bending slightly backwards thrust her hips into him. 'Did you?'

'I most certainly did, but it was a great effort to get up this morning.'

'You should have stayed, I missed you.'

He looked down at her and disregarding Stan's presence kissed her. She responded readily and if it were possible she pressed herself into him even tighter.

'Alex?'

'Yes, love.'

Stan's eyes rolled heavenwards. 'Oh Jeez.' he muttered under his breath. He gave a polite cough, 'I'll be getting on then, Mr Maxwell?'

'Oh, oh, yes, please do, my apologies, and one more thing

while I remember. How would you like a couple of days off next week and travel down to Duxford. They have a spare Jeep. Give it the once over and tell me what you think.'

'Gladly, but do we need another?'

'Yes, theirs is a Ford. I thought it would complement the Willys.'

'I see. In that case the half-track can wait. I'll make sure the running equipment is in good order to minimize problems while I'm away.'

'I shouldn't worry too much. We have an easy week ahead. There's only a London fashion house coming to do a shoot amongst some Military vehicles. Apparently camouflage is all the rage. It's a pity you're away to miss those fashion models lying around the place.'

'Are you sure you want me to go? Won't you need someone to help them on and off things? There might be a young thing looking for a father figure.'

They laughed simultaneously. 'You'll need more than a week to get into training, Stan. Stamina is what you need to keep up with the greyhounds of the modelling world.'

'Aye, happen you're right, be nice to try though.'

Alex put his arm around Jenny's shoulder. 'You know Jenny, I swear he's turning into a dirty old man. He's been around vehicles to long, that's his trouble. Let's go for a walk and leave him to his dreams.'

'We can't go too far, I have to go to the hairdressers.'

She hooked an arm into his and they wandered off in the direction of the woods.

Stan stood and watched them thoughtfully for a moment, nodded his head as if in agreement with himself, turned on his heel and went to look after his collection of older memories.

———

Lost in their own thoughts for several minutes they did not speak, each of them revelling in the company of the other. They turned off the metalled road and onto a footpath that took them into the woodland.

An eerie silence descended. The wildlife guardians of the wood silently watched the intruders in their habitat. Only the intelligent red squirrel frolicked around unconcerned, his bright eyes always alert for a tit-bit.

The two lovers walked on unaware of the consternation they were causing. Gradually, sensing they were not in danger the unseen occupants of the wood became alive once more, the interwoven sounds making a rich pattern for lovers to canoodle.

Jenny and Alex were unaware of the goings on in the wildlife city around them cocooned as they were by the nearness of each other as they walked hand in hand.

Suddenly, each feeling the other's mood, they stopped. He bent to kiss her. 'Jenny! I love you.'

They kissed passionately. 'Alex, the feelings are mutual. I did miss you this morning. Will you stay tonight, every night?'

'Yes, but are you sure that's what you want?'

'Alex Maxwell-Ross! I don't offer my body to anybody. You big Bear, of course it's what I want.'

Together they laughed and threw themselves into each other's arms once more. For a few minutes they clawed, hugged and fondled, each trying to consume the other with their passion blissfully unaware of their wildlife audience, who, smelling pheromones watched with interest the two humans lost for a moment in time, only aware of each other.

Breathlessly she pulled away. 'It's... Aah... It's time to go, Alex. I promised to be at the hairdressers by eleven and I'm afraid if we don't go now we may get caught *in flagranté delictö.*'

He looked down at her, his chest heaving. 'You're right on both counts. I don't think you're good for me, Jenny Beaumont.'

'Oh! Why's that then?' She teased him, as she knew what he meant. 'Wrong class are we?'

'Ohh... Erh... I didn't, oh dear,' he stuttered.

She laughed at his embarrassment.

'I mean.' He grabbed her and pulled her to him. 'I love you and you are a bad influence on me. You make me forget I have a business to run, you minx.' He kissed her hard. 'Come on, let's go before we are infra, whatever it is. I flunked Latin at school.'

They made their way back to the house, arms linked, without a care in the world.

They stopped at the front of the house and she leaned back to look up at him. 'Thank you Alex, I'll just pop in for my handbag and I'll be off. I'm stopping at the Stag for lunch on Lily's advice so I'll see you sometime this afternoon. You should delegate more often and take some of the weight off your shoulders.'

'You're right, I should, maybe I can persuade the youngsters to take over when they have graduated, although I think Andrew has his heart set on a practice in Edinburgh'

He waited while she retrieved her bag and said, 'Take care, Jenny.'

They kissed and he watched and admired as she drove off, handling the big turbo car with ease. 'I must tell her about speed limits,' he mused.

The drive to the village took a few minutes and she parked outside the *Stag* and breezed into the hairdressers feeling at ease with the world.

She was greeted by the practised cordiality of Sally the hairdresser. 'Good morning, you're Elaine's Mum, I can tell. You're so alike.'

'Yes, I am, but please don't tell Elaine that, she thinks everyone is saying she looks older than she really is.'

Settling into the offered chair she left herself to the ministrations of the staff and forgot the world for an hour or so.

Forgoing the recommended teacakes at the Stag she chose instead to have a leisurely lunch of salmon sandwiches washed down with a glass of red wine before returning to the castle.

On the short drive back she noticed a dark cloud had gathered over the castle grounds. 'Odd,' she thought, 'It's such a nice day. Probably a summer storm brewing,'

Swinging into the gateway she operated the remote control and proceeded up the drive feeling relaxed and happy with life. She was driving, out of character, at a steady pace, when, suddenly, as she drew level with an old gnarled oak, there was a searing, crackling flash and a thunderous explosion and a bolt of lightning struck the old tree, tearing it from its roots. It hung for a moment suspended on invisible wires, before, with increasing momentum it toppled towards the roadway.

Stunned and blinded by the explosion she braked hard. Some

sixth sense made her glance at the falling tree and realising the danger she rammed the gear lever into reverse and gunned the throttle.

The power of the engine made the wheels spin holding her transfixed for a perilous second while the tree plunged towards her.

She screamed in panic willing the car to move. At last, the wheels gripped and thrust the car backwards and the windscreen imploded as a 300-year-old gnarled branch smashed into it.

The tree enveloped the car holding it in a vice like grip and she instinctively buried her face in her hands as splinters of wood and shards of glass spun around her.

After what seemed like minutes, although in reality only seconds, everything went quiet, but the sensation of evil throaty laughter and the overpowering smell of rotting vegetation filtered through to her numbed brain.

Wrinkling her nose in disgust and with only her own thoughts to keep her from hysterics she managed to keep her self-control. 'Who could be laughing at a time like this,' she wondered. Moments elapsed as she weighed up her situation when she suddenly realised there was bright sunshine and the smell had dissipated.

'Odd,' she thought, 'that storm soon disappeared.'

There was little point shouting as no one was around. The drivers door would open only slightly, jammed as it was by debris. Then she remembered her husband's advice—'Switch the engine off first in the event of an accident.'

'What would he have done next,' she reasoned. 'Mobile, you fool. Ring someone.'

She fiddled around trying to find her handbag amongst the glass and wood and finally located it underneath her seat. Retrieving the phone she dialled the house.

'Hello, can I help you?'

The sound of his smooth warm voice reassured her. 'Alex, it's Jenny. I'm trapped underneath one of your trees down the drive. Come and get me out.'

'Stan's on his way already with a couple of helpers. I'll call him on the radio to get a move on. Are you okay?'

'Just a few scratches from flying glass, it's ruined the hairdo though. I can hear someone, it must be Stan.' She dropped the phone and shouted, 'Help! Help, I'm inside.'

'Hold on ma'am, we'll soon have you out of there, are you alright, do you need an ambulance or anything?'

'No, just a strong gin and tonic.'

'Sorry, can't oblige with that one.'

She sat patiently listening to the sounds of breaking wood and cursing as they pulled and tugged at the tree trying to get the door open.

'It's no good, ma'am, we'll have to get the chainsaw from the workshop. Are you alright for a while?'

'Yes, I'm okay.'

Stan used the walkie-talkie to contact the house and arrange the required tools and some medicinal sustenance for Jenny.

Alex arrived a few minutes later in a cloud of gravel dust with a few helpers from amongst the guests.

'Jenny, Jenny, are you alright?'

He could reach just far enough through the branches to touch her outstretched hand.

'Yes, dear, I'm okay, honestly, but my beautiful car.'

'Don't worry, we'll soon have you out of there and the insurance will sort your car out.'

'Thanks, darling, I feel better now you're here. I'll call the RAC while you're busy. They can come and collect it.'

Stan, who was stood next to Alex, nudged him. 'She's trapped by a tree that could have killed her and all she worries about is her car. That's some lady you have there.'

'You approve then?'

'I certainly do. Women like that don't arrive every day. Most of today's women, especially the young ones, would be screaming the blooming house down.'

'Thanks for that appraisal Stan, I will take due note of it.'

Stan winked. 'I'm thinking you already have, taken note that is.'

They glanced at each other and laughed simultaneously.

'Get on with it you old fogey. Let's get her out of there.'

The continuous cheery backchat through the broken window didn't allay his fears that she may be seriously injured but the chainsaw made short work of the major branches holding the door and she struggled out of the car and into his arms.

Safely wrapped in Alex's jacket she turned and surveyed the wreckage of the car. The shock of seeing how close she had come to death was unnerving and she finally lost her composure and cried unashamedly into his chest.

'Oh! Alex, look at my lovely car. He never got so much as a scratch on it and I've wrecked it. I feel so terrible, as if I've betrayed him, it was his pride and joy.'

'Jenny, darling, don't fret. Thank goodness he had the sense to buy that particular make. Any other and you wouldn't be crying on my shoulder. A couple of weeks work and you won't know the difference.'

He kept a comforting arm around her as he helped her into the Range Rover and drove back to the house.

Inside he asked Lily to make some tea.

'Can I have something stronger,' Jenny pleaded.

'No, Jenny, a warm drink first followed by a hot shower and a change of clothes. Then, and only then, we may consider something a little stronger for both of us.'

'Alex, I'm sorry too cause so much trouble. It's not fair on you.'

'Rubbish, it's not your fault. Now drink up and go and get changed.'

His mobile rang, 'Alex here.' He listened for a few seconds. 'Okay. Hold on, I'll speak to her. Jenny that was Stan. The breakdown truck has arrived and they want to know what you want doing with the car. They can take it to your home or to a SAAB workshop locally.'

'Local will do fine, but I need to know where for the insurance.'

Ten minutes saw the whole affair sorted out and a replacement hire car was arranged for delivery the following day.

'And now,' she said, 'shower and change, then we'll get that drink.'

They embraced and he kissed her on the forehead. 'Darling, I'm glad to have you in one piece, my heart's slowed down now that you're safe. I'm afraid I let my imagination run riot. I don't think I could have stood losing you so soon after you came into my life.'

She leaned on him. 'Alex. I love you. I'm so lucky.'

Reaching up she pulled his head down and kissed him. 'Don't go away, I won't be long.'

'Excuse the cliché, but wild horses wouldn't drag me away.

That evening.

Teasing her Mother had been a lifetime's fun for Elaine who never missed the opportunity whenever a mishap occurred.

'So what happened, Mum? You causing mayhem in the happy home again?'

'I don't know, dear. I was driving along feeling fine, minding my own business, when—Bang! A bolt of lightning and there I was stuck under a tree. I saw this cloud as I drove back but I dismissed it out of hand as a harmless summer shower and that's odd as well.'

'What do mean—as well?'

'Two things. It didn't rain and I am positive I heard someone laughing. It was a weird, deep, cruel laugh. It must have been my imagination working overtime but that does not explain the sudden disappearance of the cloud. The whole thing must have taken only seconds but the cloud had completely evaporated.'

Andrew chipped in at this point. 'There's probably a meteorological reason for it. Maybe the bolt used up all the energy in the cloud and the breeze did the rest.'

'You're probably right, Andrew. In future if I see a cloud I'm returning to the Stag.'

'Mum, what did you drink at lunch time?'

'Look here, young lady, don't let the family secrets out of the bag.'

They all laughed at Jenny's expense but were relieved that it was not more serious.

'That's the inquest out of the way, who's for coffee?'

'No thanks, Mum, we're joining the guests tonight. They're running a pool competition and we're representing the staff.'

When they had left she snuggled up closer to Alex. 'And what are we doing, lover boy?'

***

24

Wednesday

Alex had thought it wiser to sleep in his own room that night to give her an undisturbed sleep to aid her recovery from the days close encounter with the tree and Jenny was determined this was going to be a day without distractions. She intended no fuss and no stress, definitely no stress and the offer of breakfast in bed was to good to pass up and gave her a sound start.

A comforting arm around her would have been appreciated but she understood his logic when he said he had to get up early and wanted to let her rest.

She slid back under the quilt. It was no good, her mind was in turmoil over the events that had taken place since she had arrived. The visitations by the spiritual and her two encounters with the dark side were disturbing and she didn't want anyone to find out the reason for them.

She decided that discretion was the best course and the family skeletons were going to lie buried, at least until they were needed. The real facts may jeopardise her daughter's future, not to mention the happiness she had found with Alex.

She slipped out of bed and went over to view the damage in her dressing table mirror. 'Not bad, I expected worse.'

The scratches were small and superficial and judiciously applied make-up would soon disguise them, but the hair was a different matter. The brushing, combing and washing to remove glass splinters and bits of tree had trashed twenty pounds of hair-do.

Nothing for it, she decided, but to go back to bed with a book.

She forced herself to read for an hour until there came a point when she read the same paragraph for the third time. 'This is no good,' she mused, 'I may as well get up.'

She dressed in slacks and jumper thinking she may go for a walk later and ventured downstairs to see who was around. The place was quiet, but feeling at home in this rambling pile despite all that had happened she settled into the sofa to read the morning's garbled truth in the papers and later try daytime television.

Ten minutes of viewing was enough and she expressed her thoughts aloud. 'Oh my, this is truly awful. There must be some terribly bored people if they can watch this drivel.'

She persisted with the channel flicking a little longer but unable to concentrate she gave up and wandered down to the kitchen.

Lily greeted her cheerily. 'Morning ma..., Jenny. Over our mishap are we? Elaine told me all about it.'

'Yes, thanks, Lily, just a bruised ego and a wasted hairdo.'

'Good. Coffee okay?' She turned to see to the coffee and said over her shoulder, 'Are you doing anything special today?'

'I thought I might go for a walk.'

'Keep away from trees.'

They laughed simultaneously, one enjoying the company the other relieved by the therapeutic effect of conversation.

'Seriously,' Jenny continued, 'Alex can't understand it. He has a tree surgeon check his trees frequently and a lightning strike should do damage, but not fell a solid tree. It must have been a freak bolt.'

'Aye, nature's a funny thing.'

'Have you seen Elaine?'

'Not since breakfast. The two lovers went out with stars in their eyes.'

'They're quite taken with each other aren't they, Lily?'

Lily nodded in agreement. 'Alex is a changed man as well. He sings and hums to himself, quite the happy bunny. In love, I shouldn't wonder.'

'Can't possibly imagine why, something in the water maybe? Lily, I'm not standing on anyone's toes am I? You know what I mean?'

'No Jenny, you're not. I had thought about it, but I'm not cut out for that sort of life. I think Stan is getting ideas though, not before time.'

'Do you like him?'

'Yes, I do. He made moves as if he was going to do something about it and then he pulled back at the last minute. We've been out a few times though.'

'I like Stan, Lily. He's a little on the shy side, which is good in a man, but he's been a bachelor too long and is set in his ways. You, Lily, will have to take the lead. I know, let's me and you organise an evening down at the Stag and you ask him to join you at the last minute. I'll have a headache or something.'

'Are you sure?'

'Positive. You're going to have to lead him. You wouldn't believe the trouble I had getting my husband to ask me. In the end I organised our first date and let him think he had, and I bought my own engagement ring—the rest is history.'

'What'll I do when I get him there?'

'You sit alongside of him, close, you understand, and if he moves away you take his arm and gently pull him back, but don't let go. Then you let his hand fall on your thigh with your hand on top and you say something like, 'This feels natural,' and go on from there.'

'Oh, but I don't want him to think I want to get up to, you know—funny business.'

'He won't. You'll confuse him more like. Carry on talking as if nothing has happened and at the end of the evening suggest that he may like to walk you home. If he goes to leave you at the front door, you'll have to remind him that a goodnight kiss is in order. That first kiss is the key, but be gentle with him.'

'I'll try, but I think I've forgotten how to do things like this, it's been such a long time.'

'I know, but what to do next comes naturally. Sex is not everything, but if your feelings lead you that way, don't hesitate. If it happens, it happens, if you follow my meaning. Go with the flow as they say, Lily. I think I'll take that walk now, good luck.'

'Thanks, Jenny.'

—

She had no plan, only the need to wander which took her across the courtyard to the fence surrounding the fields opposite. Leaning against it she looked back at the house.

'I wonder,' she said out loud, 'have I a right to be here? Should I tell Alex the true purpose of my visit or would it be a big lie if I kept my secret?'

She felt a presence beside her and she shivered involuntary. There were no mysterious voices or visions, merely calmness, a feeling of a serene protective cloak.

She tried to ignore the sensation, but at the same time she was comforted. Unsure about her thoughts on the afterlife which she had previously written off as mystique and old wives' tales she turned away from the fence and made her way down the drive through the woods towards the gatehouse. She had an uncontrollable urge to see the tree that had so nearly been her demise.

They had done a good job cleaning up and had cut it into manageable pieces ready for the local wood yard to collect. The diameter of the three-hundred year old tree came as a surprise to her.

She spoke aloud, sympathetic for the arboreal life needlessly destroyed. 'You must be all of six feet across, if not more.' Giving the big trunk a pat, she added. 'Maybe we can have a sculpture made out of you.'

Curiosity assuaged she set off on a meandering course over the parkland in the general direction of the Church, breathing the fresh country air with fond memories of her husband coming back to her and how they used to love wandering around the Welsh hills.

Her special memory was how they left the car in Cilcain Village Hall car park, with its sign warning of dire consequences against those who dared, and returning hours later to collapse in the snug of the *White Horse* pub. Lager never tasted as good as the one after a good walk.

She paused at the little wicket gate that was the rear entrance to the churchyard.

'Oh, heavenly,' she whispered, 'why can't the weather be like this all the time?'

White clouds, some with a tinge of grey were scudding up from the south west making the air a little chilly when they passed in front of the sun followed by a caressing warm sensation as they moved on.

The gate creaked as she opened it and stepped into the churchyard. She was startled when the birds, who, moments before had been enjoying the mild weather, instantly ceased their chorus. Blackbirds darted for the hedges emitting their high penetrating alarm call telling their young to stay low. The Robin stopped singing and followed the Blackbird. A Thrush left its snail and hopped under the hedge and the industrious House Martins stayed hidden in their nests under the eaves of the church.

'I hope I don't scare everything like this,' she said quietly and then she remembered her hidden escort and said out aloud, 'I'm sorry, I'll only be a short while.'

The gothic church, like the castle, appeared quite new. Glancing left and right at the gravestones as she walked down the narrow path she stopped at an elaborately carved headstone bearing the Ross Coat of Arms inscribed—Christine Maxwell-Ross 1789-1866, but rather peculiarly alongside was a bare plot with only a footstone engraved, W.M.

Other graves either side were for later generations of the family including that of David Maxwell-Ross M.P—Alex's father.

To her surprise she found the church door open and inside was a plaque which told her Alexander Maxwell-Ross had donated funds to refurbish the church in 1865.

The interior was bright and airy and the stained glass windows turned the sunlight into a myriad of multi-coloured spotlights. There were vases of fresh flowers dotted around and the variety of summer colours contrasted with the light. Their perfume gave the place a wonderful rural tranquillity.

She sat in a pew in the middle of this pastoral atmosphere for a few moments conscious of the invisible presence that had been with her all morning. For no reason, she knelt and said a silent prayer.

The comforting voice of the Rev John Fraser disturbed her composure. 'Good morning. Can I help in any way?'

Jenny jerked upright, turned her head and leant away from this intruder into her thoughts.

'Oh, I'm dreadfully sorry, I startled you?'

'You did a little, I was miles away. I was out for a walk when I came into your beautiful church. Oh, that they were all this bright instead of the gloomy cold and damp churches we're used to.'

'I think that's because we are small and I have a wonderful

staff of vergers and cleaners. Is your local church that bad?'

'I think the church volunteers try very hard. The place is so large it's the devil to heat in the winter. Maybe I should re-phrase that.'

'Ha, ha... Quite apt. Maybe he's working against us and trying to drive you out.'

'I've never thought of it like that, although I would think he was more accustomed to heat. Should we be discussing these things?'

'Do you mind if I sit and talk for awhile?'

'Please do.'

He sat on the opposite side of the aisle. 'I apologise again for intruding. We are Presbyterian by the way. Does that bother you?'

'Not at all. My husband was Church of England but he much preferred the nonconformist style of service. He went to school in Gretna for a short while.'

'You speak in the past tense.'

'Yes, he died a little over two years ago.'

'I'm sorry, you were close?'

'Yes, and I do miss him. It took him eighteen months to die and it strains my religious belief. I wonder sometimes what sort of God lets good people die like that.'

'As they say, God moves in mysterious ways. Keep faith, I am sure your late husband is watching out for you'

Subconsciously she knew why she had been comfortable with her invisible shadow. 'I feel he is right now.'

'Are you staying close by or passing through?'

'I'm a guest up at the Castle. My daughter is engaged to the son of the house.'

'I believe I've met your daughter, a charming girl who takes very much after her Mother.'

'Why thank you. I really must go, they'll be wondering where I've got to. It's been nice talking to you.'

'My pleasure.' They stood simultaneously and he took her hands in his. 'God Bless You and take care.'

She returned across the parkland and the feeling that someone was watching her was overwhelming, but she resisted the temptation to stop and look around.

When she passed the offending tree she made a mental note to get Alex to do something useful with it and hurried on through the woods. Unsure why, and although it was still early afternoon she went straight to her room and the mysterious presence, her comfort blanket, disappeared and suddenly she was alone and a little saddened.

A little before teatime she woke and went down stairs. Alex was waiting, but her mind was in a jumble as she felt the need to be alone and at the same time she was happy to see him.

'Hello, Jenny, where have you been?'

She went over to him and kissed him on the cheek. 'I went for a walk down to the church and had a little rest, chatted to the Vicar and then dawdled home.'

'You met John, did you? He keeps us in line with his fire and brimstone on Sundays. That is, whenever I find the time to go as weekends are one of our busy times. He helps us occasionally when he's at a loose end by working in the guest dining room. I think he hopes to make a convert one day.'

'I cannot believe fire and brimstone, he seems such a gentle man.'

'He is really, but his sermons are quite passionate as he reminds us of our human frailties. Would you like some tea?'

'Yes please, and some biscuits, I'm quite famished.'

He jangled the bell and a few moments later Lily appeared.

'Lily, could you please bring us tea and biscuits?'

'Yes, certainly, I shan't be long.'

'Thank you. Now Jenny, tell me about your walk.'

'It was a quiet stroll. I had an urge to look at that tree, which reminds me. Can we get one of those wood sculptors to do something with those huge pieces of trunk? Make benches or something. I remember in Australia, a coast resort near Melbourne I think, trees that were blown down in a storm and the local artist had made sculptures out of the remaining trunks.'

'I suppose we could. I was going to sell it to the local wood yard.'

'I then walked down to the churchyard. I like reading old gravestones and trying to imagine the people in there, which reminds me Alex, your family plot, why isn't there a tombstone on the grave alongside Christine Maxwell.

Lily chose that moment to enter with the tea tray.

'Thanks, Lily, leave it on the centre table and we'll help ourselves.'

'There you are, did you enjoy your walk, ma'am?'

'Yes I did and thankfully the weather stayed clear today.'

Alex intervened before the two women could get into deeper conversation. 'Thanks Lily, that'll be all. Where were we, Jenny?'

'Graveyard.'

'Oh, yes, the empty plot. The story goes that when William Maxwell died they laid him out to rest in the hall. When they came to get him on the morning of the funeral his body had disappeared. They left the plot for the day his body would be found, but it's never turned up and no one had an answer to the mystery.'

'Grave robbers before he was buried?'

'That was one theory put forward, but there was no sign of a break-in.'

'How very strange.'

'Yes, and he's rumoured to be one of our ghosts. Looking for his coffin no doubt.'

'Don't joke. Do you believe in ghosts, Alex?'

'Yes and no. I used to think it was superstition, but since I started running this place there have been alleged sightings and stories by a variety of people and now I'm not so sure.'

'Lily says you have a strange room at the top of the tower.'

'Oh that. William Maxwell had his own Masonic lodge and it's rumoured that he had guests from high places here. It's a bit over the top and not at all like a real Lodge.'

'Why is it still there?'

'The room is no earthly use so generation after generation has just left it. It's considered a novelty now.'

'You said Masons, are you one?'

'Yes, and now you mention it, I have a meeting on Friday night, do you mind?'

'Not at all, if you want to dress up and have funny handshakes go ahead.'

'It's not at all like that!'

Jenny was somewhat taken aback at the sharpness in his voice in defence of his allegiance. 'But I promise,' he continued, 'I will tell all if you come here to stay. It's very interesting and they do a lot for charity.'

She went over and sat by him. 'Oh Alex, I'm sorry, I didn't mean to be rude and laugh at you.' She stroked his hair. 'Give me a hug.'

'You women! Come here.'

They clinched in a lingering embrace and fell together, lengthways onto the settee.

'Hello, hello, what have we here?'

Andrew and Elaine had entered the room unheard by the lovers.

Alex and Jenny jumped apart flustered and red faced and Jenny self-consciously straightened her jumper and patted her hair as Andrew mocked.

'I don't know, you old people can't be left on your own for two minutes and you're at it.'

'It's not what you think,' Jenny said defensively.

Andrew continued his baiting, 'Elaine, I think we should leave and come in again.'

'Oh no, I want to watch,' said Elaine, enjoying her mother's discomfort.

Andrew took hold of Elaine's arm and began pulling her away. 'No, two sexagenarians locked in passion are not for your eyes.'

'Spoil sport.'

Jenny stopped the banter with mock indignity, and said, 'Do you two mind. I'm a long way off sixty, thank you very much!'

'Methinks they protesteth too much,' said Andrew, 'Come Elaine, let's go to the kitchen and scrounge some tea off the virtuous Lily.'

Alex spoke for the first time. 'When you've made it bring some in here. Take the tea pot with you.'

The two youngsters disappeared laughing and giggling at the expense of their parents.

'What are we going to do with those two, Alex?'

'I don't know, when do they go back to University?'

'It's the summer break. We have them until the end of September.'

'We'll have to keep them busy.'

The objects of the discussion returned with a new pot of tea and sat down one in each armchair.

'Apart from snogging, what have you been up to today, Mum?'

Jenny stuck her tongue out at her daughter and said with an air of finality. 'I went for a walk!'

***

25

Thursday

'You look better this morning, Mum. Did you sleep well?'
'The wonders of modern make-up, and as for sleeping, that bed is going home with me. I've not slept so well in years.'

'That's good, I thought a bit of retail therapy would suit this morning and then if you feel alright we can go riding this afternoon. Do you feel fit enough to go riding?'

'I haven't been on a horse since you were eight and then I was only an enthusiastic amateur keeping you company.'

'You'll be alright, the horses here are docile. Alex makes sure of that as he doesn't want his guests pushing up his insurance premium.'

'Thanks for that. What do I need and have you seen Alex?'

'Any shoe with a heel and a pair of jeans and he's playing soldiers with a couple of those corporate guys while Andrew is supervising paint-balling. You know the silly games boys play that pass for macho these days.'

'Oh, I don't mind driving that tank around, that's good fun. How many times have you done it?'

'Quite often. Stan says I'm a natural and he's going to teach me stick changes or something like that.'

'You be careful, I wouldn't want you responsible for any expensive repairs.'

'Stan's good at fixing them. He says the final drives are his biggest worry, whatever they are?'

'Interesting. Let's go and disturb Lily and see if there is any coffee on the go. I'm in need of a caffeine fix.'

Lily was nowhere to be found and they helped themselves and chatted at the breakfast bar until she appeared.

'Good morning ladies, sorry I missed you. Are you all fixed up?'

'Yes, thanks,' they answered in unison.

'Good. I have a new cleaner started today and I've been showing her how we clean the shields and the armour. Good old WD40. Are you over Tuesday's little upset, Jenny?'

'Yes. I feel good considering. I wish I could say the same about the car.'

'They can fix cars, you'll see.'

'I hope so, it was my husband's pride and joy. He cherished it more than me I think. You know, boys and their toys. Look at Alex, he has a garage full of them. Lily, we are going shopping, can you tell Alex?'

'Yes, certainly.'

'Come on, Mother,' Elaine grabbed her mother's arm, 'Let's change and we'll get some mileage out of that hire car of yours.'

Twenty minutes later Mother and daughter set off for town...

—

'Elaine, I've had enough of crowds how about lunch? Every man and his dog are out today.'

'Right, Mum, what are you having?'

'My treat, shall we have a plate of those mixed sandwiches and a glass of wine?'

'Sounds good to me.'

Their order arrived and the next few minutes were spent in silence as they concentrated on their lunch before Elaine checked her watch.

'Come on, Mum, if we are going riding we had better get a move on, it's nearly two o' clock.'

'Do we have to, I'm rather enjoying this wine.'

'You're turning into an old soak, Mother, no we don't.'

'You are hard and less of the old, I prefer to be known as a lady of experience. I refuse to give in to the ravages of time and so long as I have no ill effects from this HRT I'm staying with it.'

'You're looking good on it. I hope I have your genes.'

'I think you have, right down to the birth mark.'

'Don't mention that, Mum, you know how embarrassed I get.'

'Be proud of it, dear. Men will be fascinated and fall over themselves to kiss it. I expect Andrew loves it. Tease them, show it discreetly so they just get a glimpse.'

'You're right, Andrew does, it's like a magnet.'

'It does no harm to keep others in your spell, dear. Use it to your advantage.'

'Is that how you caught Dad?'

'No. I stepped out in front of him on a pedestrian crossing without thinking and we got talking and clicked. Lucky it was a busy day or he might have been going too quick to stop.'

The idle chatter and banter continued on the drive home.

Andrew spotted them climbing out of the car laughing and giggling like two teenagers. 'Hello you two, keeping M & S in profit are we?'

Elaine kissed him on the cheek. 'Hardly a profit on the little things we buy in there.'

He bent down and whispered, 'Will I get to see them later.'

She pushed him away in mock anger. 'Andrew! Not in front of the lady with experience.'

'Ha, ha… Any particular experience.'

Jenny broke up the repartee. 'If we're going riding grab your bags Elaine.'

'I'll let you two get on with it.' Andrew gave Elaine a quick peck. 'I'll see you at tea time.'

'This is Mr Edwards, Mum. He looks after the livestock on the estate which includes the stables.'

'Good afternoon, ma'am. So you wants to go riding, young miss?'

'Yes please, can I have Sable and Dancer for Mum?'

Edwards disappeared into the stables and appeared a few minutes later with two horses in tow.

'That's Dancer, Mum. I thought you'd like a stallion between your legs.'

'Elaine!' Jenny said reprovingly. 'Excuse her Mr Edwards, I tried to bring her up like a nice girl.'

'I'm used to her little jokes, ma'am. You can tack your own young miss while I do this one for your Mum. Right ma'am, you hold his halter while I get him rigged. Have you much experience of horses?'

'No, only what I learned watching Elaine at riding school.'

'While I'm doing this you talk to him gentle like and blow softly into his nostrils. He'll recognise you after that and don't worry he hasn't got a mean bone in his body.'

She felt a bit silly talking to a horse, but she did as she was told and a few minutes later he was ready for riding.

'There you are ma'am, he's all yours.'

He led Dancer over to some steps. She had to lift her left leg a little way to reach the stirrups and when she tried to swing her other leg over his hindquarters she couldn't manage it. Determined, she tried again and a bolt of pain shot through her pelvic region.

'Ooh! I haven't opened my legs that wide since gymnastics classes at school.'

'You did alright, ma'am, are you sitting comfortable. Good. I'll adjust your stirrups. There we are, put the ball of your foot in the stirrup and off you go.'

'Are you ready, Mum?'

'As ready as I'll ever be.'

'Okay, let's go, walk on.'

Jenny tried to remember the rudimentary lessons learned years before and found that Dancer responded immediately and they followed Elaine out of the yard.

Outside the confines of the yard she wriggled a little to adjust her seating and Dancer gave her a sideways glance at the involuntary pull on the reins.

'I'm sorry, I didn't mean that,' she said guiltily and patted him on the neck.

Elaine slowed and allowed Jenny to catch up and they rode side by side chatting.

'What do you think of him, Mum?'

'He's lovely. It's like he knows what I want to do.'

'He does, they go around the same course over and over. You could drop the reins and he would take you round. How are the thighs?'

'So far, so good. I think I'll feel it tomorrow morning though, do we go far?'

'We'll do the short ride which takes us through the woods to the north and onto next doors land for a little way and then swings east in a big arc and we come back in alongside the tank track. It takes about an hour at a gentle walk.'

'That's the one for me. How are things with you and Andrew by the way?'

'We're fine and what about you and Alex? He told me he loves your company.'

'The feelings are mutual, although I have guilty thoughts about your Dad. Would you mind me living with your future father-in-law?'

'That's quick.'

'He's asked me to come and live here and you've probably guessed it's more than a platonic friendship already.'

'It's been two years, Mum, and about time you spread your wings. You should have some happiness in your dotage.'

'That's very good of you, most young people would cringe at anybody over forty making love. What's with this dotage thing, I'm a long way off a zimmer frame.'

'I know you're young at heart Mum, and you're doing Alex the world of good. I heard him singing yesterday. Not to be recommended by the way, and he's much more laid back. I have no objections so long as you're happy.'

'Thanks for that. I'm considering the move, but I will not give up the bungalow for a while. I thought I might go home at the end of the week and think it over. Will you come with me? I value your input and I want more of my own clothes.'

'Of course.'

They passed through the woods while they were chatting and began to circle round to the East.

'Who owns this land, Elaine?'

'Andrew did tell me. It's someone with a double barrel name. I think one of them was something to do with Government after the war and they've occupied this area for at least a couple of centuries. Alex's forbears bought his land and title off them and then built the house.'

'Does Alex talk about his ancestry?'

'Hardly ever unless he is asked by one of his guests. He's rather bored by it all. He did say that royalty paid a visit here in the 1850's.'

'Who?'

'I don't know and I don't think he does either.'

Their ride had taken them around the perimeter of the estate and they turned back westward and re-entered the grounds through a five bar gate. Following the well worn track they rode on until they arrived at the fence that stopped riders wandering onto the tank road.

'Let's stop for awhile Elaine. My back's beginning to ache.'

'Okay Mum. Here's a nice clearing and I think I can hear Alex coming through the woods with his toy.'

They decided to wait for the armoured monster to pass before dismounting and it was a short way off when Jenny felt the cold clammy atmosphere cloak her, but this was different, the fetid odour of decay accompanied it.

'Oh, no.'

'What's that, Mum?'

'Nothing I was having a groan.'

The two horses became fidgety and Jenny reached forward and patted Dancer's neck. 'Easy boy.'

Without warning he reared, almost unseating her, and took off at a gallop with Jenny clinging to his neck.

The tank rumbled nearer as Dancer careered toward the fence.

'Whoa boy! Elaine, Help!'

Dancer sensed the fence was too to high and his front legs stiffened in a belated attempt to stop. He skidded and crashed breast first into it. Jenny screamed as she catapulted over his head. One foot caught in a stirrup and she felt the ankle dislocate as she went over the fence into the path of the oncoming vehicle.

She crashed to the ground shoulder first and then her chest, knocking the breath from her body. Her riding hat protected her head as it hit the stony track with a resounding thud and she subsided into unconsciousness directly in the path of the oncoming vehicle.

A shouted warning by Stan came at the same instant the engine cut out. The 40-ton monster skidded to a halt rocking backwards and forwards on its suspension only yards from the inert body lying in its path.

Stan jumped off the front while Alex who was riding in the turret threw caution to the winds and jumped from the top. He staggered, executed a forward roll before coming to his feet and running towards her.

Stan got there first and went to turn her over.

'Don't touch her!' The shout came from the driver of the tank who hastily clambered out and joined them.

'I'm a St Johns Ambulanceman. Let me tend to her, you call for an ambulance with a Paramedic. Hurry!'

He reached down and checked for a pulse in her neck.

'She's alive, what's her name?'

'Jenny.'

Leaning over he held her head firmly and gave her a gentle slap on her cheek, 'Jenny! Jenny, can you hear me?'

There was no response. 'We must leave her until the ambulance arrives just in case she has neck or back injuries. They have the equipment, keep her warm, but don't move her.'

Stan threw his jacket over her and ran back to the tank. He called to the student standing in the turret opening.

'Reach behind you in the ammunition box. There's two car blankets in there. Throw 'em down quickly.'

He ran over to the still inert figure and gently laid the blankets over her with a tenderness that belied his appearance.

Alex told one of the students to run up to the house and guide the ambulance in before he went to Elaine who was standing by the fence.

'Is she alright, Alex?'

'She's breathing and has a pulse, but she's unconscious. We can't move her in case she has injuries we can't see.'

'Help me over, Alex.' She climbed over and stood with her arm around him, 'I don't know what happened. Both horses became skittish before Dancer bolted. It's not like them at all. They're so docile.'

'Something spooked them. It's curious also that the engine stalled at the very instant she landed. A miracle, it made the tank stop quicker. Someone or something was looking after her.'

They stood around checking her pulse every couple of minutes until the ambulance arrived.

A paramedic ran forward. 'Hello, my name's Helen. What have we?'

Alex quickly explained the circumstances.

Helen examined Jenny to determine the extent of her injuries before calling to her assistant to bring a collar and backboard. She looked up at Alex, 'Is she your wife?'

'No. A close friend.'

'Okay. Cup your hands under her neck and hold her head still while I remove her hat?'

Gently she removed the helmet. 'Thanks, my mate and I will fit a neck collar.'

With the help of Alex, Stan and the ambulance technician, they manoeuvred her onto the backboard with great delicacy and placed her into the ambulance.

'Will she be alright, Helen?'

'I think so, but it's too early to say what the extents of her injuries are. Wait while I hook her up to the ECG'

'Her pulse is fast, but not alarming and shock is setting in so if you're coming, jump in, we can't waste time.'

'Stan, tidy up here, will you? Elaine, are the horses alright?'

'Yes. Dancer has a cut on his breast, but otherwise okay.'

'Good. I'm going in the ambulance and I'll phone when I have news.'

'As soon as the horses are stabled Alex, I'll drive down. You'll need transport home.'

'Not while she's like this, but thanks.'

'Let's go,' shouted Helen.

Alex apologised and the ambulance set off along the track.

'Don't worry too much, sir. Her pulse is fast but not tachycardic. Her BP is above normal which is natural under the circumstances. We'll keep monitoring until we get there.'

'I understand. You do a great job, thanks.'

En-route to the hospital, Jenny groaned.

'Where am I,' she muttered?'

'I'm here, love.' Alex leaned over and consoled her. 'You're in an ambulance. Try not to move.'

'I'm hot, Alex, can I have some water?'

'Hello Jenny, I'm Helen. I'm sorry, you'll have to wait until we have you in A & E in case you have internal injuries. Don't worry we'll soon be there.'

They rushed her into the triage cubicle.

'This is Jenny, 50 years of age. She's had a riding accident. CS3 on arrival, no response, concussed for twenty minutes. I think the right ankle may be disjointed. Other injuries we could not assess and she was kept immobile throughout.'

A young Doctor took a close look at Jenny and flashed a mini-torch across her eyes. Satisfied he turned to Helen. 'Thanks Helen, any next of kin?'

'No,' she pointed to Alex, 'This gentleman is her partner.'

'Good afternoon sir. She's in good hands.'

'Can I stay?'

'I'm sorry, sir. It'll be a bit crowded in here with X-ray equipment and sundry bits and bodies. If you can wait in the relatives' room I'll send someone to keep you posted on her condition.'

'I understand. Look after her. She's special.'

'This way, sir.' A nurse walked with him and tried to console him. 'Try not to worry, sir. They're very good here. Help yourself to coffee or tea.'

'Thank you. Tell me, what's tachy something?'

'Tachycardic. It's a technical explanation for an abnormally fast heartbeat which is the body's reaction to stress and symptomatic of internal injuries, but she has no symptoms that suggest major injury.'

'Thanks, again.'

'Hello sir, I'm Doctor Hayle, if you would come with me we have your precious lady stable and thank goodness no serious injury. As a precaution we'll keep her in overnight and monitor her. I think she'll be able to go home tomorrow for some TLC. I wish all our patients were like her. Not a whimper or a moan and no histrionics. She did ask for you though.'

'What's wrong with her?'

'A severely sprained ankle and her shoulder, ribs and left arm are badly bruised. The bump on the head doesn't seem to have done any serious damage but she'll have a headache and turn all the colours of the rainbow over the next few days. Here we are, sir.

We're waiting for a bed and then we'll move her upstairs.'

'Thanks.'

'Pleasure.'

'Hi.' Alex leaned over and gave her a kiss. 'I know it's a daft question, but how do you feel?'

'I feel like an aching pin cushion. You wouldn't believe how many needles they can find to stick in you, and my ankle is throbbing to its own Rock tune.'

'I'm sorry about this Jenny. Your week so far has been less than pleasant.'

'Alex?'

'Yes.'

'Don't do anything to that horse will you? It wasn't his fault—Promise!'

'I had no intention of doing anything. He's normally so docile and laid back he could fall asleep while walking. Something spooked him. I don't think it was the tank as he's used to it. It's very odd.'

'Thank you, Alex. As soon as I'm able I'm going to ride him again. It will boost my confidence as well as his.'

'Edwards will keep him quiet for a few days and then take him for a few gentle walks. I think he's alright. Now you get some rest.'

Elaine joined them. 'Hello, Mum,' She leaned over and gave Jenny a peck on the cheek. 'What's the damage?'

Jenny gave a quick run down of her injuries while they sat with her until it was time to go upstairs.

'Bye Mum, be good and no hanky panky with those male nurses.'

'Goodbye, dear, and don't worry,' she turned to Alex, 'and don't you worry either. I'm alright.'

'I'll try not to and I'll be back early in the morning. Good night, sleep tight. I love you, Jenny Beaumont.'

They had a lingering departing kiss before the Ward Sister scolded him. 'Come along we have work to do. She'll still be here tomorrow.'

—

Friday morning

'Morning, Jenny.' Alex sighed with relief to see her sat up and smiling. 'The doctor has told me you can come home now. There appears to be no lasting damage, only hurt pride.

'Oh good, now give me a kiss and pull the curtains round while I get dressed.'

He acceded to both requests and then sat on the end of the bed.

'What do you think your doing, kind sir?'

'Waiting and helping you.'

'Outside, Alex. Modesty calls for privacy.'

'I'm sorry, I wasn't thinking.'

'That's alright, but now is too soon.'

'I'll wait outside in the corridor.'

He ventured back after forty-five minutes to see what the hold up was and met her swinging down the ward on crutches.

'I thought you'd decided to stay,' he chided her.

'Alex, you know absolutely nothing about women's ablutions. Now walk around me and make sure there are no hairs or bits on my top.'

'You're clear, where's your bag?'

'Help me with my jacket and then we must wait for the nurse to wheel me out.'

'Can't you go on your crutches?'

'No. The rules are that they have to see you safely off the premises.'

They waited ten minutes until a nurse was free to escort her to the door.

'I'm sorry about that, Mrs Beaumont, we are a wee bit busy this morning.'

'It's quite alright.'

Jenny eased herself into the wheelchair and seconds later they were on their way.

Alex refused to drive quickly. Every gear change was precise, every movement of the steering wheel controlled, and he braked far too early in Jenny's opinion. It was frustrating for a woman who got her adrenalin kicks from speed, but she didn't comment instead she loved him even more for this compassion and accepted that the future lay with him.

'Here we are, can you manage?'

'Come around and help me while I get these crutches set, and after that we'll see.'

She turned in the seat and held on to him while she slid out and balanced on her good leg.

'Right, sir knight, give me those abominable things and let's go.'

He stood and watched as she made her way into the house and mentally commented. 'That is one determined lady. I'd hate to be any of our suppliers if ever she gets to run this place.'

As soon as Jenny was settled on the sofa Lily came fussing in.

'It's good to see you back Jenny if only to brighten this lot up. It was like a morgue here this morning.'

'It's good to be back. Can I have a decent cup of tea?'

'Of course you can. Would you like a footstool to rest your leg?

'No thanks. I'll stretch out lengthways on the sofa and they can fawn around me. It's nice being pampered.'

'You shout if you want anything.'

'Thanks Lily.' Jenny turned and lifted her face towards Alex. 'Alex dear, I'm sure you have lots to do. Elaine and Lily will watch over me, you run along.'

'Are you certain?'

'Alex! Go! Elaine, how did I manage these last two years?'

'Easy Mum, there were no men to get in the way.'

Alex looked skywards and raised his arms in exasperation. 'Spare me. Women's lib, I'm off.'

Later

'Hello, love, is everything alright.' Alex leaned over and gave Jenny a kiss. 'Can I get you anything?'

'No dear, I have been spoilt enough already. Help yourself to tea. Did you lose much equipment today?'

'Very little for a change. The St Johns man was asking after you by the way. He was quite concerned.'

'I would have liked to have met him.'

'Jenny darling, there's something I would like to ask you.'

'This sounds serious. Oh, I know. Of course you can go to your meeting. I have all I need and I'll be going to bed early.'

'Can you manage those stairs?'

'Yes, if I take it slowly. They've done a good job strapping my ankle. These plastic splints give you a lot more freedom. I'll stiffen up if I don't do some movement.'

He came over to her and kissed the top of her head. 'Thank you. I'll stay if you want me to.'

'I wouldn't hear of it. When, and only when I become permanent we'll talk about it.'

'Hello, you pair.' Elaine and Andrew had entered the room. 'How's the invalid?'

'Very well, thanks very much.'

'Good. Would you mind if we went out tonight, Mum. It's quiz night down at the pub and we're half the team.'

'No, you run along and give me some peace and quiet.'

'But Jenny, I...I...,' stuttered Alex.

'No Alex, I'll be alright, besides you're not going out until after seven and it won't be long after before I go to bed.'

'So long as you're quite sure you'll be alright.'

After the previous day's escapade she wasn't sure about anything.

***

26

Friday evening.

After much persuading Alex went to his Lodge dinner at the *Stag* while Andrew and Elaine stayed until eight and then went to their quiz night at the same venue. It was sometime later and after some deliberation Jenny chose to have an early night.

She finished her cocoa, selected a variety of magazines and a book and went upstairs, groaning quietly at each step. The soreness in her ribs and across her shoulders had eased slightly, but her ankle was still hurting abominably and the accident of the previous day flashed through her mind.

There seemed no logical reason for a well behaved horse to act in a manner alien to him. She had her own ideas but they sounded so illogical she kept them to herself.

While preparing for bed she went through the incidents of the previous week which had upset her wellbeing and concluded maybe there was something in the theory of after life or ghosts. That something or someone wanted to do her harm disturbed her a little.

She put a cardigan around her shoulders with some difficulty, turned the sheets back and prepared to climb into bed when something sharp pricked her foot. She bent down to investigate and was surprised to find an enamelled crucifix attached to an elaborate gold chain.

'I've seen that somewhere before,' she said, 'I wonder who dropped it?'

She suddenly felt nervous and lonely and as on previous occasions an icy chill filled the room and the quiet detached voice of Jane Ross said, 'Keep it child and wear it at all times.'

Jenny jumped. 'Jane, where are you? Oh, do stop frightening me like that. I couldn't possibly.' Aware that she was talking to an empty room she berated herself. 'Don't be stupid, Jenny.'

She looked around, more than a little edgy now, dropped the

crucifix into her cardigan pocket and slipped between the sheets determined nothing was going to upset her further.

Mentally she thought, 'I'll ride this out if it kills me,' and in defiance she said aloud, 'I've found happiness and let no one think they are going to take it away from me.'

Concentration was difficult under the circumstances. Her mind was a whirl of crazy ideas that wouldn't come together with any rational explanation. What was not acceptable to her was a one-hundred and sixty year old family feud still ongoing in the underworld. She dismissed this conclusion as farcical and slid down under the covers in an abortive attempt at sleep.

Tossing and turning she gave up the unequal struggle. 'I think a strong night cap is called for here, or two.'

Pulling the cardigan tightly around her she clambered out of bed and went to the door where a further surprise confronted her. The corridor and the stairs were in darkness.

'Who turned the lights out, I wonder?'

The bedroom door slammed shut behind her and almost sent her sprawling. Her injured ankle took her body weight and she let out an anguished cry as she staggered forward and only an outstretched arm against the opposite wall stopped her falling.

Frightened, she gauged the distance to the top of the stairs and hobbled towards them feeling her way along the wall. Her eyes slowly became accustomed to the darkness and she was able to pick out the clock. Now that she had her bearings she moved with more confidence towards it.

At the top of the stairs she became aware of the chilliness. The experience never changed. Clammy, like a winter fog, a sweaty feeling, even though cold. The hairs on her neck bristled and she could feel the panic rising inside.

She held the banister for support when some sixth sense made her stop as she realized the great clock was tumbling towards her. Unable to turn back she twisted away from the stairs and threw herself forwards. She screamed loudly as the clock crashed down on her injured ankle and pinned her to the floor.

'Help, anybody,' she shouted, in the forlorn hope that someone had returned. 'Help! Alex! Andrew! Is anyone there?'

A chilling silence was her only reply. Using her free foot she pushed against the clock. It moved a little but the agony as the friction turned her ankle made her whimper in pain.

Realising more effort was needed she braced herself with both hands on the floor for extra leverage, lifted her body and pushed with all the strength she could muster in her good leg. The clock lifted enough for her to drag herself free as the pain stabbed upwards through her injured leg. Numbing in its ferocity, it made her dizzy and this time her scream was in earnest.

She lay in the darkness for a few moments until the pain subsided before taking stock of her situation.

'I must get downstairs,' she decided.

Rolling onto her knees and using the clock as support, she pushed herself up taking great care to keep her injured leg off the ground.

'What next,' she muttered.

Speaking aloud gave her a little comfort and helped her focus her thoughts.

It was then she became aware of the familiar stench of rotting vegetation and decay mingling with the chilly, clinging aura that surrounded her. The darkness lifted as a flickering light came from the stairwell. Her eyes widened in fear at the manifestation that confronted her.

It was of human form with the bloated ruddy features of William Maxwell, wearing a grey frock coat, white stockings, buckled shoes and a double tied neck cloth. He was enveloped in a blue, vaporous, incandescent glow and holding a six-pronged candelabra in his left hand with his right arm outstretched and pointing towards her.

This surreal apparition gave a recognisable, throaty, mocking laugh. 'The Devil delivers you to me, Ross. Strike! Fires of Moloch!'

A thunderbolt leapt from his hand and sizzled towards her.

Instinctively she ducked and it crashed into the wall behind her in a shower of molten sparks.

She screamed with terror and in desperation she turned to flee in the only direction available to her—Upwards. Hobbling, every touch of the stair sending waves of pain convulsing through her body, and using the banister for leverage to pull herself up and away from this terrible thing, she made it to the next landing.

A portrait came away from the wall and an unseen hand hurled it down on her. She turned away and leant over the rail and it bounced off her shoulders. She winced as the bruising from the previous day reawakened itself. Crying and whimpering she carried on upwards. At the next level she looked back. The apparition was still there, but closer, with the evil accompanying smell.

'You're mine, Ross!' The booming voice echoed around the inside of the tower. 'There's no escape. You'll not get your legacy away from me. It stays with the Maxwell.'

A pair of silver candlesticks on an occasional table levitated and were thrown at her by some invisible force.

Ducking down, the first one passed over her and a hastily thrust out arm deflected the second one. She screamed as it smashed against her forearm.

Sobbing she tried a door, frantically turning the handle backward and forward. It was locked and she pushed on up the stairs. The pain in her arm and ankle intensified with every movement, but determination and fear kept her moving.

A roar of laughter regaled her as she approached the next level. A wall mounted light was ripped from its fastenings and sparks momentarily lit the way as the bare wires touched. The same invisible force hurled it down on her and she ducked below the banister.

The sparks flashed onto nearby curtains and the tinder dry material immediately started smouldering.

Following the banister she reached the next level without mishap. She kept going, looking back from time to time. The clamour of smoke alarms now invaded the tower adding to the already tense and threatening atmosphere. The stairwell acted like an echo chamber and the volume increased. The kaleidoscope of sound and pain from her injuries made her nauseous.

Sobbing uncontrollably she dragged herself onward and upward. Finally, she reached the top level only to be confronted by an oak panelled door. In desperation she threw herself at it and she breathed a sigh of relief when it opened. What confronted her stunned her into immobility.

The twilight glow of luminous paint was bright enough to see the decorations of stars and occult symbols and the faded tapestry of a rearing goat hanging on the back wall. Six-pronged sconces were set at intervals and at the end of the room was an altar draped in faded blue velvet adorned with regalia unfamiliar to her. On it were two five pronged candelabrum and a jewelled sword pointing outwards.

A savage thrust sent her sprawling. A thick Persian rug absorbed most of the shock and saved her from further injury and the room echoed as the door slammed shut behind her.

For a moment she lay there breathless with the exertion of panic before she pulled herself up to a sitting position. Resting on her arms she saw the top of a pyramid painted in gold poking out from beneath the disturbed carpet.

The Reverend John Fraser and Bill Stewart the local fire chief dashed from the entrance of the *Stag* hotel.

'ALEX! ALEX!' Shouting and waving they managed to flag him down.

Alex lowered the window. 'What is it, John?'

'Alex, Bill here has received a call from the Fire Control Centre. The automatic alarm has been activated and I'm sorry to tell you there's a fire at the Castle. We'll come with you. Get a move on.'

They clambered in and with the knowledge that his special someone was alone he set off like a man possessed.

The castle was only minutes away and they skidded to a halt at the gates. Using his remote device to open them he fumed at their slowness.

Frustrated he thumped the steering wheel. 'Come on, come on!'

Bursting through with the wheels spinning in the gravel they hurtled up the drive and slid to a stop by the front door. Looking up they could see flames flickering in the tower windows.

'What's wrong with the sprinklers?' Alex called as they threw themselves from the vehicle. 'I only tested them yesterday,' and as an afterthought, 'and all the lights are out.'

Stan appeared around the corner breathing heavily from the unaccustomed exercise.

'Stan, thank goodness,' said Alex, 'can you check the

sprinkler system and the fuses while we go inside? Have you seen Jenny?'

'No, sir, I've just come back from the village. I was down by the lych-gate when I heard the alarm.'

'Never mind, do what you can.'

'No problem, sir.' He turned and hurried away to the cellar.

Alex, desperate with anxiety, raced through the front door closely followed by his companions.

'JENNY! JENNY,' he shouted.

His eyes were used to the dark and a quick check of the lounge showed there was no one there.

'Bedrooms next,' he called, 'follow me.'

With Alex in the lead they ran for the stairs where smoke was already billowing down.

'Come on hurry,' he shouted in desperation over his shoulder, 'there are fire extinguishers on each landing. Grab one as we go past.'

He almost went headlong over the clock lying across the landing. 'What the hell's going on? Extinguisher there, carry on up while I check the bedroom.'

'JENNY!' No reply. 'Oh Hell, where is she? Oh, God look after her for my sake if nothing else.'

He followed up the stairs pausing only long enough to grab an extinguisher 'Where are those damn sprinklers and what's Stan doing,' he muttered, and then, 'Thank goodness for that,' as he heard the fire brigade tenders coming up the drive.

On the next landing he caught up with the Vicar and the Fire Chief who almost had the blazing curtains under control.

'Here's another extinguisher. I can't understand why those damn sprinklers aren't working.'

'The glasses have popped Alex. It must be something to do with the control panel.'

'Come on Vicar, leave Bill to it, his boys are here now. There's another landing.'

'After you, Alex.'

The pair of them made a dash up the final flight and threw their weight at the oak door. Alex turned the handle and cursed in desperation.

'Damn, it's locked, wait here I'll retrieve an axe from one of the hydrant positions. See if you can hear anything.'

—

Jenny tumbled to the floor and the crucifix spilled from her pocket. Fighting for breath she forced herself through the pain barrier to stop herself from fainting and when she looked up she recoiled in horror. The spectre that was her tormentor stood above her.

'Welcome to my temple, Ross,' it bellowed, 'If ye are a Ross? No matter, it's a sacrifice to the Lord Satan ye are now.'

It raised its arms and looked upwards. 'Give me a sign, My Master of the Universe. Help rid me of the curse that would destroy my family.'

A thunderous crash shook the building. A lightning bolt seared around the room lighting the candles in its path and unseated two with its violence. They bounced across the floor and came to rest against the tapestry which smouldered for a short time before exploding into flames.

Jenny screamed. 'Help, someone help me. Oh Lord, what have I done to deserve this?'

'Pick up the crucifix Ross and hold it before you.'

Jenny looked up and saw the image of Jane Ross against the sidewall.

'Help me, Jane.'

'Pray child, with anything you know.'

Crash! The noise of splintering wood echoed around the room as the fire axe smashed into the door. Three more times and a hole appeared and Alex was able to get his arm through, reach in, and turn the key. Both Alex and the Vicar fell into the room with the force of their assault.

'My god, what's that,' Alex exclaimed.

'That's the image of Maxwell, your ancestor, Alex,' answered the Vicar. He pulled a wooden crucifix from his pocket and held it up. 'Pray Alex. Chant the Lords Prayer over and over and get Jenny to do it. Is that the top of a star point under that carpet?'

'Yes.'

'Keep praying while I divert attention and then pull the carpet clear and get in the middle of the star. Adopt the position of supplication and whatever happens pray as loud as you can.'

With the crucifix held out in front of him he moved slowly towards the altar. The vision of Jane Ross went before him and shouted. 'Give up this nonsense William Maxwell. You are doomed. Maybe this time we shall rid our family of your evil.'

The image of Maxwell raised his arms heavenward and pleaded. 'Help me, My Supreme Being, My Creator of the Universe! Lucifer, Prince of Darkness, rid me of this Ross usurper.'

There was no answer to his call. The aura of Christianity was to strong.

The Vicar began to chant. 'In the name of Jesus Christ, God the Father and the Holy Ghost I confidently undertake to repulse the attacks and deceits of the Devil...' He took a couple of paces closer to the altar holding his crucifix high in front of him... 'We drive you from us whoever you may be, unclean spirits, all satanic powers, all infernal invaders, all wicked legions assemblies and sects.'

Maxwell began wilting under the barrage of good directed against him.

The heat from the burning tapestry and the painted panels was becoming intense and the smoke choking. Ignoring this, Alex jumped over to Jenny and tore at the carpet to reveal the star. He pulled her into it and adopted the kneeling position.

'Do likewise, Jenny, and chant the Lord's Prayer. Come on—*Our Father, which art in Heaven, Hallowed be Thy name.* Louder!

She joined him, softly repeating the prayer. '*Our Father...*'

The Vicar advanced further. 'In the name and by the power of Our Lord Jesus Christ may you be snatched away and driven from us and from the souls made to the image and likeness of God and redeemed by the Holy Trinity—Amen.

Maxwell's ghostly image began crumbling before this Exorcism. Jane reached out towards the forgotten crucifix on the floor and it flew to her hand.

'You're finished Maxwell. Be gone from this place.' She glided forward holding the cross high before her.

The Vicar continued with his incantation. 'We drive you from us whoever you may be. Unclean serpent, you shall no more dare to deceive the human race, torment God's elect and sift them as wheat.'

The fading vision of Maxwell pushed his hands out to ward off the pressure of Christian faith.

'Leave me alone. Punish those who covet your wealth Ross. I am the truuu...'

Jane sprang forward and threw herself on Maxwell, pushing the crucifix into him.

'Jane, No!' Jenny's plea was too late.

Lightning flashed, thunder crashed overhead and then all went quiet. A spiralling mist and a musty smell were all that remained where the coming together of religions, good and evil had taken place. At that moment the sprinklers came on devouring the flames and drenching everyone.

A Fire Brigade Sub-officer called from the doorway. 'Any casualties? Come on, everyone out. Let the lads in to check. Someone turn those damn sprinklers off.'

Alex helped Jenny to her feet, picked her up and carried her from the room and left the scene to the direction of the Officer.

'Right lads, in you go and mind you move everything to make sure we have no smouldering materials.'

Later, after they had cleaned themselves up and found a dressing gown for the Vicar, they assembled in the drawing room. A breathless Elaine and Andrew, who had run back from the village, joined them.

Bill Stewart poked his head around the door. 'Excuse me, Alex, have you got a minute?'

'Yes, Bill.' Alex joined him by the door. 'What is it?'

'Can you step outside a moment?'

Alex joined him in the hall and closed the door.

'Sorry about that, but I have my official hat on. We've had to call the Police and seal off that funny room of yours.'

'What on earth for?'

'There's a body under that altar thing.'

'A what?'

'A body. I wouldn't worry too much. It looks like one of your ancestors. It was dressed in old fashioned clothes.'

'A grey frock coat by any chance?'

'Yes. Why, do you know him?'

'Can I look?'

'Yes, but only from the door. It's a crime scene and the body is lying on a large white stone with artefacts of the same material around him.'

'What artefacts?'

'A gavel and a paper weight engraved with the Masonic compasses.'

'I'll fetch, John. He's a bit of an expert on these things.'

Alex and John peered around the door of the fire damaged room at the body laid out on the stone base.

'Alex,' John said with some solemnity, 'I recognise that stone. Its brilliant whiteness leads me to believe that it comes from the quarries of Solomon under Jerusalem. Such stones were imported as foundation stones for Masonic buildings. Many believe in the theory that the builders of Solomon's Temple were the first Freemasons. The artefacts will have come from there also.'

'You astonish me. The lengths this man went to for his own private Lodge.'

Alex turned to the fire officer. 'I'll be with the others Bill when I'm wanted. I think we've just solved a one-hundred and forty-year old mystery. I'll tell you about it one day.'

Later they stood around while Jenny recited the evening's events.

'And then you arrived, Alex, just like the cavalry. Tell me, is that what you do in the Masons. Worship the Devil?'

John intervened before Alex could answer.

'Allow me to explain. The Masonic Brotherhood is a society with secrets, nothing more. Its history goes back a long way and certain ceremonies and oaths have been passed down along the way. Our oath of allegiance, besides being to protect the Brotherhood, is to 'The Great Architect of the Universe.' This is an ambiguous oath which means that who or whatever you believe made the Universe is your Great Architect. This makes the Freemasons multi-denominational and multi-cultural. The Devil was Maxwell's 'Architect' apparently. Do you understand?'

'Yes, but why all the secrecy?'

'We come from all walks of life and it is not our wish to know what you do or who you are. That you have been accepted is enough. In this way a servant can be his employer's senior within the confines of the society. Although our rules say that people should not use the Brotherhood to their advantage, being so large an organisation you're bound to get a few unscrupulous bad apples.'

'Thanks, John,' Jenny said, 'but it will remain a mystery to me.'

'John,' Alex interjected, 'What was all that chanting you were doing upstairs.'

'That Alex, was all that I could remember of the Exorcism mass. I'm sorry, but you got mostly the Latin version with my non-conformist additions. I will arrange a proper Exorcism, but I believe you have no reason to worry anymore. I think we've got rid of your ethereal visitors, good and bad. Did I recognise them as the two portraits in the Hall?'

'Yes, and I hope it doesn't affect our visitor numbers. You're all sworn to secrecy. Keep the ghost rumours going. I wonder what he meant by that Ross usurper and all the other mumbo jumbo. What was the meaning of that, John?'

'It was the plea of a Satanist, Alex, something to do with the occult.'

Jenny interrupted. 'I think I can explain the usurper business. Elaine dear, could you pop upstairs and bring my bag down for me?'

'While Elaine is away,' said Alex, 'I think I ought to tell you that they have discovered a body underneath the altar. It appears to be that of William Maxwell who went missing in 1860. In the circumstances John, can we bury him?'

'I don't know, Alex. I'll have to consult with my superiors on that one.'

Elaine returned. 'Here you are, Mum.'

Jenny took her bag and withdrew two letters. 'Alex I want you to read those and then give them to Andrew and I will say this. It was not my intention when I came here to mention these as I believe them to be history and nothing else, but under the circumstances I don't think I have any other option.'

'Mother, what on earth do you mean,' Elaine said anxiously.

'Hush dear. Give me another brandy I think I am going to need it.'

The room went quiet as Alex read the letters and with a thoughtful look on his face he passed them on.

'Please excuse me everyone. I must go and check on progress upstairs. I'll be back in a few moments.'

Jenny's heart sank. He was obviously troubled and needed time to think.

'Mum.' Elaine waved the letters to emphasise her point. 'You know these are bunkum. Like I said before—It changes nothing. And as you said—It's history and my feelings for Andrew will not alter one little bit.'

'Hear, hear.' Alex had returned. 'That circumstances and coincidence have thrown us together like this should have no bearing on how we feel for each other. I love you, Jenny Beaumont, and it is I that should be apologising for the sins of my forebears and the disgraceful abominations that have occurred this week. However can you forgive me?'

'Easy. Tear up those letters and give me a kiss and I don't care what the younger generation feels.'

'Jenny, one more thing. The Fire Officer gave me this, I think it was meant for you.' Alex looped the ornate chain and crucifix around her neck. 'She intended it for your protection.'

He sat down beside her on the sofa and kissed her with the accompaniment of cheers from their children.

One year later

'Thank you for a lovely wedding, Mum, it was wonderful. Are you and Alex going to tie the knot?'

'Not just yet, but I'm going to live with Alex and help him run the place.'

'What are you doing with the bungalow?'

'I don't know. I still feel guilty about your father. It was his home as well. Would you and Andrew like it as a bolt hole?'

'No Mum, we are joining a practice in Edinburgh. Sell it. Dad said you must go forward. He'll understand if you say a little prayer and explain.'

'You're so wise, darling, much like your Dad. Do you

remember last year when we had all that nonsense? I think he intervened on at least two occasions…'

———

…and so, Professor Mildmay, after twenty-seven years, a somewhat bizarre conclusion to the Ross family saga and the final piece of my thesis in a manner that neither you nor I could have imagined.

I've been up to the Borders to visit my cousin Jenny and she is very happy in her new role as Lady of the Manor. She did however point out to me that under no circumstances would the 1793 guinea go into the family coffers, but would continue to be passed down the female line as a token of Hope over Adversity.

Her daughter Elaine is expecting an addition to the family, which has made me determined to get my thesis published so that I may present them with another memento of their family history to pass on to future generations.

Thank you for your patience both now and in my student days, it could not have been easy.

May both you and your wife continue to live a long and happy life.

I remain yours sincerely,

Angus Lane.

THE END

For God shall bring every work into judgement, with every secret thing, whether it be good, or whether it be evil. **Ecc. Ch12 v14**

***

ADDENDUM

***Turnbull's Tavern** and **Fortune's Tavern** were the Commercial centre of Edinburgh. They worked on a similar principal to the Coffee houses in London. Banks and Business's kept a Tavern fund to entertain visitors.

[1]A **Bogle** is an evil spirit in Scottish folklore

[2]**Authors note:** It was common practice in the 19th Century for illegitimate children to take the surname of both parents. One was usually a given or middle name as against the hyphenated double barrel name.
e.g. William Maxwell Ross (illegitimate) or William Maxwell-Ross (legitimate)

[3]**Authors note:** A keen observer would notice that the 'Royal' portraits in Holyrood House are painted in oil by the same hand. One James de Witt, a Dutchman living in Edinburgh in 1684.

***Cousin Esther** – This is her real name and the case is still on file as—Unsolved.

***Caddie** or **Cawdie** from the French: Cadet.

***Caddie fund**: The caddies were a community within a community who paid deference to a Chief Caddie, who imposed fines and punishments if any of his band committed an offence.
    They also had a common fund out of which any person who happened to be robbed by a thieving caddie was reimbursed.
    How did the Caddie become associated with the Golf course? I don't know.

*The Battle of Flodden. Sept 9th 1513.

The battlefield is just a little way out of town. A stone cross on top of a green hill is all that marks one of Scotland's saddest occasions. Scotland was a graveyard after that battle, one they should have won. They lost a King, (James IV) ten earls, three bishops, eleven barons, sixty eight knights and gentlemen and many other church dignitaries that day, not to mention the foot soldiers.

***Affiliation**: The widely recognised greeting of the 'Freemasons' is by their handshake which has its own peculiarities.

**This is the actual letter from the Bank of Scotland archives. The names have been changed.

* Scott and Reid were actually paid a total of £15,000 each in 1840.

To calculate inflation from 1840 to 1995 multiply by 50.8 and then add 2.5% p.a.p.a. to bring you to the current year.

***

About the author:

My name is JB. Woods and I am a retired soldier and fibre optics industrial operative who has turned his hand to writing after researching my wife's family history which inspired, this, my first novel. I then joined the 'Paphos Writers Group' and had many short stories published in a monthly magazine and as a result of lessons learnt with them, and recalled from my school days, I now edit other peoples work in a small way.

My other exploits into the literary world are a trilogy of books called—**'REBOUND**— **'Below the Belt'** — **'Upstart'**
Fictional adventure stories of secret agent and ex-soldier **George Hunter**.

Tricia – A Gardener's daughter. The life story of a young girl in the 1840's

'Henrietta – Tales from the Farmyard' A selection of short stories for grown ups and children alike about the adventures of Henrietta the matriarch of Village Farm.

'A Cry of the Heart'— (Amber Zacharia) a ghost-written biography and account of the traumatic life story of a young woman from Zimbabwe.

And **'Gems from my Pen'** which is a selection of previously published short stories from my files plus **More Gems from my** pen this year.

© 2024

Printed in Great Britain
by Amazon